Cover Design and Formatting by Kate | Kate Decided to Design @katedecidedtodesign

Edited by Erica Rogers | Logophile Editing Services

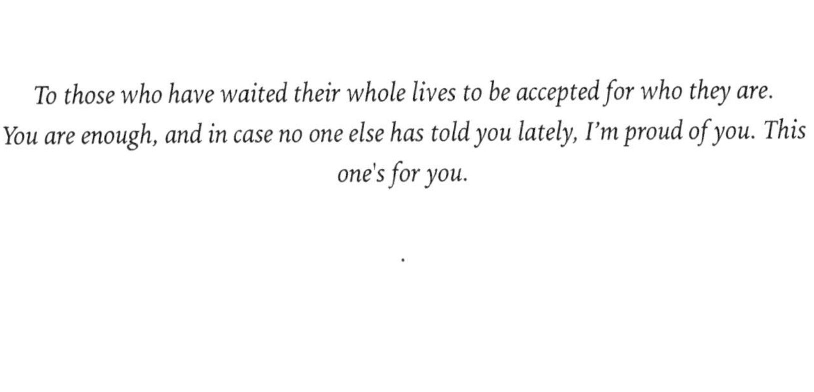

To those who have waited their whole lives to be accepted for who they are. You are enough, and in case no one else has told you lately, I'm proud of you. This one's for you.

Playlist

Trouble - Camylio
Blame It - Jamie Foxx, T Pain
Favorite - Isabel LaRosa
He loves me, he loves me not - Jessica Baio
Little Bit Better - Calen Hearn, ROSIE
Break My Bones - Matt Hansen
Something in the Orange - Zach Bryan
Sun To Me - mgk
Somebody to Someone - Natalie Jane
Espresso - Sabrina Carpenter
More Than Life - Chanin
The Girls - Megan Moroney
Chasing Cars - Ryan Waters Band
Die With a Smile - Lady Gaga, Bruno Mars
Elastic Heart - Sia
Scared to Be Lonely - Martin Garrix, Dua Lipa
Run for the hills - Tate McRae
Shameless - Camila Cabello
Hurricane - Fleurie
Yellow (Piano Version) - The Chillest
Radio - Lana Del Rey
Cornelia Street - Taylor Swift
Acquainted - The Weeknd
Ocean Drive - Duke Dumont
It's a Man's, Man's, Man's World - James Brown
Bed Chem - Sabrina Carpenter
Mastermind - Taylor Swift
Fly Me To The Moon - Frank Sinatra
I Wanna Be Yours - Arctic Monkeys
Give - SleepToken
Slow Down - Chase Atlantic
Daylight - Taylor Swift
Where Did All The Cowboys Go - Abby Anderson
SUNRISE - Forrest Frank
I Was Alive - Beartooth

Prologue

Lauren

Three months ago

New York isn't *that* different from Nashville, in that they both have some of the busiest streets I've ever been on and everyone seems to have somewhere to be. Sure we don't have subways that are confusing as shit, taxis all over the place, or skyscrapers on Broadway. Nor does New York have music playing through bar windows around every corner so loud that you can feel it in your chest, but you get it—same general vibes.

Okay, maybe they're nothing alike at all and I'm just feeling a little homesick. Sue me.

Coleson Realty, the real estate firm I've worked for since I graduated college, sent me and one other agent, Luther, to this very exclusive conference that The Fitzgerald Firm was hosting in New York this weekend, and even though I've been running around like crazy since my plane landed Thursday, it's actually been pretty fun.

There were panels for agents to attend, educating us on everything from having the right people staging and photographing homes for you, to the relationship you have with brokers to ensure your clients have the most seamless selling and purchasing experience possible. All of which are things that I've mastered since my second year at Coleson, but it was still interesting to hear from people representing the largest real estate firm in the US. Getting to talk with some of the employees from The Fitzgerald Firm, and seeing them seem impressed by *my* accomplishments, kind of had me on cloud nine. That is until I got a phone call from my mother following the last panel of the day which prompted my immediate search for the hotel bar.

I've been leaving my glorious ass print on this barstool ever since I hung up with her with no plans to move until I can't read the bartender's name tag—and I'd say I'm already getting close. Luckily I have his name memorized, so reading won't affect my ordering abilities. I'm blankly staring at the Dodgers game playing above the mirrored wall housing all the expensive liquor, suddenly wishing I was three beers and a stadium hot dog into the excitement. My phone continues to go off with texts, but I only have to glance at it once to make the decision to turn on my do not disturb. I look around me, noting that it's now dark outside and the room is far more crowded than it was when I got here.

Why are there so many damn people here?

"Mixer for the real estate convention that was going on earlier," Antonio, the very attentive bartender, answers the question I didn't realize I asked out loud. I smile at him, silently thanking him for the explanation, before turning my head back around to take in the expansive dining area once again. There are large windows that wrap around the room from the front door all the way to the wall where the kitchen entrance is, with tables of four along each wall. No comfortable booths in sight, just wooden chairs that would be killer on your back and fancy tablecloths that I know for a fact are a pain in the ass to wash every night. The few years I spent waitressing at fancy restaurants like this when I was in college are a strong reminder of how much I *dreaded* being the one to close and having to do all the dirty work.

The bar I'm occupying a stool at is absolutely massive as well—set right in the middle of the dining room with enough liquor on the shelves to supply a corner store. Not to mention every beer you could possibly name on tap and a lovely bartender who makes a mean spicy margarita. Maybe I'll get one more and see if Antonio will take me home tonight.

"Another spicy one, Antooo-nio." I wink at him, I think. Maybe I just blinked? Either way, he smiles and nods.

"Of course, coming right up." I glance down at my phone again, blinking a couple of times to help me focus on the numbers. **12:03 AM**.

Holy shit, I've been here a while. I don't even want to know how high my tab has gotten.

When Antonio returns with my drink I decide to take a lap around the room to see if I spot Luther, seeing as this *is* a mixer for the real estate convention we were attending—apparently.

I sure as hell don't remember any mention of it, but I'm here now so I might as well mingle.

Maybe I'll see one of The Fitzgerald firm reps and they'll offer me a position making millions here in New York and move me far away from the root of my crippling anxiety—my parents. My ambitions get a little out of hand when I have alcohol in my system.

I sip on my drink as I sway to the music that's coming from the speakers above me, doing one of my favorite things—people-watching. I like to think I have enough furtiveness to not classify it as lurking. Calling it people-watching is *much* classier.

The dining room is packed with people talking and laughing loudly, probably *almost* as drunk as I am. I get so lost in the music and how comfortable the room feels that I don't realize I've closed my eyes until someone approaches me, causing them to shoot open again.

"Hey doll, wanna take those moves somewhere more private?" The guy standing next to me has slicked-back blond hair, wears a pair of khakis that are creased down the front, and a sports coat, paired with a smile that sends a cold chill down my spine. Or maybe it's the gross, unwelcome hand that's wrapped around my waist making the hairs on the back of my neck stand up.

"No thanks, I'm good here." I take my index finger and thumb, grabbing his wrist to release my waist and pull away from him, looking around again for Luther, or *anyone* that looks less threatening than this douche canoe.

"C'mon. I promise I'll show you a good time." His tone is arrogant as he tilts his head, studying me. Looking at me as if I'll be missing out on the opportunity of a lifetime if I don't leave with him. In the words of our queen, Cher Horowitz, *as if*.

He reaches out like he's going to touch my hair and that does it for me. "Do not touch me." I flinch away from him, causing me to collide with another body behind me. I spin around to apologize, but I'm stopped short when the guy I've hit speaks first.

"There you are, I've been looking everywhere for you." His arm wraps around my shoulder and he gives me an unthreatening wink, causing me to pause.

Do I know this guy?

Upon further assessment, I come to the conclusion that I do not. Though the fact that I'm not getting the same danger vibes as I was with the other guy, makes it easier to play along with whatever gimmick this is. "You're not giving my wife any trouble, are you?" His piercing blue eyes leave mine and he's locked on the guy who was just trying to molest my hair. He's kind of gorgeous, actually. The stranger whose arm I'm now tucked beneath. Dark black hair, the lightest blue eyes I've ever seen, and—wait a damn minute. Did he just call me his *wife?* Is he drunk too?!

"Your...your... My apologies Mr—" Douche guy shakes his head and his face turns an odd shade of red.

"Yes, well. Why don't you call it a night before you have something to be sorry about, hmm?" I don't think I've ever heard a threat sound so polite, so *business-like*, and unbelievably sexy. The guy stares back at us like he's shocked by the fact that we're together.

Why? I have no idea, but I wish he would take his buggy little eyes and sleazy hands elsewhere.

The stranger with jet black hair and glacier blue eyes turns to face me, and when *his* hands glide over my hips and he pulls me closer to his body I'm afraid I may slip through his fingers from melting. Why I feel so much comfort with *him* is a mystery to me, but I'm not mad at it. He leans down and his lips land on mine with purpose and my entire body ignites. I try to lean into the kiss that tastes like expensive scotch and *heaven*, but stumble over his foot and spill my margarita all over him instead. I expect him to immediately pull away, or curse over the cold tequila seeping into his crisp white button-down, but instead, he lingers a little longer before pulling his lips away from mine.

"I am *so* sorry!" I gasp.

"Seems I married a very clumsy woman," he teases, immediately settling my nerves. I look around and notice the guy from earlier is long gone. I clear my throat and shift on my feet.

"Umm…he's gone." I take a step back, putting some much-needed distance between the two of us. His eyes cut to the side, seeing for himself that the guy has, in fact, disappeared.

"Good. Then my very risky efforts weren't wasted." He smiles and shoves his hands into the pockets of his dark slacks. "So what was that about anyway?" I scoff and shift my weight, popping my hip to the side.

"*Apparently,* some guys think they're entitled to anything. I close my eyes for one second and sway to the music a little bit and he thinks that means I want to dance with him…in between the sheets. Ugh, trash." I scrunch my face in disgust which draws a deep chuckle from him.

"If you want to go somewhere to dance I know of a few good places around here. I could go with you, play husband slash bouncer for you a little while longer."

"And miss the rest of this *awesome* mixer?" I joke, hiking a thumb over my shoulder. He gives me an unimpressed look, then raises a brow.

"Exactly. What do you say, Trouble… Wanna go dancing?" When he smiles at me I feel excitement prick at my skin.

"What the hell, let's go dancing." His smile deepens and he holds his arm out, allowing me to link my arm with his. I place my drink on a random table as we head towards the exit. "Thank you for that, by the way," I tell him as we walk out of the restaurant, but he keeps his eyes forward. My cheeks heat when I look up at him. His jawline is sharp, and his Adam's apple bobs when he smirks. Even in my five inch-heels I am significantly shorter than him so I doubt he can even see me looking up at him.

Thank you for the miniature-size genetics, mother. What I lack in height I make up for in personality.

"It was my pleasure." We make it into the elevator before I realize we aren't headed *out* anywhere and my brows furrow. I look up at him again just as he looks down at me. "I should probably get a clean shirt first." His smirk sends my head spinning and then he *winks* at me and completely shuts down all rational thinking. As if I'm having an out of body experience, I walk in front of him, place my hands on his chest and begin unbuttoning his shirt. His eyes grow darker as he leans against the railing, shrinking him a few inches so I can reach him better and I'm more turned on than I've ever been.

I see him swallow as he lifts his chin, watching me continue down his dress shirt until the last button is undone. My fingertips graze over his tanned skin, my eyes growing blurry as I take in the tattoo on his chest. Then his hand wraps around my wrist and he pulls my body into his, causing our eyes to lock. My heart is hammering against my chest so hard I'm sure he can feel it. Without warning his hand releases my wrist and twists in my hair instead, his lips pressing against mine with an urgency I can feel in my bones. He stands to his full height, walking us backward until he can reach the stop button for the elevator. Then he lifts me by my thighs, wrapping my legs around his waist and pressing my back against the wall. His hands are everywhere and I'm doing my best to keep up. His lips travel down my jawline and neck until they stop right by my ear again.

"We aren't going dancing, are we?" His hands slide beneath my skirt and palm my ass before squeezing it, causing me to let out a half moan, half whimper.

"No." The low chuckle he lets out sends a fresh wave of need through my entire body.

"Do you have any hard limits?" he asks, nipping at my ear.

"No." I feel his cheek press against mine as he smiles. He rears back just enough to look me in the eye. My mouth pops open of its own free will and before I know it, he bends down and bites my lip, licking the pain away right after.

"Maybe I'll find some tonight, Trouble. Hm?"

Holy shit. What have I gotten myself into?

Whatever it is at least I have the undeniable ability to, as Jamie Foxx would say, blame it on the alcohol.

I wake up to the sun just starting to filter in through the window and my head absolutely pounding. When I reach my arms up to stretch I notice a few things.

One, my neck hurts. *Two,* there's a *blissful* ache between my legs. *Three,* I'm not in my own room.

Shit. I clearly had sex last night.

I close my eyes and try to force myself to pick out even the *slightest* memory of who I may have been with last night, but outside of Antonio all I can muster up is the taste of scotch before my head starts pounding so hard I think I might actually pass out. I can handle my liquor like a champ *while* drinking, it's the mother freakin' hangovers that always get me.

The spot next to me in the king size bed is empty, though it's been thoroughly...*slept in.* I look around but see no evidence of another person in the room. My clothes are the only ones scattered across the floor, the shower isn't running so he isn't in *there*—whoever *he* is. I stand up, pulling the sheet from the bed and wrapping myself in it, as I walk around the room with my eyes squinted trying to find any details that can help me figure out what happened last night.

First thing I notice is that I'm in a higher level suite that I could never, in any of my lifetimes, afford. The view of Central Park is something I could stare at forever though. I continue my search in the bathroom, finding not one, but *three* used condoms in the trash can. Other than that, there's nothing. No toiletry bag, no suitcase, no guy... Did I get railed by a ghost or something? What the hell?

Note to self: no more tequila for you.

When I make it to the desk by the window to grab my phone from my purse I notice a note on the hotel stationary with a twenty dollar bill underneath it.

Did I whore myself out for TWENTY DOLLARS??

COFFEE'S ON ME, TROUBLE

Well... I guess I could look at the bright side. From the way my body feels this morning it was probably a good ass night. Him not being here saves me from the awkward *who are you, where am I and what happened last night* conversation, and I get free coffee out of it.

I sit down on the foot of the bed and go through my texts, leaving all of the ones from *Mother Dearest* unread, and going straight to the group chat.

TAY

Okay you boss bitch, here's what you missed while you were off taking New York by storm.

1 - Some guy high off his ass ran through the ER with only a sock on (I'll let you decide where he was wearing it.)

2 - Cece said Tay-luh so I'm officially the favorite aunt (haha, bitches)

3 - Tucker and Max are looking at a bar location in Texas this week so yee-haw for that.

SHANE

Video or it didn't happen

LEAH

Please re-read what all was on that list and specify what you want a video of before we all get a video of a man with a sock on his dick.

RUBY

She never said it was on his dick...

ME

Do you think they'll consider line dancing at Chattahoochies, TX?

RUBY

Seeing as how they wouldn't have to deal with the people as often it could be a possibility 

SHANE

Did she really say Tay-luh?

TAY

Swear to god. But I didn't video it because I'm a present auntie.

LEAH

For the love of god, where was the sock?!

ME

TAY

His left hand.

RUBY

SHANE

LEAH

I am never ever going into the ER. I'll just die.

ME

That seems rational.

I lock my phone and toss it on the bed, looking at the clock to see that I have exactly two and a half hours to get back to my room, shower, grab my coffee, and get my ass to the airport. Today I am thankful for the TSA pre-check and dry shampoo.

Dinner at my parent's house is a quarterly occurrence that I would willingly throw myself down a flight of stairs to avoid. Even though they would probably only visit me in the hospital to tell me how disappointed they are that I fell down the stairs the one night I was supposed to see them. Maybe if I'm lucky I'll be in a coma and won't be able to hear their list of disapprovals. I'm not sure why I'm even playing out this fantasy scenario while I'm sitting in my car safe and sound in front of their house, two minutes away from walking into the passive-aggressive war zone.

It's been a month since I got a phone call from my mother asking me why I wasn't promoted when Jack, the owner of Coleson Realty, stepped back from running things in our office. I was at a very exclusive real estate conference when I got the call and no matter the fact that I got chosen to go in place of Marcus, Jack's *son* and the one who was given the position, my mother was asking—*nay, interrogating*—me about, it still wasn't a big enough accomplishment to appease the perfect Mr. and Mrs. Long.

Anna and John Long have standards that Jesus himself couldn't even meet. Well, he may be the only one—regardless, they're standards I know *I* will never meet, but that doesn't stop me from trying… apparently. Because every time I try to tell myself I'm not playing the *please the parents* game, I find myself wondering if they'll be proud of my accomplishments.

Spoiler alert—they never are.

"How is work?" my father asks from his place at the head of the table. The ever-present pit in my stomach grows when the conversation begins. Because no matter what answer I give, or how well I think I'm doing, it won't be enough. I would have to tell them I'd completely taken over the company, sold every house on the market, and that they were renaming it *Lauren Long Realty* before I got even a nod of approval out of them.

"Work is good. The conference I attended last month was very exclusive and I was one of two agents from my firm that were picked to attend." I push my food around my plate, no longer hungry as I try, yet again, to say something they'll be impressed by.

"To help you see where you could be improving?" my mother asks, and I narrow my eyes. Her long dark hair is twisted halfway up, the rest falling down her back, stopping right at her shoulder blades.

"I don't think so."

"You don't think so? You don't know for sure?" My father asks in surprise.

"Luther and I are the best agents Coleson has. I highly doubt they would have chosen us to go if it were to help improve our performance." My father hums and my mother wears a look of worry that makes me roll my eyes.

"What, Mother?" I ask, causing her to purse her lips.

"I would check if I were you. You'd hate to think you're doing so well, to be left without a job." I slump in my chair, exhausted from the evening already.

"I won't be left without a job, Mom."

"You always have a place at the firm with your father if things go south."

"I won't be left without a job!" I repeat. Jesus, it's like talking to a brick wall.

"Lauren, do not speak to your mother that way." I grind my teeth together when my father raises his voice at me.

"Sorry." I sink into my chair, watching my mother out of the corner of my eye. She's the most beautiful woman I know—with dark hair, blue eyes, and the softest features that only seem to harden when I'm around.

"You know I'm only looking out for you, Lauren. Your father and I just want to ensure you're doing your best." I almost choke trying to cover up the scoff that escapes me.

We used to enjoy each other's company…right? I'm not even sure when things started to change at this point, but one day we stopped laughing together and she only ever seemed to care that I was *doing* my best, and not actually *at* my best. It's been so long since the people I care about most have even asked me how I'm doing in regards to my well-being and not my work, that I wouldn't even begin to know if I *was* if they did.

Am I okay?

"You would do well to remember who you are and show some respect to me and your mother when you're in this house." My father raises a brow at me, scolding me with just a simple look. I check my watch, seeing that it's finally eight o'clock on the dot. The extent of my required time to stay for dinner is officially up. I pull my napkin from my lap, wiping the corners of my mouth before placing it on my plate of almost untouched food.

"Yes, sir." I stand and wash my plate, cleaning up after myself as always before telling them goodbye and that I'll see them in a few months.

How is it I feel completely drained and knocked down about a thousand pegs with so little being said? I get in my car and take a deep breath, only to be surprised by a rush of tears flooding my eyes on the exhale. I shake my head and start my car, blinking them away furiously, refusing to actually cry over them. There have been dinners much worse than this one when I held my composure, tonight will not be the night I let it go. I pull out my phone and text the only other person I know will understand what I'm going through, or at least on *some* level.

ME

Why do parents start to suck sometimes?

RUBY

They expect us to be perfect in ways they never were? They see their failures in us? They want us to BE them? Because they have the great misfortune to not see what a badass daughter they have and how she's capable of taking over the world if she wanted to and does it with style.

ME

You definitely are a badass.

RUBY

Bitch, you KNOW I was talking about you.

ME

I hate these dinners.

RUBY

Come over, I'll make it up with dessert and some trashy TV.

ME

It's a work night.

RUBY

Oh I'm sorry I forgot this was the tenth grade and we had a curfew.

ME

Are you sure? Tank won't mind?

RUBY

You know he loves you too, Sour Patch Kid. Get your ass over here.

ME

Be there in ten. And he just calls me Sour Patch. No
kid. LOL

RUBY

Eh, it's your thing. Don't expect me to remember. 

I pull up to Tank and Ruby's house ten minutes later and as soon as I walk in she throws her old Bad Bunnies T-shirt at me with a pair of sweats, pointing to the couch where there's a bowl of popcorn and a spread of junk food waiting for us. Tank is sprawled out on the loveseat with Maverick, his dog, and I let out a few tears that have snuck back into my eyes. Only this time they're happy tears because I have the best friends in the world.

"Have I told you lately that I love you?" She gives me a cute little shimmy-smile combo and wraps her arms around me.

"I love you more."

"I also love you, Sour Patch, platonically of course, even if I don't know why you're crying and it's making me irrationally frustrated."

"Platonically? As opposed to the romantic way I meant that *I* love her?" Ruby says sarcastically. I let out a sad laugh and swipe my tears away, catching Ruby wink at me.

"Thanks, Tank. And thanks for letting me steal your wife tonight." I walk around the couch headed to the bathroom to change when he lifts his head to look over at me with his brows scrunched.

"You ain't stealing shit, I'm watching with y'all." My mouth pops open and I look over at Ruby.

"Guilty pleasure of his. Get changed, we'll wait for you." I rush into the bathroom, already feeling lighter than I did when I left my parents house. I don't know a lot, but I do know one thing for sure—I wouldn't have made it this far in life without my girls.

And their husbands I guess.

I can't remember the last time I felt this anxious while at work. Usually, my anxiety comes from pretty much anywhere else but here.

Stuck behind a log truck on the interstate? *Obviously.*

Seeing a text that says we need to talk from literally anyone. *Sure.*

Quarterly Sunday night dinner at my parents? *Undoubtedly.*

But at work? *Never.*

I work extremely hard to keep myself balanced and as stress-free as possible. I bust my ass at work because I like the feeling of accomplishment, I go for runs to clear my head when my brain feels too loud, and I avoid anything having to do with my parents at all costs. Work is one of the very few places I actually feel confident, in control, and on occasion, *happy.* However, today I can't stop peeling off my nail polish and staring blankly at my black computer screen in anticipation something is about to happen.

Jack and Barbara Coleson started Coleson Realty almost thirty years ago, and have done an absolutely outstanding job building this company into what it is. What started out as a small mom-and-pop style establishment, has grown into one of the most sought-after firms in

Nashville. Whether people want to buy, sell, or rent a place, they call us first.

Their oldest son, Marcus, has taken over for the most part so we don't see much of Jack and Barbara anymore. So the fact that they are both here today has me extremely on edge. I came in early, like I always do, with plans to get my schedule sorted before our team meeting, but all of those plans went straight out the window when I walked in and saw them in the conference room with someone I didn't recognize. They were in a deep, hushed conversation when I passed the door, so I kept my head down and came straight to my office. Our morning meeting begins in five minutes and I swear my clock is ticking louder with every passing second.

Tick. Tick. Tick.

"Earth to Lauren!" My eyes snap to the door, seeing Luther staring at me expectantly.

"What?" I ask, clearly having missed something.

"Girl, you are clicking that pen like you've been personally victimized by it. Are you okay?" Then he holds his hand up to his chest and gasps. "It didn't leak on that *gorgeous* blue dress you're wearing, did it?" I laugh and toss the pen onto my desk.

"Do you think it would be anywhere but the trash can if it had?" I tilt my head at him and he visibly relaxes.

"Well, then what's got you so spaced today?" He comes into my office and perches on the side of my desk, ready for whatever tea I may have to spill. This is why I love Luther. He's always ready to pour *or* absorb the tea.

Luther was going through some shit a few years ago and I was the only one that seemed to notice. Silent pain recognizes silent pain I guess. I asked him to go out with me and my friends one night for what *he* thought was a date—it wasn't—but it *was* what helped him finally come out to me. We talked for hours after leaving Topgolf that night and we've been super close ever since. He and his boyfriend, Reggie, are one of the *four* happiest couples I know and I just can't help but smile every time I see how happy he is now.

"Okay if you keep going silent on me, I'm gonna have to assume it's related to me and I don't really need that complex right now when there's a new guy that's as hot as the core of the earth in the conference room."

"So I didn't imagine that then?" I ask in a low voice, leaning in closer to him.

"Not at all. You'd have to be blind not to think so. Not even Tom Ford looks that good in Tom Ford. I've never seen a suit look like it was painted on someone before." He lets out a little playful moan and I giggle as I swat his leg with my folder full of houses I'm showing today.

"Not *that*. I just meant that there was someone in there with Jack and Barbara this morning." He rears back in shock.

"Jack and Babs are here?" The worry on his face makes the same feeling wash over me again.

"They weren't in there when you saw the guy?" My brows knit together in confusion.

"No, he—" We get interrupted when Marcus knocks on my office door, waving his finger between me and Luther.

"You are the last two I ever thought I would have to say this to but, you're late." His brows raise and he nods to the conference room. Luther gives me the *we're in trouble with the boss* look and I have to bite my lip to keep from laughing.

I grab my notebook and pen off the desk and untuck the piece of short black hair from behind my ear before walking into the conference room. Lo and behold Jack and Barbara are at the head of the conference table, and a guy who is...definitely not lacking in genetic privilege, sits next to Jack, typing away on his phone. Luther bumps my arm and his eyes roll to the back of his head and I silently scold him for thinking dirty thoughts about another man.

"Jack, Barbara, what a surprise!" I finally say, rounding the table to give Barbara a hug. She's a natural office mother when she's here, always making sure everyone is taken care of and genuinely one of the kindest people I've ever met.

"Oh my gosh, look at you. You just get more beautiful every time I see you!" she exclaims, standing to pull me into a hug. She smells like Chanel No. 5 and I know for a fact I will for the rest of the day now too.

"Which is not nearly enough. How are Sarge and Cooper?" Barbara has the cutest Corgi's I've ever seen in my life. If I were to ever get a dog, that's hands down the breed I would get.

"Oh, they're good. Sarge had to have surgery last week but you know he's a tough one. He's recovering like a champ." I cross my arms over my chest and give her a playful smirk.

"You *know*, Champ would be a really cute name for a puppy." I wink at Babs before catching a chastising glance from Jack.

"You're still a troublemaker, I see." Jack shoots me a sly grin before looking back at the papers he's flipping through. My brows knit together as something familiar flutters through my chest, but it's gone just as quickly as it appeared.

"Me? *Never*." Marcus comes in from rounding up the rest of the agents that were running late and I secretly loathe that I was one of them today. I'm never late for a meeting, and the one day I am is the day the freaking *owners* of the company are here. Mind you, I was late *because* they're here, but I digress.

"Okay, everyone. Have a seat," Marcus announces, shutting the door behind him.

When I look at the table the only open seat is next to the new guy that is *still* texting. I look at Luther and roll my eyes before pulling the chair out and sitting down, keeping my attention on Marcus and not on the loud ass typing happening next to me. Who leaves their volume turned *on* in a meeting?

Marcus starts talking about how we're moving into what is considered the *slow season* and reminding us that if we keep putting in the work, we shouldn't see too big of a difference in our numbers. Then I hear the faint *whoosh* sounds of an email being sent and something in me snaps.

My head whips to the side. "Are you serious?" The whispered scold is met with a look of indifference. "I don't know who you are or why you're even here but I do know rule number one of human decency is to pay attention when someone is talking." He leans forward, keeping his eyes—which are the most insane color of blue I've ever seen—locked on mine when he answers.

"And *who* told you I'm a decent human?" I roll my eyes and see the way his jaw tightens. He sits back in his chair still not taking his eyes off me. I don't know if he's doing it to intentionally piss me off at this point, but if so, it's working. There's nothing I despise more than people who don't pay attention when someone else is talking. Anyone who's had that sinking feeling of seeming invisible when saying something important to them and having no one pay attention would know exactly what I mean. When I finally snap out of it I realize I'm gripping my pen so hard my knuckles are white.

"Now, to move on to what I'm sure you *all* are wondering. Why are Jack and Babs here and who's the guy in Marcus's chair?" There's a collective laugh around the table, though I'm not in a very *giggly* mood so I opt for a forced smile. Jack stands up, followed by Barbara and *the texter*.

"It's good to be back in the office with you all. Reminds me of the good ole days being in the field, helping families find and eventually sell their first homes but, Babs and I aren't here to reminisce about the past. We are here because we've brought on someone new that we think will help…improve some things around here."

Honestly, Jack. Could you be any more vague?

"He's come all the way from New York to join our team and we are *very* lucky to have him. So I trust that you will all treat him with the same kindness and respect you were shown upon joining the Coleson family." The room is awkwardly silent for a moment.

"I'm a little confused. What exactly is his *position* going to be here?" I ask in what I *hope* is the kindest way possible, but if he's coming on as an agent I know people are going to be a little more hesitant to welcome him with open arms. We're already at our max number of agents and this is a pretty competitive field.

"He'll be an agent, but he'll also be weighing in on other departments that can be improving." I want to say something—

something positive or encouraging—to welcome him and show Jack that I'm gonna be a team player, but I'm just not feeling it at the moment.

"And our new agent's name is?" Luther, God bless his soul, chimes in and cuts the growing tension in the room.

"Oh, forgive me. I guess a proper introduction would be helpful." The gruff tone of Jack's laugh fills the room. "This is Mr—"

"Fitz," he interrupts Jack, smiling at everyone in the room. Though it's going to take more than a bright smile with perfectly pointed canines to get the bad taste out of my mouth about him. E-mailing during a meeting, interrupting Jack, and the entitlement dripping from his Tom Ford suit and expensive cologne that I would like to drown in if it were on literally anyone else. He smells like a rich man with good taste and I loathe myself for being so attracted to it.

"Okay. Dismissed everyone." Marcus opens the door and everyone begins chatting as they file out of the room. I take a deep breath to collect myself, push away from the table and stand with my head held high—a habit *and* a necessity since this guy is as tall as the Empire fucking State Building.

"Welcome to Coleson, *Fitz*," I say, baring my teeth as I give him my most customer service-coded smile. "I'm Lauren, Lauren Long." I offer him my hand and instead of shaking it the bastard slides both of his into his pockets and barely spares me a second glance before responding.

"Happy to be here, Sweetheart."

Chapter 3

Fitz

My little troublemaker doesn't remember me?
That simply won't do.

Chapter 4

"I think this is the one." Mr. and Mrs. Johnson stand together in the kitchen of the townhome that I have had five separate showings of this week alone. This is a new building and the surrounding community seems to be at least fifty percent new families from what I've seen during my showings this week, so it's the perfect place for these two—soon to be three—to settle down.

"You guys know how I work, there's no pressure, *but* if you're ready to make an offer we can get things moving as soon as this afternoon. I have one more showing after you guys today so I can call Amy to get things started before I ever even get back to the office."

"Yes! We definitely want to make an offer." Mrs. Johnson rubs her hand over her growing baby bump as she takes in what they hope will be their new home.

Slow season my ass, Marcus.

I've never had a slow season. I know what work has to go into keeping my sales up during the holiday months, and it always pays off. I didn't get a marketing degree for nothing, so I spend most of my time making sure I don't let opportunities fall through the cracks when I have social media at my fingertips and word of mouth doing the Lord's work.

Having chatty friends all in different lines of work really comes in handy. Those beautiful ladies hand my business card out like Halloween candy and I couldn't be more grateful for their commitment to keeping me relevant in my line of work.

Once I had someone reach out to me telling me they had some redhead—that would be Taylor—reset their dislocated arm and send them home from the ER with my card. Because, apparently, in the course of their conversation to help keep him distracted, he told her he was looking for a house and she knew just the girl that could help with that.

I hop back in my car, ready to shoot off a text to Amy about getting the paperwork ready for the Johnsons, before grabbing a coffee and heading to my last showing of the day when I realize I don't have the listing sheet for the house I'm headed to next. It's basically every single detail we could possibly want or need on a house all on one sheet of paper and I left the damn thing at the office.

"Shit," I mutter to myself, letting out a frustrated exhale before accepting the fact that I won't be getting my afternoon espresso, and head straight for the office. When I get back I see Fitz's fancy-ass Range Rover parked right out front and inwardly groan.

It's been a week since he started working at Coleson and he has been unexpectedly quiet. He just types away on his computer, only shuts his door when he takes phone calls, and as an agent, he spends *very* little time in the field. Though he has *no* problem making little remarks about other people not making as many visits as they should be.

Hypocrite.

"You have two showings marked off your schedule today, try to get them replaced."

"Be sure you're posting on your media pages more, don't become irrelevant."

"Time to go through past clients and send out equity stats and follow-ups."

Like, honestly, who died and made you king?

Oh my god, I should call and check on Jack.

"Hey Amy, let's get the paperwork started on the townhome off Indiana for the Johnsons. I don't want her to have that baby before she has the chance to pick paint colors." I smile and she claps her hands together excitedly.

"Aww, I am so glad they picked the townhouse, that place is gorgeous!"

"I know, I'm about to run again so just text me if you need anything that I may not have put in their file. Oh, and here's your final color analysis. You, my dear, are a summer." She smiles and claps her hands together in thanks as I hand the file folder and three little bottles of makeup to her. As soon as I turn to walk to my office I run into a body instead, letting out an involuntary huff.

"Oh, sorry," I shake my hair out of my face and look up, only to be met with those frustratingly hypnotic blue eyes.

"Where's the fire?" he deadpans.

"Your office, better get in there," I quickly reply. I take a step to the left and he actually has the audacity to step in front of me.

"I'm not sure I'm qualified to put out a fire." He quirks a brow, sliding his hands into the front pockets of his dress pants.

"I didn't say anything about putting it out." I press the palm of my hand to his chest and shove him out of the way as I march towards my office. I don't bother turning around to see his reaction, though I can *feel* his gaze burning into my back. As I look around my office I don't see the folder I'm looking for anywhere. I check the clock to see I have twenty minutes to get across town so I opt to print out another one instead, hoping I remember all the personalized notes I made myself on the back of the last one.

"There." I blow out a breath, closing my eyes to try and calm my anxious mind, but the more time that passes that I don't hear my printer whirring to life, the less my calming technique works. I turn around and see that my printer isn't making all those dreadful noises because it's *gone.*

"Amy!" I yell from my office, staring at the empty space with dust surrounding where my printer *used* to be.

"Yeah?" she calls back from the front of the office.

"Where the hell is my printer?"

Silence.

"Ames? I really don't have time for pranks today. Do you know where it is?" I begin walking back to the front, lowering my voice as I get closer to her desk so I'm not yelling in her face when I come to a stop in front of her desk. She opens her mouth, then shuts it again when her eyes cut to someone behind me.

"It's in my office." I turn around and see Fitz shrug, completely unbothered. Like he's not making this day considerably worse every time he appears.

"Why?" I demand, crossing my arms over my chest.

"I don't have one in my office yet and you were out at showings, so I borrowed it." His explanation comes so casually. As if it's totally fine that he went into my office while I wasn't here and took something that doesn't belong to him.

I clench my jaw so hard that it hurts, storming past him and heading straight for his office. I feel him walking behind me, even though he doesn't make a sound when he moves.

"You can't just go into people's offices while they're not here and take their stuff." I groan, leaning over his desk chair to use his computer.

"Says the woman currently in someone else's office, using a computer that doesn't belong to her." I glare at him over the top of the screen, seeing the look of amusement on his face as he leans in the doorway.

"I need my next listing printed, and since you *stole* my printer, I have to print it in here." His arms are crossed over his chest like he's got all the time in the world. Which he probably does since he doesn't *do* anything except take phone calls and get on my nerves.

"*Borrowed.*"

"What?" I snap, snatching the paper from the printer tray.

"You said I stole your printer, but I only borrowed it. I planned to return it before you got back, your little impromptu drop-in before your last showing was unexpected. I didn't think you'd be back until about four-thirty. My plan was to have it back in its home by then. Safe and sound." His completely bored tone has me itching to rebuttal, but I can't.

"I—how—" *Too many thoughts, not enough caffeine to make sense of any of them.* "Don't take my stuff." I point a finger in his face like a moody teenager before turning to storm out, only stopping when I hear him speak again.

"Make time to check your emails before the end of the day."

I'm going to murder him with his own office supplies.

With the realization that I have lost at least ten minutes of travel time arguing with him about my printer, I put my homicidal plans on hold and continue storming out. Once I'm back in my car I grab my bag from the floorboard to reapply my lipgloss and notice the folder I thought I'd left at the office is shoved under the passenger seat.

"Awesome."

So I could have gotten my espresso and avoided running into Fitz—who has managed to put me in an outrageous mood in record time. Love this for me.

Unable to fight the urge to see what email he was talking about, I grab my phone and open my mail folder, but when I open it up I find not only *one* but *three* emails from him instead.

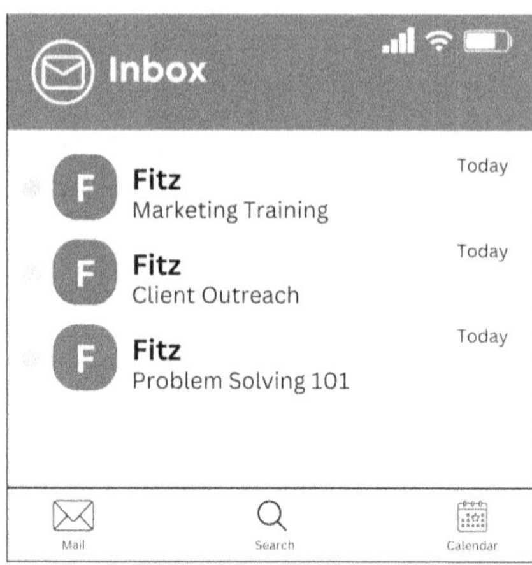

I take a deep breath, inhaling and exhaling both on a three count and when that doesn't work—I bare my teeth and scream. As if the universe knew I needed a cure for my onset anxiety attack, my phone dings with a text.

TAY

Anyone wanna move girls night up to tonight?

SHANE

Sure!

RUBY

I'm down, I'm off today so I can host.

ME

Music to my ears. I'll be there.

LEAH

Hump dayyy. 🐫 🌴

ME

More like get fucked dayyyy, and not in the good way.

RUBY

Uh-oh. Lu has drama? This must be major.

I'm not usually the one doing the majority talking when we pour it out, just the usual family issues, low-key work shit that really doesn't matter in the grand scheme of things but still bums me out, but tonight I'll have a heavy pour—in more ways than one.

Chapter 5

Lauren

"I can't tell you guys how happy I am that we didn't wait two more days to pour it out." I pour myself a generous cup full of Shane's bomb-ass margaritas and take a long sip.

"I feel that. I'm still not over my catastrophic date from Monday night," Leah agrees.

Taylor takes over the conversation next, always the queen of bringing the biggest news to the chat. She goes on talking about her trashy ex-situationship and absolutely horrendous former roommate, who are now sleeping together, apparently. Tana was a case for the health department and Zander should be flagged in a social media group somewhere—as in red flags because that's all that boy is.

"I still can't believe you ever slept with that thing," I mumble into my margarita, catching an eye roll from Tay.

"So there's that. Lauren, you go. Pour it out, baby." Leah gives me the nod to let my shit out and boy do I not hold back this time.

"*UGH*, okay. So we have this new guy in the office that came from New York, right? And since he apparently made *millions* selling some of the most upscale homes and penthouses there, he thinks he's like, the *god of real estate* or something and wants to tell everyone how to do their jobs. Like, excuse me *Mr. Real Estate,* I'm pretty fucking great at my job already. Sit down." I down the rest of my drink and slam it on the table while my best friends look at me like all the skin just fell off my face.

"Who is he?" Ruby finally asks, breaking the skin-tingling silence.

"*Fitz.* That's it. He just goes by *Fitz.* Like he's Elvis or Prince or something. I mean, come on how pretentious is that?" Taylor, the freaking five-foot-nothing Rottweiler of the group agrees with me with an eye roll I feel in my soul.

"I should just call him Lucifer. Suits his personality better but lets him keep the whole *one-name* brand going for him."

"Whose name is Lucifer?" Tank asks, swiping his keys from the island while holding their youngest son Poe in his baby carrier with their oldest son Hendrix not far behind. I don't feel the need to give Tank the full informational packet on how I'm being *mega* dramatic about this and that his name isn't actually Satan, so I just give him a guy answer. Short and to the point.

"New guy at my work." His brows bounce up to his hairline and he tilts his head judgmentally.

"Poor guy. His parents really set him up for failure."

After he tells Ruby goodbye we are left to finish our girls' night full of belly laughs, good food, and strong drinks.

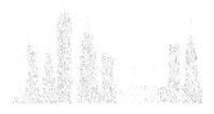

My workout playlist is playing at a volume that scratches just the right part of my brain as I push through the last few minutes of my run. New day; new possibilities. I haven't felt quite like myself since I went to New York a few months ago and I'd do anything to go back and never pick up the phone when my mother called me. I'm used to the subtle jabs at how the way I live my life isn't good enough for them, but this was the blow that took me out at the knees, and I'm not sure any of my regular remedies will pull me back together this time. I slow myself to a jog and stop at Brüman's before walking the last block back to my place.

This way I don't have to backtrack for my coffee before heading into the office.

"Morning Lauren!" Clara greets me as soon as I walk through the door and pull my headphones down around my neck. I keep my shoulder-length black hair down during my runs because feeling wind in it is extremely calming for me. I quickly run my fingers through it to settle any flyaways before smiling back at her and rubbing my hands together. It's early December and while most people would probably choose to run in a gym instead of out in the cold, nothing beats the fresh air for me.

"Good morning, Clara."

"Your usual?" She pulls out a large cup and eyes me curiously.

"You know me well." Unzipping the pocket of my jacket, I pull out the cash I had blindly grabbed from my wallet this morning and notice all I have on me is a twenty-dollar bill. I typically grab a ten so I can hand it to Clara and demand she keep the rest as change. Twenty dollars for coffee just seems a little outrageous though.

Coffee's on me this morning, Trouble.

I shake my head at the memory that violently flashes through my mind.

Lips like heaven.

The elevator.

Hands on me everywhere.

"Brown sugar shaken espresso, three pumps of white mocha, and *of course*, vanilla cold foam," Clara sings out my order with a smile and I realize I'm absentmindedly rubbing the spot on my neck that I remember being sore the day I woke up in a strangers hotel room. I quickly recover and smile at Clara.

"You really could just call my name instead of saying the whole drink, Clara. It's kind of a mouth full and I trust you with my order, you should know that by now." We share a laugh as she cashes me out and I drop a five-dollar bill into her tip jar before winking at her, placing my headphones back on, and heading home.

When I finally walk through my front door I'm immediately relaxed by the familiar scent of coconut and fresh linen. I've spent a lot of time making my home my own little safe haven— somewhere I feel happiest, a place that truly reflects who I am. It's undoubtedly my favorite place to spend my time. I set my coffee down and rush into my bedroom, stripping out of my running clothes and turning the shower on until the bathroom looks more like a sauna. I brush my hair and throw my shower cap on before stepping in and letting the steaming hot water ease the tension in my shoulders. I speed through my shower, giving me plenty of time to do my makeup and it's not until I open my emails, while finishing off my coffee on the way down to my car, that I remember I have three unopened emails from Satan himself. I can't believe I actually forgot to open them last night. I was well past the point of being able to safely read anything from him though. Especially when the reply button has no ability whatsoever to tell me I'm tipsy and about to say something that would more than likely get me fired—through a *company* email no less—so they remain unread.

And that's how they shall stay, for now.

I'm back to my regular routine of being the first one in the conference room for our team meeting today and I have the great displeasure of being accompanied by Fitz—who chooses to sit right next to me. With a room full of open chairs, he drops his stuff down on the table right beside me. I close my eyes as the gust of wind blows across my face from his folders hitting the table and swallow down my annoyance. Successful for only a moment in remaining calm until…

"Care to tell me why my emails are still unread?" His tone is arrogantly expectant.

"Because I didn't open them." I don't look up from my phone when I answer but I can feel his eyes on me.

"But you saw them, did you not?" I suck my teeth and tilt my head to the side and finally look at him, regrettably so, because the man is so gorgeous it makes me want to bleach his perfectly trimmed beard just to take him down a few pegs.

"Oh, emails from *you?* No. Must have gone straight to junk where they belong. Why? Were they important?" I feign ignorance as he studies me. Then he narrows his eyes and leans in closer—much closer than is necessary since we're the only two people in this dead silent room.

"Bitterness does not become you, Lauren." I bare my teeth and feel my chest tighten.

"Entitlement does not become *you,* Fitz." I hope for some kind of reaction. A sign that he isn't some corporate robot that is incapable of doing anything other than piss me off but he simply raises a brow at me and sits back in his seat as he keeps his eyes on me.

"You don't like me, do you?"

Duh.

"I don't know you." Trying to avoid this conversation going any further I pull my pen out of my notebook and make a note to go for a run after work tonight. No matter how cold it is, I already know I'll be in need of a little decompression run after today.

"And yet—you don't like me." I finally let the petty part of me that uses sarcasm and indirect responses as a way to deflect uncomfortable situations sit this one out and look at him more directly and confidently in what I'm about to say.

"I don't like the way you treat people."

"And how do I treat people?" If I'm not mistaken he actually looks interested in my answer, so I don't hold back with it. I toss my pen down on my planner and link my fingers together folding my hands over the top of it.

"Like they're beneath you. Less important." His jaw tightens and I can *finally* tell I've struck a nerve. Though I must say, I'm a little shocked that *this* is the topic that finally warrants a reaction from him—but I continue. "You come in here on your first day, not bothering to look up at anyone as they walk in. You continued emailing the whole time Marcus is going through our morning meeting, then you interrupted

Jack when he was trying to introduce *you*. It was the most disrespectful behavior I've ever seen pass through this office and I am shocked Jack actually hired you." He nods slowly like he's processing, and just when I think we'll see some kind of breakthrough, I'm proven wrong.

"Well, I hope you can get past this little disapproval you have of me, because we're about to be spending a *lot* of time together, Sweetheart." And with that, he stands up, collects his things, and walks out of the conference room. He stops to chat in hushed tones with Marcus before disappearing down the hallway.

Marcus comes over, sitting in the chair Fitz just abandoned, and lets out a sigh.

"Do not say it, Marcus. I'm so serious."

"Don't say what?" His brows knit together in confusion.

"Whatever you're about to say that informs me I'll be working with Lucifer for whatever god-forsaken reason he's come up with."

"I don't call the– Wait, did you just call him Lucifer?" I close my eyes in annoyance and take a deep breath.

"Don't worry about that. What did you mean? You don't call the what? The shots? Because last time I checked that's exactly what you do when Jack isn't here." He pulls his bottom lip in with his teeth, rubs a hand along his jaw, and looks across the room, clearly frustrated. "Marcus?"

"I'm sorry, Lauren. I wish I could do something, but you're doing a round of training with Fitz."

"What?! *Why?*" My eyes grow wider and my heart feels like it's fighting against my ribs. "Marcus, you know I keep up with my training, I stay up to date on everything there is to know in this business," I lower my voice to a whisper. "I'm one of the best agents you have. What do *I* need training for?"

"You don't. You're right, you are the best. I have no idea why this is happening, I was just told to inform you of your new assignment." He gives me an apologetic smile, lets me know I don't have to stay for the meeting, then stands and addresses the rest of the room.

What the fuck is happening?

Chapter 6

Fitz

I sit in my office staring at an email from my father with very specific instructions for my newest assignment, and a not-so-subtle reminder of my role in this company—*his* company. Nothing puts me in a worse mood than having to work with him, which is probably why I seem pissed off eighty-five percent of the time. Well, nothing except maybe having someone tell me to my face that I'm acting just like him.

I'd planned on breaking the news to Lauren myself about what all this training would entail, but her blatant distaste for my very existence has been slowly chipping away at my desire to get on her good side. When I asked her why she didn't like me I thought surely it was because she'd come to the realization of how we knew each other and was upset that I hadn't said anything about it yet, but oh how wrong I was. Instead, I got a full serving of humble pie and what I hated most was that she was right. The longer I'm in this business, being the puppet to a master who cares about no one but himself, the more I inherit his undesirable characteristics.

Maybe it's better that she hates me after all. Seeing as how I can't seem to wipe her from my memory no matter how hard I try; her hatred for me may be the best-case scenario. We are working together now, and sleeping with your co-workers never ends well. Or so I hear. So if she has to hate me in order for me to keep her at arm's length, then so-fucking-be it. Following that thought are the three angriest knocks I've ever heard in my life.

Trouble.

"Something I can help you with?" I glance at her over the top of my computer screen and see her tip her chin up slightly. Little vixen, wearing tights and a mini skirt I'd like nothing more than to rip right off her. Her short black hair sits right at her shoulders in loose waves, barely hitting the fabric of her black turtleneck. When my eyes finally make it up to hers, they roll in the back of her head and my hand fists at the sight.

"Telling me how to do my job, apparently," she mumbles and I can't help but smirk. She's full of fire and rage, this one.

"Well, then we have a lot to discuss." Her features turn to stone as she comes in and drops her things in the chair right inside the door.

"So where are we doing this? In here? The conference room? A cell?" I swallow down the laugh that dares to escape and lean back in my chair, crossing my arms over my chest.

"Shut the door." I tip my chin up and her cheeks turn red.

Is that fury or anticipation I see, Trouble?

She does as she asked and when she faces me again she lifts a brow at me.

"Did I pass the first test?"

"Are you just determined to make this a miserable experience for yourself or is this just part of your charm?"

"Aww. You think I'm charming?" She bats her eyelashes at me, purely out of spite I'm sure, and I realize this is going to be significantly harder for me than it will be for her. Because while she gets to keep her disdain for me during this mandatory training evaluation, I have to look at her every day for however long is deemed necessary, remembering how she tastes and the way she looks when I make her come. The eye rolls are going to have to stop or I'll likely do something completely unprofessional, and this time, unforgettable.

"Sit." She narrows her eyes into slits then walks up and takes a seat in the chair right in front of my desk. "Good. Let's begin."

I loathe my father for making me fly back to New York the day before Christmas Eve. I understand wanting me home for the holidays so my mother doesn't give him an ear full about their only son missing Christmas, but it wouldn't have killed him to have me come home a few days sooner. Every inch of this airport is packed with people in a panic over missing their flights, and more luggage than one person should ever have to look at. I pull my hood up and slump further in my seat as I wait to board, scrolling through emails to kill time.

I pull up a thread from last week, smirking at some of the fiery responses I received from Lauren. She still thinks this is some sort of punishment or the result of some kind of poor reflection on her work—when in reality, it's quite the opposite. I just find it more fun to watch her stew in her anger as I make her give me presentations on market value, interest rates, and break things down as if I'm a first-time agent or problem-solve things only people in much higher positions in the company would ever have to deal with. She's excellent at what she does, so much so none of this training is remotely necessary, but I'm not ready to stop playing this little game with her.

"Now boarding group A." I scan my ticket from my phone, sit down in first class, and let my head fall back on the seat as I brace myself for the week and a half of Christmas in hell before flying *back* out to Nashville to continue with my assignment. Two hours is not a long enough flight for me to prepare myself for this.

"Anything to drink for you sir?"

"Scotch, neat."

And probably keep them coming.

Once the plane lands and we de-board, my phone immediately starts flooding with text messages from my mother, absolutely ecstatic that I am home and I can practically hear her squealing through all the exclamation marks on my screen.

My relationship with my mother is…fine. She always seems excited to see me, but the thing about my mother is she was so desperate for this lavish life, she goes along with anything my father wants. Anything he says or does that makes him the one person on earth I wholeheartedly loathe, she cowers at his side and says nothing. Which makes it hard to have a positive relationship with her when she so willingly lets him act the way he does. Christmas at the Fitzgerald house is always extravagant, but this house, the food, and these people, aren't what *home for the holidays* should be. It should be a wood burning fireplace, Christmas carols playing on an old radio in the living room, a kitchen full of turkey, dressing, mashed potatoes and cranberry sauce, and laughter. Lots and lots of laughter—and not the fabricated kind that sells someone something over catered in food served on fine china.

I'm probably the only person in the universe who wishes their flight back home had gotten canceled today.

"Fitz!" I stiffen as my mother calls my name from the steps of their extravagant townhome. I would expect nothing less from Mr. & Mrs. New York Real Estate.

"Hello, mother." I force a smile and her features soften. I feel a little guilty sometimes that I don't get more excited about coming home. Then I remember that this *wasn't* my home for most of my adolescence and then all that guilt turns into some form of resentment, disdain, or in a lot of cases, indifference. "What's on the agenda for the night?" I ask, as she links her arm through mine as we walk into the house.

"No agenda tonight. I thought you and I might go shopping on Fifth Avenue while your father is working. Maybe spend some quality time together?" I can't think of a single time in my life my mother has ever requested to spend *quality time* with me, and even though I get the sneaking suspicion that she has some kind of ulterior motive for wanting to go, I agree. Afterall, what reason do I have not to?

"Sounds great. What time should we go?" Her whole face lights up when I don't argue the matter and a small smile makes its way onto my face as well.

"I'll have the car pick us up in about an hour. Is that enough time for you to get settled?" she asks, a smile stretched wide across her face.

"Yes ma'am." She scoffs and swats my arm.

"You and those southern manners. Your father made a mistake sending you down south," she jokes. I remain silent as I head upstairs to put my things in the spare room, knowing all too well there would have been a fight over my wanting to stay at my *own* home tonight and risk the chance of not seeing my father on my first night in town. I'll make my way home sometime tomorrow. Maybe I'll be lucky enough to get stuck there, snowed in perhaps, until my flight departs after New Year's.

"Are we ready to go?" my mother chirps as she slides her gloves on. I've missed the bitter cold of New York this winter. Tennessee is strangely warm this time of year, though most of the locals act as though their nipples will fall off if it gets any colder out. Hysterical. They wouldn't last a day in a New York winter.

"Ready." I nod, offering my arm to her. She takes me in and smiles. I've paired my black peacoat, gray knit cap, and black leather gloves with a cream cable knit sweater, dark jeans, and black leather boots, earning a nod of approval from Lena Fitzgerald herself.

My mother is nothing if not a fashion snob and has *no* trouble telling you when something doesn't match or if your colors *simply do not compliment you.* It's the one thing I like most about her because it's truly *her.* Not some personality trait she's inherited from being my father's wife. He could give a shit less about the things she loves.

We barely make it through three floors of Bergdorf Goodman before I'm ready to call it a night and go the fuck home, but I stop short when I see a pair of shoes that catch my eye.

"See something you like, dear? I never took you for a pumps guy, but maybe I don't know you as well as I thought I did." I can hear the tease in her tone and I let out a small laugh, trying to brush off the thoughts running rampant in my mind of a certain five-foot-nothing raven-haired vixen wearing a pair of black pumps and nothing else.

"Must have just zoned out I guess. It's been a while since I shopped for this long." She hums curiously as we keep walking, looking up at me expectantly.

"Something on your mind, Mother?" She sighs dramatically and then stops, pulling on my arm to get me to face her.

"Don't you ever think about settling down, Fitzy?" I wish there was a polite way to tell your mother you'd rather her call you *anything* else than the nickname of a nickname she's given you.

"Not really," I tell her honestly.

"Well, maybe it's time you do." I quirk a brow at her in question so she continues. "Honey, you're thirty-four years old. You're in line to inherit your father's company when he retires in a little over a year. If you plan on getting married or having children, now is the time to do so. Having a strong family image *is* good for business, you know." I feel my chest tighten at her words.

"Is that why I spent the better half of my life being raised by someone else? To help form a *strong* family image?"

"Fitz," she whispers, clearly regretting her choice of words.

"Is that why you brought me here tonight, Mother? To wear me down with shopping and tell me it's time I get married and have children, and for what? To maintain the picture-perfect family you and Daddy Dearest have fought *so hard* to fabricate?" I bite the words out, suddenly wishing I hadn't agreed to come here tonight.

"No! I just—" She stops to collect herself, though I'm not the least bit inclined to entertain whatever it is she will say next. "I know how taxing this job can be. You've been destined for this role since you were born, Fitz. I just thought you might like to have someone along for the ride is all... It can get awfully lonely sometimes, you know?"

Fuck.

I sigh and run my hand along my jaw. "I think we've shopped

enough tonight, don't you? Why don't we grab some hot chocolate and head home?" She smiles sadly and nods her agreement.

I carry all of her bags to the car, and we spend the rest of the evening in a somewhat comfortable silence. Both of us are more than likely clueless as to what to say after that. Part of me wants to believe she was asking about my love life out of sheer concern for me—as I'm sure any normal mother would do—but the other part is almost certain my father put her up to asking. Because she isn't any normal mother, and we don't do heartfelt shopping nights and conversations like this. So I have to be realistic in my conclusion that she's just doing his dirty work.

Skipping dinner last night was a huge fucking mistake. My stomach sounds like it's trying to wage a war against me and I have no desire to sit at the kitchen table and deal with my father on an empty stomach. Being hangry is a real thing and knowing the first words out of his mouth are going to be business-related is not something I'm prepared to deal with at seven in the morning on Christmas Eve. Doing my best to remain silent, I grab my running shoes and my wallet and sneak out the front door to head to the café down the street.

After a breakfast sandwich and cup of coffee I finally feel a little more like myself. I grab my phone from the table and begin scrolling through social media. It's like some sort of sick self torture to scroll through seeing all the happy families and couples celebrating Christmas with puppies and Christmas abroad. Then I get the urge to type a name into the search bar that I know I should stay away from.

Lauren Long.

Her handle *@lifewith_lauren* makes me smile. Her latest post is a photo of her and a group of girls. A blonde, a redhead, a couple of brunettes, and all of them smiling ear to ear around a kitchen island with Christmas-themed footie pajamas on. I find myself scrolling through the carousel of photos from the post seeing mixed drinks, what seems to be tons of laughter and before I know it I've scrolled through three months worth of her posts. There are the same three guys in a lot of her photos and I stop myself from overthinking which one she might be with. Choosing, instead, to imagine she's with none of them.

The first day I showed up at Coleson and she snapped at me, I thought she may just be uptight, but as it turns out, she just hated *me*. After her telling me why she didn't particularly care for me, I couldn't even blame her. I've watched her from a distance—where she likes to keep me—and quickly realized she's the farthest thing from what I assumed. Outside of being particularly grumpy this week, she's punctual, organized, always smiling and laughing with people in the office, she gets coffee for Amy when she stops for her own and seems to be the first person everyone goes to for help—everyone loves her—and it's pretty easy to see why.

Damn, I have got to get it together and stay away from this girl and her wildly contagious smile. Though, I never seem to see it in person.

That will have to change.

"To what do I owe the pleasure of running into *the* Mr. Fitzgerald?" I hear a familiar voice ask from beside me.

"I suppose being in the mood for a decent cup of coffee allowed you the pleasure." I lock my phone and turn to face Jessica Vanderbilt. Her name drips old money as much as the girl who owns it. She lets out an overexaggerated laugh and slides into the chair across from me.

"It's been a while. What have you been up to?" She leans forward, letting her very expensive breasts all but spill out of her athleisure wear that I'm *sure* isn't helping to keep her warm. Her hard-pressed nipples are a dead giveaway of that.

"Working," I answer, trying to portray just how uninterested in this conversation I am.

"Well of course. You're like, one of the hardest-working guys I know." Her fingertips brush along the back of my hand and my eyes lock with hers.

"Well, I would love to argue with you, for the sake of humility, but

I'm afraid I have to agree this time." She tosses some of her long blonde hair over her shoulder and sighs.

"We should get together sometime this week. Since you're here and *hopefully* not working during the holidays."

"For coffee?" I quirk a brow at her as I bring my coffee cup to my lips.

"No, silly. For dinner. I'm sure I could spare some time to let you take me out." I've known Jessica for a long time, and while she's not someone I'd ever, as my mother put it, *settle down with,* she would be an excellent distraction for me while I'm stuck with my parents this week, as she's done for me plenty of times in the past.

I'm sure they would love nothing more than for me to end up with someone like Jessica—well, not just someone *like* her. Her, specifically. The Vanderbilts are known internationally for their hotel enterprise, and while I am in no way interested in anything more than an excuse to get out from under my parent's thumb this week, she doesn't need to know that.

"How's the day after tomorrow?" I *almost* feel bad at the way she lights up.

"You know where to find me. I'll be ready at seven." She leans across the table and kisses my cheek before wiggling her fingers to tell me goodbye.

"Merry Christmas, Son." I nod to my father as he hands me an envelope with a smug wink. I already know it's some kind of check or savings bond, seeing as how the man literally only cares about money. I rip it open and look inside—a check for ten thousand dollars sits inside. *Jesus Christ.*

"Thank you, Sir." He slaps me on the back with a huge grin, which is his version of affection. He always assumes everyone shares his love of money, not knowing this check will be donated amongst the charities I give to that he doesn't know about. He would probably turn into a human volcano if he knew I gave money away the way I do. When he bothers asking what I've done with the money, I always tell him I've invested it in stocks—which sometimes I do, I am a businessman after all—-but I also care about the needs of others, a trait I did *not* inherit from him, so I like to give back to the community.

"Weston, you're next." My mother hands my father his gift from her. He opens up a new pair of diamond cufflinks and I fight the urge to roll my eyes. The man has more pairs of overpriced cufflinks than any one man ever should own.

"Lena, you did excellent, dear." I see my mother light up and then she passes him the gift I got him when we went out shopping.

"Oh, wow." His brows jump to his hairline when he looks at the designer loafers I got him. I was stuck between those and a briefcase, but figured since he won't be needing one for much longer, shoes were a better option. "These are nice, Son. Thank you." I pause at his words, then offer him a smile in return. I think that's the first time my father has ever thanked me for something.

I don't think I like it.

Once we finally finish opening presents, I manage to escape my parent's house and head home. In times like this I wish I'd bothered making friends so I would have someone to call and grab a drink with, instead of drinking alone while watching sports highlights.

Chapter 8

If I could just skip from the moment Christmas Eve eve ends and go straight to New Year's Day, I would. Christmas at the Long's is absolutely exhausting—loud, boisterous guests filling every corner of my childhood home and gifts that only prove further how little my parents know me. They buy for the daughter they *wish* they had, not the one they *actually* have. I always show my gratitude for them, though, because if there's one thing my parents and I do agree on, it's the need to exchange a gift that doesn't fit quite right. Only, in my case, it's not so much that it doesn't fit my body as it doesn't fit my taste.

Christmas Eve *Eve*, however, is my favorite tradition and the *only* thing that keeps me from hating the holidays. My girls have always been that for me. The ones that keep me grounded and show me the light when I feel like I'm sitting in a shadow cast by the person I constantly think I should be.

We started the tradition in middle school, themed footie pajamas were mandatory then and still are now. We all got to pick our favorite Christmas movie, which to no one's surprise we all had the same favorite, and we would all bring our favorite snacks. We still do all of that, only now we get to indulge in Shane's famous margaritas and we always try out a new mixed drink to see if we find a new favorite.

So far, nothing beats Shane's margaritas.

I'm sitting in bed, scrolling through the post I made last night while still half sober and I can't help but smile. If I could just live in the highlight reel that is my social media page, I would. There are so many pictures, even a few blurry ones that actually came out kind of aesthetically pleasing, of us laughing and clinking our glasses together and my favorite one—all of us asleep together on the couch while *The Grinch* plays in the background. I assume Tucker took the photo since he was the only other one in the house besides those of us asleep in the picture.

That tradition is one of the things that's stayed consistent while so much else in our lives continues to change. I've had a front-row seat to three-fourths of my friends falling in love, and watching their lives transform in every way imaginable. Career changes, building homes together, and growing their families. I simply couldn't be happier for them, even if I have to consciously fight to keep myself from going down the '*what am I doing wrong*' spiral.

I'll never be the one to say that a woman needs a man in her life to feel complete, be happy, or fulfill her purpose. All I'm saying is—I *want* a man in my life. Not just any man though. I want the kind of love I get to witness at every group outing with my friends. Every time I see posts on social media, or when one of the guys walks through the kitchen during girls' nights and can't help but smile when they look at their wife or fiancée. The way they protect them, love them and stand up for them all while letting them be completely and totally themselves. I want a man so nauseatingly in love with me that he can't imagine a life without me.

Ugh. There it is.

The one thing I'm constantly reminded I don't have is the thing I secretly crave the most.

RUBY

Cool if we grill out tonight? We didn't discuss food
during all of the firework talk for tonight.

ME

Omg yesss. Would kill for a hot dog right now.

RUBY

Well that's good enough for me and now everyone
else's opinions are irrelevant.

SHANE

Rude. But grilling out sounds fab. We'll bring buns and
chips.

TAY

We got drinks.

LEAH

Do I need to bring anything??

RUBY

Sounds like we have the basics, so just yourself,
gorgeous.

ME

See you guys tonight. 

New Year's Eve also looks a little different these days. No more going out dancing, or seeing if we can find someone to kiss before midnight. Now we hang out with the people who have become family, shooting fireworks in the backyard, grilling out, and putting the kids to bed by nine. I refuse to start the new year negatively. I'll be with my girls, laughing until our cheeks hurt and *that* is what it always comes back to. I've got my girls, what else do I need?

"I would *really* like to see you go against Tank in a hot dog eating contest." Max chuckles from his place across from mine as we all sit around Tank and Ruby's outdoor dining table with the outdoor heaters keeping us warm. I narrow my eyes and then glance over at Tank who is giving me a challenging look.

"I'd love to, but un*fortunately* I snacked all day and already put away *two* of these as well as half of Shane's burger so I'm afraid I must decline. Unless of course you want to see the absurd amount of junk food I stored away like a squirrel for winter during my Netflix binge today." Tank begins laughing, shaking his head as he sucks some ketchup off his thumb like the Neanderthal he is.

"I think she might actually give me a run for my money." I roll my eyes and sit back in my chair.

"Better you run than me, I don't think I'm moving again til' Valentine's Day."

"Will you be my Valentine Aunt Lauren?" Hendrix, my not-so-little love, asks from a few seats down.

"I can't think of a single person I'd rather have as a Valentine, Hen. Ice cream and Spider-Man marathon?"

"Heck yeah." He holds his fist out to me and I bump it—blowing it up, of course—earning the sweetest smile from him. Hendrix is by far the coolest seven-year-old I know, and the only kid I've ever found myself not feeling completely intimidated by.

"It's a little early to be choosing a Valentine, isn't it buddy? What if you find someone else you want to ask at school or something?" Tank asks. I whip my head around as my jaw drops.

"Bite your tongue." His hands go up defensively as he laughs.

"Fireworks?" Hendrix asks Ruby, bouncing in his seat with anticipation.

"Fireworks!" she agrees and they jump up from the table to get everything ready.

After shooting off the *big guy* fireworks, as Tucker called them, the kids get to experience the magic of sparklers. Cece squeals, looking as adorable as ever in her pink knit cap and rosy cheeks. Hendrix is running around the yard acting like the sparkler ninja and Poe looks absolutely hypnotized by the one Ruby is holding in the hand opposite of him. After they've emptied two entire boxes of sparklers, it's time for the littles to go in.

"Alright Munchkins, time for bed!" Tank rounds up the boys, while Max gets Cece from Shane, leaving Tucker to take the dogs in for bed. We all pile onto the outdoor couches, snuggling under the fleece blankets as the firepit comes to life between us.

We're in a fit of giggles over Leah kissing my cheek and claiming we'll ride off into the sunset together when her phone goes off and she drops a major informational bomb on us.

"You guys kissed?!" I squeal. Apparently, she and Sawyer kissed on Christmas Eve while we were all at Taylor and Tucker's house. There's a less than angelic chorus of screams and squeals coming from all of us, and just as she begins giving us the details about how they both unknowingly liked each other back in high school, and neither of them knew it, the guys come running out.

"What's wrong?" They all come almost tripping over each other out the back door.

You know, for ex-military, they're not very stealthy.

"Leah and Sawyer kissed!" Taylor screams.

"I know, but it sounded like someone was getting their eyes scratched out." I roll my lips together to keep from laughing because he's made a grave mistake letting it slip that he had previous knowledge of this very juicy gossip and *didn't* tell his soon-to-be wife.

"It might be you in a minute. What. Do. You. Mean. You. *Knew?*"

"Oh, well…" He looks to the guys for help, who both know better than to get involved.

"Nope." Tank shakes his head.

"You're on your own, brother." Max shrugs.

"Oh, I think Cece needs her Uncle Tucker." He backs into the house and blows Taylor a kiss.

"Mhm, I'll deal with you later," she mumbles.

"Promise?"

Stop being so in love already.

I turn my attention back to Leah. "So what does this *meannnn?*"

"I don't *knowwww*," she mocks. "Jackson showed up and things got kind of messy." She pulls her phone out of her pocket and shows us the text he just sent her and my heart does this weird flip. He wants her to meet him at a rooftop lounge that is *known* for its very exclusive parties, and he seems very adamant that she shows up.

After finally convincing her and helping her get ready, the excitement on her face could light up the night sky far better than any firework ever could.

So help me God, if he hurts her, I'll bury him under the hockey arena he plays in.

The weird feeling in my chest grows more prominent once Leah leaves to meet Sawyer. I don't get it though. I'm *happy* for her. All I ever want for any of my friends is for them to be happy, to find love—if that's what they want—and chase every single dream they have. I guess the realization that I'm the last woman standing alone in the group makes me feel a bit sad.

"Ok. I think I need to call it a night." I let out a sigh, pulling myself up from the couch.

"What? It's not even midnight yet!" Ruby pouts, though I can tell she's more than ready to call it a night.

"I know. I know. I'm such a party pooper, but I am desperate for sleep and if I don't leave now I will end up crashing on your couch and I do not want a pillow face in the morning."

"*Fineeee.*" She sticks her tongue out at me and I shake my head at her.

"Love you, mean it." I blow kisses at Ruby, Taylor, and Shane and say bye to the guys who all have my girls wrapped up in their arms.

"Later Sour Patch, text Ruby when you get home," Tank requests, and I can't help but roll my eyes.

"I can get myself home safely, Dad."

"I believe you. Just prove it with a text when you get there." He grins at me and I smirk before walking out the front door. I stop short when I hear a faint noise coming from beside me and look down to see the tiniest little calico kitten sitting on Tank and Ruby's front porch. I turn around and peek my head back inside.

"Tank, Ruby, did you guys get a new pet?" They look at each other with furrowed brows and shake their heads.

"No, why?" Ruby answers, turning to face me again.

"No reason. Just a stray wandering around I guess. Goodnight." I close the door and look down, the sweet little kitten barely making a sound as it meows.

Just get in the car and drive away, Lauren.

Then the damn thing rubs against my boot and I turn into butter, melting onto the ground beside it.

"Hi, baby. Where's your mama?" I pet between her little ears—then check to see if it is in fact a *her*. "You out here all by yourself?"

Meow.

"Well, that just won't do." I pick her up and look at her sweet little green eyes and before I know it, I'm walking through my front door with a kitten wrapped in my coat.

Chapter 9

Sitting in the conference room back at Coleson, Lauren sits across from me with her eyes glued to the paper in front of her. She's exhaling harder than that of a normal person who isn't moving and every now and then I'll see her pinch the inside of her arm.

"You seem particularly miserable this morning."

She levels me with a glare. "Do I ever *not* seem particularly miserable to you?" I let out a hum then notice the scratches on her arm, barely catching myself before reaching out to touch her. I grab my pen from the middle of the table instead, giving my hands something safer to do.

"Get into a fight with your Christmas tree?" I muse.

"Hilarious, but no," she says dryly. I stare at her blankly, waiting for an explanation. She lets out another hefty sigh and rolls her eyes, causing a new kind of tension to creep up my neck.

"I got a cat," she mumbles and I truly can't tell if she's angry, embarrassed, or indifferent to the fact.

"Well then maybe don't piss it off. Those look painful."

"Yeah, well, the bitch scratched up my couch, pissed on my favorite blanket, and chewed through the strap of my favorite heels, so I don't really care if I pissed her off. She pissed me off first." A smile makes its way across my face, watching in amusement as she gets so worked up over what I thought was considered one of the most low-maintenance pets to have.

"So glad my pain is funny to you. Can we get started now?"

"Whatever you want, Sweetheart." I watch her small jaw tighten at my words. "Now, before we go over the files I asked you to gather, I closed on the townhouse with the Johnsons." I pull the paperwork out and slide it across to her. "We made some—"

"You *what?*" The anger in her voice is palpable but her features remain as calm and collected as ever. It makes me want to push her buttons until I get an actual reaction from her. See how long it takes before she actually breaks.

"Closed on the townhome with the Johnsons. Has your morning coffee not kicked in yet? Pay attention." Her cheeks turn a deep shade of red but she still doesn't react. "They wanted to close over the holidays and no one else around here takes calls during the break so I made myself available to them. They took the opportunity to have me help them close before the new year."

"You had no right to do that, and without so much as telling me first? Just who the hell do you think you are?" I almost have the mind to tell her exactly who I am, but I somehow refrain.

"I thought you were eager to get them into their new home as soon as possible. How did you put it? You wanted her to be able to pick out paint colors before she had the baby? It looked like they would need to move quickly if that was going to happen."

"We're done here." She slams her notebook shut and storms out of the room.

Oh Trouble, we're far from done.

I stand and swiftly follow her all the way to her office. Just as she's about to slam the door in my face I slide inside behind her. She spins to face me after the door latches and I take the opportunity to back her into it, placing my hands on either side of her head. She tilts her head up, eyes flaring with anger.

"We're done when *I* say we're done."

"Jack and Barbara may have hired you, for God only knows what reason, but I don't take instructions from other agents."

"I'm not just any other agent, Sweetheart."

"*Stop* calling me that," she hisses.

"Now, if you're done with your little tantrum. We have houses to show today."

"*We?*" Her eyebrows jump up in surprise.

"Yes, *we.*" I let my eyes roam over her face, taking in every angry feature.

"Why? I've never shown houses with another agent. That makes no sense."

"Get your things; we leave in ten minutes. We'll take my car." I pull away from her and she crosses her arms over her chest, still not moving from in front of the door.

"You didn't answer my question," she pouts.

"That was intentional." I smirk and she rolls her eyes.

"I'll take my own car." I take a step towards her again, taking to memory the way her breath catches when I invade her space. I bring my lips close to her ear and watch her chest rise and fall more heavily.

"No, you won't. Nine minutes, Sweetheart. I *will* leave you here if you're not ready." Then I reach around her, causing her to gasp when I brush against her waist, and turn the doorknob to leave.

"Unless you want this visit to turn into one that will be considered *highly* unprofessional, I suggest you let me out now." Her cheeks heat and she takes a step to the right, allowing me enough space to leave her office. I head back to the conference room to grab my things, fighting to lose the hard-on I now have, that I'm hoping she didn't notice.

Hell, what do I care if she did? Maybe she'd do something about it and I could finally move on—get her out of my system. Is it possible that night wasn't everything I've made it out to be? I mean, if she doesn't even *remember* it, maybe I have a skewed memory of what happened between us.

It may be time to remind my little troublemaker of who I am.

Eight minutes later she's standing with her arms crossed over her chest by the passenger door of my car. Obedient little thing. I walk over to her side and her face morphs into extreme confusion.

"What's the matter, Sweetheart, never had someone open the door for you?" I pull the handle and she stares blankly inside the car for a moment then looks up at me.

"No, I haven't." The sadness that flashes in her eyes is masked quickly by the ever-present irritation she feels when she's around me, but I still see it, and fuck if it doesn't make me angry. I close the door behind her and walk around to my side.

I let her take the lead during the showings, taking notes as she does her thing. I can tell she doesn't want me here, but the moments she glances over at me with a look of discomfort vanish as soon as she turns back to her client. She's a professional through and through. She doesn't push people to choose a certain home, she doesn't hype up the higher priced listing more than the lower priced ones just to try and make a bigger commission, she gives them all the information they need then backs off but is around to answer questions without hovering and gives what I assume to be her honest opinion when they ask for her thoughts. I've never seen someone sell like she does. I can't seem to look away when she talks. I find myself pulling out my phone to check emails just to keep myself from getting caught. The last thing I need is for her to notice me staring at her and make some smart-ass remark about it. When we get back in the car I turn her seat warmer on before relaxing my head onto the headrest and letting out a sigh.

"Before you begin your critique can I at least get some food in my system first?" My brows pull together at her remark.

"Excuse me?" There she goes, rolling those damn eyes again.

"You literally did not stop watching me during every showing we had today, then during this last one you were suddenly typing away on your phone."

"So?"

"*So*, I'm sure whatever I did to lose your attention or disappoint you or whatever, is going to come up. I'd just rather not deal with the criticism on an empty stomach."

"Food first. Criticism after. Got it." She glares at me and shakes her head, turning to face out the window before mumbling something I can't quite hear.

Chapter 10

Lauren

I don't know why I'm still entertaining this stupid little assignment. I should have called Jack or Barbara the day Marcus told me I'd be doing training with Fitz. This isn't even training anymore it's…I don't even know what the fuck this is. Harassment, maybe? It's like anything and everything I need to do for work has to be run by Fitz or he has to be surgically attached to my hip while I do it. It makes no sense, and quite frankly, I'm tired of entertaining it.

We pull up to one of the nicest Italian restaurants in town and I have to swallow past the argument in my throat for him to take me back to the office so I can grab something about forty dollars cheaper. The last thing I'm going to do is tell him this place will completely wipe me of my spending budget for the week. I turn around to grab my bag from the back seat and by the time I face forward again he's at my door.

Why does he keep doing this?

He stands between the open passenger door and the back door, blocking my view of the street. My eyes bounce between his in confusion. "Am I not supposed to get out too?"

His eyes fall away from mine and down my body. "You're in a dress."

It takes me a moment to process, but when it hits me what he's doing, my stomach does a weird flip.

"Oh, thanks." I slide out of the vehicle and adjust my dress, wrapping my coat tighter around me and he holds his arm out for me.

"Are you feeling okay?" I ask, keeping my arms crossed over my chest.

"Why do you ask?"

"Because you…you're just…" I try to think of ways to explain why I'm confused without sounding like I've never been around a guy with *manners* before and quickly change my tone when I realize that there isn't one. "Never mind."

I take his arm and we walk into the building together, letting go as soon as we are inside. Maybe this is normal where he's from? To open doors and usher your co-worker into lunch like a true gentleman, even if you act like an asshole every other minute of the day. I'm used to going to lunch with Luther, and sure we link arms when walking down the sidewalk, but that's different for multiple reasons. One being that we're *friends,* the other being that I've never gotten mixed signals from him that he hates me one moment and then wonder if he's checking me out the next. It's like a mental whiplash being around Fitz and it's exhausting.

This place is very…quiet. I fear using the word romantic or even intimate because that would make me start imagining that this is a date —with the devil, no less—and I wouldn't touch that idea with a ten-foot pole. I'm used to going somewhere loud during lunch, either a deli or a drive-thru while listening to music or a podcast, or even having FaceTime lunch dates with some of the girls, but this is not like any of that. The overhead lighting is dim, each table having a small tealight helping illuminate the space, the tables are small on the open floor and the booths along the walls aren't much bigger.

"Right this way," the hostess says, leading us to our table. I continue looking around at the squared wooden columns with vintage artwork and decor hanging on them. The gorgeous chandelier hanging in the center of the room, not giving much more than a nightlight's worth of brightness, is absolutely magnificent.

"Ever been here before?" Fitz asks as we slide into either side of the booth.

"Uh, no. Can't say that I have." I pick up the leatherbound menu, another sign this place is way too freaking fancy for me to frequent the way he's probably assuming I do. He hums to himself and it immediately rubs me the wrong way. Like he's judging me for not coming to a place where nothing on the menu is under twenty dollars, knowing he came from New York and has *sold millions*—ugh, I'll never be able to get that phrase out of my head—the prices probably seem low to him. Which makes me feel inferior in more ways than I care to count today. With that thought, I quickly remember the way he became standoffish at our last showing and anxiety settles in my stomach, making me feel too nauseous to eat. I place the menu down and grab the glass of water the waitress sat down a moment ago, taking a long sip.

"What'll it be? I think the frittata affogato sounds good." He continues scanning the menu as he talks.

"I'm not hungry," I lie.

"But I thought you said—"

"Just order your frittata and don't worry about me, okay?" I tuck a piece of hair behind my ear, running my forefinger along my water glass. I try not to look at him, because those icy blue eyes of his are as seductive as they are scary, but when the heat of his gaze begins burning my skin, I break. I glance up to see him staring intently at me, his menu now closed and pushed off to the side. I watch his throat work as he swallows and just when I think he's about to say something, the waitress comes back.

"Have we decided?" I glance up at her and meet her wide smile with a small one of my own.

"Just the water for me, thanks." She nods politely at me and when I look back at Fitz his eyes are still locked on me, the weight of his stare making my cheeks heat.

"I'll have a glass of Lambrusco, the Italian Sausage & Pepper Frittata Affogato, and an order of Chicken Florentine Pasta. Thank you." He barely glances at her as she tells us she'll be back with his order shortly, then he's back to me.

"You didn't do anything wrong." My heart hammers in my chest at his words.

"What?"

"There will be no critique from me after lunch. You are one of the best sales agents I've ever had the opportunity to observe. You were excellent today." I open my mouth to say something, but shut it again when I can't think of what I want to say. I want to tell him his opinion doesn't matter to me, that I could give a fuck less what he thinks because *I* know I'm a damn good agent. But the fact that the anxious pit in my stomach has subsided along with the way I had to fight a smile at his praise tells me I'd only be fooling myself.

Damn my undeniable need to please people.

"Then why did you leave at the end of the last one?" I ask, refusing to say *thank you,* or anything that would give him the satisfaction of knowing his words meant anything to me.

"Believe it or not, something more important than crown molding and spider burners came up." I'm chewing on the inside of my lip so hard to keep from laughing when the waitress comes and puts Fitz's food in front of him. My stomach growls when the scent of the delicious Chicken Florentine sauce hits my nose and I immediately regret my decision to not order, at the very least, a salad.

"Would you like this?" He points to the dish I'm staring at and I raise a brow at him.

"Feeling gluttonous all of a sudden, are we?" I tease. His gaze narrows and his jaw works as he shrugs back into his seat.

"Just thought you might be hungry after all, but if not…"

"Fine." I roll my eyes and his nostrils flare. "Yes, I would like some. I'm fucking starving." The devilish smirk on his face makes me immediately regret my decision.

"Say please." My cheeks flame with anger as my fingertips grip the plate across from me.

I lean in closer to him until my ribs hit the table. "Bite me." Then I pull the plate to me, holding his heated gaze as I unroll my silverware and place my napkin in my lap.

His tongue peeks out to wet his lips, making me feel completely disarmed. Two can play this game, *Fitz*. I reach across the table and pick up his wine glass, taking a sip before placing it back down in front of him.

He scoffs and shakes his head. "Brat."

This time I don't hold back my smile, and I even add a little wink for flair.

Chapter 11

Fitz

"What do you mean you're coming back? The hell you are. You're not finished there." I grip my phone and fight to keep from throwing it across the room.

"Why can't we have Gerald come down for the assignment? You know he's not doing anything but scratching his balls anyway," I hopelessly argue.

"Which is exactly *why* he isn't the one I sent. This isn't some small potatoes assignment, Fitz. This might be one of our biggest—"

"I know," I cut him off with a defeated sigh. "I know. I just. I hate sleeping in hotels."

"Well, that I understand. The mattresses are shit, but just remember that the payoff at the end of all of this will be worth it."

"Yeah." Lucky for me my father can't see the look of irritation on my face right now. Once again he's speaking a language I don't care to learn.

"Why don't you come back next month and stay just about as long? Get things sorted out there so the place doesn't fall apart without you and then come back home to network. We've got some events you could attend while you're up here."

Yes, cause that's exactly *why I wanted to go back home.*

"Sure, whatever you think is best." The mantra of my life.

"I think it'd be best if you found a date for the events. Jessica Vanderbilt should be around for the Cocktails and Counseling event at the end of next month, so you'd just need to find someone to escort to the damn charity gala." My eyes narrow and I scoff.

"You already asked her *for* me, didn't you?"

"Well, I assumed you'd find some reason not to and show up alone." I clamp my jaw shut, cracking my neck trying to rid some of the tension there.

"I'm thirty-four years old, Father. I don't need you asking women out for me."

"Then learn to do it your damn self. See you next month."

Beep beep beep.

I look down and see the call is disconnected. Just as another one is coming through from my dad's best friend and business partner, Frank. I take a deep breath, trying to rid my frustrations with my father before answering this call.

"Fitz," I answer the phone, pressing the speaker button as I fall into my chair and bury my head in my hands.

"Hey there, Champ." I hate when he calls me that now. I love Frank. He's always been like an uncle to me, always supportive and shows up for every damn thing, but ever since Lauren mentioned what a good name it would make for a dog, I've wished he'd call me anything else.

"I know he can be a lot, but you know how he gets during big deals. This acquisition is no different. Once Coleson is officially part of The Fitzgerald Firm you'll be back home in no time."

That's the problem, every deal is a big deal and there's never not *a deal happening.*

"The. *What?*" My head snaps up when I hear Lauren's lethal tone coming from my doorway. Without a second thought, I end the call with Frank and make my way around my desk.

"You weren't supposed to hear that." I pull her into my office and shut the door behind us, causing her to stumble and almost drop the stack of papers in her hands.

"Yeah, no fucking shit. What acquisition?"

"Do you mind lowering your voice?" I growl through my teeth.

"Fuck you." She frowns. "Where do you get off asking me to do *anything* after I just found out you're lying to literally everyone here. Do Jack and Barbara even know they hired a *rat*?"

"I'd be more than happy to explain all of this to you over lunch like adults, that is if you'd start acting like one, but I will not ask you again to lower your voice." I glance up at my door, hoping everyone else has already left for lunch. Or at the very least, are out of earshot of my office.

"You have a stapler I can borrow?" I can practically see the thought playing out in her mind right now of her stapling the papers in her hands to my forehead.

"With the look on your face, I wouldn't trust you with an eraser at the moment, so no." I smirk humorlessly at her and she opens her mouth to say something, the color suddenly draining from her face.

"The Fitzgerald Firm," she whispers to herself, her eyes locked on mine. "Oh my *god*." My fingers twitch to reach out and cover her mouth but I've held off touching her this long for a reason, and I'm not giving in now. I can see how pissed off she is at the moment but I know as soon as I explain it to her she'll understand—hopefully.

"Your last name is *Fitzgerald*."

"Such a smart girl." I smirk and her nostrils flare. "My old man nicknamed me Fitz to get me good and branded to take over the company when it was time." She must not hear the way I loathe the future that's been forced upon me because she closes her eyes and scoffs.

"I can't believe I'm so stupid." Then she shakes her head, her eyes pop open and she turns lethal again. "Wow. Well, congratulations on the elite, upper-class life you have waiting to fall in your lap at any moment. You know, you really had me fooled lately that you may *actually* be a decent guy, turns out you've just been lying this whole time." That statement hurts way fucking more than it should. "Let your dad know if he ever changes his mind on giving you a real estate *empire*, you'd be excellent at undercover work. A plus deception, really Fitz." Her voice cracks and something in me does too.

Just tell her the truth, you idiot. Tell her it's not what it looks like and fucking tell her who you are!

I'm about to do just that when she swings the door open and the final blow hits.

"There you are, Sour Patch. You ready to go?" Some tattooed building of a guy smiles at her and she immediately relaxes.

"More than you know." She slams the folder she was holding into my chest and I watch in horror as she leaves with him. A burning rage builds inside me and I can't quite figure out what it's directed at most.

The fact that she thinks I'm an entitled, elitist asshole.

The fact that she thinks I've been lying to her—which I guess I have been, sort of.

Or the fact that she has a boyfriend.

Fuck this whole day.

I've never quite enjoyed going to bars alone. But seeing as how I'm lacking in friends here, and the one person I *thought* I was making headway with actually hates me with a fiery passion, being alone seems to be my only option. The Lucky Bastard Saloon is the closest bar I could find where the music playing inside didn't make me want to get a lobotomy on site, so that's where I'm currently drowning my rage in the most expensive scotch they had on the shelves.

If everyone is going to end up thinking I'm an elitist asshole, I might as well really own it.

I hate my father. I hate everything this company stands for and I hate that I have no way out of taking it over in a year. I hate that Lauren had to find out that way and I *really* hate the sadness I heard in her voice today accompanying the anger. The same sadness I've not been able to get off repeat in my mind since she left my office today.

I don't want to be here. I should be at home, trying to figure out how I'm going to get her to listen to me so I can set the record straight. Well, I know how to get her to listen to me, I'll trap her against a door again if I have to—I quite enjoyed that method the first time—but getting her to listen isn't going to be the problem. Getting her to *believe me* will be.

I rub my eyes beneath my glasses, which I put on halfway through the day when my contacts dried out, and drop enough cash on the counter to cover my tab, plus a hefty tip for the bartender before standing to leave. I make my way through the *very* drunk people stomping their boots against the floor just as my little troublemaker is walking through the door.

Fuck her for being so damn alluring all the time. She could spit on me—which I genuinely wouldn't put past her—and I'd probably say thank you.

Something is seriously wrong with me.

Maybe if I keep my head down I can make it out of here without running into her, and inevitably doing something stupid.

Someone starts singing along to the Teddy Swims song playing behind me and they manage to back into me while shaking their hips, promptly cutting them off. *"Don't love anyone, anyone, anyone but yourse–* Oh! I'm so sor—" I huff when she hits my chest, causing me to look up —though I immediately wish I hadn't. She gives me a split second assessment, fixating on my glasses before her features turn stone cold.

"I'm so sorry your prescription doesn't seem to be working." Not in the mood for her attitude tonight, I stoop to play her little verbal sparring game.

"Maybe you're the one who needs glasses, then you'd be able to see how many of your clients are falling into my lap." I see a fire light in her eyes and I suddenly feel exhilarated enough to remind her exactly who she's dealing with.

"Who's the friend, Lauren?" The same motherfucker from earlier slides up to her side and that ungodly feeling settles in my chest again that makes me want to throw a barstool at him.

"Friend is a stretch. We just happen to work in the same office, *unfortunately*." Something familiar crosses his face that leaves me curious—though, not for long.

"Oh, is this Lucifer?" Even in the low light of this bar, I can see her cheeks redden.

No chance in hell—pun intended—I'll let her live that one down.

Then another guy, not quite as bulky but still not lacking in muscle, also covered in ink, shows up at her other side. The two of them share similar features so I could assume they're brothers, though I am most curious about why they're both standing so damn close to Lauren.

"It's *Luther*. We played Topgolf together once—" He tilts his head, looking a little more closely at me. "Didn't we?" His question is directed at me and I'm wondering if he seriously just mistook me for the Luther I work with who could not look more unlike me.

"Um, no. We did not." His lips turn down in confusion then he brushes it off like he could care less who I am. Then I turn back to face a very blushed Lauren. The two guys surprisingly disappear from her sides, giving me a chance to step closer to her. "Lucifer, really?" She rolls her eyes, lifting a brow as she shrugs as if she's completely unphased.

I hate when she seems unbothered by me. I'd rather her feel rage, hate, lust, or *anything* else in place of indifference. I lean in to speak directly in her ear—I wouldn't quite call it a whisper since the music in here is loud enough it could make your teeth rattle, but nonetheless, she's the only one who can hear me.

"Tell me, Trouble. How did it feel, dancing with the Devil?" I glance down at her, touching her for the first time since that night when I wrap my hand around her neck and caress her cheek with my thumb. I'm looking for any hint of realization on her face, but when she narrows her eyes at me I wink at her and walk out.

Maybe another time.

Chapter 12

Lauren

What the fuck was that?

The electricity that sped through my entire body when his hand wrapped around my neck took me by surprise, even more so than what he said to me. I turn back to my friends, hoping that the rest of the night will wash the memory of Fitz out of my brain. Maybe if I get drunk enough I'll be able to forget who he is completely and I'll be able to go to work tomorrow and not daydream the entire time about slamming his head in the industrial copy machine.

"I hate that guy," I bite out, finishing off the drink I'd forgotten I was holding. My eyes roll on instinct at the thought of him. The motherfucker is literally a mole for one of the biggest real estate firms in New York, a firm that is *apparently* going to be buying out Coleson, I have no business reacting to him the way I just did. I still can't wrap my head around it and how I didn't figure it out sooner.

Blinded by his sexy smirk, hypnotic blue eyes, and the way he smells like a wet dream.

My nose scrunches at the last thought. Okay poor choice of words, but he smells fucking great and the chemicals must do something to my brain. Like shrink it.

So how do we explain the way he opened my door at lunch and made sure no one could see up my dress, or how he complimented me on my performance during our showings?

"Hey, you okay?" Ruby asks.

"I need more alcohol. Personality number two is being really loud and not making a lot of sense to personality number one who is a raging ball of emotions."

"Spicy marg it is."

God, I love her.

We're standing at the bar waiting for my drink, Ruby swaying her hips to the music and drumming her hands on the bar top, but I can't stop replaying that interaction with Fitz. The inside of my lip is already sore from chewing on it today, but I can't seem to let it go.

"Spicy margarita." The bartender sets it down in front of me and I smile at him, but Ruby answers him as I take my first sip.

"Thanks Tony!" My head snaps up and I suck in a breath.

"Another spicy one, Antoooo-nio."

"Wanna go dancing, Trouble?"

The elevator.

Buttons undone.

Tanned skin beneath my fingertips.

His lips.

"We aren't going dancing, are we?"

"Oh my god. Oh my *god*. It was him," I whisper to myself. "I slept with Fitz?!" My head snaps to the door, knowing he's probably long gone but I'm still half tempted to run after him and...I don't know start yelling at him? Ask him if he's known all this time why he's just now saying something.

But he didn't say anything...not directly. Him calling me trouble, my drink order, and the weird as shit coincidence that the bartender's name is Tony all just kind of curb-stomped the memory back into my brain at full speed.

"Karaoke time, bitches!" Shane squeals, derailing my plans.

I can't believe I slept with the mother freaking devil…and forgot about it. Kill me.

ME

I have some very very very top secret information to tell you. I need you to remain calm(ish) and whatever you do, don't tell anyone.

LUTHER

We're listening.

ME

I think I slept with Fitz…

LUTHER

I will go ahead and preface with, I did not remain calm… you owe me a new flower vase.

ME

How did you break a vase?

LUTHER

I threw my burrito, duh. Now, give me every SINGLE detail. And what do you mean you THINK?

ME

It was at the conference we went to in New York. I got a phone call that put me in a bad mood, one drink led to another and…Luther I swear to god I didn't remember anything until I ran into him tonight and it all just hit me like a party bus. I'm kind of freaking out.

LUTHER

That was not every little detail…

ME

Will you focus? I don't know if he remembers or if it's just a coincidence that what he said tonight made me remember. What if he was just as drunk as I was and doesn't remember either?

LUTHER

Are you gonna ask him? Or are you just gonna play
hard to get and pretend like you still don't remember
and let him make a move?

ME

Who said anything about wanting to do it again?

LUTHER

Be so for real right now…

ME

You haven't worked with him the way I have. The guy
is an asshole. I don't want anything to do with him. I
don't even want the memory of having slept with him
the first time.

LUTHER

Ugh. FINE.

ME

You were no help…

LUTHER

Don't you have like four straight female friends you
could consult about this? Maybe get their opinion
since I'm apparently attracted to red flags?

ME

I'm not exactly wanting to tell them I boned the guy I
claim to despise.

LUTHER

CLAIM TO?!?!?!

ME

I'm not bringing you coffee tomorrow.

LUTHER

Keep lying to yourself, honey.

ME

About what??? The coffee or Fitz?

I check my phone at least a dozen more times while we're at karaoke and he never responds. I'm gonna kick his ass for making me overthink this. Just because I slept with Fitz before I knew who he actually was doesn't mean I want anything to do with him now. The guy is literally lying to everyone at Coleson, the place I consider a second home, with people I care about like family. I have no idea when this acquisition is supposed to happen, or what that means for the current employees but I do know one thing, I won't let any of them be blindsided by the loss of a job. I'll post it on every wall of the office if I have to.

Chapter 13

It's almost a quarter 'til eight and I know Lauren will be waltzing through the door any second now. I plan on grabbing her as soon as she does, so I can set the record straight about everything that happened on Friday. I'd be worried she'd already sent a company-wide email with the news if I hadn't locked her email from working on anything but her desktop over the weekend. I'm not typically one to cross a line like that, but I'm not about to let this entire assignment go to shit just because she's pissed off.

7:45 AM

Like clockwork, she walks through the front door of the office, greeting Amy with a smile before spotting me stalking toward her down the hallway and it immediately falls.

"I'm not in the mood this morning, Fitz." She brushes past me, quickly walking into her office. She should already know better than to think I won't follow her. She shrugs off her coat and sets her stuff down on her desk, then spins around quickly, unaware I've walked in behind her, and slams into my chest. I grab her arms to steady her so she won't fall over and she gasps. Her eyes lock on mine and I notice a look in them I've been waiting to see—she remembers.

"Slow down, Trouble. I just want to talk." I smirk at her and her cheeks redden.

"Stop calling me that," she growls.

"You didn't seem to mind it so much the first time." I raise a brow at her and her lips turn down into a frown.

"No, I didn't much like it this weekend either."

She's acting like she doesn't *remember.*

My fingertips brush along her arms, feeling the goosebumps rise in their wake. I lean in slightly, catching the gaze of her wild blue eyes.

"You and I both know that's not the first time you heard me call you that, *Trouble.*"

"Yes, well. I was insanely drunk that night. You know taking a drunk girl to your room is a risky move—not a good look, *Mr. Fitzgerald,*" she snaps and my blood boils.

"If I remember correctly, I offered to take you *dancing.* I was heading up to change the shirt *you* spilled a drink on when you began undressing me in the elevator—" I back her up until her ass hits her desk, and her chest rises and falls quickly as I grip her waist. "If anyone was taken advantage of that night, it was me. Not that I minded. You were a decent way to blow off some steam for a bit." Anger bursts behind her eyes and I'm fucking delighted to finally be able to get a reaction out of her.

"Decent? Do you often use *three* condoms on a *decent* night?"

"Who said they were all used with you, Sweetheart?" Her mouth pops open and my eyes fall to her lips, running my tongue along my own as the memory of her taste floods my senses.

"Get. The fuck. Out." She presses her hand against my chest and begins shoving me backward, her eyes watering as she forces me out.

"Lauren…"

"Fuck you, you selfish, insufferable, egotistical asshole!" The door slams in my face and I look to the side, catching a judgemental stare from Luther.

"Wow… You must have done something truly awful. Lu doesn't lose her cool over *anything* in the office. I'd stay away until at least Wednesday."

"How do you know she didn't start it?" He lets out a half laugh, shaking his head as he walks into the conference room.

"Amazing. The two of you have worked together more than anyone else in this office for two months and you still don't know anything about her."

I beg to differ.

Lauren didn't attend this morning's team meeting, which was concerning enough by itself since she hasn't missed a single one in the two months I've been here. However, the fact that she hasn't opened her door again since slamming it in my face this morning, except to get her lunch order from Amy, has me feeling like I may have gone too far this morning.

Knock knock knock.

"Go away," she yells back.

Um, no.

I open the door and walk in, catching one of those famous eye rolls. "What if it was Amy or Luther? Would you want them to go away too?"

"No. I knew it was you, though," she answers, pushing the lettuce from her salad around with her plastic fork.

"Oh? How's that?" I question, sitting in the chair across from her desk, catching a glare from her as she tosses her fork down.

"Because everyone else in this office knows that my door being closed, means don't even try to come in, and to email or text me instead." She closes the laptop next to her and I notice a tissue with black smudges was behind it. Her eyes follow my gaze and she snatches it up, tossing it in the bin under her desk.

"What do you want?" She crosses her arms over her chest, sitting straight up in her chair.

"I wanted to apologi—" She holds her hand up to stop me.

"Don't." I look on in confusion.

"Um…oka—"

"Apologizing would suggest you did something to upset me. You simply proved to me that you're exactly who I thought you were. So thanks for that."

"Ah, so you've got me all figured out then, is that it?" I lean forward in my chair, watching as she mirrors my movements.

"You make it pretty easy. You come in here, telling everyone what to do like you own the place—which makes sense *now* seeing as you're about to—you make me jump through *ridiculous* hoops to prove I'm good enough to be here when everyone in this office knows damn good and well that I am. Something you would also know if you took a second to glance at my record, but no. Instead, you take the lazy way out, tagging along while I bust my ass to make sales. *Then* you steal clients out from under me for God only knows what reason. Since you *clearly* don't need the money. Then you act all gentlemanly like at lunch which was more than likely a ruse just to see if you could get me into bed again. I'm not sure why, exactly, since I was only *decent*. Hmm, boredom, maybe? The rich bachelor is having trouble picking up girls in a new city?" She taps her fingers against her lips, and it pisses me off that I want to kiss her just to shut her up. I'm practically a flaming ball of rage sitting in the chair in front of her, all while she looks as calm as ever.

"But I'll save you the trouble, *Mr. Fitzgerald.* You and I are done. In every sense of the word. I will not answer to you anymore, no matter what Marcus says. If I'm going to work with you, the order will have to come from Jack himself." She lets out a little huff, the only giveaway that she's worked up about all of this, and stands up behind her desk.

"Now get the hell out of my office." I stand up from my seat, studying her carefully as she tips her chin up at me.

Sexy little Vixen. She has no idea who she's dealing with.

I turn to walk out of her office, then think of one point in her rambling that needs immediate reconciliation. "The check for the

Johnsons townhome sale, the check with *your* name on it, is in your otherwise empty mail holder." I see her look at where the little white envelope is barely peeking out at the top before her cheeks redden with embarrassment.

"I can't wait to watch you eat your words, Trouble."

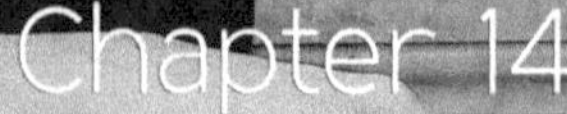

Chapter 14

What in the holy fuck does that mean?

Miraculously, I didn't see Fitz the rest of the day. I'm genuinely shocked, seeing as how he's never seemed to listen to me before. I'm the last one out of the office tonight—per usual—and just as I am locking up, headlights illuminate the front of the building before I hear a car stop behind me. My heart rate picks up when I remember I never pulled my car closer to the door before it got dark out. A decision I'm currently regretting.

I turn around, giving myself a little pep talk to look confident as I walk to my car and not as scared as I actually am. Then I see that it's Fitz in his dumb-ass Range Rover and all emotions switch to annoyance.

"Get in," he calls through the rolled down window. I walk in his direction, not because I intend to *get in*, but because my car is parked behind where he's stopped.

"Um...not no, but hell no." I smirk at him humorlessly and walk around the front of his vehicle to get to mine. I pull my keys from my bag just as I hear his door shut.

"Get in the car, Trouble." He closes the distance between us and I spin around, my eyes wide.

"What's your damage, Fitzgerald? What part of 'no' do you not understand?"

"I understand it, I just don't accept it. You can continue your tantrum later, but we need to talk." I open my mouth to give him an earful—which I can do from *outside* of his car—but he holds a finger up to my lips and I despise the way his touch makes my body react.

"Let me rephrase. *I* need to talk, I only need you to listen. Think you can manage to shut that pretty mouth of yours long enough to do that for me?"

The audacity for me to be turned on by any part of that sentence pisses me off.

He keeps his finger on my lips, raising a brow as if he's waiting for me to confirm or deny whether or not I can *keep my mouth shut and listen,* and I do something even I don't understand.

I bite him.

His finger is knuckle deep between my teeth and his glacier-blue eyes ignite.

Then he runs the tip of his finger along my tongue and I think I short-circuit completely. My mouth pops open, allowing him to remove his finger, and he runs it across his bottom lip. Then he backs up and opens the passenger door and my stupid girl brain tells me to get in the car.

"See, sweetheart. That wasn't so hard, was it?" He winks and closes the door behind me.

I regret everything.

We leave the parking lot and drive for at least ten minutes without him saying a single word. As soon as I open my mouth and take a breath to say something he looks at me, causing me to pause.

"You remember the deal, Trouble. No talking. Just listening. I'd hate to find more creative ways than my finger to keep you quiet."

I'm tempted to start talking just to see what he comes up with, then promptly remember that I hate him and question why I ever even got in this car to begin with.

Because you bit him, licked his finger, then he ran said finger across his bottom lip and you liked it…that's why.

Not a great reason, but I've done dumber things from being turned on.

Like sleeping with the guy you're sitting next to?

Okay…that's enough. I'm turning my brain off now.

Instead of saying anything, I reach over and turn the volume up on his radio. He gives me a scolding glance but I simply pop my eyes at him, still saying nothing. We drive for a few more minutes before pulling into a drive-thru.

"Two soft tacos, no lettuce, an order of cheesy potatoes, no sour cream and—" he looks over at me and squints. "A medium water. And one chicken quesadilla with a Pepsi." The person gives him his total, we pull around to pay and get our food before parking in the almost empty lot.

"Eat," he says, handing me the bag he just pulled his food from. I stare blankly at the tacos and potatoes, unable to pinpoint how I'm feeling.

"This is my exact order." I look at him as he's mid-bite.

"I know. So eat it," he says over a mouth full of food.

What does he mean, he knows?!

"What if I don't want it?" I'm starving and there's no way I *won't* be eating this food, but I'm curious what his answer will be.

"Don't be a brat. Eat the food. You're probably starving after only playing with your salad before throwing it out today." Accurate.

"Fitz. *Why* did you bring me here? I could be at home eating by myself."

Technically, I'd be eating with Ginny who is actually growing on me now that we've established some house rules and purchased her a litter box.

"While I'm sure you think your vicious, fighter cat makes better company, I do still need to talk to you, and I find people receive difficult information better when they aren't hungry."

"What difficult information?" My anxiety kicks up, causing my chest to grow tighter.

"Put the taco in your mouth and I will tell you." I roll my eyes, but oblige. Taking a taco from the brown paper bag I unwrap it and take a bite, motioning for him to begin talking.

"You think you have me all figured out, but I can assure you, you do not. And while I still plan to prove you wrong on pretty much every count, the only important thing you need to know right now is this. Yes, I'm employed by The Fitzgerald Firm, and yes, we are buying out Coleson, but I'm not a mole. I'm the acquisition manager. Jack and Barbara know exactly why I'm here because they are selling Coleson willingly. I'm simply here ensuring everything is up to The Fitzgerald Firm standard before the transaction goes through." I swallow my food and he holds my water up with a straw already in it. I hesitantly grab it from him and take a drink as I process the information—along with the fact that he's being kind of sweet right now and it's freaking me out.

"Why?" I whisper, mostly to myself, though he takes the opportunity to answer.

"Retirement is hard when you don't have a 401k and have hemorrhaged money on flips that never paid off." I drop my food in the bag and let my head fall back on the seat.

"I can't believe they didn't just tell us." My head snaps over to look at him. "Why didn't they?"

"That's a question you'd have to ask them yourself. I go where I'm told and operate under the rules set for me. One of them being: don't tell anyone who I work for, and don't mention the takeover."

"Rule breaker," I snicker, taking another bite of my taco.

"Technically, I didn't break those rules. You only found out because you heard a private phone conversation." I throw a salsa packet at him and he looks at me like I've lost my mind.

"That was on *speakerphone* while your office door was wide open. Don't make it sound like I was eavesdropping on your private conversations." He laughs, and I find myself doing the same.

The car grows quiet and I find my cheeks heating under his stare.

The street lights illuminate the vehicle just enough to see his features soften, and I catch myself wanting to lean across the console to touch him. To run my fingers along his sharp jaw, or through his hair. Dangerous territory for a girl who was told she was simply a *decent* experience to the guy she's beginning to react to in a not-so-negative way.

I clear my throat and take another drink of water, trying to get my thoughts together and remember why he is the last person on earth I should be attracted to.

"Okay. So you're not a mole, you're just doing your job, and you're *not* screwing Jack and Barbara over. That still only gets you about two percent lower on my shit list."

He chuckles and shakes his head. "That's fair, I guess."

"Take me back to my car now." I turn around, facing completely out the front window.

"Not yet." I raise a brow at him. "I need to know you're not going to tell anyone else about the acquisition. Or who I really am."

"Telling anyone else would only hurt the people I care about, I would never do that." He nods his understanding.

"I still can't believe I didn't figure it out. You literally go by *Fitz*," I scold myself aloud, hearing a surprising grunt come from the driver seat. "What's your real name, anyway?" His jaw hardens and he tosses his trash in the bag, putting his seat belt on before shifting into drive.

"Buckle up." I do as he says, simply because I don't get the idea he's going to wait for me by the way he's peeling out of the parking lot.

"I mean, surely your parents didn't name you *Fitz Fitzgerald,* that just seems redundant…and kind of mean." I begin eating my potatoes and watch as his gaze becomes more distant the further we drive.

"My name is really none of your concern, Sweetheart." The condescending tone is back in his voice, and I shake my head in disbelief. Every time I think there's some shred of decency in this man, he is so quick to prove me wrong. We pull back into the lot at Coleson and he parks a space down from my car. I look over at him, but he's staring out the front windshield, features now turned to stone and I have the urge to ask him what the fuck is wrong with him. But instead, I take a deep breath, drop my trash into the paper bag on the floorboard, and get out of the car—leaving the passenger side door wide open. I get into my car, start the engine, and look over to see him shaking his head at me. Then I flip him off and pull out of the lot. I can almost hear him calling me a brat just by the look on his face and you know what—maybe I am.

What can I say, he just brings the brattiness out of me I guess.

Chapter 15

Fitz

Man, I missed home. Being in my own bed again almost makes me never want to go back to Nashville. Though I know after a month of networking here I'll be on a plane right back there.

Making sure Lauren wouldn't ruin things for the Colesons was the last thing on my to-do list before I could pack my bags and be on the next flight out. Even though something as simple as being in my car with her in an empty parking lot made me second guess my desire to leave at all.

I can't figure her out and I like it. She isn't like the women I'm used to being around who have absolutely no mystery to them. Fakeness sure. I've seen enough of that to last a few lifetimes. But mystery? Not so much. She is confident and capable in her work but still lights up when she gets validation from others. She is painfully beautiful but her smile often acts as a mask, and while she is always doing everything for everyone else, I've seen behind the curtain when everything isn't just right with her own life. She's as strong as a hurricane and I would gladly put myself in her path of destruction just to uncover the real her.

Unfortunately, I am well aware I'm the farthest thing from what she needs in her life. More complications, smoke screens, and facades that I would never want to drag another person into. I'm a walking contradiction. Which is why I have no intentions of finding a wife like my parents have not so secretly hinted at the last two times I've seen them.

I drop my duffle bag onto the floor and fall onto my couch just as my phone begins ringing. I let out a groan but it dies as soon as I see the name flashing across the screen. I smile so big it physically hurts my face but that won't stop me.

"Well, if it isn't the most beautiful woman I know."

"Oh, hush you. What if your momma heard you saying that? She'd probably start planning a wedding right away thinking you were talking to some model or something."

"Well, Gran. She'll just have to let that dream die with her, and you're a million times prettier than all the models I know. Lot nicer, too." I hear her cackle as she shuffles around.

"How are you, sweet boy? You're not working too hard, are you?" I exhale and feel the weight of my life ease from my chest.

"Always. You know that." She clicks her tongue and I can almost see her shaking her head. I close my eyes and imagine her working around her kitchen getting everything ready for dinner while Pops tries to slow her down by turning the music up and dancing with her.

"Well, I know you'll take care of yourself so I won't mention how much I hate you working in that big city that never sleeps." I laugh at the way she still slips in her concerns after saying she won't.

"Look at you and your big city nickname knowledge. You should go on Jeopardy."

"They won't take me. Said it wouldn't be fair to the other contestants." I belly laugh and even though talking to Gran always lifts my spirits, it also immediately makes them fall.

"I miss you, Gran. Pops too." I roll my head, my eyes landing on my favorite photo in my apartment.

"We miss you too, sweetheart. You know we're always here when you have time to visit."

"Yeah. Maybe soon." I'm sure she doesn't believe that. I wouldn't believe me either. It's been far too long since I've been back to see them.

"Well, dinner is just about ready so let me hang up this phone. I just wanted to check on you."

"Wait wait wait. What's for dinner tonight?" I ask, my mouth already watering in anticipation.

"Chicken and dumplings, cornbread, and veggies." I hold my hand to my chest and let out a dramatic, agonized groan.

"You're killing me, Gran. How am I supposed to eat my takeout and enjoy it now?"

"Honey, I don't know how anyone ever enjoys that mess." I can hear the judgment in her voice and laugh.

"Talk soon. I love you."

"Love you too, bud." I click the red button and drop my phone in my lap, staring at the apartment I couldn't wait to return to and wondering why I missed it so much. It's quiet and lonely, two things I despise about my parents' home.

Maybe I'll get a house plant.

I'd say a cat, but after seeing Lauren's arms after she took ownership of one, I think I'll pass on having anything living.

Not like I'd have the time to care for a cat in New York, anyway.

Let's be honest. A ficus and a cat both have an equal chance of making it out alive with me.

Of all the things my father does that makes me hate him, setting me up to take Jessica Vanderbilt to these events is near the top of the list. After the last time I was in town and saw her and this, she's definitely going to get her signals crossed.

"Jessica, you look lovely." I force the words out as I give her a tight smile and she beams back at me.

"You don't look too bad yourself, Fitz." Her long, blonde hair is pulled back in a bun that looks so tight it's giving *me* a headache. She has a small clutch in one hand and *me* in the other. I twist my neck and try to loosen my bowtie, my skin itching to be released from her grip. We make our way around the room, speaking with every important person on my father's list, and catching adoring glances from both of our mothers. I feel like my skin is on fire when Jessica leans her head on my shoulder.

"Mr. Fitzgerald, Ms. Vanderbilt, over here." I look over and before I can object Jessica puts on her best model face, reaching up to place her hands on my chest and the camera flashes.

"I'd say we're pretty good together," she whispers as we continue making our way through the crowd.

"You certainly play the part well." Her face scrunches but I try to ignore it.

We continue walking through the venue as she talks. "It doesn't have to be a *part*, you know. We could try this thing for real. I mean our parents would be ecstatic and we have fun together." She stops and looks up at me, causing me to exhale in frustration. "You do like me, don't you Fitz?" There are very few times I'll ever wonder why I'm not of high enough importance to have a hit out on me because now would be an excellent time for such a distraction. I open my mouth to speak, but Frank shows up and interjects himself at the perfect moment.

"There you are. There's someone your father wants you to speak with."

"Excuse me," I politely remove myself from the trap that is Jessica Vanderbilt and nod at Frank to lead the way.

"Who is it?" I ask, preparing myself to turn on the charm.

"Clay Holmes." I stop walking and look at Frank.

"Like the pitcher for the fucking *Yankees*, Clay Holmes?"

"Yes. That's the one."

"Why the hell is he at this event?" I question, looking around the room.

"Not entirely sure, but I heard he's looking to buy a house and I told him I knew just the guy to make it happen." He smiles at me and I can't help but laugh.

"Frank, you're awesome." I see a light in his eyes and he nods before beginning to lead the way again.

"Glad to know you're still into baseball," I scoff and rear my head back.

"One does not simply *stop* being into baseball, Frank." Once I see Clay a few tables ahead I clear my throat and put my professionalism back in place. No matter how shocked I am that I may be the one helping a Yankees pitcher find a new house, I have to act like I would with any other client.

"Clay, this is Fitz. Fitz, this is Clay Holmes." Frank introduces us and I extend my hand to him.

"Great to meet you, man. I hear you're the man I want on the job when looking for a house?" Clay shakes my hand and smiles and I laugh off the praise Frank must have been singing for me.

"I do my best. What are you looking for?" We chat for nearly twenty minutes about what he's looking for and then exchange contact info so I can send him the listings I find that I think will interest him.

"Thanks, man. I really appreciate you taking on the job." Clay smiles, offering me his hand again.

I shake it and shrug. "It's what I do."

He laughs and nods his understanding just as Jessica strolls up beside me. "There you are."

I catch myself just before my eyes begin to roll and force a smile instead. "Here I am."

Un. Fucking. Fortunately.

"You ready to go?" My brows pull together briefly before I catch myself and smooth my features. Why is she acting like we're leaving together? And why is she interrupting my conversation without so much as introducing herself. I'm only here with her to present myself *better* and she's being rude as hell right now. I've got to get out of here. *Alone.*

I turn to Clay with a fake smile on my face. "Well, I guess I'm leaving now. Give me a call when you're ready to get things moving."

"Literally, right?" Clay laughs, holding up my business card as he backs away from the table. Once he's moved on to another conversation, well out of earshot, I level Jessica with a stare.

"What the hell was that?" I bite out, grabbing her arm and pulling her to the side of the room.

"I just thought since we talked to everyone we needed to, we could get out of here. Maybe grab a drink and then…" Her hands run over the lapels of my jacket in a much too seductive way to be standing in a room full of my peers. My hands shoot up and grab her wrists, stopping her as she lets out a small gasp.

"I was in the middle of a very important conversation, which you not only interrupted, but you also made no effort to introduce yourself or apologize to the person I was speaking to." Her lips turn down into a pout.

"What? The baseball guy? He wasn't on the list."

"For fuck's sake," I mumble to myself. I grip her hands tighter to ensure I have her attention, though to any watchful eye, it may look endearing. "You say this doesn't have to be a *part,* but you have no idea how to interact with people in a real way. You don't bother speaking to people who aren't labeled as important and are oblivious to simple conversational manners. What on earth makes you think I would ever want to settle down with someone as spoiled and entitled as you?" She pulls her hands away from me with a huff.

"Says the guy in a seven thousand dollar suit that's next in line to inherit a real estate empire." I don't even like this suit. Though, that doesn't change the fact that she's *right,* and I think I hate that even more than this suit. "Are we leaving or what?" She crosses her arms over her chest with a pout.

Unbelievable.

Chapter 16

Lauren

"Okay. I have to tell you guys something." I crack my front door open just enough to see my four best friends standing outside waiting to be let in. There's a mix of terror and confusion on all of their faces.

"Something you can't tell us in the warmth of your home? Possibly with a drink in my hand?" Leah shifts on her feet, fighting the cool night air.

"I just know you're going to have a lot of questions and I wanted to get it out there first thing."

"Mhm. Yeah, sure. Hurry the hell up, I can't feel my toes." Taylor nods her head, urging me to get on with it.

"I got a cat." They all stop moving and almost comically all look at me with the same expression. "Say something."

More silence.

"Open the damn door." Ruby shakes her head, pointing behind me. "I gotta see this baby." I open the door further, exposing a snuggled-up Ginny in my arms.

"Oh my gosh!" Shane whispers, covering her mouth with her hand.

"Stop it right now." Taylor drops all of her things inside the door and pulls her out of my arms. "Hey, little sweetie. What's your name?"

"Ginny," I answer, shutting the door and crossing my arms over my chest.

"So you got her during a *Ginny & Georgia* re-watch," Leah states.

"Duh. But it still suits her." I shrug, petting Ginny between her ears.

"You—start the margs, you—start explaining." Ruby points to Shane first then at me, plopping down on the couch next to Taylor who is trying to suffocate Ginny with her affection.

"You remember when I was leaving on New Year's Eve and asked if you got a new pet?"

"*Yes.*" Ruby's eyes widen. "You took my porch cat?" I snort and grab a blanket from the back of the couch and wrap it around myself before joining them.

"You didn't even know she existed. Stop acting like I stole Maverick." She giggles and we all start giving Ginny the attention she demands.

"So what made you decide to take a stray cat home?" Leah asks, clearly suspicious. I could tell them it was because I was feeling lonely and sad that I was the only one without someone to ring in the new year with, but instead, I do what I do best. I lie.

"Didn't like any of the things my parents got me for Christmas, so I got Ginny for myself." The room falls quiet for a moment like it often does when the topic of my parents comes up. Then Ruby lets out a laugh that scares Ginny, causing her to run into my lap.

"Oh my god, your parents are the *worst!* What did they get you this time?" she groans.

"A set of porcelain ballerinas and a dress my grandma wouldn't even wear."

"I'm going to light their Christmas tree on fire next year," Ruby deadpans. I pick up Ginny and snuggle her under the blanket with me, feeling her purr against my legs.

"Or break in and steal the fuses for the lights," Leah says excitedly.

"Or take all the little forks and spoons so all they have left are the big ones," Taylor adds. I roll my eyes and laugh at all of their attempts to make me feel better.

"Someone change the subject, please," I beg. Taylor picks Ginny up again and snuggles her to her face.

"Tucker is one hundred percent going to try and steal this cat."

"Then we just won't tell him about her," I tease, scratching her under her chin as we all burst into laughter.

"I do not understand why that man will not get a pet. He already tries to steal Maverick every time he sees him," Ruby laughs.

"Which is basically every day. He must be exhausted in his attempt to steal everyone else's animals," Shane adds, bringing the tray of margaritas and glasses to the coffee table.

"I don't get it either! I have told him a million times to just pick one and he keeps saying no. He's a mystery, that man of mine." Taylor takes a sip of her margarita on a shrug.

"I honestly love that you have a cat. She's adorable," Ruby says as the other girls are wrapped up in conversation about something Sawyer did for Leah—I think. I zoned out thirty minutes ago.

"I know. I kind of love her." Ginny rubs her nose against Ruby's fingers. "And she's clearly a fabulous judge of character." I smirk.

"*Right?!* I was just thinking the same thing!" Ruby and I laugh together, snuggling deeper into the couch.

Sitting at my desk I refresh my emails for about the twentieth time, and like every time before, nothing new appears. Our morning meeting ended an hour ago and I've already managed to update my online marketing campaign, send current equity fliers to my old clients, and return all the messages that were left for me on Sunday. Fitz has been gone for a month and I loathe myself for even mentally admitting this, but I'm freaking bored without him here making my life a living hell. I didn't realize how boring this job is when someone isn't challenging me at every turn. It's been a full month of no one emailing me about absurd scenarios and how to fix them, new marketing ideas, no one questioning the amount of showings I have scheduled for the week, and no one making my heart race—purely out of anger, of course.

"Trying to see if your ass print will mold to the chair if you sit there long enough?"

Fuck you, heart, for leaping at the sound of his voice.

I look up and see Fitz with a brow raised in my direction, leaning against the doorframe to my office.

"Why? Gonna try to steal my chair if it does?" The smallest hint of a smirk plays at his lips and I can feel one of my own trying to surface.

"So, what? I leave for one month and you lose all momentum to stay at the top? Come on, Sweetheart. I trained you better than that, didn't I?" He gives me a condescending wink and my will to smirk is quickly replaced by an annoyed eye roll.

"Careful, *Mr. Fitzgerald*, you'll fall off that high horse of yours." I snatch my folder from my desk, conveniently it's time for me to leave for my showings today, and stop right in front of where he's blocking my exit. "You and I both know I was already what this company needed before you ever got here. I think you just enjoy my company. It's... *decent*...don't you think?" I pick a piece of fuzz from his suit, flicking it away with a mask of indifference as his jaw suddenly flexes.

"Decent, indeed," he says through bared teeth. He stands up straight, towering over me as he does, and looks behind me. Then he hums to himself and silently walks away. I frown, looking back to see what he was looking at, and my mouth pops open when I notice a perfect ass print slowly losing its shape in my chair.

Stupid memory foam chair.

As soon as I'm left alone again I notice the way my heart is thumping and my cheeks feel warm and I let out a groan.

"Seriously, Lauren? *No.*" I scold myself as I head to Brüman's for my morning coffee.

Chapter 17

Fitz

I'm going to rue the day I ever told Lauren Long she was only *decent* in bed. The word is already beginning to haunt me, though now's not exactly the time to tell her she was anything but *decent*. My father has all but ruined New York for me, and the month I *thought* would be spent enjoying being home, wound up being a month-long marketing and *image-building* trip to hell. I'm pretty sure Jessica Vanderbilt, and all of her less-than-desirable characteristics, thinks we're now betrothed or something of the sort. If my entire life didn't revolve around the fact that I'm meant to take over my father's company in a year I would disown them and disappear. However, doing that would result in me losing everything I have in the process, and though that doesn't sound half bad most of the time, I wouldn't be able to do a lot of the good things I can in the position I am in now. Things I'm not willing to give up.

I sit down at my desk, watching as that perfect ass of hers saunters out the front door. I get the idea to follow her and insist I go with her to her showings—to ensure she hasn't lost her edge in the month I've been gone, of course—but before I can move my phone begins going off repeatedly.

JESSICA VANDERBILT

New York is missing you already. It was nice having
you back for a whole month.

JESSICA VANDERBILT

You can deny it all you want, but we make a good
team.

I will deny it because it's impossible to be a good team when your teammate makes you want to lose the ability to hear half an hour into an event because her fake laugh is worse than styrofoam cups rubbing together.

MOTHER

You and Jessica make a lovely couple. Maybe you can
come back more often and you two spend some time
together. Outside of networking events of course. 🙂

ME

Not a couple, mother. A mirage. Fabricated by you
and my sperm donor, no less.

MOTHER

Don't shut down the idea just because you're being
stubborn, Fitz. Remember what I said about this life
being lonely.

ME

Yes, mother. I'm quite familiar with how lonely your
home feels even when it's full of people. I have work to
do. We can discuss this later. Or never again. I'm fine
with either option.

I take the liberty to ignore Jessica's texts since I am, in fact, *not* obligated to her in any way, shape, or form, and run a hand through my hair. It's about time for a haircut, but did I have a single spare moment to get it done while I was in New York? No. Of course not.

How early is too early to start drinking around here?

I managed to make it until four o'clock at work before peeling out of the parking lot on two wheels in search of a place to get a drink. I walk into the first bar I see—and while the name is absolutely absurd, it's a lot quieter than any other bar on the main strip—so I'm willing to take the chance of getting robbed or beaten to death by the group of bikers smoking outside to enjoy a drink in peace. Their vests read *Drengr* with a shield and crossed axes on the back and they're all looking at me like —well, like a guy in a three-piece suit walking into a biker bar.

Only it's not a biker bar it's… I have no idea what the fuck it is. There are photos of bikers, service members—active and retired it looks like—there's more viking-esque decor on the walls, a neon sign that says *Chattahoochies* above the bar, pool tables to the right with a jukebox playing "Simple Man" by Lynyrd Skynyrd next to them and…a fucking *dog* sitting in a booth to the left.

"What the fuck is this place?" I ask, mostly to myself, sitting down on a barstool.

"Mine." I look up and see a man scowling at me like he wants to throw me *and* the barstool I'm sitting on right back out the front door.

"It's very…" I still don't even know. It's fucking cool as shit, and so much different than most of the other bars around here, but I doubt he'll believe anything I say by the way he's glaring at me right now. I clear my throat and unbutton the top of my dress shirt instead. "Macallan, neat. Please." He nods and grabs a coaster and a glass, pouring the drink as he studies me.

"You lost?" He chuckles, making me relax a little more in my seat.

"Um, no. I came in here on purpose, believe it or not."

"How come?" I take a moment to bask in the hushed chatter from people around the bar and the low volume of the music coming from the jukebox. Appreciating the fact that I can actually hear liquid being poured into a glass in this establishment.

"I like the quiet." He hums his approval, or agreement, I'm not entirely sure which, then puts the bottle back on the shelf.

"You're not from around here." It's a statement, not a question and I laugh.

"What gave me away?" I ask sarcastically. This time when he looks at me a flash of realization comes across his face before his eyebrows raise and he busies himself with moving empty bottles from the place next to me.

"You're wearing a three-piece suit and look like the tornado from Oz spit you out on the sidewalk."

I tilt my head in disbelief. "You talk to all of your customers like this?" My brows draw in as I finish off my drink.

"Depends on the day. Typically, yes." What an unusual person. He smirks and I admire how straightforward he is.

"Outstanding." I pull a one hundred dollar bill from my wallet, dropping it on the counter and nodding as I go.

His eyes widen and he looks up at me. "Have a good one," I say, nodding at him. He nods back at me and keeps working, and on my way out I recognize a familiar giant of a person walking through the front door. He glares at me then gives me a playful smile before making his way behind the bar, greeting the guy who was just serving me and I inwardly groan.

I guess Lauren's guard dog just so happens to be friends with the guy who owns the only bar in town I have the desire to visit again. I'm still unsure of his actual relationship to her and it pisses me off that I'm bothered by not knowing.

Chapter 18

Girls' night got canceled this week due to Leah being out of town with Sawyer, Shane being sick, and Taylor covering someone's shift at work. However, Ruby and I thought it would be simply absurd to miss the opportunity to hang out in our sweats and help Poe work on his crawling.

"He's so close. He's got the Army crawling down, he's just gotta get those little knees up!" I encourage him in my best Auntie Lauren voice. "Come on, Poe. You got this, buddy." His drool-filled smile makes me laugh and I scoop him up into my arms.

"How is holding him going to get him to crawl?" Ruby asks with an eye-roll.

"Simple. He doesn't need to crawl. He has me, and my legs are *super fast.*" I run in place as the little baby giggles fill the room.

"Um..." Tank enters the room holding his phone in one hand, rubbing the back of his neck with the other. "Allen had a stroke." A skin-pricking chill runs through my whole body. I sit down with Poe in my lap and stare blankly as Ruby asks questions.

"What? When?"

"Um. Earlier today I think. He didn't make it. Sawyer just texted and said Leah broke up with him as soon as he dropped her off at her mom's tonight. Did you guys not know about any of this?" I feel a pit forming in my stomach and a nauseating feeling washes over me.

Allen is gone?

"I gotta go." I shake my head, wiping a tear from my cheek. I set Poe down and kiss his head, snatching my purse from the counter. I think I say bye to Ruby and Tank, but before I make it to my car I hear the front door slam again.

"Hey, hey hey. Give me your keys." I look up at Ruby and start sobbing uncontrollably.

"Why wouldn't she tell us? We should be there for her! And for Loretta. Oh my god. She's been alone this whole time wai—waiting for her to get back?! Why wouldn't they call us!" I suck in a shaky breath and she pulls me close to her chest.

"I don't know. I'm sure they had their reasons. If I had to guess, Leah looks about like you right now, so maybe she just needed time to process it first." She continues trying to console me and I feel like an asshole for even saying any of that. Of course they're processing and needing time together before telling us.

"You're right. I'm just… We always go through things together. I just don't want them to be alone, you know?"

"It's okay. They've got each other, and you've got me, okay? No one is alone in this. Ever." I think back on all our childhood memories that Allen was a part of, how he would always try to scare us during our Halloween movie marathons that Leah hated, or how he would randomly sing on Saturday mornings to wake us up. He was the best dad to Leah and loved Loretta so deeply. I squeeze my eyes shut as the warm tears roll down my face.

"Why do the *good* parents have to go so soon?" I whisper.

"I wish I knew, babe. I really do." Ruby gives me a sympathetic look and pulls me tighter for one last hug, then we rush over to Leah's mom's house.

It's not fair.

Allen was a great man—an amazing father and husband. He loved me, Shane, and Taylor like we were his and Loretta's own children, he always helped others in need and had a way of mending Leah's broken heart when no one else really knew how to.

They deserved more time with him.

Leah has been unreachable since his funeral, and it's caused a panic within my heart that I can't shake. We know she's home because we still have her location and her car hasn't left her driveway, but she's in pain and she's choosing to suffer alone, and it's taking everything in me to let her. Not only did she lose her dad, but she lost the guy she's in love with—again. By choice or not, that's got to be hard.

She shouldn't be alone right now. Which is why the cavalry is standing outside of her door with coffee in hand, praying that she'll let us in.

Knock knock knock.

We wait a few beats then I hear the vague sound of something sliding on the other side of the door.

"She hasn't responded to any of our texts. We don't even know if she's alive at this point." I know it's dramatic, especially since I just heard her on the other side of this door—I think.

"She's grieving, it's a lot to endure—especially by yourself." Shane tries to reason with me, but I'm not having it.

"Exactly! She shouldn't be alone. We should be in there with her." Shane sighs and leans closer to the door.

"Leah. Sweetie, we wanted to check on you. We don't have to stay or anything, but can you just let us know you're okay?" I frown a bit when she tells her we won't stay because I'm so close to breaking into her house and planting myself in a corner somewhere so I can keep an eye on her, it isn't even funny. My heart is pounding harder with every second she doesn't respond. I just need to hear that sweet, assertive voice of hers.

"Le, baby girl. I'm about five seconds away from busting down this door. Please. Just any sign of life? Knock once if you need us and twice if you're okay but want us to leave."

Please knock once.

Knock. Knock.

I sigh in relief anyway, knowing she's there and that she's heard us. She knows she isn't alone, and that when she's ready we'll swoop in and be there for her.

I look around and I'm the first to sit down on the small step by the door, sipping on my coffee as the others follow suit. We stay for a while, enjoying the spring breeze as we occupy her front porch. Tennessee is finally starting to kick out the bitter cold and get little hints of warmer weather, which is always my favorite time of year. I roll my head along the sturdy wooden door, imagining what things look like on the inside.

Has she been eating? Has she showered? Does she have enough toilet paper and tissues? I wonder if Sawyer has come to check on her. I'll kick his ass if he hasn't. Big burly idiot.

When all of our coffees are empty, we nod in agreement that it's time to go. After they all say their *I love you's* and walk down the front porch steps, I press my forehead against the door and sigh.

"I love you, Leah. You're so much stronger than you probably think you are right now. You'll get through this, I promise and we'll be right here when you're ready to open the door." I tap the door gently, then head down the stairs. Knowing tonight is a dinner I'd give anything not to go to.

"So sad about Allen," my mother says, taking a sip of her wine.

"Mm, very." My father barely looks up from his food to respond as anger simmers in my chest.

"Loretta looked absolutely dreadful at the funeral, did she not?" I look on in disbelief at the absolute gall.

"As opposed to *what*, Mother?" I snap.

"Excuse me?" She looks up at me, a completely clueless look on her face.

"How is a woman who's just lost her husband supposed to look? Radiant? Flawless? Slightly distressed? Only needing to dab away a bit of smeared makeup but otherwise composed?"

"Lauren, that's enough," my father warns, but I could care less what he thinks is enough.

"No, Dad. It's not. The woman just lost her husband, her best friend, her soulmate. Of course she looked dreadful, she's *grieving*. Should we expect no tears whatsoever from you when Dad goes? Will you care more about how you look at his funeral than the thought of him never coming back home?"

My father drops his silverware on his plate. "Lauren Long, that is *enough*."

"You know, I actually agree with you this time." I stand up so quickly my chair almost falls over, and look at my parents. "I hope someday I find someone that loves me the way Allen loved Loretta. Someone I couldn't imagine losing because they make me feel the way he made her feel. They had an admirable love, and she's just lost the other half of that love. Shame on you for speaking ill of her appearance, Mother. I hope your next round of Botox fails you the way you've failed me." My mother's face goes stone cold.

"Well, you certainly would have fit in better with that family." She goes back to eating as if she's completely unphased by everything that just conspired and my heart physically aches. I storm out of their house and make it to my car with my chest heaving as I try to catch my breath while my blood continues to boil beneath the surface of my skin. I can't believe I just said that. I know this night is going to come back to bite me in the ass, and I probably should have just kept my mouth shut, but I just…couldn't.

Chapter 19

Fitz

In the month since I've been back, Lauren has been more unlike herself than I've ever seen her before. It's unsettling and quite frankly, starting to piss me off. She's not showing up early, her eating habits have changed, she barely mumbles a word when I press buttons I know would usually cause her to blow up in my face, and she hasn't so much as cracked a smile since the day I got back and it's infuriating how much I miss seeing it. I'd even settle for one of those god-forsaken eye rolls right now. Anything to know she's still in there. So to find out, I do the only thing I know to do to get a response out of her.

"What the fuck is this, Lauren?" She flinches at the mention of her name. Not sure I've ever called her anything other than Trouble—except the condescending *Sweetheart* I throw around every now and then.

"A sales report, Fitz." God, her voice sounds as empty as she looks.

I scoff, "A sad excuse for one, maybe. What's going on?" She remains expressionless and stares at her computer. No typing. No scrolling of her mouse. Just staring at a blank screen as she remains silent.

"Let's go." Her eyes lazily drag up to mine.

"Where?"

"Tell you on the way." Pain settles between her brows and she shakes her head.

"No." The fact that there's no fight in her whatsoever is alarming.

"Is whatever is going on with you really *so bad* that you're willing to just give up like this?" Her eyes slice back to mine. There it is... *anger*.

"Fuck you, Fitzgerald." She snatches her bag from the floor beside her and rounds the desk. "Stop acting like you know everything about me. You don't know a damn thing so why don't you make my life a little bit better and stay the hell out of it." My hand wraps around her arm before I can think better of it and her jawline sharpens as she glares up at me.

"No." Surprise flashes across her face as quickly as she yanks free of my grip, then she slams her office door behind her, closing me in.

I'll fucking get her back. No matter how pissed off she gets at me in the process.

I take advantage of being alone in Lauren's office, doing my due diligence to snoop while I have the chance. She's an insanely organized individual, which is why I'm taken aback by how messy her desk is right now. There are papers and half-empty energy drink cans all over it. I walk around and glance over everything, careful not to mess anything up. In case by some slim chance, she's one of those wild ones who knows when her mess has been messed with. Then I see a green pamphlet that stands out amongst all the white papers surrounding it, so I pick it up and read it.

In loving memory of Allen Gates

Well, fuck.

I toss the program back down on the desk and sigh. I have no idea who this guy is, or what he may have meant to her, but the fact that it was sitting on top of her desk— a month after the date of the funeral arrangements listed on the back—tells me there's a good chance this is why she's been off.

I am an asshole—and this time I don't feel good about it.

I gotta get out of this damn office.

As soon as I open the door Luther is standing in the hallway, looking at me with wide eyes.

"Something I can help you with there, Luther?" His face morphs into one full of shock and a little bit of…sass?

"Whatever you did kicked a little bit of life back into her, which I guess is good, but buddy you pissed her the hell off."

I smirk to myself and pat him on the shoulder. "I can handle her."

Hall's Gym.

Maybe this place will be better than the less-than-desirable gym in my hotel. I hike my bag over my shoulder and walk through the door, immediately met with the smell of sweat and sanitizer.

"Welcome to Hall's," a guy behind the front desk greets me as I take in the space. I am already more pleased with what I see than when I first walked into the stale gym in the basement of my current residence. "First time here?"

I nod, dropping my bag at my feet. "Yeah."

"Well, are you looking for a guest pass for the day or a membership? A membership gives you access to our new boxing area and the sauna." I look at him in anticipation for more, but his eyebrows raise as he waits for *my* response.

"Uh, I guess just give me a membership then." I flip my wallet open and pull out some cash to pay for the year—whether I'm here for another month or the rest of my life—which feels like a possibility with as many months as I've already been here. This acquisition feels like it's taking a lot longer than most, but I haven't had the energy to care why. Plus, I don't really mind it. I've found something, someone rather, to entertain my time while here. After filling out the membership information I take my things and head onto the floor. I'm halfway through my workout when I see three familiar faces walk through the door and one I don't quite recognize.

"Who's going in with me today?" The guy who picked up Lauren from work a couple of months ago asks the other three.

"I'm not even saying anything because you know I'm out until the season is officially over," the guy with longer hair answers.

"I think getting my ass handed to me yesterday was enough to last me at least a month." *Bar owner.*

"As much as I have always dreamed of beating the shit out of my little brother, I'm getting married in a few weeks so I'd rather avoid having my beautiful bride yell at me for getting blemished." The red-headed guy slaps him on the back and he groans.

"Pussies. All of you." I almost snort when he slaps them all in a row with a towel he just pulled from his bag.

"Oh my god, dude. Did you dry your fucking ball sweat with that towel? Why does it smell like that?!" The older brother covers his nose and slaps him in the back of the head.

"That's what a *man* smells like, dude. It's understandable you don't recognize the scent." I realize I've completely stopped my workout to eavesdrop on this conversation like a fucking creep, but it did give me a good laugh—and the urge to spar with this complete stranger. Fuck it, how bad could it be?

"You need someone to spar with?" I ask, approaching them from the weight bench I was just working at.

"Oz. What are you doing here?" How clever.

"Working out somewhere better than the stale gym in the hotel I'm staying at."

"The fuck did you just call him? I thought his name was like… Lucy or something?" the red-headed guy says.

"Lucifer," the guard dog corrects, staring at me with his arms now crossed over his chest.

"Uh, hey. I'm Sawyer," the guy with long hair introduces himself. The most unthreatening of all of them so far.

"Hey man, it's Fitz, actually, but I admire Lauren's term of endearment choice." The red-headed guy barks out a laugh at that.

"My bad man. I'm Tucker." He holds out his hand to shake mine. I nod and shake it, looking over at the broody one.

"I could keep referring to you in my head as *The Bar Owner* if you'd like—" He huffs and it *almost* looks like he smirks.

"Max." He holds up a fist and I bump it, turning to look at the last man standing. Who does *not* offer me his name.

"So you want to spar then?"

I shrug in agreement. "Let's do it." I notice as the other guys share glances with each other but think nothing of it and glove up. Not even five minutes in the ring and I'm on my ass.

"Jesus Christ," I mumble and the dog finally cracks a smile. Of course he's pleased with my pain.

"What's the matter, Big Money? Daddy never taught you how to fight?"

The fuck is wrong with this guy? And no, he didn't, dammit.

I get back up and we go another few rounds where I actually get a couple of good shots in. Pleased with myself; I let my guard down, apparently, and he gets one last hit in and I go down hard. I lie on my back, breathing heavily with no desire to get back up. I toss my gloves, sit up with my arms draped over my knees, and look up to see Tucker offering me his hand.

"Probably should have warned you that you were getting in with a former Marine with like, ten years of martial arts training."

Goddamn. Yeah, that would have been useful information.

"Yeah. Maybe mention that to the next guy."

"So, how do you know Lauren?" Sawyer asks, the others clearly listening for the answer too.

"We work together," I answer simply.

"Did you steal her favorite pens or put a push pin in her chair or something?" Tucker laughs and I give him a confused look. "Must have done something shitty to earn the nickname *Lucifer*." I chuckle, thinking of my little troublemaker getting worked up enough to call me the devil.

"No, but she thinks I tried stealing her printer."

"Why?" Max asks, clearly confused.

"Because I borrowed it one day when she was out of the office." I shrug.

"Well, maybe don't touch shit that isn't yours."

"I was going to put it back. If it makes you feel better, she yelled at me for it." I offer as some sort of peace offering, seeing as how my very existence seems to bother this guy almost as much as I think it bothers Lauren sometimes.

"I'll let you guys get back to your workout. I'm sure I'll see you around." I start exiting the ring, mumbling, "Sorry in advance for that, I guess." As I pass the guy whose name I *still* don't know. When I make it to my gym bag, I pull my phone out and see a text from my father.

DAD

June 10th, sales conference. Be back on the 8th, ask Jessica to go with you. People like the look of you two.

Would it be an overreaction to throw my phone into oncoming traffic and claim I never got the text? I'd rather peel my own skin off with a vegetable peeler than take Jessica Vanderbilt to another social event.

Chapter 20

Tank

"Yo, what the hell was that about?" I watch as Fitz grabs his gym bag and leaves Hall's, turning back to face Tucker.

"What do you mean?" I start taking my gloves off as he gives me a bored look.

"Don't act like you don't know what I'm talking about. You never go that hard in the ring anymore, clearly, you have something against that guy." I grind my teeth, remembering the day I went to pick Lauren up from work.

I sit on the bench and sigh as they all stand in front of me waiting for an explanation. "Look, all I know is when I went to pick Lauren up from work she came out of his office fucking *crying* and I have no idea why."

"You didn't ask her?" Max asks.

"You know how Lauren is. She's fucking tough as nails, shit doesn't make her cry, and when it does, she brushes it off like it's nothing. She put on her brave face when she got in the truck and I could tell from the way she was keeping the conversation on anything but work that she didn't want me to ask about it. So I didn't."

Sawyer rubs his hand over his jaw. "So you don't know what happened while they were in his office?"

I finish taking a drink of water and slam the lid shut. "Nope. Which pisses me off. Any time I see that guy I wanna grab him by the throat and ask him what he did but…it's not my place."

"Okay, well maybe next time you fill us in on the fact that some asshole at her work made her cry. That way we're not blindly polite to the guy." Tucker holds his hand out in the direction of the door and I laugh, standing to move to the weight rack.

"That's on you for being so fucking nice all the time."

Max follows me, grabbing the 45s as we begin curling. "I met him at the bar the other day, he didn't necessarily strike me as the threatening type."

I blow out a breath as I try to keep count of my reps. "Maybe he isn't. But she wasn't coming out of that office crying for no reason. So until she can set the record straight, I'm not letting my guard down with him." I watch in the mirror as Sawyer and Tucker give agreeing looks.

"Fair enough. We've got her back," Tucker says, placing weights on the squat rack.

Lauren is Ruby's best friend and has been like a sister to me for almost as long as I've known her. I see how she puts on a brave face, I hear her tell Ruby about the shit she's gone through with her parents, and the last thing she needs is some asshole giving her shit at work. I'm always going to have her back because I know no one else does. Well, the girls do, sure. But when it comes to someone needing their ass beat, that's more my speed than theirs. Though I wouldn't put it past my wife to give him a run for his money in the ring too.

Chapter 21

My heart sinks a little at the subtle reminder that I'm the only one without a date to Taylor and Tucker's wedding. Then my phone rings at the same time I go to unlock it and I accidentally answer before I see the name on the screen.

Shit.

"Hello." I take a deep breath, preparing myself for whatever is about to come through the other end of this call.

"Lauren, it's your mother." I roll my eyes and drop my bag in the chair next to me.

"Yes, Mother, I know. I've had your number saved for quite some time now actually."

"Well, I just wasn't sure. You could have me saved as some obscene nickname or not bother saving it at all so you can decline the call due to it being an unrecognized number."

"Did you need something?" I ask, not having the energy to entertain her dramatics this morning.

"Well, ever since dinner the other day where you mentioned wanting someone in your life, not as much like your father and I than your *friend's* parents, but someone nonetheless, your father and I have been talking—"

"It's a little late to put me up for adoption, Mom." Even joking about it still stings.

"Your father and I have been talking and he heard that the Henderson's son, Miles. Do you remember Miles?" I shake my head, my eyes popping in annoyance because does she even realize it is seven thirty in the morning?

"No, Mom, I can't say that I do."

"Well, your father and his father got to talking and Miles is still single, he owns his own accounting firm, graduated from Berkeley, and is *very* handsome."

…

"Lauren?"

"Yes?"

"Well, what do you think?" This might be the first time I have ever heard my mother sound *excited* while on the phone with me.

"Are you trying to adopt *him?*"

"Lauren Long, can you be serious for one minute. Your father gave him your number and he's going to be contacting you soon—today even —to ask you out." The way the end of that sentence sounded like she was seconds away from a cartwheel is alarming, but the fact that my parents are trying to set me up—with one of my father's business partner's *sons* no less, makes me want to throw up.

"Mom, I have to go," I say urgently, hoping she'll think it's unrelated to our conversation, even though it is solely because of this conversation that I need to get off the phone.

"Okay. Well, let me know what he says. Oh, this is so exciting."

Beep beep beep.

Not even a full thirty seconds after we hang up, my phone chimes with a text alert.

UNKNOWN NUMBER

Hey there, this is Miles Henderson. I was told there was a lovely lady at the other end of this number that might be interested in a date this weekend? I'm out of town on business right now, but I'll be back Friday night. Send me an address and I'll pick you up around 7.

I stand in my office staring at my phone screen, not even having unlocked my computer yet and I already want to scream. I run through a million different responses I could send him, declining the date that's being forced upon me, then think of all the misery I would suffer at family dinners for turning down someone my parents hand-picked for me from their social group without even a first date. I grip my phone so tightly in my hands that Siri beeps, *how can I help?* The robotic voice asks and it does me in—I rear back and throw my phone, causing it to crash into a photo hanging on the wall, shattering the glass and dropping to the floor. I'm not even concerned about the noise since I'm the only one here this early. My heart is racing, a cold sweat breaks out over my entire body and I'm trying to think of a calming technique to reel in the anger I am feeling, but my mind is completely blank.

I hold my head, my face settling between my elbows, and fight back the tears about to unleash hell on my makeup. The more I try to steady my breathing, the more ragged it becomes.

"Look at me." Hands land on my elbows and startle me. I look up and see Fitz. "Breathe."

"I'm. Fucking. Trying." My voice cracks as I try talking back to him.

"That's it, Trouble. Give it to me." He smirks and it pisses me off.

"Get the fuck out of my office," I scream at him, pointing to the door.

"Go ahead. Scream at me. Tell me to fuck off. Tell me how much you hate me. But for God's sake, let it out." Then I do something unexpected.

I slap the shit out of Fitz, immediately gasping and holding my hands to my mouth when I notice he already has some bruising there.

"There you are." He smirks at me and my eyes quickly become wet with unshed tears.

"I am so sorry. I don't—" I blink a few times, quickly letting my tears fall and I can feel my shoulders sag—then they begin to shake. "What the fuck is wrong with me?" I laugh through the question, running my fingers through my hair as I walk farther into my office and away from Fitz.

"I'd like to know the same thing." I look at Fitz in surprise and let out a half laugh, half scoff.

"Wow, where do I start? My best friend just text me asking if I can share a boyfriend for her wedding, my parents literally told me I would have been better off being someone else's kid, they disapprove of pretty much everything I do with my life, and as much as I wish that didn't bother me, it fucking *does*. So when the one time they are excited about something happening in my life it's, of *course*, something that's being orchestrated by them and I don't have the fucking balls to say no, thank you, but I do not want to date the accountant from Berkeley you picked out for me." I watch as he processes everything that just spewed out of me and I'm slightly mortified that I just gave this guy any more ammunition to use to make my life hell than he already had. It's as if I was a Diet Coke and someone dropped emotional Mentos down my throat—I couldn't have fought the explosion that followed if I'd wanted to. The other part of me feels a little bit lighter that I got all of that out but now I'm waiting for him to say something, anything, and it's making me more anxious by the second.

"Your boyfriend doesn't seem like the sharing type." I pause at his words.

"What?"

"Well, you said your friend texted you asking if you could share him for a wedding? He doesn't strike me as the sharing type. Very... territorial." His jaw flexes and my brows draw together as I shake my head.

"No, I have to share my other friend's boyfriend's arm when we walk down the aisle because *I* am the only one that doesn't have a date. Or in this case a significant other that is related to or lifelong friends with her soon to be husband." I hate the bitterness I feel in my words as they leave my lips, but it's not like it matters. I'm talking to Fitz for God's sake, if anything he'll just throw my single girl meltdown back in my face during one of our petty work arguments and no one else will know how I really feel about it.

"The guard dog isn't your boyfriend?"

"The *what*?" My eyes pop curiously.

"The guy who picked you up here the day you heard me on the phone talking about the acquisition."

"Tank? God, no. He's married—to my best friend." Something flashes across Fitz's face and I swear I see his shoulders drop. As if he's just relaxed for the first time since walking in here. I get a sobering feeling when he looks at me, the noise in my brain becomes quiet as I study his softer features. The way his eyes widen slightly when he isn't actively trying to annoy me and the way his dark hair is so much longer now than when I first met him.

"I'll be your date." I let out a laugh and shake my head, rolling my eyes and when they refocus I see his eyes have narrowed again, his jaw tight and he's closed most of the space between us. "Something funny, Trouble?" I swallow down my laughter, feeling the weight of that nickname hit me at full force.

"Why?"

He shrugs. "Purely selfish reasons, of course."

I scoff, "Of course." I mull it over for a moment, giving the inside of my lip hell as I bite it so hard trying to tell myself this is a horrible idea.

"What kind of selfish reasons?"

"You'll owe me a favor." That could be a very simple statement or a very dangerous one. Still, I can't help but think spending an evening with Fitz might be better than being there alone. Sure I'll have my girls, but they'll eventually start dancing with their dates and I'll be left to man the bar and that bit is getting a little old. I'll be thirty in a couple of months, for crying out loud, it wouldn't be the end of the world to take a co-worker as a date to a friend's wedding, would it?

"So it's just a favor then, not a real date," I state for extra clarification. His smirk damn near has me refusing this whole thing.

"Unless you *want* it to be."

My eyes roll on instinct. "In your dreams, Fitzgerald." His last step brings us so close I can practically feel his growl against my chest.

"If you keep rolling those damn baby blues at me, Trouble, I might just be inclined to make them roll for an entirely different reason." I can practically feel my heart beating through my cheekbones and before I can say something stupid, someone clears their throat in the doorway.

"*So* sorry to interrupt." *Luther*. "I saw your coffee sitting out here and thought you must have set it down and forgot it." Fitz has yet to move from in front of me, so I squeeze past where he's got me practically pinned against the wall and smile at Luther. I open my mouth to say something and he holds a finger up to stop me.

"Mm-mm. Later." Then he cuts his eyes over to where Fitz is now turned around with his eyes on me like I'm his next meal. By the time I turn around, Luther is gone.

I clench my jaw and walk behind my desk, pulling my small mirror from my bag to fix the makeup I smudged while having a nervous breakdown earlier.

"Next Saturday, six o'clock. Don't be late—and wear something nice." I glance over at him and see that devilish smirk on his stupidly handsome face and almost roll my eyes again. Though I think better of it when I remember what he said just before Luther came in. I swallow hard and put my small mirror back in my bag. "I'll send you the address."

"It's a date." This time I don't stop the eye roll that happens before they land on the drink Luther brought in. My brows scrunch together and I pick it up.

"Wait," I say mostly to myself, though it causes Fitz to halt in the doorway. "I didn't get coffee this morning." *Did I? Am I losing it and forgetting that I stopped for coffee?*

"Thought you needed a little bit of your spark back. Caffeine should do the trick, right?" He winks and then disappears down the hallway as I take a sip of the coffee that is my exact order made to perfection. I stand in my office replaying my morning and finally have to shake my head to clear it.

Well, he definitely brought a little spark with him this morning, but it didn't come from the damn coffee, that's for sure.

Chapter 22

Fitz

Being someone's date to a wedding but not *going* to the wedding together is definitely a first for me. I guess that comes with the territory of being the date of a bridesmaid who had to be at the wedding location the entire day. I pull up to the address Lauren emailed me and pause when I realize it's a gravel road in the middle of nowhere. Either she organized my death, or I'm extremely overdressed for some backwoods wedding. When I pull around the circle driveway I see that the address on the whitewashed brick house matches the one logged on my GPS so I park my car and make my way around the back.

"Holy shit," I mumble to myself. The most elegant-looking backyard wedding I've ever seen lies in wait along with a party tent just down the hill. I check my watch and see that I have a few minutes to find my seat before the ceremony begins. As soon as I'm settled I feel my phone vibrate in my jacket pocket.

TROUBLE

Are you here yet?

ME

Have you ever known me not to be punctual?

TROUBLE

That's not an answer.

ME

Yes, I'm here.

I don't see the three little dots appear again so I lock my phone and put it away, just as Tucker and the other guys make their way up front. I catch a less-than-thrilled look from Tank but choose to ignore him until the girls begin walking out a few moments later. The first girl out is the blonde from all of her photos, followed by the dark-haired girl with tattoos, and then the other brown-headed girl with tight curls. When Lauren walks out in a fitted blue dress with a dangerously high slit up the leg I feel my breath halt in my lungs.

Fuck me, she looks sensational.

I can't take my eyes off her, which makes it easy to notice the way she and another bridesmaid are talking through their teeth to each other. When her eyes land on mine, I give her a wink and she immediately looks away.

"Who gives away this bride to be?"

"Oh, she makes her own choices, her mother and I just support her in them." The crowd shares a laugh and I find myself smirking at the statement as well. I wonder what that's like? Having parents that just... *support* you in life? Parents that allow you to make your own decisions, possibly with encouraging guidance, but in the end you're the one in control of your own life. The couple exchange vows, and all the while I can't stop watching Lauren. She looks at her friends in adoration, subtly wiping a tear away as Tucker finishes his vows, and it makes me wonder what her soft side looks like.

The ceremony concludes and everyone makes their way to the reception tent while the wedding party takes photos. I've been here for an hour and a half and have yet to talk to my date. I'm beginning to wonder why she was so upset about not having a date when she clearly doesn't seem to have the time for one. Then I hear the DJ announce the couple and the rest of the wedding party walks in with them, smiling and clapping as Tucker dips Taylor in the middle of the dance floor. Finally, Lauren starts walking my way.

"I was beginning to wonder if you invited me here simply to ignore me the whole night." As I expected, those deep blue eyes roll around, only this time they pop in what looks like fear at the end. I can't fight the smirk that finds its way to my lips and wouldn't even if I could. "Remembering what I said about rolling your eyes at me, Sweetheart?"

Her features shift and she squares her shoulders. "No."

Little liar.

"Sure, you're not." She turns away from me to watch her friends share their first dance and crosses her arms over her chest.

"I didn't invite you here." I look down at her with a frown. "You said you were beginning to wonder if I invited you here to ignore you. But you invited yourself." She shrugs.

"Well, don't make it sound so rude," I tease, catching a sassy glare from her. "What I did was out of the kindness of my heart." The sass thickens.

"I believe the words *'purely selfish reasons'* were used? I hardly call that kind." I step in front of her, obscuring her view of the dance floor.

"Are you going to be trouble for me tonight, Sweetheart?" My tone must rub her the way I hoped it would because she averts her gaze. People begin clapping and I assume the first dance is over. The music grows louder and she finally meets my eye again.

"I'm *going* to get a drink. Excuse me." I shake my head as she saunters away, her hips swaying with attitude at every step. She stops to give Tucker a hug and they speak briefly before she makes her way over to where all of her friends are gathered near the bar. I'm never uncomfortable at events like this, but my lack of familiarity with this particular one is making me second-guess my brilliance in offering to escort her here tonight. Especially since she's spent all of five minutes talking to me and has already run off in the opposite direction.

I'm quickly pulled from my thoughts when I feel a light tap on my arm. "Hi there, I'm afraid I don't recognize you. I'm Marilyn, the mother of the bride." I give her a smile and set my scotch glass, that might as well be part of my hand at this point, down on the table.

"Hello, Marilyn. We haven't met before but it's a pleasure. I'm Fitz, Lauren's date." Her eyes widen slightly at the mention of the word *date*.

"Oh my, well. I see her good taste expands further than her wardrobe and friends... I hope." She gives me a knowing look that is both charming and confusing. "You better treat that girl well. I may not share their DNA but all of those girls over there are my babies." We both look over to see Lauren joining the girls as she continues, "And she's got a whole lot of people looking out for her." I feel a nudge on my bicep and see her nod nonchalantly at where the groom and the rest of the pack are looking at us. Unease settles in my chest and I must say, it's a feeling I'm not too fond of.

"Yeah, I've noticed that." I nod to the group and smile back at Marilyn. "It's been lovely meeting you, Marilyn but I'm going to take a chance on asking a beautiful woman to dance with me." She simply nods and smiles before turning to talk to someone at the table next to us. The conversation between the girls is quiet, but not quiet *enough*.

"...and he offered to come with me." Lauren's small shoulder lifts and Taylor jumps in.

"As an arch nemesis does, *naturally*."

That's my cue.

"Could the arch nemesis steal you for a dance?" I see her body stiffen ever so slightly, finding a little too much pleasure in the reaction she has to me. Negatively or otherwise. She turns around and her eyes fall to my outstretched hand.

"Is this the part where you grab the cake cutter and bring me to my demise?" A laugh rumbles out of me and I'll be damned if she doesn't smile too. I spin her onto the dance floor and the look of shock on her face is priceless.

"Don't tell me you assumed I couldn't dance."

"Okay, I won't." I pull her body flush with mine as we continue to sway to the music.

"Enlighten me, Trouble. This feisty little attitude of yours— are you like this with everyone or is it something you bring out just for me?" She takes such a deep breath that there's not an inch of space between us.

"Hmm, I'd tell you, *but* I'd rather not give you the satisfaction."

"So it's just for me then." I smirk at her and she glares up at me.

"Interesting that *that's* the answer that would bring you satisfaction." I spin her around once, quickly bringing her back in.

"What brings *you* satisfaction?" I tip my chin in her direction.

"Dirty." The flirty way her eyebrows raise and the tone of her voice has my blood traveling south.

"Sweetheart, if you want it to be, it can be. You can tell me every dark and dirty desire you have and I would explore every one of them with you." Her eyes pop and her cheeks flame. "But I simply meant, in life. What brings you satisfaction?" That addicting look of desire falls from her face, replaced instead by confusion.

"Oh," she says, dropping her eyes as she thinks. "Giving you frown lines." I don't think I've ever wanted to bend someone over my knee as much as I have this little troublemaker.

"Brat," I mumble into her ear, noticing the goosebumps spread down her arms.

Interesting.

"Asshole," she bites back through her teeth.

Lauren left me at our table almost an hour ago to accompany her girlfriends on the dance floor, and I haven't seen her since. Which isn't something that would typically bother me, if it weren't for the angry-looking man stalking toward me.

"Lucy!" he practically grunts as he falls into the chair across from me. "What the hell are *you* doing here?"

"It's Fitz," I correct him.

"I know." He smirks humorlessly at me. I let out a sigh, giving up any hope of him ever using my real name.

"I'm here as Lauren's date. Was that not obvious by the dancing earlier?" His nostrils flare and his jaw flexes.

"How exactly did that happen?"

Anger bubbles in my chest at his question. "Excuse me?"

"Just wondering how she goes from hating you to you being her date to her best friend's wedding." I lean forward, resting my elbows on my thighs.

"Ever consider that it's none of your damn business?"

"Listen, you fu—" He's quickly on his feet, but someone steps in between us before he can get another word out.

"Simmer down, please. Taylor will kill you if you cause a scene at her wedding." She turns to face me and extends her hand. "I'm Ruby."

I'd be lying if I said I wasn't a little bit terrified to accept it.

"Fitz," I offer a small smile and shake her hand anyway.

"Well, I hate to interrupt you boys, but ours have a bedtime so we gotta get going." She nods towards the exit and before things can become awkward, or worse—hostile, they say goodbye and take off in the opposite direction.

Why the hell does this guy care so much about me being here with Lauren? What the hell did I ever do to him?

"Hey there, *date*, you ready to go?" I look up to see a smiling Lauren, her forehead glistening with sweat from dancing so hard and her hair slightly disheveled. As if she's been continuously running her hands through it.

"Are you drunk?"

"Yeah, so? Isn't that how you like me anyway? People find I'm much more agreeable when I have a few drinks in me." She's so…unstable? The poised, fierce, controlled hurricane I'm familiar with looks like a soft breeze could blow her over at any moment, as her arms flop at her sides as she speaks.

"How often do you get drunk like this?" She shrugs and sinks into a chair, practically melting onto the table as she props her cheek up on her palm.

"Whenever we go out. Sometimes on girls' nights. On work trips, apparently," she mumbles the last part before reaching for my scotch glass to finish it off. I grab her wrist and stop her before she can.

"Please tell me you're never left alone when you're like this."

"Aww. You worried about me, Fitzgerald?" I can tell she's trying her best to glare but it's not working.

"Do you understand how reckless that is? Anyone could—" I stop myself and rub my hand across my mouth as she snatches hers back and stands up so fast I fear she might actually fall over.

"Could what? Take advantage of me?" My blood boils at the thought, causing me to loosen my tie as I stand to face her.

"Exactly." I can smell the tequila on her breath as she stares back at me. Beautiful blue eyes completely empty.

"So, what? It's only okay when it's you reaping the benefits of my drunkenness?" I lift her up and throw her over my shoulder, completely aware there's a fifty-fifty chance she'll vomit all down the back of my suit. When we finally reach a quiet place on the outside of the reception tent, I place her feet on the ground and back her into the support beam.

"I didn't *know* you were blackout drunk that night. If I had, I would have stopped you in that elevator."

"Regretting it now, are we?" Tears fill her eyes, causing my chest to tighten. Fuck.

"No. But, I would have waited til you were sober enough to remember the first time I fucked you, and I sure as hell won't let you forget the next time I do." Her eyes pop and she rushes past me to empty the contents of her stomach in the grass.

Well…I've never gotten *that* reaction before.

Chapter 23

Lauren

Is it possible to have an aneurysm from drinking too much? I should probably look into that as soon as I can open my eyes all the way. I reach for my phone and peek them open just enough to see the time. My hand brushes against something cold when I place my phone back down and I roll my head to look again—seeing a glass of water and a bottle of aspirin.

Thank you, last night me.

I sit up and grab the bottle of pain reliever, popping two in my mouth before reaching for the water when I notice a little note underneath.

Coffee will be delivered at 10, Trouble.

I check my phone again, not remembering the time from two minutes ago, then I drag my ass out of bed since it's already five after. I don't know how punctual the coffee delivery service he's using may be, but I *do* know I'm not a fan of watered-down coffee. I swing the door open and feel a wave of nausea wash over me again at the sight of *Fitz* standing outside, holding my coffee.

He looks hot as shit, wearing a pair of slacks with white sneakers and a fitted T-shirt, meanwhile, I resemble an ugly step troll in a baggy T-shirt, insane bed head, and a pair of underwear as he looks me up and down.

"Morning sleeping beauty." He hands me my coffee and strolls inside my house, uninvited.

"Shut up," I groan, shutting the door behind him. "And come in, I guess?" I follow him into *my* kitchen as he makes himself comfortable on a barstool while I hold my iced coffee.

"How hospitable of you." He smirks at me then jumps when Ginny hops up onto the counter. "Ah, the killer cat."

"Better watch out, she's a great judge of character." I snort.

"Explains why she attacked you." The smirk on my face falls.

"We worked it out." I roll my eyes and take a sip of my coffee. Then the little bitch starts *purring* and rubbing her head against his arm. My mouth pops open as she practically melts onto the counter in front of him.

"Well, would you look at that? She *is* a good judge of character." He grins at me and I glare back at him.

"She must be having an off day," I say, picking her up from the countertop. "Traitor," I whisper in her ear before putting her back on the ground. "Is there a reason you're here?" When I turn to face him his eyes are drifting back up from my ass, causing a blush to spread across my face like wildfire.

"Coffee, remember?" He nods to the cup in my hand.

"Is watching me drink it part of the agenda or?" I leave the question open so he can fill in the blanks.

"No. I am here to cash in that favor you owe me." I slump over on my counter, giving him a clear look of annoyance.

"I'm very clearly hungover right now. Can we maybe talk about this some other time?" I whine.

"As much as I'd love to accommodate your misery, this is kind of a time-sensitive matter."

"*Ugh.*" I slide my coffee to the side and lay my head down on the cool countertop as I hear him stand up from his seat.

"Water?" I assume he's asking for some and point him in the direction of the refrigerator. I hear it open, then the crack of a water bottle lid.

"I need you to be my girlfriend." I snap to attention, staring at him across my kitchen island.

"What?"

"Well, fake girlfriend, I guess." The bothered look on his face is something I'll have to revisit and assess at a later time because my head has barely stopped pounding enough to even understand what the hell he's asking me to do.

"Again, *what?*"

"My parents are trying to force me into a relationship with a woman I whole-heartedly loathe, and every time I go to New York—for any reason, but especially for work events—they invite her as my plus one on my behalf. I figure they can't exactly invite a date for me if I bring my own."

"Fitzgerald, I am so *not* in the right headspace for this conversation right now." I lay my head back on the counter as he continues.

"If I had the time to discuss this when you were less…grouchy, believe me, I would. However, I am supposed to fly out for an event this weekend and time is of the essence if I'm going to inform my parents I will be bringing my own date instead of the one that makes me consider willingly walking on hot coals just to escape her." I don't bother picking my head up when I speak this time because the cool surface is actually working wonders for my headache.

"I am not *grouchy,*" I argue. "And you hate me too, so why trade one woman you can't stand for another? Just take the girl your parents like and get it over with."

"You'd be surprised by how little I hate you, Trouble." I gasp when I hear Fitz *behind* me and spin around so quickly it makes me dizzy. He takes a step toward me, even though there's not nearly enough room for him to do so, making my back hit the edge of the marble.

"What do you say? Be my girlfriend?" My stupid girl heart flutters at his words and that's enough to tell me this is a horrible idea. I'm already starting to notice the nice things he does more than the annoying, bossy things. Not to mention he's everything I try to avoid in a man. Rich, entitled, and too damn charming for his own good. So in reality, maybe it's a harmless task. How hard could it be to get through an event or two as his fake girlfriend? With a *real* relationship off the table, it shouldn't be that challenging to pull off a fake one.

"Whatever. It's just one event, right?" His brows pull together.

"Um, no. I just needed you to be available by the first event."

"So, how long is this favor going to last, exactly?" For the first time ever I see Fitz look *nervous*.

"A year." My eyes pop.

"A *year?!* I'm gonna throw up." I lean my head forward to stop that from happening, unable to care that it's now resting on his shoulder.

"Yes, I seem to have that effect on you lately." My head snaps back up.

"Oh, *please* tell me I didn't throw up on you last night." I close my eyes, praying to anyone who will listen that he says no.

"You don't remember?"

"Don't start. I barely remember my own name right now, okay? There's a lot happening this morning."

"No, you didn't throw up on me. But I got to see the show while you let it out in your friend's backyard."

"Oh, thank god."

"So, is that a yes?" I mull it over for another minute because that's an entire *year* of my life pretending to be in a relationship with someone I can't stand ninety-five percent of the time. That's insane, right? I mean, sure I wouldn't be alone, rewatching *Gossip Girl* for the ten *thousandth* time while my friends repopulate or travel the Earth with their husbands, and it would keep me from having to accept unwanted dates from my parent's co-workers ki—*oh shit*. I was supposed to go out with that guy this weekend. I will literally never hear the end of this from my parents if I don't have a good reason for blowing that guy off. Whatever the hell his name was.

Well, I guess I found my reason to agree to this insanity. Though there's no chance I'm letting him think it's going to happen that easily.

"Are you still in there?" Fitz uses two fingers to tap me on the forehead and I swat them away.

"What's in it for me?" I cross my arms over my chest, brushing against his since he's still standing unnecessarily close to me.

"I thought you understood this was an owed favor for me escorting you to the wedding."

"Okay, that was *one* night, this is a *year* of my life. Did you really think I just didn't have any other potential plans for the next 365 days?" I lift my brows in anticipation as he stares back at me.

"Whatever *potential plans* you had for yourself over the next year, I promise to make it worth your while to…postpone them." The arrogant assurance to his tone makes my skin tingle.

"How so?"

"Say yes and find out."

Note to self: Don't make decisions while hungover and high on the smell of rich boy cologne.

"I have one condition." He gives me a curious glance. "No one can know it's fake."

Because how embarrassing is that?!

"Even better," he agrees.

"Fine. One year." I hold out my hand and he smiles.

"We'll see." He grabs my hand and pulls me flush against his chest and I curse my body for the way my nipples harden against the thin fabric of my T-shirt. "Didn't your parents ever teach you not to make deals with the devil, Trouble?" I swallow hard past the lump forming in my throat, allowing my eyes to lock with his.

"I have a bad habit of doing the opposite of what my parents tell me to." He leans in and my entire body is frozen as his lips inch closer to mine.

"Of course you do." He kisses my nose and my entire brain turns to static. Then he grabs his water bottle from the counter and walks towards the door. "We fly out Thursday, make sure Ginny has a sitter. We'll be gone for a week." He turns to face me once more. "See you soon, Sweetheart." And with a wink, he's gone and I'm left wondering what the hell I just signed up for.

Chapter 24

Lauren

I'm pretty sure I haven't moved an inch over the last hour and a half. My stomach is growling, Ginny is staring at me like I might be a ghost, and I can't stop thinking about Fitz.

Stupid, handsome, *be my fake girlfriend*, Fitz.

"I'm an idiot. He's killed all of my good brain cells, Gin."

Meow.

She gets it.

Knock knock knock.

What a perfect time for company. I still look like a bridge troll and now I'm starving. I kiss Ginny on the nose, pausing when the memory of Fitz doing the same thing to me flashes through my mind.

Knock knock knock.

I shake my head to clear my thoughts and head for the door, freezing when I open it.

"Mom?" I couldn't hide the shock on my face if my life depended on it.

"Please tell me you don't make a habit of answering the door in such scandalous attire." She's clutching her handbag like *it's* appalled by my appearance too.

"Um, no. Typically my attire includes pants, it's just been a…weird morning." She's walking through the door before I can even finish my sentence.

"I sure hope you have a good reason for blowing off Miles Henderson this weekend." *Miles! That's his name.*

"Yeah, Mom. I was kind of busy being a bridesmaid. In my best friend's wedding." She actually scoffs. As if that's not a valid enough reason.

"Yes, I was there for the ceremony, Lauren. Miles would have made a lovely date. He's very likable, and didn't I tell you he graduated from Berkley?"

"You did. Which I'm sure is very impressive to someone, however, I wouldn't care if he was *Mr. Berkley*, I don't need you and Dad trying to set me up with someone."

"Well, wouldn't it be better than being alo—What in God's name is that?" She freezes when Ginny hops up on the counter next to me.

"That's a Ginny." I smile, scratching underneath Ginny's chin, earning me a very loud symphony of purrs.

"A cat?" She scrunches her face in *obvious* disapproval.

"Yes."

"It's on the counter."

"Yes."

"Cats don't belong on the counter. They belong on the floor. Or an alleyway behind a restaurant searching for scraps in a dumpster." My mouth drops open in surprise.

"That's amazing. That's exactly where I found her!" Her eyes pop as she tries to figure out if I'm lying. "I mean, I know it's not ideal. I could have adopted from a shelter or something but the poor thing was just covered in garbage and my heart couldn't take it. I had to bring her home."

"You're joking." It's almost a plea for me to tell her that I am.

"Yes, Mother. I found her at Tank and Ruby's house."

"Oh." I see her visibly relax and close my eyes to keep them from rolling. I'm annoyed by the fact that Fitz has made me realize how often

I do that. "You will call Miles today and apologize and *if* he happens to be forgiving enough to reschedule the date, you will *go*."

"Um, no."

"What do you mean, *no?*" Ginny runs into the other room, likely frightened by my mother's tone and I envy that she has the option to do so.

Here we go. Moment of…fake truth.

"I mean no, I won't be going out with him. I'll apologize for the misunderstanding but that's about all I can offer you."

"What misunderstanding?" I imagine she would have frown lines if her Botox injections didn't keep her from showing emotion.

"I'm seeing someone else, Mom." Her body language changes as she looks at me.

"Who?"

"Um, his name is Fitz." She rolls her eyes.

"How pretentious."

Oh fuck meeeee. Am I turning into my mother?

"It sounds like he works at a skateboard shop or a Dairy Queen or something."

"No, he doesn't."

"Well, what's his full name? What does he do? How long have you two been together?"

"Um, slow down. Don't they usually let people answer during interrogations?" She finally lays her handbag on the counter, not before eyeing it for Ginny first, and crosses her arms over her chest.

"This isn't an interrogation. I'm just curious. Why didn't you tell me about him when I told you Miles was going to call you?" I cross my arms and begin pinching the inside of my arm, a nervous habit I've had for as long as I can remember. We didn't exactly discuss our backstory so I guess I'm winging it and he's just going to have to go along with whatever I pull out of my ass.

"Because it wasn't really official yet but we've been…hanging out, I guess for a while. He's also in real estate—"

"*Hanging out,* how romantic." There goes that all-too-familiar attitude again. I don't say anything else, I can't. I don't want to keep lying unnecessarily so we just stare at each other awkwardly. Then she grabs her handbag and turns to leave.

"Are you sure he doesn't work at a Dairy Queen?"

"I've worked with him every day for seven months, Mom. I'm sure." She gives me a judgemental look but says nothing else until she reaches the door.

"I'll inform Miles of the misunderstanding. Would hate for you to embarrass yourself with the story about the skateboard shop owner."

Cue the eye roll.

"And keep that disgusting animal off the countertops, Lauren. You have no idea what kind of diseases it may have."

"Bye, Mom!" I yell, throwing my head back with my eyes closed, praying she actually leaves. The door latches behind her and I'm at least grateful she isn't the *'slamming the door'* type of mother, since I've only just realized my headache is gone. I take time to fill my favorite Tumblr full of ice water before snuggling onto my couch with my favorite blanket and Ginny takes that as her cue to curl up at my feet. I unlock my phone and chew on my thumbnail as I stare at the group chat. The last thing sent was a video of Hendrix putting on a show, lip-synching to an AC/DC song with one of Tank's old Guitar Hero guitars, wearing underwear, a pair of sunglasses, and crew socks. I watch it again and giggle then blow out a breath as I begin typing.

ME

Is everyone sitting down?

RUBY

Just plopped down on the couch.

SHANE

Teaching an art class but I have a chair nearby. 👁

TAY

On the road, so yes.

LEAH

I can beeee.

ME

Fitz and I are…dating.

SHANE

The floor is now the canvas.

TAY

Tucker is now lecturing me about gasping while he's driving.

RUBY

Dayumm. Sneaky little thing.

LEAH

🙂 Detailssssss.

ME

Sorry to disappoint you, but there's not really any. Not yet. It's new, but we made it official this morning.

TAY

AS IN HE STAYED OVER AFTER THE WEDDING AND YOU SEALED THE DEAL THIS MORNING?! THIS MORNING?

ME

Um, no. He brought me coffee though.

SHANE

I think that's even more romantic. 🙂 But coffee is my love language soooo. ☕

LEAH

Look who found their way over the line between love and hate 😊

ME

Let's pump, nay, slam on the breaks. No one is in love. Just…lets call it exploring the other side of the line.

RUBY

So you guys HAVEN'T slept together 🐐

Shit.

I hate lying to my friends. They're the only ones I have ever been completely transparent with, but keeping the secret of me and Fitz, our history, and our current situation, feels like the least humiliating way to go about this. A year from now when this is all over, they'll just think I'm a regular heartbroken girl. So I see no need to let them in on the expiration date of this fake relationship.

ME

Dirty details another day. I'm still nursing a hangover and I need sustenance.

TAY

Time to call Fitz then. 😏

RUBY

Tucker better double wrap it this week. Sounds like someone is in heat.

TAY

🐐

SHANE

💀

LEAH

Oh, geez. 🐐

I lock my phone and toss it to the side. I'll tell them about the trip to New York later. Time for a nap.

Chapter 25

She said yes. I can't believe she actually said yes. I had an entire presentation in my head ready to try and convince her, but she surprised me and agreed. I felt like I was two feet taller when I left her house. Though I'm not sure why, it is fake after all. For now, at least. I pick up my phone to call my father after finishing my workout, and for the first time in my life, I'm happy to be the one to call him. Mostly because I know what I have to tell him will piss him off.

"Fitz, what's the matter?"

"Hello to you too, Father. Nothing is wrong, why do you ask?" He clears his throat and changes his tone.

"Oh, well, good then. How are you?" I can't remember the last time my father asked me how I was doing.

"Um, I'm fine. I was actually calling to inform you I will be bringing someone with me to the event this weekend so there's no need to involve Jessica again." I hear him scoff and have to fight off the urge to hang up on him. Seeing as I'm the one who called him in the first place.

"Jessica has already been invited to the event. You will take her as planned. It'll look bad if you cancel on her at the last minute."

"It's not last minute, the event isn't for four days, and isn't it also a bad look to take someone who *isn't* my girlfriend to all of these events just for the sake of public image?"

"You don't *have* a girlfriend." I can feel the deviousness in the smirk on my face.

"Well, I'll let you try that theory out when you meet her on Friday. I gotta go."

"We're not done, Fitz—"

Click.

Yes, I believe we are.

I booked our first-class tickets to New York the minute I left her house Sunday morning, ensuring I didn't pick the *first* flight out since my little troublemaker doesn't seem to be a morning person. It's quarter to eight when I pull in front of her house to pick her up, shocked to see she is sitting on her front porch with a cup of coffee in her hand, and a rolling suitcase next to her. Her carry-on is attached to the handle of the rolling bag and she's wearing a small fanny pack across her chest. She's wearing a ribbed lounge set, biker shorts with an oversized hoodie, and sneakers that look like they'd slide off and on pretty easily.

Someone is an experienced traveler.

"Morning, Sweetheart. Ready to go?" She rolls her eyes at the nickname and stands up to face me.

"I've been ready for hours. I get anxious on travel days."

Well, fuck my nice gesture to let her sleep in. I guess she is a morning person.

"Noted. I'll book earlier flights from now on. This all?" Her cheeks redden and she offers me a small smile when I grab the handle of her suitcase to carry it to the car.

"Yeah, thanks." After everything is loaded I open the door and much to my surprise she quietly gets in, only speaking to say thank you when I go to close the door behind her.

"So, what's the itinerary this weekend?" she asks, tucking her foot beneath her ass as she turns to face me.

"Well, Friday is a convention I am speaking at. It should be pretty low-key, but you'll be there with me. Just simple girlfriend stuff, sit front row during my time slot speaking on media marketing and how to use today's technology to help real estate careers, have lunch with me, basically just *be* with me." I glance over to see her face is a beautiful shade of red and she shifts in her seat to face forward.

"Yeah, okay. Sounds simple enough." I take a deep breath and the scent of coconut and something a little more...I don't know, minty maybe, hits my nose. God, she smells like— "What about Saturday?" I clear my throat, getting my mind back on track and growing a little more nervous now.

"Saturday is...my dad's birthday." I can see her head whip around, her short black hair flying around her face.

"You're launching our relationship to your father, who wants you with someone else, mind you, on his *birthday?!* Are you insane?" I start to smile and earn a slap on the arm from her, making me laugh.

"Ow," I say sarcastically.

"Fitz! This is a horrible idea!" she laughs the words out. A mix of fear and humor in her tone.

I shrug. "He'll be fine. I already told him about you."

"What?" I look over to see her perfectly shaped brows pulled together.

"I just mean, I told him I had a girlfriend I would be bringing with me this weekend. He doesn't think you actually *exist*, but I assume it'll be pretty hard to deny when you're standing right in front of him."

"He might not be able to deny it but he can ignore it. I wouldn't be surprised if the other girl is there waiting for you when we show up." She snorts and the thought makes my skin feel like sandpaper.

"You won't be ignored. Not if I have anything to say about it." He would do it too, wouldn't he? He'd invite Jessica and try to make me look bad if I ignored her after all the times we've been seen together in the last few months. Suddenly the sandpaper feeling is gone and it feels as if a silk blanket is covering my arm.

"You okay?" I look down and see her tiny fingers curled around my forearm, and when my eyes meet hers a fire spreads throughout my entire body. I want her to touch me more. To feel this sense of calm everywhere. She looks so concerned about me and that makes me want to do something completely irrational.

"All good," I assure her, forcing a small smile. When she goes to move her hand I quickly reach for her fingers, bring them to my lips, and kiss them, then I place her hand back on my arm and we remain silent the rest of the way to the airport. I expect her to try and move her hand at some point, but she never does. When we finally get our bags checked and get through security my phone alerts me that our flight is already boarding.

"See, this is why I get to the airport at least two hours early," she says, anxiously chewing on the inside of her lip. I squeeze her cheeks together with one hand, forcing her teeth to release the skin.

"You're going to start bleeding if you keep doing that." She rolls her eyes and my dick stirs. *Yeah, I know. I think she's doing it on purpose at this point too.* "And two hours is way too fucking long to be at an airport. What the fuck do you do while you wait?"

"Read. Watch a show on my phone. Listen to music. Nap—" I look down at her and frown.

"You *nap*? Alone. In an airport?" She glares at me and I can't quite tell what she's thinking.

"No. I only nap if I'm traveling with someone. I do actually care about my safety, you know?" I give a look of disbelief and she swats my arm again.

"Could have fooled me, Sweetheart." She turns to face forward as we move further up the line to board.

"Well, at least I don't have to worry about that anymore." She shrugs.

"What do you mean?" She looks up at me and bats her eyelashes and fuck me for falling for it.

"Didn't you hear? I have a *very* protective boyfriend to look out for me now." She wraps herself around my arm, making that same feeling from the car spread through me again. "Now I can nap anytime, anywhere." I huff out a laugh but pause when she doesn't remove herself from my side. I'm not used to this side of her. She's actually playing into this role pretty damn well and we aren't even in New York yet. She better be careful. I might enjoy her calling me her boyfriend a little too much and never let her stop.

Chapter 26

God, I missed flying first-class. I may be a practical girl who likes to spend her money intentionally, but I think one of my intentions just became flying comfortably for the rest of my life. The legroom alone is enough to sell me on it, not to mention the added bonus of only having one seat neighbor. Speaking of which, mine smells as good as he looks and it's taking everything in me not to press my nose into his chest just to savor the scent a little longer. He smells the way you would imagine a man who looks like Fitz would smell—expensive and delicious.

"Can I get you anything to drink?" the stewardess asks, looking right past me at Fitz.

"Water please." My face captions must be turned on because he gives me a sexy little smirk and grabs my hand. "Anything for you, Sweetheart?" *Asshole.* He knows I hate when he calls me that. I roll my eyes and feel him squeeze my hand, making me lift a brow at him. Daring him to challenge me.

"Same for me." When we have our drinks I settle into my seat and turn to face Fitz. "Okay. We have a lot to discuss."

"Such as?" He looks at me as he locks his phone and drops it into his lap. I can't help but notice the gesture. Our first encounter, well what I *thought* was our first encounter, was me going off on him for being on his phone while someone was talking. I guess I got my point across.

"Well, our backstory for starters. It was very awkward when my mother started asking questions the other day and I had no idea what to tell her."

"You told your mother about us already?" The look of shock on his face reminds me I never told him about the date I was supposed to go on the night I asked him to be my date to Taylor's wedding.

"I kind of didn't have a choice. Do you remember me mentioning the guy she and my father were trying to set me up with?" He nods. "Well, I think she intended for *him* to escort me to Taylor's wedding. I never texted him back about the plans for that night and she showed up Sunday shortly after you left to let me know how rude it was. So I had no choice." I shrug and his eyebrows rise.

"Alright then. What did you tell her? So we can keep the story the same for everyone." I scoff remembering how she responded when I used the phrase *'hanging out'* in reference to what Fitz and I had been doing until things were official, but *hating each other* didn't exactly feel like the right selling point.

"I just told her that we only recently made things official and that we'd been hanging out and then she cut me off and told me you probably worked at a Dairy Queen." He laughs with his whole chest and it makes me smile.

"And what if I did? Does she not think I would be a good boyfriend and bring you enough free ice cream?" The sarcasm in his tone makes me laugh but I avoid answering.

"Anyways, that's all I really told her before she left." I shrug, realizing how sad it is that my own mother isn't interested in the guy I'm seeing. Outside of thinking he has, what she considers to be, an unacceptable job.

"Okay well, we can work with that. But we have to say something other than *hanging out*. We aren't fifteen."

"Okay, well what do you suggest because *talking* isn't much better either."

"We just tell the truth," he says, like it's just the most obvious answer in the world.

"The truth? The truth is that we slept together 10 months ago, you started working with me, made my life a living hell for seven months and now we're fake dating."

"Okay, smartass, a half-truth. That we've been working together for a while and were interested in each other and now we're dating." I narrow my eyes.

"Fine. But you were interested first. And you had to win me over." I tip my chin up and he leans over the armrest between us, making my heart skip a beat.

"Ah. Made me work for it, did you?" My eyes fall to his lips and I absentmindedly lick my own.

"That's right." He nods slowly, his lips turning down. Then he beckons me closer and I freaking lean in. We're practically nose to nose and now his eyes are the ones to drop.

"And just how hard did I work for it?"

"Hmm. *Decently* hard. I'd say it took you at least *three* times to get it right. The first two just…mm, didn't do it for me." His glacier eyes ignite and I can't help but be proud of myself for *finally* pressing *his* buttons. He takes a deep breath and his nostrils flare as he sits back in his seat.

"You're very lucky this *is* all fake, Trouble." He rubs his hand along his jaw and despite hardly being able to look away from his arms, I frown.

"Why?" He leans back in, his lips closer to my ear this time.

"Because if you were *really* mine, I'd fuck that bratty mouth of yours until you could recall that night properly." My heart hammers against my chest so hard I feel like it might jump out the window. Then, before I have to scramble to say something to hide how flustered I've become, the overhead speaker dings and the crew begins going over the safety procedures.

I've flown plenty of times before so I don't worry too much when I completely zone out during the informational portion but I'm reeled back in when I feel Fitz's hands around my waist. I look down at the same time my seat belt clicks.

"Looked like you were a little…distracted. Safety first, Sweetheart. You're not getting out of this that easily."

"You think I would rather die in a plane crash than pretend to date you?" I level him with a stare.

Like, be so for real right now.

"Most days, yes." I roll my eyes, pull my headphones out of my carry-on, and put them over my ears, staring straight at him without saying a word as I select today's playlist. I smile when I look down to see Adele is up next on the mix. Then I close my eyes and lean my head back on my seat. Though I only get about two songs in before he does that godforsaken forehead tap thing again.

"I will bite your fingers off if you keep doing that."

"That seems a bit dramatic, don't you think?" I pull my headphones down and pause the song playing.

"What's up?" He clears his throat and shifts in his seat.

"Well, while I'm glad we got our backstory covered, there are other things we should discuss." I cross my legs, able to fully face him in this big-ass first-class seat.

"Like what?"

"Pretty much anything. We should probably get to know each other a little better, don't you think?"

"I'd say I know you *pretty* well." I give him an unamused smirk and he just nods.

"What's my favorite food?"

"What?" I scoff.

"My favorite food, what is it?"

"That's not fair. I know you in work ways. Not in friendly, personal ways."

"What about my coffee order? Birthday? How long I've worked in real estate? Where I went to college?" I stare at him as he rambles off question after question that I don't even kind of know. "These are all things a girlfriend would know, Trouble."

"Okay fine. Point made. Do you want to go back and forth with the answers?" His brows draw together.

"What do you mean?"

"Like you tell me your coffee order then I tell you mine—well, apparently you already know mine—but for the other stuff, and we just go down the list like that until we're very well acquainted. We could put it in a shared note on my phone so we can look back if we forget." I pull my phone out of my bag and open my notes app as he studies me—his expression is one that I can't quite read.

"Brown sugar oat milk shaken espresso. You won't drink it if they forget the vanilla sweet cream cold foam, though they almost never forget. Your birthday is September 5th. You graduated from UT with a marketing degree and got your realtor license while in college, interning at Coleson until they could hire you on full time. You eat clean most of the time, chicken wraps, salads, or other rabbit-like food, at least for lunch, but then there are times when you'll only eat tacos or a cheeseburger from the diner down the road. How am I doing so far?"

"What the fuck?" I am certain that was not supposed to actually come out of my mouth. "Why do you know all of those things? *How* do you know all of those things?"

"I pay attention."

"To me?" I hate that I sound so surprised by the fact that someone has bothered paying attention to me. What I like. My routines.

"Yes, Trouble. To you."

"Why?"

He ignores my question and continues talking. "My favorite food is pizza. Specifically, this place called Milano's—" He goes on telling me about the way no one makes pizza like them, and how he would kill for a slice of meat lovers with extra cheese. My stomach is growling now but I'm still having trouble coming out of the haze of having someone tell me, so directly, that they pay attention to me. "I'm taking you there as soon as we land," he concludes.

Holy shit this man is passionate about pizza.

I absentmindedly nod and he lets out a dramatic sigh before grabbing my phone from my hands.

"Something tells me you're not going to remember anything I'm saying right now." He begins typing the details of his love of pizza and I roll my eyes.

"Meat lovers smothered in cheese and something about Bruschetta, I think."

"I'm impressed. I only barely slipped that detail in." He smirks and continues. "My birthday is June 25th—"

"What! That's like…soon!"

"It's not a big deal. I don't really celebrate my birthday, I just know it's one of those facts couples seem to know about each other, so…" he trails off with a shrug.

"How come?"

"What?"

"How come you don't celebrate your birthday?" I wrap my arms around my legs, hugging them closely to my chest.

"I used to. Just haven't for a while." I can tell he doesn't really want to talk about it and for the sake of staying positive during this flight, I leave it alone.

Though I'm very curious why he doesn't *anymore*. Did something bad happen? Did he just grow out of the celebration? Does he not have friends to celebrate with? That doesn't seem too far-fetched since he literally lives at work. I mean, I do too but my friends were sealed to me in sixth grade so that's a little different.

I grab my phone back from him and add his birthday to my calendar with a little heart next to it—very fake-girlfriend-esque of me. "Okay, I think I can take it from here. What else? Where did you go to school?"

He cracks a smile. "Um, Berkeley."

"Shut up. No, you didn't." I drop my phone in my lap, thumbs hovering over the screen to add it to my notes—though I'm sure I'll *never* forget that.

"You're surprised?" he questions.

"Not surprised just... It *had* to be Berkeley?" I laugh and his eyes soften.

"Silver lining. I'm not an accountant," he offers as reprieve, and my lips purse.

"But you could be, couldn't you?"

"What makes you say that?" I shrug and readjust my position again. God this is going to be a long flight if I'm already fidgeting.

"You just give off like...really smart guy vibes. Like, multi-major smart."

"Is that the same as saying I have a good personality? Are you complimenting my intelligence while simultaneously insulting my appearance?" he teases

"Yeah, right." I snort, immediately feeling my cheeks redden.

Maybe I will *just jump out of a window.*

The soft smile he gives me makes me relax a little then he pulls my headphones back up over my ears, leaving them open just enough so I can hear him say, "Get some rest, Trouble. We'll be hitting the ground running when we land." Then he winks at me and pulls his phone back out, leaving me to my music.

Chapter 27

I didn't realize how addicting it could be to watch someone sleep. But from the moment she let out that cleansing breath and her head rolled onto my shoulder, I haven't been able to look away. She's such an expressive person; mostly negative expressions when I'm involved, but expressive nonetheless. To see her face completely relaxed, free of frustration, pinched brows, or a scowl, she looks…happy. Peaceful. The captain's voice comes across the overhead speakers announcing our descent, though it's quiet enough that she sleeps right through it. I reach across and tuck her hair behind her ear, then pull it back out when I remember how many times I have watched her untuck it. She must not like that for some reason.

"Hey, Trouble. We're landing," I whisper, giving my shoulder a gentle shrug to help wake her, kissing her forehead as she begins to stir.

What the fuck. Why did I do that?

"Mm-mm," she argues, nestling further into my neck.

I'm going to have to spend a little extra time in my seat if her lips get any closer to my neck. How is she even comfortable right now?

I clear my throat, trying to help wake her faster. "Lauren." Her eyes finally flutter open and she pulls her head back. Those same sleepy eyes widen when she realizes what she was just doing.

"Oh my gosh, I am so sorry. I just...I have no boundaries when I sleep." She's practically pressed into the opposite side of her seat, which is probably the best place for her given how I'm feeling right now.

"I'll remember that when planning our sleeping arrangements." Her head falls lazily in my direction and she's frowning.

"What do you mean?"

"I only have one bed in my house."

"You have a couch, right?"

"Yes."

"Planning done. You'll sleep on the couch." She gives me one of those sassy ass smirks and I shake my head in disapproval. "Time to go, Mr. Fitzgerald." The amusement falls from my face at lightning speed but before I can tell her, yet again, to not call me that, she's up and reaching for her bags.

I think the hell not.

I slap her hand away from the overhead bin. "I'll do that." Her mouth pops open, to argue with me, no doubt, then snaps shut again. Moving enough to allow me to get the bags before she leads the way off the plane. As soon as we're back in the airport, I hold our bags over my shoulder and wrap my free arm over her shoulders. She tilts her head up to look at me, the back of her head resting perfectly in the crook of my elbow.

"Showtime, Sweetheart. Never know who may be watching." Then I give her a wink and she puts one arm around my waist, lacing her fingers through mine with her other. My stomach twists into a million knots when her fingers intertwine with mine.

It will get easier, right? Wanting this to be real, and knowing it may never be.

At first I wasn't sure she would last a year, but now I'm afraid *I* won't. While we walk she pulls her phone out and a wave of texts begin flooding her screen. She scrolls through them and when she giggles, I let my curiosity get the best of me and peek down.

If you joined the mile high club I'm going to be so
jealous. Tucker doesn't fly so that'll never happen for
me and I am gonna need hella details.

I like the way you think, Tay.

I smirk to myself, but it quickly falls when I see the reply she's typed out.

Who says I wasn't already part of it before this trip?

Yeah, fuck this conversation.

When we finally make it to baggage claim I pull the Dodgers hat from my bag and put it on.

"Wow." I look over at Lauren, who has a perplexed look on her face.

"What?"

"Are you like…trying to disguise yourself or is this a fashion choice?" I frown at her.

"I can't tell which answer will get me into less trouble, honestly."

She laughs and crosses her arms. "No, I like it. I've just literally never seen you wear a hat in Nashville."

I shrug. "You've never really seen me out of the office." She hums her agreement. "Come here." I tilt my head, beckoning her over to me. She gives me a curious glance, then takes a small step towards me, giving me the chance to whisper, "My dad's partner is over there."

Her eyes widen. "What do I do?" she asks nervously.

"Relax, Trouble. Just follow my lead and act like you don't hate my guts." She rolls her eyes like I was hoping she would, and I grab her face with both hands, letting my fingers rest along her neck as my thumbs caress her cheeks. "What did I tell you about rolling those eyes at me?"

Her hands come up to grab my arms, rubbing them lazily as her eyes bore into my soul. "You said you'd show me better ways to make them roll."

Fuck. I guess I forgot who I was playing this game with—a vixen who doesn't back down. I spin her around, pulling her back flush with my front, wrapping my arms around her, and dropping my lips to her ear. To anyone watching we look like any other couple in love, and not two people wound so tight they would probably cause an atomic-sized explosion in the middle of this airport if they just gave into their feelings. I hear her gasp when she feels my length press into her back and I smirk.

"You'd do well to remember that." I must catch Frank's eye because he gives me a surprised look before starting toward us. I take the opportunity to whisper one last thing in her ear before he makes it to us. "You're driving me fucking crazy already, Trouble."

"Fitz!" I keep my grip on Lauren firm, not wanting her to move and expose just *how* fucking crazy she's driven me.

"Frank. Good to see you." I shake his hand, seeing his eyes fall to Lauren. "This is my girlfriend, Lauren. Lauren, this is Frank. A close family friend and Dad's business partner." Frank's eyes widen in surprise and he does an atrocious job of trying to cover it.

"Oh, Lauren. Of course. Nice to finally meet you."

"Nice to meet you, Frank. Fitz has told me so much about you." She rests her head back on my shoulder and I feel my heart stutter.

"Well, you can't believe everything you hear, right?" He laughs nervously and it's becoming more awkward by the minute.

"We can't wait to catch up with you more this weekend, but we better grab our bags and get going. So great to meet you, though."

"Of course, you as well." Just like that, Frank leaves.

Well, she made that quick and painless.

"You're magic." The statement rolls bluntly off my lips.

"What do you mean?" she laughs.

"I have never been able to have that short of a conversation with anyone. Not without feeling like an asshole for cutting them off."

"Oh. Must be part of my charm. Casual misery and short conversations." She smirks up at me before pressing her ass gently into my groin, making my eyes flare.

"Just checking to see if it's safe to move yet." I glare at her. "All good. Frank must have scared him off." She walks over to the conveyor belt of luggage and taps, very loudly, on hers. "This one is mine." Then she stands like a perfect little statue waiting for me to get it for her.

How does she make being obedient seem so defiant? Like she's looking for any reason to press my buttons. Payback for all the ways I've pressed hers over the last seven months, maybe?

"Look alive, babe. I'm starving." My dick twitches at the nickname as my stomach growls at the idea of food. I grab her bag, then find mine and we're in a car headed to my place ten minutes later.

"Tour now or later?" I ask as I unlock the door to my apartment.

"I will literally die if I don't eat something in the next twenty minutes. Later is fine. I'm sure you have a standard bachelor pad or maybe a fake plant in the corner or something. I'd rather you show me this pizza place you want to get married, or buried in. Probably both with the way you went on about the cheese."

"Oh my god, you're chatty when you're malnourished." I roll the suitcases right inside the door and drop our carry-ons next to them before shutting the door again to lock it.

"Feed. Me," she growls. I hold back a laugh and nod.

"Let's go, gremlin."

I walk in front of her and hear her mumble, "Oh you ain't seen nothin' yet."

With Milano's being within walking distance of my place, and one of my best-kept secrets of New York, we are at a table and eating within the time limit allotted before Lauren claimed she would turn into a corpse. Watching her put away three slices of pizza and washing it down with a diet soda is a sight to behold. I don't think I've ever been so attracted to another person. Savage little thing.

"Pizza good?" I tease as she chews with her mouth so full she looks like a squirrel. She gives me a middle finger and keeps eating as if I never said anything at all. "Good."

"I hope you know I am unbelievably pissed off at you." I sigh and toss my napkin down on the table.

"Tell me, Sweetheart. What have I done this time?"

"I'll never be happy with pizza from anywhere else. You've ruined me for all other pizza, you asshole. I *love* pizza." I can't help but smirk because I think she's genuinely mad about this.

"I guess I'll just have to make sure you get your fix every time we're in New York then, won't I?" She leans back in her chair and crosses her arms.

"That's fair…I guess."

"Ready to go?" I nod to the door and she nods in agreement.

"More than. I am desperate to wash the smell of airplane off myself." I pause on our way out when the thought of Lauren naked in my shower invades my mind.

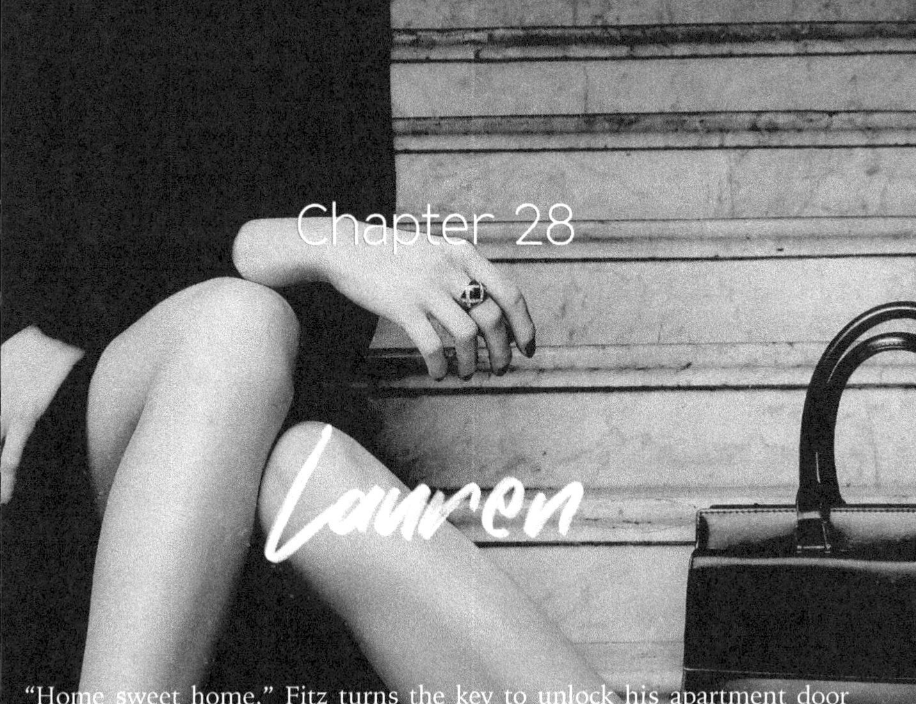

"Home sweet home." Fitz turns the key to unlock his apartment door and I'm suddenly brought to the realization that I'm going to be staying here. With him. As his girlfriend—well, *fake* girlfriend. Although I must say I have been doing a hell of an acting job since we got off that plane. If real estate ever stops being fun maybe I'll be an actress.

We walk through the door and I'm surprised by the way it doesn't feel...cold. I half expected a couch that doesn't look even remotely like it was made to be sat on, abstract black and white art on the wall, and something that screams *bachelor pad* lingering in the corner, like Joey's big, white dog from *FRIENDS* or something.

Instead, I'm met with warm tones of beige, navy blue, and rust. A painting of a farm with a single tree out in the middle of a field as the sun sets in the distance, as well as a plush area rug that Ginny would *live* on. The entertainment center has one shelf full of books, one with DVDs, and another with records on display. I almost roll my eyes, thinking it's all for show, then I see it. On the opposite side of an old wooden piano, a record player sits on the other side of the room, on a table with another massive stack of records. Not for looks at all, you can tell by the way they're scattered about that they get used.

"If you're done judging who I am as a person from the look of my living room, I can show you the rest of the place." I look up to see Fitz standing against the wall with his arms crossed over his chest, smirking at me with those stupidly perfect white teeth.

"I'm not judging." I shrug, only partially lying. I am judging him, but in a completely different way than I thought I would be. I'm just too surprised by that fact and exhausted, to think of anything clever to say.

"Kitchen is here, obviously." He points to the kitchen right across from the living room. "This is the half bath, right next to my office." I peek inside and see the single desk in the middle of the floor, which is immaculately clean, with a black leather chair behind it. There's no rug, no plants, not even any artwork. Just a filing cabinet in the corner and the desk. There is a small suede futon on the wall opposite his desk, but it's still a lonely-looking office.

"What's up there?" I point to the spiral staircase and look up towards a loft.

"Nothing, actually. Maybe some storage bins. I never really had much use for the extra space. I thought about making it a record room, but I prefer to have it in the living room. Easier to access when I'm in the kitchen.

Hmm. Interesting.

"Show me the shower next?" His relaxed features become more rigid before he leads me through the next door.

"Right this way." We walk into his bedroom and I frown. "There's only one shower. In the master bedroom." I swallow past the slight discomfort of knowing I'll have to shower so close to his bedroom and try to play it off.

"Makes sense." I refuse to give him the satisfaction of knowing how painfully aware I am of how small of a space we're about to be sharing. No matter if it's only for the weekend; if the plane ride and little stop at baggage claim were any indicator of how Fitz is going to play his part in all of this, I'm in for a *tension-filled* weekend. Maybe it won't be like that the whole weekend though. This whole thing is for show, right? Meaning things like that will more than likely only happen when watchful eyes are around and not when we're behind closed doors.

We walk into the bathroom and he turns on the light, my eyes pop when I take in the massive space. "There's room over here for your stuff, I don't know how much you packed but I don't use much so take all the drawer and counter space you need. Just leave me room to brush my teeth, would you?" I glare at the back of his head as he walks closer to the shower. There are two sinks in the vanity and the largest walk-in shower I've ever seen.

"No tub?" I frown as I voice my observation. When my eyes meet his again he's just...staring at me. It takes him a moment to finally answer.

"No. But there's two shower heads in there with excellent water pressure so hopefully that makes up for it." I peek into the shower and see the two shower heads on either end.

"A shower with room for two, why am I not surprised?" I scoff, immediately embarrassed when I realize I said that out loud.

Oh my god, I have got to stop doing this. Especially around him.

I quickly turn and walk towards the vanity, getting myself far away from the shower and, by association, any stupid comments that may come flying out of my filterless mouth. I stop at the counter and my eyes immediately find Fitz's in the reflection, like a moth to a dark-haired, blue-eyed flame. He slowly walks up behind me, stopping just short of his body touching mine. His head tilts to one side, his eyes lazily raking over me. Then he reaches up, silently tucking a strand of hair behind my ear, and I completely stop breathing. The feather-like touch of his finger brushes my jawline, and my stupid eyes flutter closed. The heat from his body disappears before I finally open them again, and I find him standing in the doorway, smirking at me.

"Enjoy your shower."

"I still have to grab my stuff." I start walking towards the door but stop when he stands up taller.

"I can bring it to you." I narrow my eyes at him and cross my arms over my chest.

"You're gonna bring my stuff into me…while I'm *in* the shower? Absolutely not. We're *fake* dating, Fitz, remember? Seeing me naked is *not* part of the agreement." That smirk of his is back, with the hint of devilishness that makes me weak in my stupid knees.

"If I wanted to see you naked, Sweetheart. I'd only have to close my eyes." My mouth pops open as he walks away. He returns a moment later with my bags, setting them outside the door with a knock before disappearing into another part of the apartment. I hate that he remembers that night and I don't. Not entirely, at least. Sure I had parts of it come screaming back to me after running into him that night at the saloon, but he seems to have a much more solid memory of it and I wish I could just crawl through his brain and see it through his eyes.

"When you're done, I'd also like a chance to shower. Before the hot water runs out." I roll my eyes and lock the door. Barely catching the last thing he says before I head for the shower. "Mind those eyes, Trouble."

Un-freaking-believable.

Well, he was right about one thing—the water pressure in here is enough to make up for there not being a soaking tub. I take a deep breath as I step out of the shower, letting the eucalyptus scent from my shampoo fill my senses. I can't accurately describe the sensation I get from having minty fresh *hair*, but it's invigorating. I don't even feel like I've been up since five AM. I'm wide ass awake now and somehow, hungry again. I finished applying my lotion, moisturizer, and frizz-control hair oil before realizing I only brought my hygiene bag into the bathroom. Meaning all of my clean clothes are in the bedroom. I unlock the door and swing it open, drawing in a sharp breath when I see Fitz filling the doorway.

"Jesus Christ, have you been standing there this whole time?" I hear him inhale, watching as his nostrils flare and his eyes darken before I realize I'm standing in front of him in nothing but a towel. I hug it closer to me as if it will help combat whatever thoughts are swarming his mind right now, and try to explain. "My clothes are in there." I nod to my suitcase lying open on the floor behind him. He lets out a noise that is something between a growl and a hum, inching closer to me.

"If you don't want me to see you naked, Trouble, take your clothes with you when you shower." He moves past me into the bathroom, causing me to robotically turn, switching places with him. I narrow my eyes, ready to mouth off to him—maybe ask why the hell he was trying to become one with the fucking door before I was even out of the bathroom—but I catch the slightest glimpse of a tortured look in his eyes that causes me not to.

"Uh. Sorry," I whisper before he slams the door in my face.

That's fair.

I'm still not sure where I stand with Fitz. I've spent so long hating him for coming to Coleson's the way he did, for lying, for micromanaging the ever-loving *hell* out of me, and the way his arrogance seems to carry him through life.

Never mind. I remember exactly where I stand with him.

So why the fuck did I agree to be his fake girlfriend for a year?

"Ugh!" I turn around, grabbing my vintage *Journey* T-shirt, underwear, and pair of shorts from my bag before opening my towel to change. As soon as I begin to drop it, the bathroom door swings open again.

"Did you—"

"*Fitz!*" I screech, quickly wrapping the towel back around me. I spin to face him, thanking the universe that I was at *least* turned away from him, and see his jaw hanging open. "What?!"

"Sorry. I thought I heard something." My eyes pop as he stares at me hungrily.

"I was airing out my frustrations." His brows furrow and he doesn't say anything in response. "Is it safer if I get myself dressed in the living room?"

"Probably so."

"Fantastic." I snatch my clothes from the bed and storm into the living room, slamming his bedroom door shut behind me.

This was a horrible idea.

Chapter 29

Fitz

Why I thought this plan would go smoothly is absolutely beyond me. It's one thing to have to share an apartment with only one bed with her, but sharing a shower, having her scent cover every inch of this place, and seeing her in nothing but a towel is enough to kill me. I'm never washing my sheets after she sleeps in my bed if it smells the way she did when she walked out of this bathroom.

God, she looked beautiful.

Short black hair still dripping wet, tanned skin that looks as smooth as velvet, and the mix of mint and coconut that make me want to bottle up her scent for my own guilty pleasure. My cock throbs as I stand motionless in the shower, letting the water beat down on me as I indulge in every wicked thought I'm having about the little troublemaker in the other room. I fist my length and begin to pump, with the same memory playing in my mind that always helps me imagine it's her hand and not my own.

Her hands make quick work undoing the buttons on my shirt, and before I know it I'm pulling her soft lips back to mine. I've never been a fan of tequila, but if the taste of it is the taste of her—tonight I'm a fan.

"We're not going dancing, are we?" She looks as desperate for this to happen as I am and it has me praying she doesn't change her mind.

"No." Thank God.

When we finally make it back to the room I'm staying in, while the leak in my apartment gets tended to, I can't unlock the door fast enough. Once we're inside her hands move to my belt and I can't help but smirk as she slides her hands into my boxers, while those big, blue eyes practically brand me.

"Eager to please?" She bites her lip and nods. As soon as the back of my legs hit the foot of the bed, she drops to her knees. She hooks her fingers into the waistband of my boxers, pulling them and my slacks down, freeing my cock from the only thing between it and those perfect fucking lips of hers. Her tongue peeks out to wet her lips and she looks up at me, and I wouldn't be surprised if I shot cum across her face just from that look alone.

"Take your shirt off." Yes ma'am. Her hand wraps around my length, and I can't stop the groan that follows. Her hot tongue strokes me from balls to tip, then she spits on my cock and my mouth hangs open like an idiot. She swallows me down inch by inch, but when she cups my balls and opens her throat to allow me in further, I swear I see fucking stars.

"Fuck!"

This woman sucks cock like it's a sport and she's not to be beat. Her hand moves in sync with her mouth and I completely lose myself in the way she makes me feel. I fist her hair and pull her head back, seeing her tear-streaked cheeks and mouth dripping with spit, and I can't decide if I want to shoot a load down her throat or bend her over this bed.

"I wasn't done." She tilts her head at me in disapproval.

Guess I'll be bending her over after I come down her throat. She sticks her tongue out, her own little way of asking for my cock back, and I feel my balls begin to tighten. She takes every inch greedily, and I don't even ask where she wants it. I saw the look in those devious blue eyes, she's gonna swallow every single drop I give her.

"Fuck, Trouble."

"Yeah?" My eyes fly open when I hear her voice, but what I don't expect is to see her, standing with the door wide open, her hand still on the knob, and her mouth hanging open.

God, what I wouldn't give to put her on her knees right now.

Her eyes move slowly from my cock, locking with mine, and it's all I need to finally find my release. "Fuck," I mutter, as I finish harder than I have in…what was it? *Ten fucking months.*

Holding her gaze as ropes of my cum hit the wall is an erotic experience I've never had before. The redness of her cheeks and the way she watches it happen, in no rush to leave, apparently, brings a tired smirk to my lips. "See something you like, Trouble?"

That snaps her out of whatever trance she was in and her spine practically snaps straight. "Lock the door next time, Fitz!" Then she slams it behind her and my smile grows.

Once I'm done, I wrap my towel around my waist and make my way into my room to grab my clothes. Because let's face it, I'd be more than delighted if she ripped my towel off me the way I wanted to do to her just a little while ago. I grab one of my old college T-shirts and a pair of sweatpants and head to make a pot of coffee. Lauren is sitting at the barstool in the kitchen, staring into the living room when I emerge from the bedroom. She's either sleeping with her eyes open or she's extremely captivated by something because she doesn't even look my way when the door accidentally hits the wall. Though it may be an active choice not to look at me, I never can tell with her.

"Are you one of those people that can sleep with their eyes open?" I inquire, moving to the cabinet with coffee filters.

"That painting is so pretty." She continues staring at the picture hanging behind my couch. "It looks like the kind of place you'd go to just…escape. Don't you agree?" I look over to find her pretty blue eyes on mine and I fear if I'm not careful, I could give this woman the power to absolutely destroy me. If I haven't already.

"I do." She's silent the entire time the coffee is brewing, and since I'm exhausted after my shower, I remain silent as well. I've never enjoyed awkward silences. But this isn't an awkward silence, it's a comfortable one. She's so fixated on the painting across the room that I get to sit back and just look at her. Taking in every feature from her long eyelashes to the slope of her nose to the way—

"Why are you staring at me?" She's still fixated on the painting, so how does she know? As if she can read my thoughts she answers. "I can feel you looking at me."

"That's…insanely creepy." She finally looks over at me with that sassy expression I know and love.

"Creepier than staring at someone's side profile to kill time?"

"Touché." Her eyes narrow and I move to start making two cups of coffee for us. I glance up at her a few times in the process of moving around the kitchen, seeing that there's clearly something on her mind. "What?" I finally ask, setting her mug in front of her.

"I could have sworn you said my name earlier." I raise a brow at her. "Did you?"

"Yes."

She pauses for a moment, her eyes narrowing. "Why?"

"You saw what I was doing, Trouble. You really want the answer to that question?" I reach into the fridge for the caramel coffee creamer, setting it down by her cup.

"You really should lock the door when you're in the bathroom." I lean forward, resting my forearms on the countertop.

"No one forced you to come in." I lift a brow, seeing her cheeks heat ever so slightly.

She grabs the creamer from the counter, her features hardening. "So, what time do we have to leave tomorrow?"

I smirk at how desperate she is to change the subject. Even though she's the one that brought it back up, to begin with. "It's an early event. We will need to leave here around 7:30."

"Okay. Sounds good." She takes a sip of her coffee then glares at me. I swear she doesn't know how to look my direction comfortably. "You're not going to like…tell me what to wear, are you?"

"You seem to know your way around a closet just fine." She nods but looks almost…confused? "Do you *want* me to tell you what to wear?"

"No. I don't think so."

"How about this? If you're not sure about what to wear and *want* my opinion on what you pick for the events, you're more than welcome to ask."

"Ask you if you like my outfits? Yeah, okay," she scoffs.

"Spoiler alert, Trouble. I'm always pleased with how you look. Whether it's in that plaid mini skirt, that should be illegal for you to wear in the office, or this thin T-shirt with wet spots from your hair dripping on it. You have my stamp of approval." I tap one of the wet spots on her shirt and her cheeks heat again. She tries hiding behind her mug, taking a small sip before looking around the room.

"Umm. I think I'm going to head to bed. It's been a long day." She slides off the barstool and looks from the bedroom door back at me. Her mouth pops open then she closes it again, deciding against whatever she was going to say.

"Night, Fitz."

"Goodnight, Trouble. Sweet dreams."

Will I never learn that I cannot drink coffee before bed? Because it's nearing two in the morning and I can't stop tossing and turning. The bed is cold, something I normally love, but tonight it's chilling me down to my bones and I have no idea where any extra blankets are in Fitz's house. My feet feel like ice and I left my fuzzy socks at home, so in a nutshell. I'm miserable. I've talked myself out of going out to the living room to ask Fitz for more blankets at *least* ten times. I already took the man's bed, the last thing I want to do is seem ungrateful, or like I need *more* from him. I turn once more, trying to tuck myself in like a burrito to keep myself warm, but when an even colder part of the sheet hits my legs, I can't fight it anymore. I shoot out of the bed and quietly open the bedroom door. I'm not sure why I'm worried about being quiet since I'm going to have to wake him up anyways to ask him where a mother freaking blanket might be hiding in this place. When I round the corner and the couch comes into view, I see Fitz sitting straight up on the couch, rubbing his eyes.

"You're still awake?" I ask in surprise.

"Uh, yeah. This couch is nice, but was clearly not made to be slept on." He laughs, then his brows pull together. "Are you okay?" I'm not sure why that question seems to have such an impact on me. Maybe it's the genuine concern in his tone when he asks.

"Oh, yeah. Uh... I'm just a little cold. Do you have any extra blankets hiding somewhere?" I fold my arms over my chest, remembering I'm not wearing a bra. Add how cold I am and my nipples are practically high beams against my thin T-shirt.

"Oh, I actually don't." My expression morphs into disbelief.

"You don't *own* blankets other than your bed cover?" He chuckles and it seeps into my brain causing a wave of calmness to wash over me.

"I know. I'm a Neanderthal. I get insanely hot when I sleep so I've never had a need for them." He stands from the couch and begins walking in my direction. I almost forgot how hot he looks in his Berkeley T-shirt and *gray* fucking sweatpants. Walking around looking like every girl's wet dream. "Come on." He bends down and before I know it, I'm thrown over his shoulder.

"Fitz!" I squeal. "What are you doing?" I feel the dip of the bed seconds before he's laying me on my back, hovering inches above my face.

"Taking you to bed." I mindlessly lick my lips, watching his eyes follow the movement. "What kind of boyfriend would I be if I didn't help my girl get a good night's sleep?" My clit throbs and I bite my tongue to distract myself from the ache between my legs.

Fake, Lauren. Fake girlfriend.

"Fitz, we can't—" My words die on my lips when he kisses my nose.

"We could." He dips down closer to my ear. "And we *have*." Then he leans back, letting his knuckle brush against my nipple, though he doesn't acknowledge it as he stands up, strips off his sweats, and T-shirt, and climbs back in bed.

Oh my god. Oh my god. Oh my god.

"But tonight, I only meant that I'm going to keep you warm." I finally take a full breath, though I can't identify the feeling in my chest when he moves away.

"You can do that with your clothes on!" I argue, trying not to stare at his abs and the way his forearms flex as he moves.

"Body heat works best without them."

"Oh," I manage to say, catching a smirk that makes me want to crawl under the bed and hide. Just in case he can somehow see how much I need to get off and gets any ideas. He pulls the covers back, lays down on his back, and holds his arm out to one side.

He wants to CUDDLE? I thought he just meant I could tuck my feet under his ass or something.

"We are not cuddling." He sighs and sits up straighter in the bed, running a hand through his already messy hair.

"Look, I don't ask for much. But I am exhausted from traveling, I have to be up in three and a half hours for this conference, and I just want to know that you're taken care of. So will you please just lay your ass down, tuck your popsicles for feet under my calves, and go the hell to sleep?" I stare at him, completely speechless. "I promise as soon as the conference is over I will take you shopping for as many blankets as you can hold. Heated ones even, if that's what you prefer."

"No, it's fine. I mean…one will be fine." I can do this. It's just cuddling. It's just Fitz. In his boxers. Telling me he wants to take care of me. What the fuck am I supposed to do with that information? Why does he care? I thought we were just…using each other? People who use each other don't care about shit like that. Do they? I guess I wouldn't know, I've never fake-dated someone to help them take ownership of a company before. Maybe this is exactly what they do.

Fantastic, now I have a headache.

There's no way in hell I'm asking him for medication though. Not after all of this.

"Come on, Trouble. I even said 'please'." I roll my eyes and scoot down under the covers, carefully and hesitantly resting my head on his chest. Just as I'm about to roll the other way and insist I'll be fine, he wraps his arm around me, and I'm frozen. I lay my hand on his stomach, feeling his abs flex beneath my fingertips. Then I feel his lips against my hair and my eyes feel heavy.

"Sleep," he whispers before kissing my head, but as I wait for him to pull away, he doesn't. He stays pressed against me, and I finally start to relax.

"Hey Fitz?" I whisper into the darkness of the room.

"Yes, Trouble," he mumbles sleepily.

"Thank you."

"Mmm."

Chapter 31

I watch as the minutes tick by, completely unbothered that my alarm went off half an hour ago. Normally I wouldn't be able to sit still or stop thinking about everything on my morning checklist that I need to be knocking out, but this morning? This morning I have Lauren's body wrapped around mine, listening to her breathe as the sun starts filtering in through the floor-to-ceiling window in my bedroom. I have no idea what's going to happen with this agreement we made. How long will she stick around, playing house and pretending to be my girlfriend, all while holding some sort of disdain for me in her heart? But there's one thing I am sure of, and that's that I won't move until she does. I continue twirling strands of her short black hair through my fingers until she starts to move. She wiggles a little bit before her alarm starts going off, almost like her internal clock is already starting to wake her.

She pushes herself up, her hand staying on my chest as she rubs the sleep from her eyes. She freezes a moment later, peeking her eyes open.

"Fitz!" she gasps, turning around to grab her phone from the nightstand. "You're late! You were supposed to wake up half an hour ago. Weren't you? Or did I do that math wrong?" She switches between checking her phone and burying her face in her hands, but all I can see is the way the sunrise around her looks like something I wouldn't mind waking up to every day. I pull her back over to me, catching the confused look on her face before she's back under my arm—the same way she fell asleep last night.

"No one should start their day in a panic, Sweetheart. Take a deep breath." I stop and wait for her to do so. It takes her a minute but she finally does. "Another one." Again, she obeys.

"Okay, but you were supposed to be up already, right?" she asks, though I'm surprised she hasn't tried to move again.

"My alarm went off about thirty minutes before yours, yes." She lifts her head just enough for her eyes to meet mine.

"Then why aren't you *up?*"

I smile down at her and shrug. "I wanted to stay in bed." I see the corner of her lips barely turn up before my phone goes off and she jumps. I look down to see my father's name lighting up the screen and I have the mind to toss it out the window. Motherfucker just interrupted what I *think* was about to be one of the first smiles Lauren has ever given me.

I'm gonna bleach his favorite suit for this.

"Sorry, I have to take this."

"Yeah, of course." She slides out of bed and I watch her every move until she closes the bathroom door behind her. I close my eyes and my head falls back onto the headboard as I bring my phone to my ear.

"Yes?" I don't bother hiding the aggravation in my tone and boy does he notice.

"Whatever stick you've got up your ass this morning, remove it before you show up to speak at this conference. Are you on your way to the hotel?" I look at the clock to ensure I didn't somehow spend over an hour looking at Lauren.

"It's six thirty in the morning. No. I'm not headed to the hotel."

"Well, don't be late. It makes us look bad when the host of the event isn't there when people begin to arrive." Yes, because an event that doesn't begin until 9:30, and doors don't open until fifteen minutes before that, requires me to be there at six thirty in the fucking morning.

"We won't be late."

"We?" I pinch the bridge of my nose, fighting the oncoming headache.

"I told you I was bringing someone with me this weekend. My girlfriend. Remember? The one you don't think exists." Lauren walks through the room, just as I'm reminding my father of this detail he managed to forget, pursing her lips and giving a little eye roll. I can't wait to see how she handles him. All that fierce, strong attitude handling the awful Weston Fitzgerald. I raise a brow at her, making her eyes widen because she knows she's been caught. I can't help but smile when she holds a hand up to cover her eyes.

"Got it?" My dad's voice interrupts my moment with Lauren—again—and the smile falls from my face immediately.

"Sure. See you later." I hang up the phone with no idea what it is he thinks I *got*, and I genuinely don't care. I roll out of bed and join Lauren in the bathroom, seeing her with a fluffy headband that has a bow on top.

"Shut up. It's so I don't get product in my hair." She holds a finger up at me then continues rubbing something foamy all over her face.

"I wasn't going to say anything. But I do have to pee, so…" She looks over at the toilet then back at me, but not before her eyes fall to my cock that is, in fact, hard as fuck. I smirk when I see her throat work with a swallow.

"Yeah, sorry. Give me two seconds." She shakes her head and turns back to the sink, rinsing the suds from her face before reaching for the hand towel to pat it dry. She leaves the bathroom, but about five seconds into me peeing I hear her voice so clearly I could have sworn it was coming from right beside me.

"So, to reiterate, I just hang with you today? Sit front row, smile, clap, goo-goo eye my ass off. Anything else I need to be prepared for?" I shake my head and laugh at the fact that this woman is having a full-blown conversation with me while I'm pissing.

"Um. No, not really. Nothing I can think of anyway."

"Nothing else your past girlfriends have done you can think of?" I flush the toilet and wash my hands while I think about how to answer that.

"Nope." She gasps when I suddenly appear behind her.

"Come on, Fitz. Give me something. You're acting like you've never had a girlfriend before." She laughs.

I tap the tip of her nose with my index finger and wink. "Such a perceptive girl." I move past her, heading to my closet to grab my clothes for the day, but I don't miss the way she posts up against the door frame, glaring at me with her arms crossed and her fuzzy headband still firmly in place.

"I don't buy it. You've *never* had a girlfriend?" I look over at her, doing my best to portray how much I *don't* want to have this conversation and her hands shoot up. "Fine. I'll drop it." Ten minutes later she comes out of the bathroom with her make up done and her hair still wavy but...tamed. She stops at her suitcase and looks at me, not saying anything as she takes in my tan slacks, blue dress shirt, and brown shoes.

"I thought I was supposed to be checking *your* outfits," I tease as she carefully thumbs through her clothes.

"I have to make sure we coordinate." My brows pull together as I finish buttoning my shirt.

"Like, matching?"

"*No.* Like coordinating. I can't wear colors that clash with yours. Couples should complement each other. We should look like we...I don't know. Belong together." She pulls out a dress that's almost an exact match in color to my shoes and belt, as well as a blazer and pair of heels that match the color of my shirt. "This should work." I grab one of the shoes from her hands and hold it up to my chest.

"These shoes are almost the exact same color as this shirt. How the hell is that even possible?" She snatches the shoe back from me.

"Do. Not. Touch. My blue. Suede. Shoes." She heads for the bathroom. "Elvis would roll over in his grave. The audacity," she mumbles under her breath.

Pops is gonna love her.

"Ready," she announces as she emerges from the bathroom and I check the time. 7:15 AM. She might be the only woman I have ever met who can get ready in under an hour. "But I am starving. Please tell me breakfast is next on the list?"

"Anything you want, Sweetheart."

Chapter 32

Lauren

If there's one thing I knew not to leave behind this morning, it was my confidence. It's how I excel at my job, it's how I face my parents when I'd rather do anything else, and it's how I am going to make it through pretending to be Fitz's girlfriend in front of his colleagues and his freaking *parents*. I think I might throw up.

"Sweetheart, you might want to breathe." I glare at Fitz from the passenger seat.

"Don't tell me what to do."

"I'd pity the man that tried," he mumbles and I hold my head a little higher.

Damn right.

We pull up to the hotel where the event is being held, and I take the chance to check my hair and make-up while he parks. Before I can shut the mirror and unbuckle, he's at my door, opening it and offering me his hand.

"I'm not sure I'll ever get used to seeing you be…nice."

"Really?" he muses, shutting my door behind me. He starts walking in front of me, then I notice his hand outstretched behind him—waiting for mine. I place my fingers in his palm and his hand quickly envelopes mine. He moves to intertwine our fingers and something resembling butterflies, flutters to life in my stomach. He leans into me and whispers, "I'd say I was pretty nice last night. You woke up nice and toasty, didn't you?" He pulls back just enough for his eyes to meet mine and I shake my head at him.

"I—" I'm cut off when a dark-haired man in a three-piece suit approaches us.

"Fitz," the man says sternly, but Fitz lets his eyes linger on me a bit longer before turning to face the man. He looks upset, but I can't tell why.

"Father." *Oh, that explains it.* I have to keep my expression under control because I was not expecting this man to be his *father.*

"You're late." Fitz checks his watch, looking back at him with a blank expression.

"It's 8:15. I'm an hour early." They stare at each other for long enough that my anxious need to fill the silence kicks in.

"Hi, I'm Lauren. It's a pleasure to meet you." I offer him my hand and he looks down at it before barely shaking it. Ew, my seven-year-old godson has a better handshake than him.

"The girlfriend, I presume?" I try to ignore the disapproval dripping from his tone, but it's damn near impossible.

I force a smile. "You presume correctly."

"Well, maybe next time you can get him up on time. Remind him that being late isn't good for his image. If you even care." He looks me up and down and I feel my face grow warm with embarrassment.

"Don't speak to her like that. I'm fully capable of getting myself up and here on time, as I've done for every other event I've ever been to." He takes a step closer to his father, invading his space as his jaw tightens. "And if you can't speak to her with respect, then don't bother speaking to her at all," Fitz growls back at him and it takes me completely by surprise. I squeeze his hand and after facing off with his father a moment longer, he finally looks down at me. "We're going to make sure everything is ready in the conference room." He barely gets the sentence out before he's pulling my hand, guiding me down the hallway.

I look behind us, seeing his father now outside on the phone, then turn back to Fitz. "What the hell was that?" I pull my hand away but he grabs it back quickly, his grip tighter now, but not so much so that it's painful. It's firm, like he needs it.

"Your unfortunate introduction to the man from whom I get my name." I stop for a moment and take him in—seeing the anger in his eyes, the way his chest looks tight, and how his nostrils flare as he looks back at his father. "I am so sorry he spoke to you that way. I knew he'd probably have some issues with me bringing someone he didn't hand-pick for me, but that—" the anger builds as he rubs his free hand over his mouth. "That was unacceptable." I've never seen Fitz like this before. Sure I've seen him upset, but this? This is something completely different. I know the feeling of having parents that make you want to be anywhere, or any*one* else, and from my very brief introduction to his dad, I fear that may be a common denominator between us.

"Hey." I reach up and guide his eyes back to me, cupping his cheek in my hand. "Look at me. This is why I'm here, right? When you feel… whatever you're feeling right now. Find me and clear your mind. I'm sure I won't be far." His Adam's apple bobs as he swallows and his chest finally relaxes. Then he grabs either side of my face and leans in, making my breath stall, yet again, before he kisses my nose. He grabs my hand again, intertwining our fingers and his thumb caresses mine, leading us to the conference room. He's making a habit out of kissing my nose, and I'm not sure I like how comfortable I am with it.

I've always considered myself a good businesswoman. I learn my trade and excel in every avenue of it. But I only treat *business* like business, not my entire life, friendships or relationships. I fear I've met my match in professionalism with Fitz, because he's flawlessly taken on his promotion to fake boyfriend, not holding back in the role. Whereas I foolishly thought things wouldn't change that much. If the lines are already blurring, and we've only been at this, officially, for 24 hours, then I'm gonna be screwed trying to keep my head straight for the next *year*. He kisses my nose and holds my hand in public like it's the most natural thing in the world. Meanwhile, I can't decide if I still hate him or not. Today is not the day to debate that though. Today I'm in full fake girlfriend mode. Which shouldn't be too hard to do since I get the feeling the best way I'll be able to be here for him, is to distract him from any interactions with his dad.

After ensuring everything is in place in the room Fitz is speaking in, he takes us to the registration table to get our name badges. They're laminated and have little VIP ribbons in the top corner that give us access to the open bar and a mixer later tonight. I can't imagine having to do this on a regular basis, it seems absolutely exhausting. Sure it was fun when I got to come to my first one last year, but it's a lot different on the other side. They sell out of these tickets months in advance and the speakers do two different events—keynote speaking and a panel with the other colleagues.

"I'll take one last question before it's time to wrap up." Hands shoot up all across the room and I watch as Fitz picks someone out. Pointing to a man a few rows behind me.

"Why is social media marketing such a big deal for real estate? I mean, if people want to look for a house, chances are they're going to visit the website to begin with, right? I understand having an app to download to make it easier to browse, but why social media?" I practically choke trying to cover up my half scoff, half laugh, catching the attention of the man of the hour. Fitz raises a brow and smirks at me, and I feel the embarrassment all over my face.

"I'm going to let my associate, Ms. Long, answer that question for you. Ms. Long is one of the most educated people I know in the sense of media marketing. Lauren." He holds his hand out, motioning for me to take the floor, but I'm still shaken from the complement he just gave me. I finally recover and scowl at him, standing up and taking the microphone from the girl who randomly appears with one.

"Oh, thank you." I hold the mic up, addressing the whole room. "Social media marketing has resulted in a 60% increase for most real estate companies that utilize it properly. Think about it, you've been pondering the idea of moving for a while, dreaming up where you'd like to live. Maybe you and your partner, roommate, or family have been discussing it, but you don't think your dream home is out there. One day, you're scrolling Instagram, or any other social site of your choice, and you stop when you see it—your dream house. With a perfectly manicured lawn, the two-car garage you need to keep from fighting over who has to park in the rain, and even a doggy bath in the mudroom for Fido. You click the link and a few weeks later, you're in your new dream home."

The guy scoffs. "Yeah, but like. how often will that actually happen?"

"I've had fifteen clients this year tell me they came across my company's listings while scrolling on social media. It's a big deal. If you don't trust me, trust the stats." He sinks back down into his seat and people begin clapping. I hand the mic back to the girl, Aimee—aww, that makes me miss *my* Amy—and catch a wink from Fitz before I take my seat.

"Well, I think I know who will be speaking at the next event. Thank you, Ms. Long, for that insight on social media marketing." The smile on his face is truly captivating as he claps and dismisses the room for lunch. I remain in my seat, waiting for him to move before I do, but he practically falls into the chair next to me.

"Wow. That was amazing." I look over at him and see the smaller, playful smirk on his lips.

"Just shop talk." He shrugs it off like it's nothing.

"You seem so passionate about what you do, and you're so charming while you're up there." I glower at him. "Oh my god, you're an even better actor than I am."

He frowns. "What do you mean?"

"The passion, the charm…it's *clearly* all fake."

"Oh *really?*"

"Obviously. You're completely charmless and I've only ever seen you be passionate about pizza, so…" I shrug with a bored expression.

He slaps his thighs with a groan. "Okay. I think it's time to feed you." He stands up, offering me his hand.

I take it and follow behind him. "Why?"

He looks back at me with that wicked smile. "You're meaner when you're hungry."

"I'm not mean," I mumble, rolling my eyes as his arm wraps around my shoulder.

"Yeah, and I'm a natural blond," he whispers into my hair before planting a kiss on the top of my head.

Chapter 33

Fitz

I managed to grab the only table with two chairs for Lauren and me to eat our lunch at, hoping it would keep anyone from interrupting us. I'll take any chance I can get to try and show her I'm not the villain she's thought me to be for the last few months.

"So are we going to this mixer tonight?" she asks, taking a bite from her chicken wrap. I notice the bit of ranch on her cheek and quickly grab a napkin to dab it away.

"I wouldn't hear the end of it if I didn't show up, so yes. We will go, but we don't have to stay long."

She shrugs. "I don't mind." I watch as she rolls her ankle around beneath the table and wonder how the hell she works every single day in heels that tall. "The last one the firm threw was pretty fun—what I remember of it at least." My eyes bounce up to hers and she smirks at me.

"I'm not sure I trust your judgment of fun, given just how little of it you remember." I raise a brow at her, fully expecting an eye roll or glare, but she looks back at me with a twinge of guilt in her eyes.

"I hate that, you know?" She looks around the room and takes a sip of her Diet Coke, setting it back on the table before her eyes meet mine again. "Not remembering. Any time I think about it I catch myself wishing I could pull a clear memory from that night." My stomach knots in anticipation. I never would have guessed that she willingly thinks of that night at all. Outside of all the times I've blatantly reminded her of it.

"I—"

"Fitz!" The styrofoam noise of a voice rings out to my left and I look up to see Jessica Vanderbilt walking up to our table.

That's it. After today I'm taking Lauren home, locking the door behind us, and silencing our phones so people will stop fucking interrupting us.

I shoot a regretful look Lauren's way and her brow raises. "Jessica, how are you?" I look up at her but don't stand, trying to set a boundary that she clearly cannot see. She bends down, breasts practically spilling out of her top as she kisses my cheek, resting her hand on my shoulder.

"I'd be better if I hadn't spent most of my morning looking for *you*." I look at Lauren who is watching in amusement as this whole interaction unfolds. "Who's this?" Jessica turns to Lauren but Lauren's eyes are still on me, waiting for me to answer.

"This is Lauren. My girlfriend."

Jessica's face immediately turns sour. *"Girlfriend?"*

Lauren reaches her hand out to Jessica with a soft smile on her lips. "Pleasure to meet you." Jessica returns the gesture with a snarky smile and turns to face me.

"Well, how awkward for her." Jessica winks at me, then disappears before I can ask what the hell she means by that.

"Friend of yours?" Lauren asks, grabbing her drink from the table.

"Hardly." I look around the room, expecting to see my dad in the corner somewhere lurking to see how I would handle having Jessica approach us.

"I don't know, she seemed awfully friendly." She still has that amused look on her face and it hits me, she wasn't even a little bit bothered by what just happened. I would have thrown a guy out the window if he'd come up to Lauren acting that way.

"You think this is funny?"

She shrugs and cracks a smile. "I mean…come on. She might as well have sat in your lap and flipped me off. It was a little comical."

"Unbelievable." I shake my head.

"So who was that? She looked familiar but I was too blinded by your obvious frustration to look closer." She picks her wrap back up, taking another bite as I answer.

"Jessica Vanderbilt." Her mouth pops open, partially chewed chicken wrap on full display.

"The *model* and hotel empire heiress, Jessica Vanderbilt?"

"I'm amazed I understood any of that, but yes." She finishes chewing, washing it down with a drink before sitting back in her chair. "She is also the person my father has invited on behalf to every single event we've hosted the last few months." She blinks an unnatural amount of times after hearing that. "You okay there, Sweetheart?"

"Shut up for a second." She processes a little longer and her expression changes. "So you mean to tell me the girl you were supposed to bring as your date, or actually date, or whatever the plan was, is a girl meant to inherit an entire chain of hotels. Meanwhile, you're supposed to inherit the largest real estate company, not only in New York but across the country? And you thought dating *me* would cause your parents to let go of that dream?"

"I *thought* if they saw me making the decision to settle down for myself; if they saw me running my life the way they think I should, but with someone *I* chose, they would trust that I'm capable of running a company."

She stares at me blankly then abruptly pushes away from the table. "Excuse me." She's up and heading down the hall before I can even try to stop her. The last thing I need is to cause a spectacle with my fake girlfriend at the *first* event we attend together, so I let her go. My father would have a field day if that were to happen, and I am sure I would never hear the end of it. I stand up, slowly following the direction she went in, but she's nowhere to be found.

How does she move so fast in those shoes?

I check my watch and see that the panel I'm on is starting in ten minutes. She was supposed to be front row for that, same as before, but I'm not so sure that will be happening.

"Lose her already?" My teeth grind together when I hear Jessica's voice.

"No." I turn to face her and place my hands on my hips.

She lets out a breathy sigh, taking a step closer and dusting the shoulders of my sports coat. "Some girls just can't handle a challenge, Fitz. You need someone a little tougher than that by your side. Let's face it, you're going to have women fawning all over you for the rest of your life. You're smart, sexy, and super successful. I can handle that. But can she?"

"Well, I'm handling *you* pawing at him when he just told you he was taken, so I think we'll be just fine." Lauren slides her hand in mine and wraps her other one around my forearm, making my body immediately relax. Jessica's eyes watch it happen and she scoffs.

"Being jealous and being able to actually handle women throwing themselves at him are two completely different things." Lauren takes a step closer to her, with a lethal smile on her face.

"Believe me, I'm not jealous. If Fitz decides he wants to partake in activities with the desperate women throwing themselves at him, then by all means, they can have him. Jealousy isn't an issue when you have trust." Jessica frowns when her eyes meet mine. "Now, I believe we have a panel to get to, if you'll excuse us."

I clear my throat, trying to compose myself after watching Lauren put Jessica in her place like that. "You ready?" She nods and we leave, not bothering to say anything else to Jessica. If she wants to play dirty, then so be it. Only I don't think she's going to like the way we play the game. Because I have a new partner, and we play *very* well together.

I thought Lauren might be ready to call it a day before the mixer even started, but she has eased into the night flawlessly. She's smiling and talking to associates and attendees alike, every one of them seemingly captivated by every single thing she says. I get it, I am too. Which is exactly why I want to throw her over my shoulder and take her home. I already find myself wanting to be greedy with her and I'm not even sorry. I never have been one to share well. I blame it on only-child syndrome.

"Chapman, Henderson, how are you both doing tonight?" I ask, inserting myself into their conversation.

"I think we can agree our night is going pretty well." Jefferey Chapman, the absolute scum of New York gives Nico Henderson a suggestive look that has my blood absolutely boiling. "That is fantastic news. I'm afraid I need to steal my girl away though." The frown on both of their faces tells me everything I need to know about *why* their night was going so well.

"We didn't know this was your girl, Fitz," Nico pipes up, and I get the unfamiliar urge to punch him in his smug face.

"Now you do." I smile, holding out an arm to guide Lauren in the opposite direction.

"Nice talking to you both." She gives them a smile bigger than any I've ever had directed at me, which only pisses me off further. I place my hand on the small of her back and we make our way through the room.

"What the hell was that?" I growl under my breath.

"Um. Talking?" she states as though it should have been obvious.

"Looked a lot like flirting to me." She stops dead in her tracks and I turn to face her.

"You better be talking about their end of the conversation and not mine." She looks as angry as I am now.

"I don't know. Am I?"

She scoffs, shaking her head in disbelief. "What do you want from me Fitz? I'm here, aren't I? I'm playing the girlfriend. I'm marketing for *your* company, I'm stepping in when a boundary-blind model starts pawing at you, and you're mad at *me*? For what?!"

I can't tell her. She would laugh in my face. Or think I'm crazy. Or both.

"You're right. I'm sorry. I may have overreacted."

"May have?" She looks at me with that *are you kidding me* stare and I grind my teeth.

Running my hand through my hair, I step closer to her, my voice low. "I overreacted, okay? Are you happy?"

Her face hardens. "No." She turns and walks away, leaving me feeling completely clueless as to how I'm going to fix this. I'm about to go after her and fumble my way through an apology when my father appears beside me.

"I need to speak to you, privately."

"Now isn't a good time." His hand shoots out to stop me when I start to walk away.

"It wasn't a request." He nods to a room off the main ballroom and we head that way. When the door latches behind us I feel a cold chill shoot down my spine. "What the hell did you say to Jessica tonight?"

"You invited her, didn't you?" He puffs his chest, and it's all the answer I need. "I told you, *twice*, that I was bringing someone this weekend. Not just anyone, my girlfriend. Someone I'm actually serious with. Did you honestly think I would just leave Lauren behind and run off to escort Jessica instead?"

"You and I both know you've never been serious about anyone. I don't see this ending any differently than the string of women you've fooled around with in the past." The look of disgust on his face has my blood boiling. "She's got nothing to offer you, son." I bare my teeth, trying to remain calm.

"And how would you even know that?"

"I ran into her in the hallway earlier while you were speaking with Jessica, the woman you *should* be here with." I close my eyes to keep from rolling them. "I asked her about herself and she told me what she does. She's a sales agent… That's it! She didn't say much about her parents, got all smiley when she mentioned that all she does in her extra time is hang out with her friends," he practically spits out the words, a humorless laugh following. "She's probably just some gold-digger that will distract you from your work and spend all your money."

"She might have just been nervous to talk to you after the way you spoke to her earlier."

"Well, then you need to find a woman with a backbone, Fitz! You'll see soon enough; she's all wrong for you."

"That's your opinion." He gives me a bored look and I fight the urge to shove everything he's ever given me back in his face. "You don't even know her. You have no idea what she has to offer me."

"I know it won't be enough," he says confidently.

"You're never going to accept the choices I make for myself, are you?"

"Maybe when you start making the right ones. Which better be soon, you're getting promoted in two months. Time to get your shit together, Fitz." I nod, watching the man I am supposed to look up to most tell me I'm still not good enough.

"You may not let me make many of my own, but *Lauren* is my choice. Like it or not, she's not going anywhere. Not if I have anything to say about it." I walk out of the room and slam the door behind me. Worrying that after the way we left things, I may *not* have a say in it anymore.

Chapter 34

Lauren

I was having a pretty good day. Getting to put Jessica Vanderbilt in her place was entertaining as hell. Hearing Fitz speak, and getting the chance to speak on the subject of social media marketing myself was thrilling, and the mixer was actually a hit. I was talking to two guys about the changes they've been seeing in numbers regarding upstate housing recently, when Fitz came up and went all cave-man on me, getting mad that I was being nice. To *his* fucking associates at that. And my day just kind of went to shit.

LUCIFER

Where are you?

ME

Home.

LUCIFER

Did you suddenly inherit the ability to teleport?

ME

YOUR home. 

I probably should have said it that way the first time.

I see the text bubble pop up and disappear twice before it stops without another word from Fitz. Ten minutes later he's walking through the door. He stops in the threshold with his hands planted firmly on his hips. I look at him from where I'm mixing cookie batter at the island with my brows raised, waiting for whatever it is he's about to say.

"How did you get in here?"

"I took the key off your keyring. You probably shouldn't leave your keys in your fancy ass car, by the way. Someone could steal it." I scoop some of the batter onto a baking sheet, watching as he runs his hand through his hair.

"I have a tracker on it. I'd find it. Which reminds me..." I give him a suspicious look when he starts stalking toward me. "Give me your phone."

"No," I argue, seeing his eyes land on it sitting on the counter. Before I can even try to beat him to the punch, he snatches it, holds it up to my face to unlock it, and starts clicking the screen.

"Asshole."

"Brat."

"What are you doing?" I try to look at the screen but he keeps holding it higher so I can't see.

"Sharing your location with myself."

"What? No. That's an invasion of privacy." I try to grab it again, but he lifts the phone over his head, causing me to fall into his chest.

"Still have me saved as Lucifer in your phone, I see." He brings it back down, showing me my own screen, where he has our text thread pulled up.

"Well, you're still the devil, so..." I smirk at him, but all of the confidence backing my quick wit is swept out from under me when he grabs my neck, his thumb caressing my jaw.

"Trouble, the devil would blush if he knew the things I wanted to do to you." I clear my throat and pull away from him. Though I don't make it far.

"Would banishing me from New York so other men don't talk to me be on that list?"

He lets out a frustrated breath. "Not even close." The way he's looking at me has about a million questions fighting for dominance in my mind, but I'm not ready to ask any of them. More like I'm not ready for the answer to any of them. So I choose the easiest one.

"Do you like chocolate chip cookies?" I tuck a piece of hair behind my ear, grabbing the bowl I discarded while trying to get my phone from Fitz. I finish filling the baking sheet with little globs of cookie dough as Fitz strips out of his sports coat.

"Does anyone *not* like chocolate chip cookies?" he counters.

"You'd be surprised. Statistically, almost the same amount of people don't like pizza."

"Well, that's just insane." I smile to myself at how serious he sounds. I get the cookies in the oven and set a timer on my phone before turning to see Fitz staring down at his. "Unbelievable," he scoffs, lifting his head with a satirical smile.

"What's the matter?" I grab a water from the fridge and take a sip as he continues shaking his head.

"My father's birthday party got moved to next week."

"Oh, okay." I put my water bottle on the counter and lean forward, trying to figure out why he seems so bothered by that. "So, are we coming back next week then?"

"Yep. Seems like it." He unbuckles his belt and whips it out of the loops so fast it makes a popping sound. "I'm going to change." He storms into the bedroom, slamming the door behind him.

What the hell was that about?

TAY

It's practically a crime that we have seen 0 photos posted while you're in New York with your hunky hunky boyfriend.

RUBY

Does being sisters-in-law come with some sort of telepathy? Because you read my mind.

SHANE

Send themmmmm.

LEAH

If you need help picking which ones to post you have
an entire board of directors here ready to help. • •

I bite my thumbnail, fighting the guilt that's creeping into my gut. They've seen no pictures because there *are* no pictures. And there *are* no pictures because this is all fake and I can't keep up with how the hell I'm supposed to act with him. It's easy when we're around his colleagues and I know what I'm supposed to be selling. But when we're having lunch or even a simple conversation at his apartment, I have no idea what version of myself I'm supposed to be. So maybe it's time I just be myself? The best way to sell this relationship is to treat it like I would any *real* one, with the minor detail in the back of my mind that it comes with an expiration date. Plus that may make the guilty feeling of lying to my friends shrink. With my mind made up that I'm just going to be *me*, I take a deep breath and switch to the mindset that this is all real.

ME

Today was totally insane. We have taken no pictures
together, shocking I know. But as soon as I have one
on my camera roll it's headed straight to this chat.

TAY

Who even are you?

RUBY

Will be impatiently waiting for any and all photos.

LEAH

What's his place like?

ME

I feel like I am living in an episode of FRIENDS. But
like, if they had MONEY money.

SHANE

That's a good thing, right?

ME

Lol. Yes! it's amazing. Gotta bounce, cookies are done. 🍪

RUBY

You made him cookies?! Oh this girl is in LOVE love.

ME

You'll always be my one true love.

TAY

Rude.

SHANE

How dare.

LEAH

We can still hear you, you know?!

I laugh out loud before locking my phone, but I practically jump out of my skin when I see Fitz standing in front of me, his lips turned up in a small smile.

"Something funny?"

"With them? Always." I nod to my phone, sliding my hands into the oven mitts. Once the cookies are on the stovetop I turn the oven off and face Fitz again. "Cookies will be ready to eat in five!" I smile and Fitz's features go soft as he visibly swallows. "What?" I feel my cheeks heat to an ungodly temperature as he pushes off the counter and walks over to me, tucking a strand of hair behind my ear. My eyes fixate on his, but he's watching his own movement as he plays with my hair.

"There's something I didn't tell you earlier." His icy-blue eyes finally find mine. "You have the most amazing smile I've ever seen in my life." It's taking everything in me to stay focused and not get lost in the smell of his cologne or the way his eyes hypnotize me.

"Um. Thank you?"

"And I'm afraid I didn't handle it well when you smiled at those guys during the mixer earlier, when I've never been rewarded with one of your smiles."

Oh.

"And even though I'm not sure if that one was for me or for the cookies, I'm claiming it as my own." My eyes roll playfully and his hands begin traveling down. From my cheeks to my arms, until they settle on my hips. "I acted irrationally while you were doing me a favor, and I truly am sorry about that. I promise it won't happen again."

"If this is going to work, if we're really going to sell this, you're going to have to trust me. I can handle myself, and I'm not the kind of girlfriend who cheats. Regardless of the fake title. For as long as people are supposed to believe I'm with you, I'll be with *you*. Okay?"

"Okay," he agrees. You could cut the tension in the room with a knife, but in an effort to keep things light tonight, I grab my phone off the counter, pick up two cookies from the baking sheet, and hand him one.

"Smile." His eyes bounce around and he smiles directly at me. I almost fall over laughing and when I finally look at him again, his face has completely lit up.

"What?! I literally did what you asked me to do." I keep trying to compose myself but every time I think about it, I start laughing again.

"I meant for a picture!" I hold my phone up and the realization hits him.

"*Oh.* Well, say that next time so I don't look stupid." I giggle when he wraps his arm around my waist, turning us to where he's standing behind me, his chin above my head and a smile on his face. I hold my phone up and—holy shit he's cute.

I snap a few pictures as he takes a bite of his cookie and I do the same with mine. It's an entire photoshoot at this point, and I can't stop giggling the whole time. When we're finally done, he takes his thumb and wipes chocolate from the corner of my lips and I watch closely as he licks it off his finger.

"You're quite the baker, Trouble. These are delicious."

"Thanks, so are you." He raises a brow at me and I reach up, licking the chocolate off his cheek. He shakes his head at me with a smirk that makes me want to lick him pretty much everywhere else.

Oh my god, when I decide to be myself I just really fucking send it, don't I?

Chapter 35

This woman is going to be the death of me.

I never imagined I would die so happy.

She's finishing up in the shower, the minty smell from her shampoo floating through the air, and it's taking everything in me to stay away from the bathroom today. She comes out with damp hair, her travel clothes on, and her suitcase packed and ready to go. I remembered what she said about early flights so we're heading out at a brisk 5:30 to get to the airport.

Our Uber pulls up to our entrance and I busy myself with grabbing our bags from the back. When I pull out her rather large suitcase I realize we were only back in New York for a single day.

"I'm sorry our trip got cut short."

"Don't be sorry. I had a good time. One day I'll actually *see* New York while I'm here, but you can't control your own schedule. Or so it seems."

"How many times have you been to New York?"

"Only twice." She glances up at me and I see the mischief behind those pretty blue eyes. "And wouldn't you know it, some part of The Fitzgerald Firm took up every single second of my being there." She nudges my arm with her elbow. "I'm teasing. Well… I mean, it's true, but I'm not mad about it."

"How about this? I'll show you New York properly the next time we're both here."

"Sounds like a plan." She smiles softly at me but is unusually quiet the rest of the time. We drop our bags off and make it through security twenty minutes before our plane starts boarding. I don't plan on ever letting her fly anything but first class, mainly because I like the fact that it's just the two of us in the row and I get her attention all to myself. However, this flight I got none of her attention because she fell asleep approximately five minutes after we were in the air.

"Hey, Trouble, we're landing." I kiss her nose and she scrunches it in the cutest way before rubbing it with her fist that's hidden beneath her sweatshirt sleeve.

"Did you just kiss my nose?" The sleepy frown on her face makes me smile.

"Would you rather I yell your name on a plane full of people?"

"Hmm," she hums, giving me a suggestive look. Making me curious what exactly was going through her dirty little mind. I get déjà vu walking into the airport with her, only this time she insists we part ways so she can grab us coffee while I go to the restroom.

"I'll meet you there in a sec. Here."

"What's this?" She holds the cash up with a frown.

"You know the drill, coffee's on me, Trouble." I wink at her and she gives me a sassy glare.

"Wow, and I didn't even have to put out for it this time," she teases. I watch her walk through the airport like she owns the damn place. She seems so different. So light, confident, dare I say…happy? I smile when I see her hold her phone up to take a photo of the coffee shop before heading to the bathroom. I check my texts when I stop outside the restrooms, seeing the message that came in from my mother last night, having that same sense of irritation roll over me when I read it again.

MOTHER

Dad's party is rescheduled for next Thursday at 5pm.
Attire is still black tie. The venue scheduled
maintenance on the same day we had the place
rented out. They gave us a 50% refund, the imbeciles.
Anyways. Don't forget to get your father a nice gift and
why don't you come to this one alone. We have things
we need to discuss.

Two more months. Only two more months of having to go along with my parent's bullshit before I'm the one in control of my own future. I pocket my phone and head to the coffee shop, stopping short when I'm gifted the gut punch of seeing Lauren hugging another man, smiling at him like he lit every star in the sky.

I'm so not in the mood for this today.

"How long are you in town for?" I hear her ask before I clear my throat and get their attention. Her head whips to the side and her smile falls when she sees me.

Well, that fucking hurts.

"Fitz. Hey." Her cheeks turn red when she looks back at the guy then over at me again.

"Hey yourself." I force myself to muster up a smile. "Who's your friend?"

"Hugh Burgess." The charming bastard introduces himself, holding his hand out to me.

"Fitz." I nod, giving him a firm handshake.

"Fitz, huh? How very poetic." He laughs. He has this carefree and confident air about him that makes me kind of hate him. "Okay, Love. I have to be going, but call me when you're free this week." My eyes pop and I look at Lauren who is smiling and *nodding.*

"I will."

You will the fuck not.

"So great seeing you." He puts his hand on her shoulder and squeezes before offering me his hand again. Would it be completely irrational to...I don't know? Break it. "Lovely meeting you as well, Fitz."

He's barely out of earshot and I'm practically fuming. "So…who's the French motherfucker calling you *Love?*" Her eyes pop and she begins looking around before pulling me off to the side, careful not to spill her drink.

"Lower your voice, would you?" She glances around again, ensuring we have privacy in the little alcove we're standing in on the other side of the coffee shop. "He's a friend of mine, and he's from Australia, not France." She gives me a puzzled look.

"A friend?" I ask skeptically.

"Yes."

"A friend you've slept with before?" I watch her cheeks redden again as her eyes widen and a shred of her confidence disappears.

"Why exactly does that matter?"

"Well, if you tell me he's a friend of yours like *Luther* is a friend of yours, then I can accept the little nickname and the possible plan-making. If he's a friend of yours like *I'm* a friend of yours, then it matters."

Her chest is rising and falling more rapidly when she answers. "And if he's not a friend of mine like Luther is?" My jaw tightens, waiting for a clearer answer, and she crosses her arms over her chest. "We have… intimate knowledge of each other." A humorless laugh leaves me as the jealousy in me grows in leaps and bounds.

"You're not meeting with him this week."

"Fitz, he's just a friend. I haven't seen him in *that* way in a really long time."

"Then a little bit longer won't kill you, will it?"

I'm hyper-aware of how insane I sound right now, but that doesn't change the fact that I kind of want to go find him and punch him in the forehead.

"What the hell is your problem?"

"My problem is that now I can't stop picturing you with him, Lauren, and I don't fucking like it." She stares up at me, those big blue eyes full of surprise. I'm not sure how. I don't bother hiding the way she affects me. If she doesn't realize all the ways that I want her, then she simply doesn't want to.

"Fitz—"

"Let's get out of here. I'd rather not have an audience while you finish yelling at me." I grab the bags from her hand and walk a few paces, putting my coffee in the same hand as the bags so I can stop and reach behind me. Praying that her hand will fill mine. That she'll give me some shred of hope that I didn't just ruin this because I was fucking *jealous* and pissed off at my parents. My chest is tight with anticipation until I feel her cold hand slide into mine and I feel the tension in my shoulders start to ease.

I will not fuck up like this again, but it's time she knows exactly where I stand when it comes to her being mine.

Chapter 36

Lauren

Neither Fitz nor myself have spoken since we left the airport. I've been trying to figure out how I feel because part of me says his behavior at the airport should have me running in the other direction, but the other part of me feels…wanted. I'd never say it out loud, because I fear it would sound even more pathetic than it does in my head, but seeing him kind of freak out over the idea of me with another man makes me think of Max, Tucker, Tank, and Sawyer. The four guys would have acted the exact same way, had someone been a little too friendly with any of their girls and they witnessed it.

I mean, he did tell me last night that he got jealous when I was talking to those guys at the mixer, and I *did* tell him that for as long as we are in this agreement, I would be his. Maybe he felt like I was betraying that trust I asked him to put in me. I look over at Fitz, who is zoned in on the road as he drives in the direction of my house.

"My problem is that I can't stop picturing you with him, Lauren, and I don't fucking like it."

He called me by my name. That has to mean something, right? I've been *Trouble* or *Sweetheart* for as long as I've known him, unless he's introducing me to someone, of course. For him to use my real name feels the same as when your parents use your middle name when you're in trouble—it's unsettling. Him shifting the car into park pulls me out of my own thoughts, but he doesn't say a word as he gets out, opens my door, and grabs my bags from the back.

"Thanks," I mumble. I go to grab them from him but he stops me.

"You know the rule, Trouble. You don't touch your bags. I'll take them up for you."

Trouble.

He sets the bags inside the door, his feet never leaving the doormat and my heart sinks. Ginny runs over to us and I smile, picking her up and snuggling her.

"Ginny girl! I missed you!" Her purrs are insanely loud for five whole seconds before she jumps down, rubs against Fitz's leg, and then runs back into the house. "She's so low maintenance." I laugh, seeing a smirk play at Fitz's lips, but the humor doesn't quite reach his eyes.

"You want to come in?" I ask, leaning against the door to allow it to open further.

"Do you *want* me to come in?" The defeat in his tone makes me even more sure.

"Yeah, I do." He nods and walks inside, kicking his shoes off to the side, and I do the same. We make it to the island in an awkward silence before I finally get the courage to speak first.

"Fitz?"

"Yeah, Trouble?"

"Why didn't you like the idea of me with someone else?" The pained frown on his face makes me backtrack. "I just mean... It was a long time ago, me being with Hugh, did you really think I would sleep with him when I'm supposed to be with you? After I told you I wouldn't do that." He takes a deep breath and I have no idea what answer to expect from him.

"I didn't, and don't like it because I've been able to picture you with no one but *me* ever since I had you. Today, seeing you with him, put a new picture in my head. The possibility of you wanting to be with someone else, and it shattered the illusion I've been living in."

"I don't—"

"You don't remember that night, but I haven't been able to forget it. For almost a year now, every time I see your eyes roll, all I remember is how it felt to be inside you. Every time I have to get myself off, I see you on your knees for me, begging for every drop of cum I had for you. Every time I see you play with your hair, all I can see is the way it fanned out on my pillow when I would sink inside you. You're rooted in every single part of my mind. Having to act like that wasn't the best fucking night of my life just to keep you from running for the hills has been *torture*." I can hardly breathe when his hand reaches for my hair, tucking it behind my ear. "You were anything but *decent*, Trouble. I would have kept you in my bed forever had I not gotten called away before you woke up the next morning. Then when I finally saw you again, you didn't remember me. All the while, I've not been able to think of anything but you. I wasn't ready for the illusion to end if you decided you wanted to be with someone else. That's why I snapped."

I can't breathe.

"I need some water," I barely whisper, causing Fitz to fly into action. I stand motionless as he moves around the kitchen to get me a drink.

"Here." He hands me the water and I practically chug the whole thing. I finally meet his eyes and feel as though my knees could give out at any moment.

"You... Do you—" Shit, why are words so hard right now.

"Breathe, I'm not going anywhere." He runs his hands along my arms, helping to center me while simultaneously sending goosebumps along my skin.

"You make all these flirty comments, but then you walk away. I always thought it was part of your game to get under my skin. Do you still want me? In that way?" If he said no I would probably just go fling myself off the roof.

"Yes."

"Then why haven't you done anything about it? Why haven't you made a move?" The look he gives me is one that will be ingrained into my memory forever.

"I needed to know you wanted me too, Trouble." Consider caution officially in the wind.

"I do."

"You do?" I nod, a little more eagerly than I meant to, and he's got me on the counter before I can say another word. His hands are resting on the curve of my ass and his nose is grazing my ear when I hear him inhale softly. "Tell me that you want me."

"I want you, Fitz."

"Fucking finally," he growls in my ear. The ferocious way he kisses and nips at my neck, while his hands palm my ass before moving underneath my shirt, has my panties soaked within seconds. He rips my shirt off and kisses down my neck, against the slope of my breasts, and down my stomach. "You know the rule, Trouble. You tell me to go and I take what I want." He hooks his fingers into my shorts, and I bite my lip in anticipation.

"Go." It comes out breathy and I don't even care. I need this. I need him. He rips my shorts down, taking my underwear right along with them, discarding them before he hooks his arms around my thighs, pulling me to the edge of the counter as he kneels for me. I prop my feet up on the barstools on either side of him and his mouth is on me a second later.

"Fuck," I moan. I can feel the motherfucker smirk against my pussy and I roll my eyes. The moans coming from *him* as he completely devours me have me closer and closer to coming undone. Then he moves—plunging his tongue inside of me, sucking my clit into his mouth then kissing it so softly it has my head spinning.

"Fitz!" My body is screaming, begging for release. He looks up at me and the way his face is glistening with my arousal is exhilarating.

"Say please, Trouble." He squeezes my thighs and blows on my clit, making me jump.

"Please, Fitz. I need to come." I grab a fistful of his hair and *his* eyes roll, finally making me understand what he gets so worked up about. I guide him back down, and he doesn't argue. His tongue is back on me and the electric feeling I get every time we touch, completely ignites, causing my toes to curl. I keep a hold of his hair, grinding my hips against him and he matches every movement. Causing the most intense orgasm I can ever recall having, to rip through me.

"Fuck, Fitz. Yes!" He lets me ride out every last wave of pleasure before giving my clit one last kiss, and stands up.

"I've been craving the taste of you for *ten. Months.*" He slides a finger inside me, staying only long enough to be a tease, and I moan at the loss when he pulls it away. "Don't make me wait so long for another taste, will ya?" He sucks his fingers clean and grabs my shorts from across the room, sliding them up my legs until I feel the dampness of my underwear. He pats my hips and kisses my nose, leaving the scent of my arousal lingering before he walks away.

"Wait. Where are you going?" I frown, folding my arms over my chest.

"Giving you time."

My frown deepens. "For what?"

"To make sure you won't regret this before we go any further. Because if I have you again, I'm never gonna want to let you go." He opens the door and my stomach twists.

"I'm not going to regret it," I call after him.

"Get some rest, Trouble. I'll see you soon." Then he closes the door and I'm left with the realization that I miss him already.

Shit.

Chapter 37

Lauren

"I don't like how busy you are with your new boyfriend," Taylor whines, and my mouth pops open. "You didn't text us like, *at all* while you were in New York. I've become accustomed to hourly texts, or Insta story updates or *something!*"

"OK, hold on a minute. I've had to deal with every single one of you bitches getting boyfriends, then fiancés, then husbands. Not to mention the dogs and the babies, whom I love with my whole heart, and you're gonna get mad when I've had a boyfriend for five whole minutes because I didn't send you a picture of my breakfast?" The whole room is silent as I wait for her answer.

"Yes."

"Well, that sounds about right," I mumble and the room falls into a fit of laughter.

"God, you're high maintenance." Shane shakes her head at Taylor, who just shrugs as she finishes pulling the takeout containers from the bag.

"High maintenance is still maintainable." Taylor winks at her.

"Okay, but tell us everything. How was it?" Ruby's eyes bounce in anticipation.

"It was good. We were pretty busy the whole time. Obviously." I pop my eyes at Taylor and she rolls hers. "He took me to his favorite pizza place when we landed and it was to die for. The conference went well and I actually got to answer one of the questions at the end of Fitz's presentation. The party we were supposed to go to got moved to next week and after checking my work schedule I realized I'm supposed to be training someone so I don't think I'll get to go, which I'm bummed about, but it was a good trip. Until we got to the airport, but everything is fine now."

"I'm so glad you had a good time and getting to speak must have been fun!" Shane encourages from her place at the table. Her little baby bump is starting to show up now and I still can't believe her and Max are having another baby.

"Bitch, back up. What do you mean until you got to the airport? What happened?" Leah asks.

"Did you get strip searched?" Ruby asks.

"Why on *earth* would I get strip searched?"

"Well, what else could go wrong in an airport?"

"I can think of a few things other than getting strip searched!" Ruby shrugs and I shake my head and laugh.

"Woman, what happened!?" Taylor waves a hand at me and I suddenly cower.

"We, uh… Ran into Hugh." I shrug, forking a bite of my food into my mouth. I see Ruby's eyes widen and everyone else shares a look of confusion.

"My old boss, Hugh? Why would that be a problem?" Shane asks, taking a sip of her water.

"Well, yeah, no. It would have been fine if I'd been like, '*This is my friend's old boss, I met him once at an event she took me to in California, I haven't seen him in almost four years*'." I notice the way Ruby is fighting back a laugh and I want to push her off her chair.

"How *did* you introduce him?" Taylor's getting suspicious and my sweet, sweet Shane still looks just as lost as before.

"As a friend…" Eyes begin to widen around the table. "That I may or may not have slept with before," I mumble the words out quickly as I bring my Diet Coke up to my lips.

"YOU SLEPT WITH HUGH?!" Shane screams, with no regard for who else in the house may hear her.

"Oof. Yeah, I'm sure that went over fabulously," Leah snickers, just as Tucker and Tank come storming into the kitchen.

"Umm. Who did?" Tucker asks, looking around the table. Four fingers are suddenly pointed straight at me.

"I hate you all." I roll my eyes and turn around with a guilty smile on my face. "Hi."

"Damn, Sour Patch. The old guy? Really?" Tank teases and I glare at him.

"He's literally like three years older than Tucker and Max?"

"Yeah, well, they're old too." Tucker slaps the back of Tank's head and they start fighting, like full-on wrestling, in the kitchen.

"Boys! Take it in the living room. We're gossiping." Taylor points them towards the living room and they oblige.

"I cannot believe you slept with Hugh! When?!" Leah's eyes light up when she asks and I cannot believe I am finally telling them this.

"Well the first time—"

"The *first time?* How many times were there?!" Shane is absolutely losing it right now and I must say, it's kind of funny to see.

"The first time was when you and I went to Cali together. I ran into him while I was at the gym, and one thing led to another…"

"I knew no one worked out for that long! You're dedicated, Lu, but not *that* dedicated."

"*Anyway…*" I continue, "then when we went back for your showcase we hooked up again. I saw him a few times after that but I didn't know what I wanted and he knew *exactly* what he wanted, so it just wouldn't have worked." I shrug.

"What did he want?" Taylor asks.

"He wanted to settle down. He said he wasn't getting any younger and he wanted to have someone to spend the rest of his life with, to share his art with, and maybe have a kid to pass it all down to. I really admired his dream, but I just knew I wasn't the one that it would come true with. I was what? 25? 26? I wasn't even kind of ready for that life back then," I scoff, waving a hand dismissively at the idea of me settling down back then.

"And now?" Ruby asks, and when I meet her gaze it levels me.

"And now... I'm with Fitz. It's new but...we'll see what happens." They start in with the *aww*s and squeals about how *their girl is ready to fall in love*; when in reality I still have no idea if that's what I want. The only thing I'm sure of is that it feels good to be with Fitz. So I'm going to do something I never do and stop the thought process there—for now, anyway.

"Honey, Can I talk to you for a minute?" Tank peeks his head in the room and Ruby frowns in confusion.

"Uh, yeah. Sure. Be right back, ladies. Don't talk about anything fun without me." I look over at Tank, but instead of being met with one of his goofy smiles, or him playfully flipping me off, there's a look of concern on his face—and before they disappear, I notice it's directed right at me.

Well, hello anxiety. You weren't invited tonight.

The conversation around the table switches when Taylor and Leah ask Shane about labor pains and what it feels like to grow a human, but I'm more curious to know what the hell has Tank looking so worried. Unable to steer my mind in another direction, I excuse myself from the table and head to the bathroom. I have no intentions of eavesdropping, but that doesn't stop me from pausing when I hear my name come from one of the spare rooms.

"I'm worried about Lauren dating this guy." I'm practically frozen in place when I hear the words leave Tank's mouth.

"What?" Ruby laughs. "Why?" I can tell she seems completely unbothered, which makes me glad it's not a shared opinion.

"You remember back when she had some work done on her car? I went to pick her up for lunch before picking it back up at the dealer?"

"Yeah?"

"I walked in to get her and she was coming out of his office and she looked really upset. Almost hurt, from the look in her eyes."

Oh my god, he remembers that?

"Hurt? Like he *hurt her?* Hurt? What the hell, Tank? Why didn't you tell me about this then?" Ruby sounds pissed off.

Great job, Tank. You got Ruby in fight mode.

"No. Not physically hurt. Well, I don't know, maybe—" I don't even give him time to finish that sentence before I storm into the room.

"I can take some of the guesswork out of that answer for you," I offer quietly, giving Tank a grateful look. "I didn't mean to overhear your conversation, but I did stop when I heard my name because you looked really concerned a minute ago and I don't want you to be. Not when it's not necessary." He folds his arms over his chest and his brows pinch together.

"So we don't have a reason to worry? He didn't hurt you?" Ruby asks for clarification.

I sigh and check behind me to see if anyone else has wandered this way. "I was upset that day, *really* upset and I was emotionally hurt, yes, but the whole reason behind that was a big misunderstanding."

"I don't understand." Ruby shakes her head so I continue. I explain the phone call I overheard and how angry I was that Fitz had been lying to everyone. How I thought he was a mole, only to find out he's an acquisition manager, and that Jack and Barbara weren't losing everything, but choosing to sell so they could retire. I tell them how he took me to get food that night and explained everything and that we worked through it.

I mean, I'm still kind of working through it, but that's irrelevant.

"But he still lied about it," Tank states, clearly not quite as accepting of the explanation as Ruby, who has visibly relaxed.

"He didn't have a choice, it's in his contract not to talk about it." I shrug. Tank takes a deep breath, making him look even bigger than he already is.

"You know I'm just looking out for you, right?" Tank asks, and my heart squeezes in my chest. *I will not cry. I will not cry.*

"Yeah, I know." I smile, fighting back the tears.

"You trust the guy?" I pause and Tank notices. "Lauren—"

"Yeah. Yes. I trust him." I shake my head, cutting him off. Seeing as how other than that one small incident Fitz hasn't given me a reason *not* to trust him, I don't see why I shouldn't.

"Okay then. But if he hurts you, you have like four guys willing to make him disappear, just remember that." He smiles and waves me over for a hug.

"Tank, I mean this with my whole heart, I don't think after the Mark situation, I'll ever forget that." Ruby and I are both tucked under Tank's arms giggling when I feel him shaking his head.

"I stand by what I said. Then, and now."

"Okay, you big softy. We're going back to girls' night. Go check on our sons and make sure Hendrix isn't trying to ride Maverick again." Ruby slaps Tank's ass and we stand in the spare bedroom together.

"He means well." I smile at Ruby, knowing she's probably worried I thought they were talking behind my back or something. Some might jump to that conclusion, but I know them better than that.

"I know, Rubes. I'm grateful to have you guys looking out for me." I rest my head on her shoulder and we stay like that a bit longer, before returning to the round table of chaos.

"I can't believe you told them about Hugh." Ruby bumps my hip with hers.

"It was time. I can't believe *you* almost didn't hold it together. They'd kill you if they found out you knew and didn't say anything."

She shrugs. "Hey, it wasn't my business when I walked in on you guys at the hotel, and it wasn't my business after."

Ruby Landry, the very definition of a ride or die.

Chapter 38

Fitz

It hasn't even been twenty-four hours since I left Lauren's house and told her I would give her some space, and I'm already going crazy without her. I've done nothing but replay her telling me she wanted me while remembering the way it felt to finally make her come again. To taste her again. So why the hell has she not texted me once since I left her house that day? Did she just need to get me out of her system? I sure the hell hope not, because I'm almost positive she'll never be out of mine. This is going to be the longest Sunday night of my life. I flip through the channels, stopping on some late-night show before pulling a pillow over my head to try and force myself to sleep.

I slept like absolute shit last night.

I tossed and turned all night, checking the time every hour on the hour, until I finally deemed it appropriate to get up at 5 o'clock to go for a run. I pushed myself harder today than I have in months, which felt great—even if it's directly related to the fact that I have so much built-up tension I can hardly see straight. By the time I got home and showered, the coffee shop Lauren frequents, and by frequents I mean she might as well live there, was open and I went to grab her favorite drink. Knowing the day is eventually going to catch up to me, I grab a double espresso for myself, before heading to the office.

"Morning, Fitz! Welcome back." Amy smiles at me from her place behind the front desk.

"Good morning, Amy. Good to be back." I give her a polite smile and head straight to Lauren's office, my shoulders dropping a bit when I see she isn't in it. I look around and notice her bag is sitting in its usual place beneath her desk, and frown.

Where are you, Trouble?

I hear her laugh almost immediately, and when I turn around I see her leaning against the desk in Marcus's office. I'd *hate* to be rude and interrupt them, so I go into Lauren's office, set her coffee in the center of her desk, and walk over to lean on the small table against the left wall to wait for her.

"You're terrible," she laughs again, her voice floating closer to her office. "Don't you go getting me in trouble, now."

I'm going to punch him in the teeth for making her giggle like that.

She walks into her office, making it only a few steps before she stops, seeing the coffee on her desk, and frowns.

"Morning, Trouble." She jumps back, sucking in a breath as her hand shoots up to her chest.

"Jesus, Fitz. You scared the hell out of me. What are you doing in here?"

"Waiting for you to finish your riveting conversation with Marcus." Sarcasm drips from my tone, causing her to shake her head as she walks to her desk.

"In the corner like a poorly trained stalker?" I smirk and walk over to close her door, not missing the ways her eyes settle on it before they find mine.

I slide my hands into the pockets of my slacks. "Hear any good jokes lately?"

Her brows pinch together. "What?" She clicks something on her computer before standing upright.

"Something must have been funny to earn a laugh like that from you." Her eyes roll as she makes her way over to her printer and I move quickly behind her.

"No jokes, but jokes aren't the only thing that makes me laugh," she says, popping her hip to the side as she waits for her old-ass printer to get this page out.

"Good to know." My voice is low and she jumps when she feels my nose brush across her hair. "I'll get one of those laughs out of you one day, Trouble. But right now I'll settle for your moans."

She spins to face me, her ass bumping her printer when she does. I see her swallow as she studies my face. "Fitz—"

"Do you regret it?" I ask, caressing her cheek with my forefinger.

"What?" she breathes.

"I gave you time to think, and I've been going crazy not knowing what's going on in that beautiful mind of yours." My hands travel down her body, my fingers teasing the hemline of her dress. "Do. You. Regret. It?" She shakes her head and my lip twitches into a smile. "Tell me," I demand.

"I don't regret it, Fitz," she whispers, something flashing in her eyes that's unfamiliar to me.

I slide my hand beneath her dress, feeling the smooth surface of her skin. "What made you laugh?"

"You can't be serious?" She breathlessly laughs.

"I'm very serious." Her breath shakes when I brush along the wet...

lace?

She's going to be the death of me.

I continue rubbing her clit through the lace, making her eyes flutter. "Barbara got a new puppy." I stop and her eyes open fully again.

"A puppy?" I frown. "That's what you were laughing at?" I take a chance and slide my fingers inside of her panties, feeling how wet she is, and when she doesn't pull away, I slip one inside her, pleasantly surprised when she lets out a little whimper.

"Marcus said—"

"I'd prefer you not say another man's name while I'm playing with your pussy, Trouble."

"Then stop asking me questions about why I was laughing in his office while your fingers are inside me." The way she manages to still cop an attitude with me while she's literally dripping down my fingers has me harder for her than ever before. I slide a second finger in and she lets out another one of those beautiful moans.

"You're lucky I don't put you on your knees right here and remind you who you belong to."

"Who said I wouldn't get on them willingly?" I curl my fingers and her hips press into me, her eyes rolling as she bites down on her lip. I brush my nose along her jawline, all the way up to her ear. Nipping at the lobe.

"Do not fucking tease me right now." Her hypnotic blue eyes meet mine and she grabs my wrist, guiding my fingers out of her. Then she reaches into a basket behind her, grabs a clip out of it, and pulls her hair back. "Lauren," I warn.

"That's *Trouble* to you." She puts her palm flat against my chest, pushing me back just far enough to allow her room to kneel. Before she does, she makes a show of undoing my belt and pulling my shirt out of my slacks. When her fingertips travel along my abs I instantly relax.

What is it about her touch that calms me immediately every time?

Then she gets on her knees, pulls my cock out, and spits on it.

I think that's in the top three of my favorite things she does.

I look down at her, catching a glimpse of those baby-blue eyes, and this euphoric feeling washes over me when I realize…she's going to remember it this time. Then she fucking winks at me, and I lose any hold on reality that this is all for show. Because right now, it's just us in this office. Right now, there's no one to sell a relationship to, and she still has my cock so far down her throat her eyes are glistening with unshed tears. Because right now, she *wants* it.

Knock, knock, knock.

"Lauren?" Fucking Marcus. I *wish* he'd walk in here right now.

I fully expect Lauren to jump up and demand I right myself, but the little troublemaker just keeps sucking me off.

"I know the rule, but I needed to finalize this—" This time when Lauren's eyes roll I see the annoyance in them, but it's towards Marcus this time, not me. She's annoyed that someone is interrupting us, and the fact that she still doesn't stop has me losing my fucking mind.

"She'll be with you in a minute." My voice booms across the room, silencing Marcus on the other side of the door. When I look down again, seeing the smirk in her eyes that she *would* be wearing, if her mouth weren't preoccupied. I take the clip out of her hair and fist it myself, setting a faster pace for us. She moans around my cock and slides her hand under her dress.

"Fuck, Trouble!" It comes out louder than I mean for it to, but fuck it, I don't care. I'd gladly let every person in this office know not to bother even looking in her direction, and that I won't be looking in theirs. In my mind, there is only *her*.

Her last little moan vibrates around me, and it sends me over the edge. I hold her head steady as ropes of my cum shoot down her throat at the same time her hips buck against her own hand. When I pull my cock out of her mouth, she reaches up with her clean hand and wipes her mouth. Then stands up and slides the fingers glistening with her arousal into my mouth. I groan, wrapping my hand around her wrist as I suck them clean, swirling my tongue around them careful not to waste a single drop.

"I remember who I'm with, Fitz. You might not like that I laugh with other guys, but I assure you…You're the only guy moaning my name while I blow you in my office." She winks at me and walks around her desk, picking her coffee up and taking a sip. "Thanks for the breakfast. And the coffee."

Holy shit.

"Fitz?"

I blink and raise my brows. "Yeah?"

"You might want to put your dick away, I *do* have a meeting with Marcus in five." I glare at her and growl, following her instruction to put myself back together.

I leave her office, completely speechless, catching a curious glare from Marcus on my way out. I head to my office, already knowing I'm not getting shit done today. I listen to the vibration of their voices through mine and Lauren's shared wall, until Marcus leaves her office, keeping the door open when he goes.

I forgot about her closed door rule—that worked out in our favor today.

A few minutes later I receive an email from Lauren.

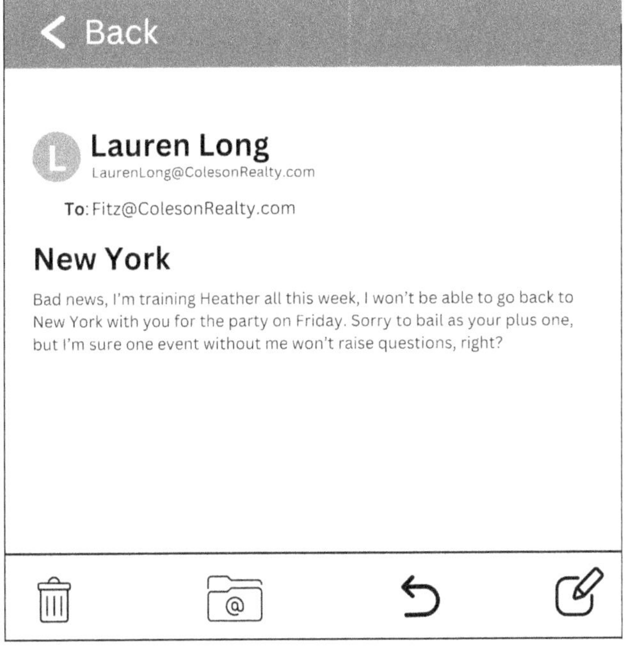

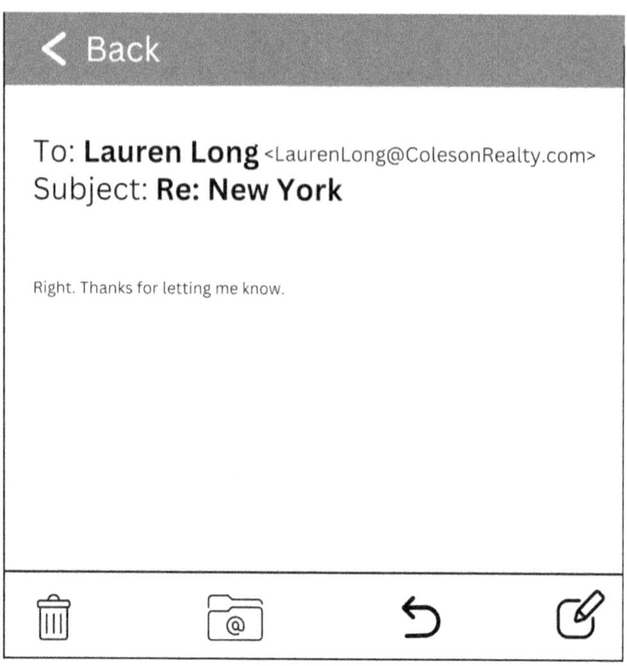

Happy birthday to me.

Chapter 39

Lauren

I lay in bed staring at my ceiling, unable to shake the feeling that something is off about today. Meanwhile, Ginny is curled up on my chest, sound asleep. My alarm starts ringing and I roll my head, staring at it sitting on my nightstand just out of reach. I strain every muscle in my body trying to get it without waking Ginny, but when I turn the alarm off and my screen lights up with a reminder, I shoot up in bed like I've just been electrocuted.

Reminder: Today, June 25. Fitz's Birthday.

"Shit!" I click on my calendar and stare at it with my mouth hanging open. Once I'm past the fact that I forgot his birthday was this week, my eyes fall to the second event on today's calendar, synched from my email.

Mr. Fitzgerald's birthday bash. 6 pm.

"Shit." Ginny is officially awake now, due to my movement *and* me talking to myself. No wonder he seemed so upset when he got the text about the party being moved. They moved the party to *his* birthday. I can't believe I didn't make the connection before now. I've been so busy training Heather this week, and with Fitz getting called away to finalize a small acquisition they had happening in Connecticut before going back to New York today, it wasn't even on my radar.

I start chewing on my thumbnail trying to decide what to do. I know he said he doesn't celebrate his birthday, but that doesn't mean people shouldn't still feel special on the day they came into the world. Unable to figure it out on my own, I grab my phone and click on Ruby's contact.

Ring. Ring. Ring.

"Come on, you have two kids I know you're awake," I mumble to myself, waiting for her to answer.

"Hey, Aunt Lauren!" Hendrix says, picking up the phone.

"Hey, my guy. How's it going?" I smile listening to Poe scream happily in the background.

"Mom burned the pancakes." Is all he says and I laugh when I hear Ruby call him out on his bullshit.

"I burned *one* pancake, you little stink. Give me the phone. Go tell Dad to come finish these. It's his damn recipe anyways." Her voice is getting closer to the phone as Hendrix gets farther away.

"Damn is a bad word." If there's one thing Hendrix is gonna do, it's tell you when you've said a bad word.

"Get out." She mumbles something else inaudible before finally addressing me. "Hi!" she says in an overly chipper voice.

"Good morning, beautiful, badass, mother of chaos. How are you this morning?" I'm met with silence until…

"Did you do something slutty? Why do you sound so happy?"

"Not today," I tease.

"Ohh, tell me everything. Tank can burn the rest of the pancakes."

"Another time, I need your advice." She actually *boo's* me, and I roll my eyes, letting her get it out.

"Fine. What's up?"

"So, today is Fitz's birthday. *But* he's out of town. I was supposed to go back to New York with him for a party, you remember?"

"Yes."

"Well, I got put in charge of training someone this week and told him I wouldn't make it, but that was before I realized it's *his* birthday. And he's having to spend it celebrating his dad, who I'm pretty sure he hates."

"Oh, relatable."

"Right?"

"So what do you need advice on, exactly?" she asks, bringing me back around to the point.

"Is it too weird or too soon in the relationship to go to New York and… I don't know, surprise him?" I feel my cheeks warm at the thought of going to New York without him knowing ahead of time.

"Aww! No, I don't think so. I mean, you've been there with him before, it's not like you'd be crossing any lines or like he didn't want you there since that was the plan to begin with."

"Yeah, I guess you're right." I pull my knees under my chin, feeling my stomach twist anxiously.

"But if you don't want to go, I'm sure he wouldn't hold it against you. What does your gut say?"

"That I really want to go."

"Then go!" she encourages. I can practically hear the smile on her face.

"Ok! I'm gonna go." My heart begins to race, and my brain is not far behind.

"Oh my gosh, this is so exciting. What are you going to do?!"

"I have no idea, but making sure I can get a flight so last minute is step one. I'll keep you updated." I check the clock on my nightstand and start thinking of everything I need to do, deciding it'll be best if I make a list.

"Ok. Love you bye!"

"Love you, bye!" I immediately click into my flight app to see when the next flight to New York is for today. "2 o'clock?!" I triple-check that it's the *only* available one before buying the ticket and making a list of things to get done before then.

- Email Amy that I won't be at work today
- Coffee from Brüman's
- Find a dress for the event tonight
- Get Ginny a travel carrier
- Everything shower

"Ginny. Pack your bags. We're going to New York."
Meow.

I got everything on my to-do list done in just enough time to make it to the airport thirty minutes before boarding. I say a quick prayer that we don't have any delays since I'll already be cutting it close to the time Fitz will need to be at his dad's party. I have no idea what I'll do if he's already gone. I come up with a backup plan just in case that happens, and pet Ginny's chin through the mesh on her pet carrier as the pilot announces we're ready for take off. My hands are sweating and I have this nervous excitement rushing through me, making me feel like I've had about a thousand milligrams of caffeine today. I pull my headphones on, turning to my travel playlist to help calm my nerves.

Between the subtle vibration from the plane, and the soothing voice of Adele, I close my eyes and the next time I open them it's because I feel a tap on my shoulder. I remove my headphones when I see that it's the stewardess. Damn, I really do sleep best on planes.

"Ma'am. We're going to be landing soon." I smile and thank her, looking at the older woman next to me who is doing a crossword puzzle, suddenly missing the way Fitz wakes me up on flights. When I check my phone I see that my service is back and texts are piling in. Most from the group chat, one from Ruby and one from Fitz. My stomach does a somersault when I see his name and I try to ignore that fact.

LUCIFER

I tried calling you at the office several times today and missed you every time. Don't kill yourself working too hard, Trouble.

ME

You know me, if I don't do the work, someone else will try to.

I quickly remember that Fitz has my location shared with himself and I turn it off.

LUCIFER

Such a hard worker.

I don't realize how hard I'm smiling at my phone until the crossword lady informs me it's our turn to de-board. I lock my phone, grab Ginny and my carry-on, and dart through the airport, hoping I can, by some miracle, hail a taxi and get back to Fitz's place before I run out of time. However, by the time I'm finished with all of my stops, I look at the time and curse to myself.

It's already past 6. There's no way he isn't already gone.

Time for plan B.

When we pull up to his building I pay the taxi driver and look at myself in the reflection of the doors and sigh. I can't believe I'm actually doing this. I shake my head, quickly shifting my focus back to the task at hand. *Getting into his house without him here.* When I walk in the doors, I realize my plan is going to fail miserably. This is a housing complex, not a hotel. There's no front desk person to help me like I'd thought there would be while making this plan.

"Man, my brain isn't working today," I mumble to myself, starting to feel defeated. Then I see my answer—a maintenance man. I readjust my grip on all the bags and boxes in my hands and rush over to him.

"Hi!" I wear my kindest smile when he looks up at me and his eyes soften.

"Hello there." His white hair and frail-looking hands make me think of my grandpa.

"I'm so sorry to bother you, but my boss asked me to drop these things off for him before he left at six o'clock and traffic was a nightmare and I didn't make it in time, obviously, and I left my set of keys to his place in my desk and I can't exactly afford to get fired so I was wondering…could you help me?" I look at him in desperation and he smiles.

"Which floor?"

"Oh, thank you so much—"I glance down at his name tag. "Ernest. I would hug you but I would probably drop Ginny." I nod to Ginny's cat carrier and he laughs.

"Rain check then." He gives me an unthreatening wink and I smile.

"8th floor."

Ernest saves the day! Now, time to get to work.

Chapter 40

I have very strategically planned out my evening. I will show up, find out what "family matters" need to be discussed, and take some photos with my father for the press, I'm sure. Then as soon as they've sang happy birthday to him and brought out what I'm sure will be an overly extravagant cake, I'm out of here. I never celebrate my own birthday, so I sure as hell don't want to be celebrating *his* today. I walk into the venue, which has been decorated with gold and black accents in every single corner, preparing myself to get into business mode.

"Let the countdown begin," I mumble to myself, working my way through the crowd to find my mother. It's a much edgier venue than I would have expected my parents to book, though you can barely tell through the elegant decorations masking its true form. They sure have a knack for covering up the true potential of things by drowning it in their own…*vision*. There are small bar tables spread around the room for people to stand at, stark white couches placed around the room for people to sit on, and the upstairs loft area looks to have a mix of the same couches as well as a few small tables. The loft is also where I spot the open bar, so I make a note to head there after speaking with my parents.

"Fitz!" *Speak of the devil.*

"Happy birthday," I tell my father with a forced smile.

"Oh, it's really just another day, you know?" He laughs and I clench my jaw.

"Where's Mom?"

He looks over his shoulder and shrugs. "I'm not sure, why?"

I frown at him. "She said that I needed to come alone because we had a family matter to discuss."

He clears his throat, shoving the hand not holding his drink into his front pocket. "Oh, yes. Of course."

The look on his face tells me everything I need to know. "There's no matter to be discussed, is there?" His mouth pops open, and for the first time in my life, I'm curious what he has to say for himself. Before I can find out, my mother waltzes over with a few familiar faces.

"Oh! Wonderful, you're both here!" She turns and waves someone over, but I continue glaring at my father, who is strategically avoiding eye contact with me. "Look who I found!" I look over and have to keep myself from audibly grunting.

"Let's all take a photo."

I shake my head and go to move, but Mother grabs onto my arm. "No, Mo—"

"Oh, come on, Fitz. It's your father's birthday. We're making memories!" she insists. I swallow down every emotion trying to surface at her words.

She quickly rearranges people and wouldn't you know it, Jessica and I are standing dead center with our parents flanking each side of us. If Jessica were in white it could be a fucking wedding portrait. She grabs onto my arm and tilts her head to where it almost rests on my shoulder and my whole body tenses. The camera flashes numerous times, then our parents move and I go to do the same, but Jessica keeps a hold of my arm. I look down at her to tell her to let go, but she smiles up at me and the camera flashes a few more times.

"I think we're done here," I tell the photographer. He nods and heads in the opposite direction. Then I look back down at Jessica. "As are we." She frowns, but I pull my arm away and head straight for the open bar, not caring what has her pouting tonight.

"Scotch neat." The bartender pours my drink and I quickly empty the glass. Tonight is not the night for sipping. I slide it back to him, giving him a nod and he smiles, pouring me another. "Good man." I drop a twenty-dollar bill into the tip jar and lean over the railing of the loft overlooking the party happening below.

I can't believe I actually fell for the reason my mother told me to come alone. I know my parents never discuss important family business during social events. That with the fact that the Vanderbilts will always be invited to parties my parents throw, I should have seen right through it. I pull my phone out and check Lauren's location, noticing that it's no longer shared with me and a small panic settles in my chest. I type out a quick text to check on her.

ME

Where are you? Why is your location turned off?

TROUBLE

I'm out.

Well, that's vague and only answers one of my questions.

I'm about to follow up with the question she's clearly avoiding answering when another voice stops me.

"What's gotten into you, lately?" I close my eyes and take a deep breath, hearing Jessica beside me. I slide my phone back into my pocket, reluctantly deciding I'll have to deal with Lauren later.

"What do you mean?" I don't bother looking at her, as I finish the rest of my second scotch. She leans against the railing I'm currently propped up on and tilts her head, trying to get my attention.

"You seem like you don't even want to be near me. We used to have fun when you'd come into town. At the very least you'd look at me at social events with something other than disdain. What's changed?" I finally look over at her and her hand rests on my arm.

"A lot has changed. What I don't understand is why you're still trying so hard to get my attention when you clearly no longer have it." She pouts a little, then she smiles.

"Because I know I could get it back if you just gave me a chance."

I scoff and turn to face the party again. "You're relentless, aren't you?"

"You never cared about that before."

"Well, that was before," I snap, wishing more than anything that this conversation would end.

"Before what?" She might as well have stomped her foot and huffed with the childish tone she uses with me.

"Before…" I push off the railing, hardly believing my own eyes when I see *her*.

My little troublemaker.

She looks fucking breathtaking in a floor-length black gown with a slit running dangerously high up her thigh. Her hair is pulled back with a few pieces hanging down in the front. There's only one long sleeve, the other arm completely exposed and she looks so beautiful I wish I could stare at her forever.

"Excuse me," I mumble to Jessica, pushing past her to rush down the stairs and get to my girl. I get stopped for a few handshakes and *hellos* on my way to her and I suddenly wish my family didn't know so many people. When I finally see her from behind I smile, despite the fact that she's talking to Nico Henderson again. I walk up behind her and slide my hands around her hips, feeling a sting when she slaps them. She spins around with a scowl on her face that quickly morphs into the most beautiful smile I've ever seen.

"Fitz!" she exclaims. Then she does something that fucking breaks me and puts me back together all at once. She throws her arms around my neck, kisses my cheek, and whispers, *'Happy birthday'* in my ear. My arms tighten around her and my eyes fall closed, feeling the sting of tears trying to form. Nico disappeared into the crowd at some point, leaving the two of us alone.

"Thanks, Trouble." When we finally separate, I get the chance to fully take her in. She looks even better up close. "What are you doing here? I thought you were training Heather this week?"

"I wasn't going to miss seeing you on your birthday, Fitz. They can live one day without me." She shrugs, smirking at me. There's a twinkle in her eye tonight that I'm not sure I've ever seen before. She looks like she's up to something and I'm more than curious to know what it is. "Oh, excuse me. Could you take a photo for us please?" She stops the same photographer from earlier, handing him her phone from her clutch. He gives her a confused look, probably wondering why she's handing a guy with a camera worth thousands in his hands, a *phone*. "I'm sure yours is better, but do you mind?" He lets out a low laugh and agrees, backing up and angling the phone. She looks up at me, and I smile, taking the lead by wrapping one arm around her waist and holding her hand with my other.

"There you go." The photographer hands her the phone back and gives me a curious look. Then he shakes his head and walks away.

Weird.

"This is some party, huh?" Lauren looks around the room, prompting me to do the same.

"Yep."

"It's a shame they covered up so much of the natural beauty of this place. I feel like maybe they chose the wrong venue for this particular party." I look at her in awe because she just fucking gets it. "Sorry! That was probably so rude." Her hand flies to her mouth and her eyes widen, making me smirk.

"I couldn't agree more. So, what were you and Nico discussing?" I nod in the direction he went.

"Well we hadn't been talking long, but he did ask me if The Fitzgerald Firm was looking for any brokers to work with."

"What did you tell him?"

"Nothing. You came up right after he asked so I didn't get the chance to say anything."

"Hmm… Go tell him that we are and to send his resume to you." Her eyes pop and she looks around nervously.

"To *me?* I can't do that. I don't even work for The Fitzgerald Firm."

"No, but you're dating the soon-to-be owner, and I trust your judgment."

"You do?"

I nod and scan the room, seeing Nico by the open bar upstairs. "He's at the bar. Go grab yourself a drink. *One* drink, and let him know."

"Why did you put emphasis on how many drinks I can get?" She glares at me and I raise a brow at her.

"Maybe I want to see if you'll obey." I watch her face closely as her eyes grow wild. I lean in closer, pressing my lips to her ear. "Because I'm taking you home *sober* tonight, Trouble. That's why." She tips her head up to look at me, grabbing the lapels of my tux.

"Correction, *I'm* taking *you* home tonight, Fitzgerald." She winks at me and I realize that's the first time I haven't minded her calling me by my last name. Simply because of the anticipation I feel from her words.

"Make it a quick conversation." I practically growl in her ear, kissing her nose before she makes her way upstairs. I watch her as she goes, admiring the way that dress shows off every curve that I can't wait to get my hands on later.

"I told you to come alone." I turn around and see my mother looking at me in disapproval.

"Hello, Mother."

"You couldn't follow one simple instruction? I told you—"

"You told me that we had a family matter to be discussed. Which, after speaking with Dad, I realized was a lie. And I *did* come alone. Not because you told me to, but because Lauren had to work this week and thought she couldn't get away."

She scoffs and folds her arms over her chest. "So then why is she *here?*" I look up to the loft, seeing Lauren's eyes land on mine at the same time. She smiles and winks at me, then goes back to chatting with Nico.

"Because she didn't want to miss seeing me on my birthday." My voice is low, mostly because I still can't believe that's the reason she came. I glare over at my mother, seeing the uncomfortable, *almost* sad look on her face. "Enjoy the party, Mother. I'm taking my girl home." I leave her standing there, heading upstairs to grab Lauren, but when I see her handing Nico her card, I choose to stay away until she finishes her conversation. She smiles and excuses herself, walking straight over to me.

"Hey, you okay?" Her face is full of concern as she sets her glass on a nearby table.

"Why do you ask?"

"You just seem…off."

Oh, I am. More than she could possibly know.

I deflect answering by asking my own question. "Why did you say you would be the one taking me home?"

Her face is immediately full of mischief. "It's a surprise."

"Let's go." I nod towards the stairs and she walks in front of me, then stops and reaches for my hand.

I don't think she'll ever understand how something as simple as holding her hand makes everything else feel right. As we're on our way out, I hear my name from somewhere behind us, but I don't bother turning around.

"Fitz!" I glance at Lauren, seeing her look over her shoulder before she turns back to me with a frown.

"Who is that?" she whispers. I keep my eyes forward as I push the exit door open.

"My mother."

Chapter 41

Lauren

I was so nervous walking into Fitz's dad's party, unsure he would be okay with me showing up unannounced, but the response I got when he saw me immediately calmed my nerves. The way he squeezed me a little tighter when I told him happy birthday, and the look on his face when I told him I came just to see *him*, made me confident that my decision was the right one. My heart starts racing and the grip my teeth have on the inside of my lip grows tighter the closer our car gets to Fitz's building. I hope he likes everything.

When we pull up to the front, Fitz slides out first holding out his hand to help me get out behind him. When we walk in the door I spot Ernest in the far corner, locking the storage room door.

"I'll be right back," I tell Fitz, running over to where Ernest stands. I tap him on the shoulder and when he turns around his eyebrows raise as he takes in my appearance.

"My goodness. You look beautiful." His wobbly smile warms my heart.

"You have time for that hug now?" I smile at him and he nods. I wrap my arms around him and his frail hands pat lightly between my shoulders. When we pull away he looks behind me, causing my gaze to follow where Fitz stands with his hands tucked into his dress pants.

"That the boss?"

"That's the boss," I confirm, turning back around to face Ernest. "Thank you so much for your help earlier."

"It's no problem. You seem like a hard-working girl. He better treat you right." I laugh and he gives me a wink before he slowly makes his way across the room. I join Fitz again and he presses the button on the elevator with a curious look on his face.

"Anything I should be worried about there, Trouble?" I roll my eyes and laugh, stepping inside the elevator with Fitz's hand on the small of my back.

I turn around to face him. "You're crazy, you know that?" The doors seal shut and before I know it he's pushing me against the wall, his hands gripping my waist with need.

"And losing a little more of my sanity every time I'm around you." My heart begins to race, distant memories of past elevator rides with Fitz dancing through my mind. I open my mouth to say something, anything to cut the tension, when the elevator does it for me.

Ding.

The doors slide open on the eighth floor, and I grab Fitz's hand, leading him out. We make it to his door, but I stop him before he can even try to open it and he gives me a curious glare.

"Give me your keys." His face grows more suspicious, but he pulls them out of his pocket and hands them to me. "Stay right here."

"You're leaving me at the door? Like a stray dog or a postal package?"

"Hey, I picked Ginny up off a porch, I'll come back for you too," I tease. "Don't come in. I'm serious." I point a finger at him and he holds his hands up.

"I'm here until you say move." I smile and go inside, locking the door behind me…just in case. I run around trying to set everything up as quickly as possible, not wanting to leave the birthday boy feeling like a package for too long. I re-start the James Brown record that was playing last, then run over to the door, checking what his view will be when he comes in. I let out a satisfied breath, happy with my work. Before I open the door, I remember to pull out my phone and take a few pictures of everything.

"Close your eyes," I say through the door. He doesn't say anything in return. "Are they closed?"

"Yes, Trouble. They're closed." I bite my lip and open the door, grabbing his hand as I guide him through the doorway.

"Okay, slowly follow me. Keep your eyes closed." When he's finally far enough inside for me to close the door, I move to stand beside him, still holding his hand. "Okay. Open them." I keep my eyes on him as he opens his, blinking a few times to help his vision adjust and I see his throat work as he swallows. He stays quiet, which only makes me more anxious, as he looks at everything I've done.

"You did all of this for me?"

I look at my work again, smiling. "Well, yeah."

There are colored balloons weighted down on either side of his kitchen island, with big, gold, numbers three and five in the middle of them. A handmade banner that says *Happy Birthday, Fitz* sits on an easel beneath them. Two of my favorite bottles of wine, two glasses, and two large pizzas, from the same place he took me on our first night in New York, off to the side. I even have an ice cream cake in the freezer and candles in the cabinet to sing *"Happy Birthday"* to him later. When I look at him again his bright blue eyes, which are practically glistening, are already on me, and I smile. I don't think I've ever seen Fitz look so… vulnerable.

"Happy birthday, Fitz."

"I—" he shakes his head, looking at it all again, and then my heart leaps into my throat when he turns back to me.

He grabs either side of my face and his lips come crashing down on mine, stealing my breath and silencing every worry I had in my mind about today. I fist his tux jacket, pulling him closer and savoring the feeling of his lips on mine. He tastes like scotch and kisses me with a hunger I've never experienced before. His tongue dips into my mouth and his hands caress my body until they settle on my lower back. I wrap my hands around his neck, silently begging him not to stop.

His lips never leave mine as he finds the zipper on my dress and slowly starts pulling it down. When the zipper stops, he slides the right sleeve down, letting the dress fall to the floor. His lips move to my neck and he wraps my legs around his waist and carries me over to the kitchen island where all of his birthday things are set up. The marble is cool against my ass, causing me to suck in a sharp breath when he sets me down. He stands up, taking one small step away to be able to look at me, and my cheeks heat under his gaze.

"You are so beautiful." I pull his lips back to mine, missing the way they feel, and his hands wrap around my waist. I can feel every muscle in my body relax at his warm touch and my mind feels so much lighter.

He pulls away, resting his forehead on mine. "You're the only thing I want for my birthday." His hands cup my cheeks, our eyes locking. "Can I have you, Trouble? All of you?"

I bite my lip, trying to hide my smile. "Say please, Fitz."

"Please, baby?" Something happens in that moment, causing my body and heart to crave him in a way I've never craved another person before.

"Yes." I pull him back to me, his lips landing on mine again as my fingers move quickly to unbutton his shirt. He pulls his tie off and his shirt and jacket are the next to go. I pull away, looking at his sun-kissed skin, letting my fingertips trail from his shoulders down to his fingers. He interlocks them before kissing me again and every single time has my heart beating harder. He eventually hooks his fingers into my panties and I lift up enough for him to slide them down. His kiss travels from my lips to my stomach, until he's low enough to see just how desperate I am for him.

"Your pussy is so pretty when it's crying for me." He steals my breath away the minute his tongue flattens against me and my head falls back, making me unable to focus on anything but him. The way he teases me, the way he kisses every inch of me, his hands on my thighs, the scruff from his five o'clock shadow adding to the pleasure. When he sucks my clit into his mouth, I snap.

"Fitz, please." He kisses me so gently, as his eyes meet mine.

"What do you need, Trouble?"

"Your cock." He stands up immediately, hovering over me.

"You ready for me?" The hungry desperation on his face has my senses on overdrive, and my hands are already working to unfasten his belt.

"Yes!"

"Are you the pill?" he asks and I nod my head.

"Are you clean?" His hand caresses my cheek and his jaw ticks as he nods.

"All clear. Plus, I haven't been with anyone since you." I stop my attempt to unbutton his pants and look up at him, too shocked to say anything. My mouth pops open just barely, and he bites my lip, finishing unfastening his pants. He lets them fall to the ground and steps out of them, fisting his cock and lining himself up to my entrance.

"Hold on tight, Trouble." He plunges into me and my nails dig into his shoulders. I let out a moan and he sucks on my lip until I can catch my breath to kiss him back properly. He fucks me hard against the countertop, digging his fingers into my ass and swallowing every single cry of pleasure I give him. His hands move to unhook my bra, and he moves only long enough to discard it with the rest of my clothes. I lean back on my hands, letting my tits bounce as he hits a spot no one else ever has. Not even my drawer full of toys has accomplished a sensation like this.

"Fitz, yes! That feels so good."

"You take me so well," he practically growls before taking one of my nipples into his mouth, sucking it until I'm tingling all over. I feel my pussy contract around him and he pulls my head back up, forcing my eyes on his. "You gonna come for me, baby?" I nod my head, desperate for the release. His hand moves between us, putting just enough pressure on my clit to send me over the edge.

"Yes, right there, right there!" I whimper, seeing the fire in his eyes.

"Kiss me while you come for me, Trouble." I wrap my hand around his neck and pull his lips to mine, tasting myself with every swipe of my tongue across his. I wrap my legs around him, realizing only now that I'm still wearing my heels, allowing him to thrust even deeper into me. My moans are muffled as our tongues collide, and my body feels like it's floating when I come for him.

"Come for me, Fitz," I whisper against his lips, before biting his bottom one.

"Anything for you." He thrusts into me harder, making me see stars before he buries his face in my neck and I feel his cock pulsating inside of me.

He stands back to look at me, gently tucking my hair behind my ear and letting his forefinger caress my cheek. "I'd celebrate my birthday every year if I got to celebrate it with you."

Rip my heart out, why don't you?

Chapter 42

Lauren comes back from the bathroom wearing one of my Fitzgerald Firm sweatshirts, with the sleeves rolled up at her wrists, her hair still up but in a *just fucked* mess, and a pair of my gym socks. I, however, am in nothing but my black boxer briefs as she skips over to me, throwing her arms around my neck. I'm shocked when she reaches up on her toes and kisses me. Her lips are so soft, and her touch so gentle, I wouldn't mind living this night on a loop for a little while.

"Are you hungry?" she asks, tilting her head back to look at me.

"Starving." She bites her lip and grabs my hand to pull me behind her.

"I picked up your true love in food form, but it's clearly going to need to be reheated. I hope that's okay."

"Of course." I watch as she preheats the oven, pulling out a pizza pan and placing a few pieces on it, before grabbing the bottle of wine. I take it out of her hands and she frowns.

"Wait…was that drink at your dad's party the only drink I get to have *all* night?" I laugh and shake my head.

"No, I was just coming to pour our drinks. You've done enough for me today." I assure her, pinching her chin.

"*Hardly,*" she argues. "I'm a huge birthday girl. If you don't feel absolutely spoiled, then I have failed."

"Do people spoil you on your birthday, Trouble?" She smiles and nods.

"Yeah, my friends never let me down in that department." There's a vacant sadness in her eyes that I can tell she's trying to mask.

"Have other people let you down in that department?" I frown.

"It doesn't matter if they have or not. I know who to surround myself with on days when I want to feel good...when I want to be happy." I wrap my arms around her, resting my chin on her head.

"I'm sorry I brought it up, I just wanted to make sure you've felt just as special on your birthdays as you've made me feel tonight." I feel her smile against my chest.

"You haven't even opened your gift yet." The devious little smirk on her face has me curious what on earth she might have gotten me. She puts the pizza in the oven, sets a timer on her phone, and grabs the big ass bag off the floor that's been hiding behind the counter.

"Oh my god, you weren't joking." My eyes widen when I see the bag that's half her size.

"I never joke about birthdays." She holds the bag out to me and claps her hands. "Open it!"

"So bossy."

"So slow." I grin and start pulling the paper out of the bag. My brows pinch together when I pull out the first item. "A Taylor Swift record..." I look up at her and am terrified to react because I don't know if this is supposed to be a joke or not.

"I noticed you didn't have one yet," she says simply.

I choose the safest route with vague gratitude. "I certainly do not. Thank you." I look at it again, seeing the title *Midnights* written across the top, not sure what I'm supposed to do with this. Then she bursts into a fit of laughter. "What?" I'm starting to laugh now too simply because hers is so contagious.

"It's a gag gift, Fitz...Well, sort of."

"What do you mean, sort of?"

"Well I'm obviously going to make you listen to it with me because it's a *masterpiece*, but I didn't think you'd be like… jumping up and down excited about it."

"I'm gonna stop you right there, I don't get *jump up and down excited* about anything. The closest thing to make that happen would be seeing you naked, and if you're naked, I'm probably naked too and no one wants to see me jumping up and down like that." She gives me a seductive look and I shake my head at her.

"There's more, but the rest aren't gag gifts so if you don't like those then just…lie to me. Which is the only time in your life you'll hear me say those words." I reach into the bag and pull out another record, though this one is a Frank Sinatra collectible. I look up at her and she's chewing on the inside of her lip again.

"Sweetheart, this is amazing. Where did you find this?"

"You really like it?" She looks so hopeful.

"Of course, I do."

"I noticed last time I was here that you had a Christmas one but he has so many good non-Chrismtas songs that would sound amazing on vinyl." I look at it again, turning it over to look at the songs listed. "There's more." She jiggles the bag and I laugh at how impatient she is. I pull out the next item—a heated blanket.

"We already bought a blanket." I frown and her face falls.

"You've been without a woman in your life for far too long, there is no such thing as too many blankets. But there *is* such thing as too few, and that's where you're currently at."

"Noted." I look in the bag and see one last item, pulling it out with another confused look on my face.

"Turn it around." I turn the small package around and see a handwritten note taped to the back of the card game.

I want to get tUNO you better. Xo, Trouble.

I bark out a laugh reading the pun and she smiles. "I know it's cheesy, but it's also true, so…" She shrugs, letting a few pieces of stray hair fall from her bun.

I brush them out of her face, leaning closer to her. "Then I'll tell you anything you want *tUNO*."

Her hand shoots up to cover my mouth. "I instantly regret making that joke, please don't ever say that out loud again," she says through another fit of giggles.

"Fine," I mumble into her hand. She moves it when I stick my tongue out and lick her. She tilts her head in disapproval. "Thank you, Trouble. I think this might be the best birthday I've ever had." Her hand caresses my cheek, flipping it over to do it again with her knuckles.

"You're welcome." Then she presses her lips softly to mine, right before the timer on her phone goes off. "Pizza is ready!"

"I'll pour our drinks." She practically bounces over to the oven and I catch a glimpse of her ass when she bends over to pull the pizza out. When she stands back up and looks over at me, her hair back down in her face, my heart constricts painfully in my chest.

I fear I've fallen in love with my fake girlfriend.

"So, how does this work?" We're having a full-blown picnic on my living room rug, pizza and wine off to the side as she shuffles the deck of UNO cards.

"You've played UNO before, right?" she asks.

"Yes."

"Okay, so basically anytime you have to draw, you have to tell the other person something about yourself the other doesn't know. Skips skip your turn to ask a question, and reverse changes the order meaning you get to ask two questions in a row. Got it?"

"Did you make these rules up?" I ask, seeing the genius behind it all.

"Yes." She continues dealing the cards.

"Hm. Smart girl." She glares at me. "I'm serious." Her glare disappears.

"Oh. Okay. You ready?" She readjusts her position, grabbing her wine in her free hand.

"Let's do it. How do we know who goes first?"

"Fitz, it's your birthday. You go first, duh." We both set about three cards each down before I have to draw one. She does a little dance in her spot, taking another sip of her wine before setting it on the coffee table next to us.

"Something I don't know about you, go!" I think about it because I'm just not realizing how much there is we don't know about each other.

"Uhh, okay. I wear glasses."

Her eyes narrow on me. "Try again, genius. I already know that."

"How?" I try to recall a time I've worn them around her and come up empty.

"The night we ran into you at Lucky Bastard, you were wearing them."

"I was?" I frown, catching a confused look from her.

"Damn, and you say shit about how much *I* drink." I roll my eyes at her and she tells me to pick something else.

"Okay, uh… I played baseball in high school." Her mouth pops open and she looks me up and down. "You okay?"

"Yeah, just putting *buy Fitz baseball pants* on my to-do list for tomorrow."

"No, thank you." I take a sip of the wine Lauren picked, and I have to admit, it's actually good as hell.

She playfully scoffs. "Are you saying you wouldn't wear baseball pants for me?" I think about it for a minute.

"Just the pants, right? Not a whole uniform."

"No, that'd be weird." She scrunches her nose and I reach across and pinch it.

"Well, I don't know, you might be into that sort of thing." She starts laughing at me and I start sifting through my cards again. "Is it your turn yet? Mine has gone on way too long."

"Not my fault your first thing was something I already knew," she mumbles under her breath, playing her cards until she has to draw one.

"Finally." I sigh in relief.

She fires off her fact without hesitation. "I secretly went to cosmetology school before getting my degree in marketing."

"Why secretly?"

She shakes her head, wagging her finger at me as she finishes off her glass of wine. "No follow-up questions."

"I don't like these rules." She shoots me a sassy look and I pull out a reverse. "Yes! You again."

"Ginny was named after a character on one of my favorite TV shows because I was in the middle of a binge re-watch and was lacking in creativity." A second later I see movement out of the corner of my eye and jump. "Speak of the devil."

"Yes?" I tease, and she rolls her eyes at me. Ginny walks up and begins rubbing against my calves. "Hey there Gin. Where the hell have you been hiding?" I look over at Lauren and her cheeks have turned red.

"I put her in the bedroom when we got back." I'm curious for a moment if she knew where tonight might lead, but the fact that she locked Ginny up in another room along with that sexy lace number she had on, I think she just might have. "Your turn." I look down to see I have no cards and draw, thinking of another thing to tell her.

"The first, and only, tattoo I got when I turned 18 was a bull." She pours herself another glass of wine, topping mine off as well.

"Why a bull?"

"No follow-up questions," I remind her.

"Ugh, fine." The card I laid down was a draw two so it's immediately her turn.

"In eighth grade I memorized every single state flower and bird."

"*Please* let me ask a follow-up question," I beg, making her giggle.

"No! I was so weird and that's all you need to know." She hops up and takes the wine bottle to the recycling bin before returning to our game. Meanwhile, Ginny curls up on the couch and looks like she's going right back to sleep. I thought kittens were more active than this. "Okay, we're running low on cards so make your next one good," she yells from the fridge, and I look over my shoulder, only to see her hidden by the door of it.

"Do you want me to say it while you're in there?" I hear her mumble something to herself and then I hear something click.

"Uh, no. Just wait for me. Hey, can you close your eyes again?" I glare in her direction, fully aware she can't see me, then I do as she's asked.

"They're closed." I hear her shut the doors, followed by a cabinet and a drawer and I can't for the life of me figure out what she's doing.

I can feel her near me and a few seconds later she says, "Open them." The space around us is illuminated by two small candles, a three and a five, and she starts to sing *"Happy Birthday"*. As if tonight couldn't be more perfect, I see her face lit up by the candlelight, and her smile makes my heart beat just a little faster.

"Make a wish, Fitz." I'm not typically one to believe in wishes, but if there's a chance in hell this one will come true, I'm taking it.

I wish I could keep you forever, Trouble.

Then I blow out the candles and she sets the cake down on the coffee table next to us. "I hope this is okay. I was kind of stuck on what flavor to get, so I felt like cookies and cream was a safe bet. Maybe that can be your next fact because we did *not* discuss that on the plane ride here, and what girlfriend doesn't know her boyfriend's favorite ice cream flavor?" She stops mid-ramble and gasps. "Oh my god. Can you even eat ice cream? You're not like, lactose intolerant or anything are you? Do you even like ice cream?" I grab her face and kiss her to shut her up—something I've dreamed of doing more times than I can begin to count.

"I am not lactose intolerant. I do like ice cream. Cookies and cream was an excellent choice. You did good, Sweetheart. Thank you." I caress her cheek and see her relax a little more.

"Okay, good." She smiles. "Last card?" She looks down at the deck and I nod, picking mine back up, thinking of something else I could tell her that she doesn't know yet. I toss the cards down and she looks at me, puzzled.

"My real name is Vincent. Vincent Fitzgerald." The smile on her face, and the way it reaches her eyes, etches her deeper into my heart than she already was. She crawls over to me, straddling my lap before running her cool fingers through my hair. I can feel her short nails scrape along my scalp in the most soothing way before her hand comes down to rest on my cheek.

"Well then. Happy birthday, Vincent."

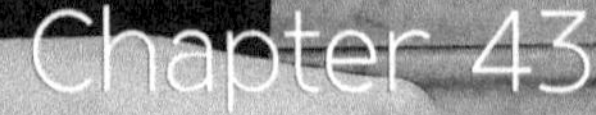

Chapter 43

Vincent Fitzgerald already has more of my heart than I've ever been able to give another person, and I don't know what to make of that. Last night was one of the most incredible nights of my life. From the look on his face when he walked through the door, to the late-night talking over a silly little made-up card game, I don't think I've smiled that much with a man…well, ever.

When I roll over and reach my hand out where his body should be, I feel that the bed next to me is empty, and a familiar feeling overwhelms me. I sit up, looking around the room, squinting when the sunlight filtering through his bedroom window shines right in my eyes. I get up and slip on the T-shirt I was wearing last night, then head to the bathroom before going to look for him. I hear the faint sound of a piano playing coming from the living room and when I walk in, I see a shirtless Fitz sitting at the old piano in the corner of the room, his hair a mess and a cup of coffee not far from his reach.

I tiptoe further into the room, trying to place the familiar tune, smiling when I figure it out. When I find where he's at in the song, I slide onto the bench next to him and begin to sing along to "Yellow" by Coldplay. The look of shock and amusement on his face when he looks at me causes my cheeks to redden. I watch his hands move over the keys and continue to sing until the song comes to an end. I can't help but bite the inside of my lip nervously as he watches me.

"Morning, Trouble."

"Good morning." He cups my cheek and kisses me, then turns around, straddling the piano bench to face me, so I mirror his movements.

"Where did you learn to sing like that?" The smirk on his face makes me feel like a middle schooler with their first crush—completely awestruck.

I shrug, playing a few keys with my right hand, catching another shocked look from him. "My parents had me in music lessons at six and piano at seven, up until I was a senior in high school."

"Why'd you stop? Did you not enjoy it?"

"I don't really know," I answer honestly. "I think I got to a point where I just went against most things my parents wanted for me, or *from* me, and even if it was something I enjoyed, I didn't want to give them the satisfaction."

"I can understand that," he mumbles and I look up at him again.

"Yeah… I thought you might." I smile softly at him, prompting him to grab ahold of my legs, pulling me closer to him. My legs drape over his hips, as he presses his forehead to mine.

"Have I told you just how much I loved spending my birthday with you?"

"Really?" I whisper, his hands cupping either side of my face.

"Really." His soft lips meet mine again, but this kiss is different than any we've shared before. It's slow and full of purpose. With every swipe of his tongue, my body yearns for more of this—more of him. My hands wrap around his neck, my thumbs moving lazily as he pulls my body closer to his, until there's no space left between us.

Ginny is sure not to let our moment last for too long, jumping up on the piano scaring the shit out of not only herself but me as well. I jump back and gasp, just as she meows and takes off into the other room.

"Jesus Christ," Fitz says, also a bit startled by the noise. I can't help but burst into laughter over it. "She's a little menace." He points to his room and my mouth pops open.

"She is not! She's an angel."

"An angel that clearly had some kind of concentrated catnip at about 3 AM. Did you not hear her in here? I fully expected it to look like I had been robbed when we woke up this morning." I laugh again, knowing that he's right but having no intention of telling him so.

"That's when she likes to exercise."

"She needs a new routine then. Or a kitty Bowflex or something. Shit." I roll my eyes and look over to see his gifts from last night are out and opened on the coffee table.

"How long have you been up?" I ask, moving to pick up the Frank Sinatra vinyl.

"Not too long, just wanted to get up before you to make some coffee." He shrugs, grabbing his mug from the piano and taking a sip as he stands next to me.

"Do you really like your gifts? You won't hurt my feelings if you say no. I know this is all…new." Ok, I would be a *little* hurt if he said he didn't like the Sinatra vinyl, I actually thought really hard about that one.

"I love them. Seriously. You know I'd tell you if I didn't." I look up and see the old version of Fitz I got so used to back in Nashville and my eyes roll again. He sets his coffee mug back down and pulls the vinyl out of my hand, putting it on the record player before he comes back with his hand outstretched.

"Dance with me, Trouble." I give him a sassy look, then slowly place my hand in his. I let out a gasp, followed by a giggle when he pulls me quickly into his arms. Holding one of my hands out to the side, his other rests on my lower back. He spins me around his living room, singing in a not-so-terrible voice, "Fly Me To The Moon" by Frank Sinatra. He boops my nose and winks at me, singing some of the lyrics with a surprisingly smooth voice. Making it hard to focus on anything other than the way he so confidently leads me around the room. My cheeks are practically cramping from smiling so hard when the song comes to an end and he dips me.

"Not bad. Maybe I should have let you take me dancing that night after all." I smirk at him and he raises a brow at me.

"We may not have made it to where we are now, had we only gone dancing, though."

I frown, confused. "What do you mean?"

"Now I can dance with you in the living room *and* the bedroom." He bends down, throwing me over his shoulder. When my shirt slides up, it reveals that I have nothing underneath it.

He slaps my ass and then— "Ow!" I squeal when he bites my ass.

"Sorry, Sweetheart, but you look absolutely ravishable."

"It's ravishing," I correct him, just before I get thrown onto the bed.

He smirks at me. "Not this time, baby."

"Shake a leg, baby. So much New York to see, so little time," Fitz calls from the door as I finish tying my shoes.

"Don't rush me! It stresses me out."

"Well, I have plans to de-stress you later, but only if we make it out of the apartment on time." My stomach flutters and I stand, throwing my fanny pack over my shoulder.

"Ok, boss. I'm ready to go."

He looks me up and down and laughs. "You look like a tourist."

I glare at him. "Then allow me to look for a new tour guide." I walk past him, placing my hand on the doorknob and turning it before he slams his hand on the door to keep it shut.

"Don't be a brat," he warns.

I look up and challenge him. "Or what?"

"I'll keep you locked up here all day."

I slide my hand up his T-shirt, running my fingertips along his abs before teasing the waistband of his boxers. "Mm. Don't tempt me with a good time." His hand slides off the door, heading straight for my neck, when I pull it open. "Is Rockefeller Center on the list? I've been dying to see it in person."

He growls in response. "You drive me fucking crazy, you know that?" I wink and blow him a kiss as he follows me out the door.

When Fitz said he had a whole day planned for us, I had no idea just how well he had planned it. We took more photos than I care to admit in Times Square. He surprised me with a picnic lunch in Central Park. We even went to the MET and the Statue of Liberty, before ending our day of touring at Rockefeller Center.

"Huh." I stand back and look at the busy streets, hearing Fitz laugh from beside me.

"It's a lot more magical when the tree is lit for Christmas."

I turn to face him, crossing my arms over my chest. "Yeah, I think that's the image I had in mind when wanting to come here."

"Then I'll have to bring you back for Christmas. Start shining your skates now." He wraps his arm around my shoulders, planting a kiss on the tip of my nose. "Okay. You see enough of New York yet?" he asks, and I exhale so hard I feel my whole body sag.

"Yes. I am exhausted." The smile on his face makes me curious.

"Good. We have a couples massage in forty minutes. Let's grab a coffee on the way."

Oh my god, this is the best day.

Our flight back to Nashville is delayed, and even though I am exhausted from this weekend with Fitz—in all the best ways—I don't mind sitting in the airport with him. We got stuck sitting on the floor since every seat in our boarding section is full, so we're propped up with Fitz's back to the window and mine against his chest. His arms hang lazily over me while I scroll through the photos I took this weekend. The one of us from his dad's party makes us look so high class, which feels absolutely insane. Then I select the picture of his apartment set up with everything I got him for his birthday, the video of me singing *"Happy Birthday"* to him, a photo of Ginny sleeping on his back—before her midnight aerobics started—one from Times Square, and another of my favorites from our picnic in Central Park. I click out of the app and set my phone up against my carry-on with the camera on a timer, then I look up at him and before I can say anything, he leans down and kisses my nose, making me smile.

I don't know what to make of him. Most guys hate taking pictures or have something to say about you wanting to capture every single moment, but Fitz never has… I wonder if he's just programmed that way from having to be in photos for business so often. I grab the phone and click on the picture, smiling so hard I feel my cheeks getting warmer.

"That's a good one." I agree and click back over and finish making my post, captioning it; *Surprising the birthday boy in New York, 10/10 recommend. Nashville here we come.*

"You are insanely good at marketing, you know that?" I shrink at the simple reminder that that is exactly what this is. Marketing a relationship for better business. "Hey, look at me." I turn around and see Fitz with his phone out.

"What are you doing?" I frown.

"For someone who took pictures all weekend, I'm surprised you have to ask." I glare at him and hear his camera click, causing my eyes to widen.

"Fitz! I wasn't ready." He keeps clicking away, earning more and more frustrated looks from me.

"Oh my god, you look so pissed." He laughs, causing me to giggle—against my will.

"I am!" I go to grab his phone and he stops me by linking our fingers.

"I got you now, Trouble. Whatcha gonna do?" I lean forward and lick his camera lens and his mouth pops open. "Ok, now you're just being a brat." He wipes the lens off on his hoodie, still not letting go of my hand.

"You bring out the brat in me, Fitz. Your suffering is self-inflicted."

"Well, as long as you're *my* brat, I can handle it." He smiles, pulling me back to him, and I suddenly forget why I was even mad. He kisses the top of my head, moving his lips so I can hear him. "Are you?"

I look back at him. "Am I what?"

"Mine."

"You tell me." His hand wraps around my neck, and he kisses me like there's no one else in the airport but us. My body practically melts into his, loving the way he claims me with his lips.

"Yeah, Trouble. You're mine."

"Fuckin' better be," I mumble under my breath. Though our close proximity doesn't allow me the distance needed to keep him from hearing.

"Don't worry, Sweetheart. I'll prove to you, *again*, just how mine you are as soon as I get you home."

"Why wait?" I glance over to the bathrooms right across from where our terminal is and I see the spark in his eyes as soon as his jaw tightens.

"Get up. Now." I shiver with anticipation as he lifts me to my feet. He grabs our bags, including Ginny in her cat carrier, in one hand and mine with his other, walking with purpose toward the family restroom.

Who the hell am I? And what the hell am I doing?!

Chapter 44

I'm hard before we ever make it in the door of the family restroom, ready to prove to her that I'll claim her anytime and anywhere, all she has to do is say the word. I drop our bags and lock the door, seeing the wild look in her eyes with only the slightest hint of reservation.

"I'd give you an out to change your mind, Trouble, but I don't exactly want to sit on a three-hour flight while my cock is hard as fuck, thinking about sinking into that sweet pussy of yours. So I'll give you the option, on your knees, or bent over the sink." She walks over to the sink, placing her hands on the edge, looking at me in the reflection of the mirror.

"Such a smart girl." I walk over to her, sliding her leggings and panties down, smirking when I see how soaked she already is for me. "So wet for me." I pull my sweatpants down, and tease her entrance with my tip, seeing her eyes grow heavy with desire.

Her hands grip the sink tighter as she presses her ass back into me.

"Greedy."

"Yes! Just fuck me already, stop teasing me," she grumbles. I pull away from her, fist my cock and pump a few times.

"And still a little bratty."

"I thought you didn't care if I was bratty if I was *your* brat." Her gaze pierces my soul and I swallow hard. "So then make me yours and fuck me before we miss our flight!"

I lean over her, my cock resting comfortably between her legs. "Say please, Trouble."

"*Please!*" she whispers, pulling all of my restraint away. I plunge into her, drawing a gasp from her that only makes me want to see just how many beautiful noises I can get from her before we leave this bathroom. I grip her hips, fucking her relentlessly as her back arches and her eyes fall closed.

"Look at me," I demand. Her pretty blue eyes open; still full of desire when they meet mine. "You still gonna be a brat?" Her mouth pops open just as I hit that sweet spot that renders her speechless, only allowing her to answer when I pull away.

"Probably," she finally says, with a devious little smirk on her beautiful face. I lean over her, sliding my hand beneath her shirt to pull her bra down, palming one of her perfect tits.

"And who's brat are you?" I nip at her ear, thrusting into her again, gently as my other hand reaches around to rub her clit. There are far too many clothes between us for my liking.

"Yours," she whispers, her eyes still on mine in the mirror. I grip her waist again, holding her in place as I pick up my pace.

"Say it, baby. Who's brat are you?"

"Yours!" she moans, and every time is like another hit of a drug I'll never get enough of.

Mine.

"Say my name, Trouble. Scream it for everyone in this damn airport to hear."

"Yours, Vince! I'm yours." I almost stop in my tracks at her words. Her eyes fly up to mine in the mirror, both of us breathing heavily.

"I'm sor—" I cut her off, spinning her around to place her on the counter, ripping her leggings the rest of the way off. I spread her legs and sink back into her, grabbing her neck to pull her lips to mine. Her fingers grip my hair and she spreads her legs even wider for me, erasing any space there was between us. I know she's close when her lips part and her pussy squeezes me like a vice.

"Say it again," I growl in her ear, thrusting into her harder, hitting that sweet spot over and over again until she's shaking.

Her head falls back. "I'm yours, Vince. Please, don't stop," she cries and it's the most beautiful thing I've ever heard in my life.

"You feel fucking amazing." I rush the words out before claiming her mouth again, letting her milk me until I've emptied every drop of my cum inside her. The bathroom is filled with the sounds of our breathing while my forehead rests against hers. I pull out, using my fingers to push my cum back inside of her when it dares to drip out. "Mine." I raise a brow at her, but her eyes are completely sated as she smiles back at me.

She hops down from the counter and glances at the toilet then back at me. "Can you uh, face the other way?"

"Why?" I give her a curious glance and she rolls her eyes.

"I don't want you to watch me pee," she says, like it should be obvious.

"After what we just did, you're going to be pee-shy?" I tease. She points to the door and I shake my head. "Ridiculous." I do as she asked, hearing her pee and flush before she finally gives me the okay to turn back around.

"Oh my god. Do you think Ginny is going to be traumatized?" Her eyes widen and she looks down at where Ginny is staring straight at us through the mesh in her pet carrier.

"If she made it through this weekend without calling her kitty therapist, I think she's probably okay with this." I raise a brow at her, and her cheeks turn red. Suddenly a montage of a naked Lauren on every surface I could fuck her on in my apartment plays in my mind.

"Kitty therapist," she scoffs, pulling me back to the present. When we open the door we catch glances from a couple outside with their two kids, and I look at Lauren and she looks at me. I hold Ginny up and smile.

"All yours." Then I grab Lauren's hand and head back to our terminal.

"Did you just try to make it look like we were in the family bathroom for our *cat*?"

Our cat…

"Yes."

"That's genius," she whispers, making me smile. We make it back just in time to be the last ones to board, and Lauren gives me a mischievous look when we get on the platform. I slap her ass and let her go in front of me, getting our bags in the overhead cabin before sliding Ginny under the seat in front of mine.

I let out a tired exhale when I finally get in my seat and when I roll my head to look at Lauren, her eyes are already on me. I give her a wink and she starts biting on the inside of her lip. I reach over and pull it out, knowing something has her anxious.

"What's the matter?" I sit up straighter, giving her my full attention.

"Nothing, just uh…" She looks around the plane and then leans in a little closer. "Were you okay with…with, you know?" This might be the first time, outside of the peeing situation of course, that I've ever seen Lauren look *shy*. I get the mind to push her buttons and make her squirm, the way I did when I first got to Coleson's, but this isn't something I want her feeling uncomfortable about. So I lean closer, whispering in her ear as my hand rests on her thigh.

"Was I okay with you calling me Vince when I was claiming you in an airport bathroom?" I watch her throat work as she swallows and her eyes cut over to mine. Her head nods so subtly I almost miss it. "Yes, Trouble. I was okay with it."

"Did you…like it?" She's choosing her words carefully, which is new for her since she usually says whatever the hell she wants to me.

"Yeah, actually. I did. You're the only one to ever call me that, and I'd be happy if you remained the only one."

"So, if it…slips. That's okay?" I smirk at her and grab her chin.

"Call me Lucifer, call me asshole, call me Fitz, or call me Vince. If you're calling, baby, I'm gonna answer." I press my lips to hers, feeling her beautiful smile against my lips when I pull away.

"Okay," she whispers.

"Okay." I smile back. Then I buckle her up, and she wraps herself around my arm, settling into the flight back to Nashville.

I only hope this doesn't all go away when we get back to business. Because this trip was definitely full of pleasure.

Chapter 45

Lauren

RUBY

Your post from this weekend is freaking perfect. 🫡

TAY

Why haven't you brought this hunky boyfriend of yours around yet? What are you hiding? 🫣

LEAH

I know she didn't elope after giving me shit about eloping when Sawyer and I got engaged.

SHANE

New fear unlocked, our last single friend getting married without us.

ME

It was such a fun trip. So glad I didn't chicken out. Tay, did you not JUST give me shit about him taking up my time??? and now you wanna hang with him? Please make up your mind. Leah, marriage is so far off the table, the table is still a tree. Shane, I would never do that, if I'm getting married, my girls are gonna be there. No questions asked. But again, we are NOT there.

RUBY

Girls night this week. You have a lot to fill us in on. We have yet to get the dirty details, and I refuse to be denied any longer.

TAY

Finally, someone with the right priorities.

SHANE

Max is asking if it's girls night, group hang or what?

LEAH

We're good with whatever.

ME

Girls night.

TAY

Why don't you wanna do a group hang?

RUBY

Tank asked about guys' night. We take the kids and the boys hang.

RUBY

He said Lucy is invited, of course.

I'm gonna throw up. Why is Tank inviting him? Not that Tank isn't a great guy, but he's only nice to like, eight people. I'd be lying if I said I wasn't terrified on Fitz's behalf.

I decide to switch to a single chat with Ruby since she and I are the only ones aware of what went down during the last hangout.

ME

Is he inviting him to interrogate or harm him?

RUBY

No! I don't think so…

ME

Ok, Rubes. That's kind of something I need you to be sure about before I tell my boyfriend he's invited to guys' night. Maybe knowing ahead of time whether it'll be his first or his first AND last would really help me calm down.

RUBY

He said no, he's not going to kill him. He said he'll play nice.

RUBY

Plus, Tucker, Sawyer and Max will be there.

ME

Yes, the three other guys he promised would help make Fitz disappear if he hurt me. That makes me feel so much better

RUBY

Lu! Has he hurt you?

ME

No…

RUBY

Then do we have anything to worry about?

ME

No… 😏

RUBY

Very good, now take a deep breath, and maybe a fucking shot, and get back in the group chat.

ME

GIRL GANG GROUP CHAT

ME

Ok! I'll let him know. When, where and what time?

SHANE

We can do girls night with the kids here, Mav and Ginny are welcome too, of course.

RUBY

The guys said they'll meet at Chattahoochies at 6 Tuesday. Is that good for everyone?

TAY

Good with us.

LEAH

Sawyer has something Tuesday, can we do literally any other night?

SHANE

We can do Monday or Friday.

ME

LEAH

We can do Monday!

RUBY

Monday works.

TAY

Works for us too.

ME

You guys realize the more people we add to this little family of ours, the harder it's going to be to find time to hang out, right?

SHANE

Well, you're the last one to add a person, so we'll just learn to make it work like we've been doing the last four and a half years. 

"You okay, Trouble? You look like you're going to throw up. Or pass out. Maybe both. Let me get you some water." Fitz walks over to my fridge and grabs a bottle of water for me. How do I tell him I'm worried some of my best friends are going to harass him or make him feel left out or beat the shit out of him without either making myself sound crazy, or making them sound like terrible people. When, in reality, they're just like…super protective.

"I'm fine." I didn't try hard enough to sell that, but he doesn't mention it. He simply moves in front of me and grabs my face.

"We're going to have a good time tonight, okay? Don't worry about me fitting in with your friends, I'm pretty good at adapting in new environments. Plus, it's not like it's the first time I've met them." He kisses my nose and turns to grab his keys off my counter, but almost as soon as I relax from his touch, I'm tense again.

"What do you mean you've met them before? When? Where?"

He looks at me with concern on his face. "You are really freaked out by this, aren't you?" I shrug, not wanting to lie, but not really wanting to talk about it, either. "Why?" He frowns. "Is it because you think I'm not going to fit in, or am I not the kind of guy you want to take around your friends?" My mouth pops open, shocked that he even said that.

"What? Fitz, no."

"I wouldn't blame you if you didn't. I mean you've said from the beginning how much of an asshole I am."

I storm over to him. "Fitz, no. Those were things I thought when I first met you."

"And what about now, Trouble? What do you think of me now?" His features are hard and all I want to do is help soften them again.

"I think I like the version of you I've been getting to know, and I want my friends to get to know him too." I reach up, cupping his cheek as he nods.

"You mean that?" The pained expression on his face makes me feel bad that my stupid anxiety ever made him question whether he was good enough to get to know my friends.

"Yes! I'm sorry I got so weird. I just…really want this to work. I want you to like them just as much as I want them to like you. They can be a little…rough around the edges."

"Yeah, I'll say," he scoffs. I frown when he agrees with me.

"What do you mean by that?" He shakes his head, brushing off the last statement.

"Nothing."

"That was not nothing," I argue as he checks his watch, kisses my head, and starts for the door.

"It's nothing, Trouble," he sings out, walking farther away from me.

"Vince!" He stops mid-stride and turns around, his features softer now. "Please don't lie to me. If it's really nothing and you were just saying that, then fine. But if something happened to make you agree with me, please tell me." He sighs and walks back over to me.

"A little while back, I was at a gym in town, not too far from my hotel, and I saw the guys there. I had met Max at the bar already, and I remembered seeing Tank at the office one day when he came to pick you up and I…may or may not have offered to spar with him." My eyes pop.

"And you're still *alive?!*"

"I think he took it easy on me." He laughs.

"Oh my god." My hands come up to cover my mouth. "Was that the week you came into the office with a busted lip and a bruised eye?" The look on his face is answer enough for me. "Why didn't you tell me?"

"That I got into a fight with a guy I saw pick you up from work, simply because I thought he might be your boyfriend and I was jealous? All while you still hated me. Didn't think it would really matter. You probably would have told me I deserved it."

I smirk at him and throw my arms around his neck. "You're right, I probably would have said that." He rolls his eyes and rests his hands on my ass.

"Go have a good time, and I'll see you later, okay?" I nod in agreement and he kisses me quickly. "Grab your bag. I'll walk you to your car."

I take a deep breath, then do as he's said. Once he's closed my door behind me, I take a deep breath before turning my key.

Everything is going to be fine.

Chapter 46

I can't remember a time I've ever gone out for a drink in something other than a suit and discussed something other than business, golfing, or someone's mistress. Going out for drinks in my world is always business or scandal related and I hate it with every fiber of my being. I pull up to Chattahoochies and lock up the Rover, sliding my keys into the front pocket of my jeans, shaking off any nerves I may have about this actually being an ambush by Lauren's friends. I must say, I much prefer the jeans, sneakers, and plain white T-shirt I have on for a night out than the suit I'm usually wearing when I grab a drink after work.

I see the guys standing at the bar, laughing about something, as soon as I walk in the door. They turn to face me as soon as it closes behind me and I'm surprised to see some of them actually smiling.

"Lucy! Get the hell over here." *Well, guess I'm stuck with that name forever now.*

"How's it going man?" Tucker holds his fist out and I bump it, nodding at Sawyer as I do. "Can't complain." I slide onto a barstool and Max pulls out a glass, pouring me a scotch. It's awkwardly quiet for a minute then Tucker breaks the silence, picking up in the middle of a conversation I was clearly not a part of.

"So how is this going to work anyway? We can't do teams if there's five of us."

"Matty is going to meet us there. I realized our dilemma about half an hour ago and figured I'd invite him too." Sawyer chimes in, setting his beer bottle down on the bar.

"Smart." Tucker snaps and points at him.

"Umm. What's happening?" I frown and see Tank smile, which is unnerving.

"Paintball."

"Ah," I say, finishing off my drink.

"Don't be too nervous, city boy. We'll take it easy on you." I take the jab quietly and smirk. After all, the result of our little sparring match probably has him thinking he's got me all figured out.

"I appreciate it, but I think I can handle myself."

"Let's get going then," Max says, clapping his hands together.

"You can ride with us. They're taking the bikes." Tank nods towards Max and Tucker, who are heading out the back, as Sawyer walks towards the front exit.

"Cool."

Tank comes in hot with directions, "Okay, so we're doing this in teams. Sawyer and Matty with me, Lucy, you're with Tucker and Max." *Why am I not surprised?*

"Sounds good."

"We got you, Rookie. If there's anyone you want covering your six, it's us." Tucker slaps me on the ass, taking me completely by surprise. "Let's do this."

"If he doesn't shoot you for that shit, I will," Max mumbles to Tucker, but I manage to hear it and have to stifle my laugh.

Halfway through our time in the field, someone yells, "Every man for himself." Splitting our teams up. I shake my head with a laugh. Why does this feel like some sort of hazing, or initiation of sorts? I get a hit on Tucker first, then Max, I make it a point to take a few shots on Tank when I spot him—just to make sure I didn't miss—then get Matty and Sawyer last. When the game ends my shirt is completely covered in paint, but so is everyone else's.

"Dude, where the hell did you learn to shoot like that?" Tucker asks me as we're turning our gear back in.

"I spent a lot of time hunting with my grandpa when I was younger."

"Holy hell. Color me impressed." He gives me a pat on the back, and we return to the rest of the group. "Spurs?" He looks around the group, and everyone mumbles their agreement.

I recognize the name. Lauren likes their food during her…less healthy weeks.

When I slide into the back seat of Tank's truck, I see him glance at me through the mirror. "What?"

"Nothing." He starts the truck, looking straight out the windshield as we wait for Sawyer to finish talking to Matty outside.

"You don't like me." He grumbles in response, and his eyes cut over to mine. "Look, our girls are best friends, apparently, so why don't we just address this now? That way Lauren doesn't have to freak out every time we're supposed to hang out together."

"Why was she freaking out?" He frowns, and it's then I see the genuine worry in his eyes.

"I don't know man, you tell me. She was clearly worried about us all hanging out, but out of all the guys here, you're the only one who doesn't seem happy about it. So do you mind filling in the blanks?" His jaw hardens and he shakes his head.

"Lauren is like family to me. I don't care much for people who hurt my family, and I don't know you all that well yet. Meaning I'm not so sure you won't hurt her again."

"Again?" I cut him off, confused by what he means.

He sighs, shifting the conversation. "Look, you don't have to worry about me, and neither does Lauren. You and I can be friendly, and everyone can play nice, but I believe that trust and respect are things to be earned, not expected."

"I agree, no one should blindly do either of those things if it hasn't been earned, but what do you mean by hurt her *again?* When have I hurt her?"

He shakes his head. "I don't feel like the details are mine to discuss."

The fuck?

"Then I'll talk to her about it."

"Good." His tone is clipped, like he doesn't want to discuss this any further.

"But let's get one thing straight." His eyes meet mine through the mirror we've been communicating through. "I would *never* intentionally hurt her. And I plan to apologize my ass off for whatever I did in the past to hurt her, if necessary. I'm crazy about her. So much so I'm actually scared to tell her for fear of running her off." I see him smirk, exhaling in a way that could be interpreted as a laugh, causing me to relax a little bit.

"Good. Then you and I shouldn't have any problems. Sorry, for the hazing," he mumbles the last part as he turns the volume up on his radio and I laugh.

"Sorry about that. Let's go, I'm fucking starving." Sawyer climbs in and slams the door shut.

"Yes, dear," Tank jokes, and while the two of them go back and forth talking about god only knows what, all I can think is…what did I do to hurt Lauren?

"Max? Is that you guys?" I hear a voice call from somewhere in the house. I look over and see him smile, then a second later tiny little footsteps come barreling down the hall.

"DADDY!" Max scoops up the little blonde-headed girl with a big ass grin on his face.

"Hey, my little sunshine."

"I'm still a little salty that she took my nickname." A grown-up version of the little girl rounds the corner, smiling up at Max before tucking herself beneath his arm.

"You know you're my Sunshine, first and forever." I look over at the little girl, who has her head bashfully resting on Max's shoulder and smiles. She buries her face in her hands and her mom laughs.

"You two, get a room." Tucker groans dramatically, hugging the woman. Then he growls like an animal and takes the little girl out of Max's arms.

"How's my favorite little monster doing?" He tickles up and down her back, making her giggle before disappearing further into the house.

"You must be Fitz, I'm Shane, Max's wife. It's nice to officially meet you." She smiles, extending her hand, and I quickly understand where her nickname stems from.

I smile, shaking her hand. "Pleasure to meet you."

"Lauren and the other girls are in the kitchen stuffing their faces with chips and queso, you're welcome to some if there's any left." She laughs.

"Thanks." I walk in the same direction Tucker went, finding the kitchen full of laughter and baby giggles. There's another little boy hanging on Tank's arm like a spider monkey, and a baby sitting in the lap of who I recall to be Ruby, Tank's wife.

"Get in here, Lucy. Make yourself at home." Tank's overzealous welcome makes me want to roll my eyes. The other dark-haired woman slaps his arm, and Lauren turns around with a frown on her face, then smiles when she sees me, waving me over to her.

"Fitz, this is Ruby, Taylor, and Leah."

"Hi," they all basically say in unison.

"Tucker is holding Cece, Max and Shane's baby girl. That little guy there is Poe, Tank and Ruby's youngest son, and this is Hendrix, their oldest."

"Nice to finally meet everyone." I nod, catching a glare from Hendrix.

"How do you know Aunt Lauren?" Hendrix asks.

"She and I work together and we're uh…dating." I look at Lauren and see her grinning, seeing how uncomfortable I am trying to answer that question with a child.

"Dad, is that the bastard from Aunt Lauren's work that made her cry?" My eyebrows jump to my hair and the room falls silent. Not even the kids are making noise, which just makes it more dramatic.

"Hendrix!" Ruby scolds him, as Tank wraps his arm around Hendrix to cover his mouth with his hand.

"Son, we're gonna go learn how to whisper, okay?" Tank drags Hendrix with him into the other room, and I stand there, not knowing what the fuck to do or say after that.

"I am so sorry about him, he's always been one to just say what's on his mind. He comes by it honestly, between me and his dad, I'm afraid." She raises her eyebrows at Lauren and takes a sip of her drink.

"No, I understand. What's that saying? If you want an honest opinion, just ask a child?" Ruby laughs, giving me a grateful glance, but when I look back down at Lauren, her smile has left.

"Did you um… Are you ready to go?" she whispers, looking at me for confirmation.

"Why don't we stay? I'd really like to get to know your friends a little better."

Her face lights up. "Really?"

"Of course." I smile at her, looking around the room to see that everyone has made themselves busy again. "But, uh…can I talk to you outside really quick?" She nods and stands up, telling the girls around the table that we'll be right back.

"We have cameras outside!" Shane yells, making Lauren's eyes widen at her. The girls are all giggling and Shane shrugs. "Do with that what you will." Lauren rolls her eyes and we walk through the backdoor.

Chapter 47

Lauren

Leave it to my precious godson to make it known in the first five minutes of Fitz being introduced to my friends that he, at one time, made me cry. Not only that but that Tank knows about it and called him a bastard for it. Oh my gosh, this is literally the worst thing that could have happened tonight. No, maybe not. Hendrix could have come up kicking him in the shins, so I guess that's a win.

I was sure Fitz would want to leave, and probably ask me what the hell that was about, but the fact that he wants to stay? I'm not quite sure what to make of that. I'm practically pinching the shit out of the inside of my thigh worrying about it.

"Lauren, what is going on?" He grabs my hand and I turn to face him.

"I hate it when you call me that," I mumble, hearing him laugh.

"Sorry, Sweetheart." I glare at him because he knows that's not much better. "What is going on?" His brow furrows and I shrug.

"Nothing."

"Nothing? Well, I don't think being called a bastard by a six?"

"Seven," I correct.

"Seven-year-old really qualifies as *nothing*. Start talking." I exhale shakily, wishing more than anything Tank hadn't seen how upset I was that day. This could have all been avoided had I just had a little better grip on my emotions. Which I *thought* I did, but clearly my friends can see right through me.

"The day Tank came to pick me up from work, was the same day I overheard you on the phone talking about the acquisition." A look of realization washes over him, but I continue when he says nothing. "While I thought I was hiding my emotions pretty well when I left the office, Tank knew something was wrong. It wasn't until you and I became '*official*' that I overheard him telling Ruby he wasn't sure he trusted you, simply because he knew that something happened while I was in your office that day, and it hurt me." He nods, taking in the information.

"Did you tell him it was a misunderstanding?"

"Yeah, I told him everything I could to make him understand. I'm sure Hendrix's comment has to do with something Tank said about you *before* I set the record straight, I just... I hate this. I hate that Hendrix thinks you made me cry, I hate that Tank saw me upset that day, and I hate that the first night you met my friends it ended up like *this!* All because I couldn't just tough it up about something as dumb as my job." Tears sting my eyes and my voice is starting to crack.

"Look at me." He holds my face in his hands, wiping a fallen tear with the pad of his thumb. "I am so sorry that something I was involved with hurt you. You had every right to be upset that day, and you didn't do anything wrong by reacting, do you hear me? You're allowed to care about your job, and the jobs of your co-workers, and be upset about thinking they would lose them. You're allowed to be pissed at me for not telling you about the acquisition—even though legally I wasn't supposed to." I let out a small laugh at that. "You are allowed to feel whatever the hell you want to feel, and you have nothing to apologize for." I smile at him and his face morphs into something a little more playful. "So what if Tank and his son think I'm a bastard that made you cry? I was a bastard for making you cry, but they're not the ones that I'm worried about proving myself to. They'll come around when they see just how important you are to me, and realize I would never do anything to hurt you." I shake my head and he smiles.

"Now, let's get back in there and show them just how awesome I really am." I laugh so loud I catch the attention of Riley, who had been further out in the yard somewhere. She comes running up to us and Fitz jerks a little.

"Do not tell me you're scared of dogs," I tease him.

"Just the ones that move like ninjas, where the hell did this one come from?" He starts looking around and I laugh again.

"This is Riley, she's Max's service dog." I pet behind her ears and she lays her head in my lap.

"I think I saw her at the bar before."

I smile, thinking of Riley and Maverick's booth. "You definitely did. It was either her or Maverick, Tank's dog."

"You said she's a service dog? What for?" I look up at him and smile.

"Let's go inside and he can tell you himself." He kisses my temple and we head back inside.

The rest of the night goes off without a hitch, and I couldn't be happier that Fitz wanted to stay. The guys hang out around the island talking about all of their occupations, Max and Tucker tell the story about how they enlisted in the Navy together and were able to serve on the same SEAL team, Tank tells him briefly about his experience in the Marine's, completely beaming when he starts talking about The Veterans Center he now runs with Asher—a guy he served with in special ops. Sawyer claims his occupation sounds boring in comparison, making Fitz agree about his life in real estate.

"Okay, quit hogging the new guy, we want to know about him too," Taylor yells as the guys start cutting up about something.

"You might just want to talk to your husband about his life some more, mine pales in comparison." Fitz comes over, standing behind my chair, playing with a few strands of my hair.

"Well, then tell me all about your boring life. We need to get to know our bestie's new man." I look up at him and smile, and he winks at me.

"Alright then. What do you want to know?"

Taylor taps her chin. "Hmmm. Where did you grow up?"

"New York." He sounds like he's ready for a round of rapid-fire questions, which is definitely a possibility with this group.

"Damn, you've lived there your whole life?" Ruby asks from where she now stands next to Tank.

"Yep. Born and raised."

"Did you always want to go into real estate?" Shane asks next.

He sucks air in through his teeth. "Uh, I always knew I would *end up* in real estate."

"Oh, he *so* wanted to be a cowboy or an astronaut or something." Taylor laughs, picking up on the way Fitz answered, and everyone joins in—Fitz included.

"I definitely wouldn't have chosen to go to college for business, marketing, *and* accounting degrees. But hey, at least I am not lacking in wall decorations for my office."

Max snorts and takes a sip of his beer. "Yeah, fuck that. I'd do two more tours before going through all that shit."

"Do you travel a lot for work?" Leah asks, turning back to face Fitz.

He slowly nods. "*All* the time."

"Do you enjoy it? I would imagine it would be exhausting having to travel all the time. For fun, it's worth it, but for work, it sounds… taxing."

"Eh, it can be. There are some weeks I'd rather chew off my own arm than get on another plane, but, I don't know." He shrugs, looking down at me. "Some assignments are better than others."

"So what is it you do? I would assume you're not selling houses across the country, that would take like…a lot of different licenses, right?" Shane is squirming in her seat and I would bet my morning coffee that her ass has fallen asleep.

Fitz clears his throat and when I look up at him he's giving me a concerned look.

Oh, shit. Right.

"He's an acquisitions manager, as well as an agent in New York," I answer for him.

"Acquisitions manager?" Taylor frowns. "Wait, is that why you're at Coleson?"

"He's legally not allowed to talk about it, but yes. The Fitzgerald Firm is buying out Coleson from Jack and Barbara. They need to sell to be able to retire without going bankrupt—and I trust that this information stays in this group." Everyone agrees, zipping their lips, nodding, or giving carefree shrugs—as if to say *who am I gonna tell*?

"Wow. It's so crazy to think that if Jack and Barbara never decided to sell you two would have never met." Leah smiles and my cheeks grow red when I feel Fitz's eyes on me.

"Isn't it?" he agrees, and I know I'm in for an ear full when we leave here.

"Okay, my ass is falling asleep in this chair. Let's move this party to the living room, shall we?" Shane stands up, shifting back and forth on her feet.

Ha! I freaking knew it.

I stand up to follow, and a cold chill shoots down my spine and my mouth begins to water.

Shit, I'm about to throw up.

"Uh, actually guys, I think we're going to head out." Fitz wraps his arm around me and everyone turns to face us.

Ruby's face is full of concern when she faces me. "Oh, no! Lu, you look like shit."

"Well, at least we know where Hendrix gets his truth-telling abilities from." I laugh, making her roll her eyes.

"Do you need anything? You need me to give her a ride?" Ruby looks at Fitz for his response.

"Nah. My car is still at the bar, I'll drive hers and get her home."

"Okay. Call us if you need anything but we know she's in good hands." Shane smiles at us and I offer a small one in return before the nausea returns.

"Let's go, Trouble." Fitz kisses my forehead, then waves to everyone. "It was really great meeting everyone."

There are multiple voices telling us bye, telling Fitz it was nice to meet him, and proclamations being made to do this again soon, and no matter how sick I feel right now, that brings a smile to my face.

We barely made it back to Lauren's place before she was practically falling out of the passenger seat to throw up. The color has completely drained from her face, making it absent of that usual rosy color I've grown to love. She made it to her bathroom to brush her teeth, but almost threw up again halfway through it, then went straight to her bed. She lies down on the foot of it, still completely dressed with her shoes on and everything, as her eyes begin to flutter closed.

"I hate throwing up in front of you. It's so not cute," she mumbles into her comforter as I slide her shoes off.

"Go to sleep, Trouble." She dozes off and I leave her room, shutting the door behind me before pulling my phone out. I check the time and say a prayer that the person I need to call isn't already sleeping.

Ring ring ring.

"Hello?" I smile when I hear her voice.

"Hey Gran."

"My boy. Is everything okay?"

"Yes and no."

"Oh? What's the matter, sweetheart?" I look back at Lauren's closed door.

"Well, my girlfriend is sick and—"

"Young man! Is *this* how you're telling me you have a girlfriend?" I smile as she calls Pops into the room, yelling about how I have a girlfriend and didn't call to tell them sooner. "Well, you're bringing her here for us to meet her soon, right?"

"If you want to meet her, I'll bring her up there soon."

"Damn right, you will." My mouth falls open in shock.

"*Gran.* I've never known you to be a swearing lady," I tease her and I can picture her face turning red.

"Well, I've never known you to call any woman you've been with your *girlfriend.* This is a big deal." I look, once again, at the closed door Lauren lays behind, with a sense of tranquility washing over me like rain.

"Yeah. It is."

"Okay then. You said she was sick?" I hadn't realized how comfortable I'd gotten calling Lauren my girlfriend without the weight of the "agreement" we made in the back of my mind, reminding me this all has an expiration date. Things got so real so quickly for me, I'm no longer sure if she's still just playing along—and playing *really* fucking well—or if she feels it too.

"Vincent Fitzgerald. Are you listening to me?"

I clear my throat and try to remember anything Gran said while I was spaced out. "Sorry, Gran."

"That's okay, dear. I know you're probably worried about her. I was just asking what was the matter with her. What kind of sickness?"

"Um, she threw up earlier and she looks really pale."

"Did she feel feverish when you touched her?"

"I don't know. Should I know what that feels like? Her hands are always freezing, but her forehead is always warm, but not hot. How do you know if someone has a fever?" There's silence on the other end of the line so I look down to make sure we didn't get disconnected. "Gran?"

"You're going to do just fine taking care of her, sweetheart. If she's hot to the touch but says she's cold, she likely has a fever. If that happens, she can sweat it out or try to get her in a lukewarm bath, and fever reducer is sold at stores over the counter so that won't be hard to find. Make sure she stays hydrated if she keeps throwing up. Chicken noodle soup and crackers with some ginger ale always does the trick—you should remember that." I smile, remembering all the times I got sick and Gran would make me her famous chicken noodle soup and run me a bubble bath to help my muscles relax after contracting from vomiting so much.

"I do. Thank you, Gran."

"You're more than welcome. So…what's she like? This girlfriend of yours." I smile, feeling a wave of emotion creep its way up my throat as I try and put into words what Lauren is like.

"She's…amazing. She's incredible at her job, she's an amazing friend, and has such a big heart, but she's funny and witty. I mean, she puts up with my shit and still sticks around, so that says a lot about her." That makes Gran laugh. "She's like…you know how it feels to watch the sunrise? How captivating and calming it is to watch something so beautiful just… exist? That's what she's like. She's the sun to me."

"Well, I can't wait to meet her. Call me if you need anything else, but I think you're more than capable of giving her what she needs, Vincent."

"Good night, Gran."

"Good night, my sweet boy." I hang up the phone and swing into action, looking through her fridge and cabinets to see if she has any of the things I need.

She doesn't, of course. I check in on her one more time, placing a trash can right beside where she's lying and tuck a piece of hair behind her ear, but when I hear her snore I know I should be in the clear to run to the store and make it back before she needs me again.

Her fridge is fully stocked with sports drinks and ginger ale, chicken and vegetables for homemade chicken soup, and ingredients for one of

Gran's special recipes for when she can keep food down again. I even grabbed some bath salts and bubble bath for her, and a new blanket just because it's soft as hell and I wanted her to feel it. I strip down to my boxer briefs, then help her out of her clothes, leaving her in nothing but her underwear while I look for a T-shirt to put on her. She makes little noises as I pull the shirt down over her head and lift her to take her to her side of the bed, taking the trash can with us before putting her phone on the charger and climbing into bed too.

Ginny climbs back up on the bed when I'm finished relocating Lauren, curling up in the bend of her knees, and while the two of them sleep, I turn the TV on, keeping an eye on Lauren just in case she needs me. I don't even feel sleepy, but the next thing I know, I'm waking up to the sound of Ginny meowing so loud you'd think she was stuck in a trash can. I look at the clock, noting that it's just after 5 AM.

"What is your damage, porch cat?" She walks into the kitchen and meows again, clearly summoning me to follow her. Then she paws at her empty bowl.

"You are just like your adoptive mother, you know that?" I pour food in her bowl and she starts chowing down. "There you go, girl." I head back to Lauren's room and pull her curtains closed, not wanting the sun to wake her up in a couple of hours when she should be resting. Then I slide back into bed next to her, and she rolls over, laying her arm on my chest. Then she lets out a little sigh and I smile, kissing the top of her head before dozing off with her.

Chapter 49

I wake up covered in sweat, my hair thrown into some makeshift bun, with little pieces falling out on all sides, and wearing a T-shirt that I don't remember changing into last night.

"Hey beautiful, you feeling okay?"

I look over at Fitz with a pouty frown. "I feel gross."

"Are you still nauseous?" he asks, touching my cheeks with the back of his hands, moving to my forehead, and then down to my neck.

"Not at the moment, but that's subject to change." I roll my neck and stretch my shoulders. "My body hurts though and I'm starving." I look over at him, only to see that handsome-as-hell smirk on his face. "I'm sorry. I'm sure I'm fine. You didn't have to stay."

"Shh." He leans forward and kisses my forehead. "Where else would I be?"

In your hotel room, far away from me and my vomit?

He stands up, and I take the opportunity to admire his physique. I've seen Fitz naked or in his boxers plenty of times—his summer-tanned skin, his tattoo, his toned muscles, and messy black hair all make my mouth freaking water—in a good way. Today, something just seems different, and I can't quite explain why.

"Come here." He scoops me out of bed and my arms fall around his neck.

"Fitz, put me down. I smell like the inside of a gym bag," I complain, secretly hoping he doesn't listen—he doesn't. He walks into my bathroom, and I immediately smell eucalyptus. When we make it to the tub, he places me on my feet and I see my soaking tub full to the brim with bubbles. I look at it and back up at him, my eyes trying to betray me by watering.

"Suddenly decide you needed a bath?" I try joking with him. His face remains serious as he reaches down and grabs the hem of my T-shirt, pulling it over my head. He wads it up and tosses it to the side, and I try to ignore how his movements affect me.

"No, Trouble. I'm taking care of *you.*" He slides my panties down next, and I take a deep breath to steady myself. His hands rub from my calves all the way up to my hips, and when he stands back up, I look down to see he's just as turned on as I am.

Is it normal to be this turned on when you're sick? Aren't I supposed to feel like death, or want to be a blanket burrito?

If so, I am far from normal…

He holds his hand out and helps me step into the bath, and I hum in appreciation of the hot water, soothing my muscles. I sink down, letting my neck rest on the edge of the tub. When I look back up at Fitz, his eyes are dark and his gaze travels from my chest up to my face. He smiles when he reaches my eyes and moves to kneel behind me. He takes my hair down and goosebumps spread across my skin. He massages my head, then grabs my brush from the counter, gently combing through the tangles.

"Mmm, Fitz. That feels so good." His lips move beside my ear and I lean my head back.

"Good. You deserve to feel good." My eyes flutter open, finding his already on me, and I feel this ache in my chest for him. Which seems so crazy since he's literally right here.

"Fitz?" I whisper.

"Yes, Trouble?"

"Touch me." I see his jaw flex, and his throat work as he swallows.

"Where?"

"Everywhere." His hands move from my hair, down to my neck, leisurely rubbing his thumbs in a circular motion until he slides them to my shoulders, doing the same thing. When he moves them down my arms, his thumbs barely brushing the side of my breasts, I gasp. He rubs all the way down to my wrists, and back up to my shoulders, before his hands move to my chest, slowly sliding down to my breasts. He massages them with the perfect amount of pressure, gently pinching each of my nipples before moving down to my stomach. I want to tell him to go back to my breasts, but I can't manage to form words when his hands are working this kind of magic on me.

Suddenly, his hands disappear and all I can do is frown before he appears at the other end of the tub, reaching into the water to grab one of my feet.

"You're not ticklish are you?" he asks, and I smile and shake my head.

"Not on my feet," I tell him, making him quirk a brow at me. Then he begins massaging my feet and I make a note to never pay for another massage so long as I have Fitz and his magic fingers. He switches feet, rubbing them all the way up my calves before putting them back in the water, then he's at my side.

"Feeling better yet?" He tucks a strand of hair behind my ear and I bite my lip, nodding.

"Yes." His eyes narrow as he studies my face.

"What is it? What do you need?"

"Will you get in with me?"

"Anything you want, Sweetheart." The contempt that used to accompany that nickname, is no longer there. Instead, it actually sounds endearing when he says it, and my heart flutters. He stands up, dropping his boxers, and I slide to the middle of the tub, giving him room to get in behind me. The water sloshes as he steps in, rising closer to the edge when he settles in. Then he grabs my shoulders and pulls me back to his chest. I lay my head on his shoulder and he kisses the top of it, running his hands along my arms.

"Do you need me to take you to the doctor today?" he offers, making me smile.

"I don't think so. My stomach just feels a little queasy, but I don't think it's anything serious. Maybe food poisoning? I've never had it before but my enchiladas last night did taste kind of questionable."

"Where did you guys eat?"

"Food truck on Main Street," I tell him, feeling him pause.

"Well, no wonder you got food poisoning."

"Hey, food trucks and gas station food are severely underrated."

"You are unbelievable." I can hear the laugh in his voice and I turn around to look at him, all joking matters aside.

"I was going to say the same thing about you." His eyes soften as he moves one hand from the edge of the tub to cup my cheek.

"And why is that?"

"You stayed, you took care of me."

"Is that really so hard to believe?" His free hand begins to travel over my body again, his thumb flicks my nipple and I guide his hand to palm my breast like he did earlier. "You like that?"

"Mmhm." My eyes fall closed again, and he moves his hand between my legs. They open for him immediately, giving him access to slide his fingers inside me. I wrap my hands around his arms, the need for more of him growing stronger with every pump until I can't take it anymore. I sit up, prompting him to slide his fingers out. I turn around and face him, reaching for his cock under the water, loving the hunger that flares in his eyes when I wrap my hand around him and begin pumping.

"You don't have to—" I cut him off before he can say anything else.

"I want to." He licks his lips, staying quiet and allowing me the freedom to continue. "I want *you*."

He grabs my waist and pulls me closer until my hands are on his shoulders and I'm perfectly positioned above him. "I'm yours for the taking, Trouble." He fists his cock and lines himself up to me, and I lower myself onto him.

"Fuck," he hisses. "You feel amazing."

"Really?" I don't mean to say it out loud, since I usually keep my insecure thoughts to myself, but it just…slips.

"Baby, your pussy was made for me. Nothing feels as good as when I'm inside you." I bite my lip, rocking my hips as he presses harder into me. His grip on the tub is turning his knuckles white and I love knowing that I'm the one making him feel so good. That I'm the one that's pushing him closer to the edge every time I tighten my walls around him.

I stop rocking my hips and start bouncing up and down instead, without a single care in the world how much water is spilling out of the tub every time I do.

"That's it. Just like that." Every time he speaks my climax inches closer and closer. I reach up, squeezing my breasts, and pinching my nipples, craving the sensation as I continue riding him. "Look at me," he demands, making my eyes fly open. "You're so fucking pretty, baby. Keep playing with those perfect tits while I fill your pussy with my cum." His hand slips between us, putting the pressure on my clit that I need to come.

"Yes, yes, yes," I whisper. My body begins writhing with pleasure as he grips my hips, keeping the pace that I'm slowly losing control of. I take the place of his hand, playing with my clit to bring my climax to completion, and when I think I can't take anymore, he thrusts harder, hitting that spot inside of me that makes me want to scream in delight.

"Fuck, Vince!" I hold onto his shoulders, as he slows down, his cock pulsing inside of me as I'm filled with his cum. He wraps his arms around me, my head resting on his shoulder as I sink into his embrace.

"I'll never get enough of you, Trouble." I roll my head and kiss his neck. "Now, let's get in the shower so I can wash your hair."

I sit up and frown at him. "Why are we moving to the shower?"

"Because as soon as I pull out of you, there's a chance I'll be washing your hair with my cum."

"Right." He leans up, biting and kissing along my neck, as his cock pulses inside me again.

If this is a dream. I hope I never wake up.

After our shower, Fitz insisted he bring me my food in bed, told me to pick a show to watch, and that he would take care of everything else. He comes back in with a bowl of soup that smells absolutely amazing, a pack of crackers, and a sports drink, as well as one of my tumblers full of ice water.

"I got you water too 'cause I haven't seen you drink much in the last couple of days."

"Are you real?" I poke his face and he smiles, making me question the fact even further because who is actually this hot *and* sweet?

"Stop, you'll give me a big head then yell at me for my ego." I purse my lips and turn back to face the TV, pressing play on the show I picked.

"Hmm…true."

"There she is." He laughs and I look at him in confusion.

"What do you mean?"

"It's been a while since your little attitude showed up, I was starting to think you were sicker than I thought."

"I guess you've just been keeping it fucked out of me."

"Is that it?" I smile and shrug, seeing him shake his head at me. He hands me the bowl of soup and I blow it off before taking a bite, completely mind blown at how good it is.

"Oh my gosh, this is amazing." I scoop another bite in my mouth, watching his face light up. "Where did you get this from?"

"Gran's old recipe. Always did the trick when I was younger." I look over at him, putting the bowl in my lap.

"You *made* this?"

He shrugs. "Yeah." My mouth pops open, but no words come out. I don't even think my own mother ever made me anything other than microwaved Campbell's soup when I was sick growing up. "I have another surprise for you for dinner, but I wanted to make sure you could keep food down before making it. It's not a dish you want to…lose." His face scrunches and I laugh.

"I don't deserve you."

"Trouble, you deserve so much more than me." I place my bowl on my nightstand and crawl onto his lap, tucking a still-wet piece of hair behind my ear. I cup his face in my hands and plant a soft kiss on his lips. No words are exchanged, we simply kiss, then he tucks me under his arm, I grab my bowl of soup, and we watch Netflix until we fall asleep.

Best. Tuesday. Ever.

Chapter 50

Fitz

Lauren watches from the barstool as I finish placing the pie crust onto the top of the chicken pot pie I'm making for dinner. I have to admit, I'm pretty proud of my work, and I think Gran would be too. So long as it comes out tasting like Gran's, I'll be happy.

"So…you can cook." I throw the kitchen towel over my shoulder and face her, after setting the timer on the microwave.

"Yes, I can cook." Her eyes narrow on me.

"I hate to say this, but I totally took you for the type to order takeout on the nights you're not at some fancy-ass dinner making big business deals."

I can't help but laugh at how accurate that is most of the time. "Well, you're not entirely wrong. Actually, you're kind of spot on. When I'm in New York that's exactly what I do. When I'm here, I basically live on room service or restaurants near my hotel since my father didn't put me up in a room with a kitchen. Apparently, he thinks I should be able to survive in a room with a mini fridge and a microwave for what? Seven months?"

"You haven't had a home-cooked meal since you came here?" Her eyes widen and I shrug.

"And long before that. I don't typically cook for myself."

"Why not? That soup was the best soup I've ever had and if the smell of that pot pie says anything about how it's going to taste, then you're a solid cook." I smile at the praise.

"Cooking was something I always did with Gran and Pops—mostly Gran—but cooking alone just made me feel…well, lonely."

"Did you spend a lot of time with them growing up? Your grandparents?" I hop up to sit on the counter next to where her barstool is and sigh.

"Most people don't really know this, since I was always brought around for the big, photo-worthy moments with my parents, but Gran and Pops practically raised me. My parents were off taking the real estate world by storm and left my upbringing to them until around the time I was in high school. Then my father started taking me to events with him, grooming me to take over for him someday." She makes a disgusted noise and I look down to see the angry look on her face.

"They never even *asked* you what you wanted to do in life, did they?"

I laugh at the very idea. "No. I was an only child so the family business going to me just…made sense. I was excited about it for a while, the way they talked about the lifestyle I'd have was every kid's dream, but things changed when I got to college. The comments about how I needed to handle my workload better, that I needed to prioritize the company if I wanted to be a good leader some day, and that I needed to stop spending so much time at Gran and Pop's house or I'd never get accustomed to the life I was *meant* to live. Meanwhile, the life they were trying to pull me away from had become what I wanted."

"Fucking assholes."

"Yeah, well…I quickly turned into one of those assholes." I drop my gaze and her hand appears on my leg.

"Hey, that's not true." I'm grateful for her trying to make me feel better, but she's still wrong.

"It is, though. I lost so much of what I actually liked about myself, becoming who my father wanted me to be—*him*. I started hanging out with CEOs or their kids, depending on who was closer to my age.

Which is how I got involved with Jessica Vanderbilt. We would party every weekend, and I sat idly by and watched as so many shady deals were made amongst some pretty powerful businessmen, simply because that's where my father wanted me to be." I look at Lauren, trying to gauge her reaction, but she's just…listening. Not cutting me off, correcting me, or making excuses for my behavior. She just listens. It's refreshing. "When I finally got sick of all the partying, I cleaned up my act, stopped hanging out with those people—the ones I knew were shady, anyway—and I started focusing on work the way my father always wanted me to and poured every ounce of myself into the business. I was outselling every other agent at the firm, I was training multiple teams in marketing while assisting the accounting team when they needed it—"

"God, that sounds awful."

"Yeah." I laugh, humorlessly. "And it still wasn't enough for him. You know I've never once gotten my father's stamp of approval. For anything. The bastard works more than he's home with my mother, so I stayed at work all hours of the night. He's a shark in sales and jumps on properties before anyone else gets the chance, so I started making offers people couldn't refuse, just to secure a place he wanted. He's selfish and entitled and I became his fuckin clone, and he still isn't satisfied."

"Vincent Fitzgerald, look at me." I look over at her, trying not to smile. I love it when she gets bossy. "You are *nothing* like your father."

"How can you say that? When I've just told you everything I've done to become like him?" I look at her in bewilderment.

"Because you may be telling me everything you've done in the past that you think makes you like him, but I've *seen* everything you do that makes you the complete opposite of him." I scoff, not believing her. "The first night I met you, you saved me from some handsy stranger trying to get lucky. You offered to take me dancing to let me have a good time and protect me from other scumbags without an ulterior motive. You went as my date to my best friend's wedding when I was upset about being the only one without a date—"

"Well, to be fair, there were selfish reasons behind that one." I wink at her and she smiles at me, rolling her eyes.

"You also missed work today to stay with me while I was sick. You stocked my fridge with food and drinks, you made me homemade soup and chicken pot pie—which smells absolutely amazing, by the way. You drew me a bath and…took care of me. You're not a selfish man, Fitz. Now, hold on to your dish towel because I'm about to say something nice, but you might just be one of the most selfless people I've ever met."

"You might be the only person who's ever seen that side of me."

She rests her chin in her palm and gazes at me. "It's one of my favorite sides of you."

I slide off the counter to grab a drink, walking back over to lean against the counter next to her. "One of? What's the other side you favor?"

"Dat ass." She slaps my butt and I burst out laughing, pulling her from her seat and into my arms.

"You are so weird," I mumble into her hair, as I try burying my face in her neck. She giggles and wiggles around until her arms are draped over my neck. I brush her hair out of her face, and her features soften.

"So, what did you want to be when you were younger?"

My heart expands when she becomes the first person ever to ask me that. "A cowboy." She laughs out loud and I smile from simply seeing her happy.

"If you're serious, Taylor will never let us forget she was right about that." I barely kiss her lips before her phone starts vibrating on the counter. We look over at the same time and I see the name *Mother* appear on the screen. She lets out a frustrated breath before walking over to pick it up, hesitating before she slides the icon to answer it.

"Hello?" I watch as she rolls her eyes. "Yes, Mother. I didn't forget." She pulls the corner of her lip in with her teeth, chewing on it. Then her face falls and her mouth pops open. "But I—" She falls silent again and her eyes meet mine. I'm instantly on edge when I see the worry on her face. What the hell is being said on the other end of this call that's making her look like…well, like she looked last night. "Okay. I will. Bye."

"What's the matter?" She slides her phone back onto the counter, crossing her arms over her chest.

"Um, my mother was reminding me about our family dinner this Friday." When I look into her eyes they're distant, unfocused on anything as she stares into the living room.

"Oh?"

"Yeah…" Her eyes finally meet mine. "She told me to bring my new boyfriend with me."

"Is that a bad thing?" I frown, unsure why she seems so worried by it.

"It's just… I wasn't expecting it. That's all."

"I'm sure everything will be just fine." I kiss her nose and see her relax.

"It's just that—"

I move my finger to her lips to stop her. "I'm not scared to meet your parents, Trouble. So you shouldn't be either."

"I'm not scared I just—" The oven timer goes off, stopping her again.

"Why don't you *just* let me feed you, rub your feet, and help you forget how anxious you are about this dinner, okay?" I offer, seeing her glare at me.

"Well, I'm smart enough to know not to turn that down."

I can't believe I'm actually going to meet her parents. Her meeting my father was bad enough, maybe this will make up for the poor parent introductions. Seeing as how I can't imagine any interactions between her and *my* parents will ever go well. I'll just have to charm hers enough to make her see that she has nothing to worry about.

Chapter 51

Lauren

I have thought of about fifty different ways to get Fitz out of going to this dinner tomorrow night, and all of them would make it insanely obvious that I don't want him to meet my parents. Which would probably raise questions, and since I don't want to lie about anything else in my life, I'd have to tell the truth and at that point he might as well just meet them. I click my pen repeatedly as I stare blankly at my computer screen. The fact that I don't even have the motivation to work today because I'm so worried about this has me tense and irritated. I've got a knot in my neck the size of a golf ball and no matter how much I try to get it to go away, it just keeps coming back with a vengeance. My phone vibrates on my desk and I look down to see Fitz's name pop up on the screen.

FITZ

You look…troubled.

I look up to see him standing down the hallway, facing me with his phone in his hand, as one of the tech guys stands with a laptop in his hands in front of him.

ME

Just a knot in my neck I can't get rid of. I see you're back to your old ways of texting while someone is speaking to you. 😌

FITZ

Well, he's not talking, he's waiting for this computer to load to ask me a question and insisted I stay right here because it would be "really quick"

ME

I'm more surprised that you listened.

FITZ

Well, I can't beat the view from here.

I bite my lip, smiling down at my screen.

FITZ

Stop biting your lip. It drives me almost as crazy as you rolling those pretty blue eyes.

I look up to see a smirking Fitz, and of course, roll my eyes.

FITZ

What happens when you roll your eyes, Trouble?

ME

You give me a reason to.

FITZ

Do I need to come in there and make good on my promise…again.

ME

You wouldn't.

I watch him from my office, then look down and wait for the text bubbles to pop up but they don't. A moment later I hear my office door shut and look up to see a very hungry-looking Fitz locking the door.

"Fitz, what the hell?! You scared me to death." My hand flies up to my chest and he makes his way over to my desk, laying his palms flat on the top of it, his icy-blue eyes burning a hole in mine.

"You're a fucking tease, you know that?" I smirk and stand up from my chair, walking around to where he's standing before running a hand down his back.

"I would never." My tone causes him to turn and face me. I'm about to walk back over and open the door, ushering him back to his IT guy, but he grabs my wrist and pulls me around to face him. Then he takes several calculated steps towards me, causing me to back further and further into my office.

"But you *do*. Every single day. Wearing these dresses that accentuate every delicious curve you have. In these heels I'd like to have wrapped around my head…or my waist." He finally stops when I bump into a table, and my chest is heaving with every breath. The scent of his cologne surrounds me, intoxicating me. He smells so good I just want to strip him out of his damn suit and wrap myself around him.

He picks me up, causing me to squeal, and plants my ass firmly on top of my printer. "Fitz, what are you doing?"

"I need you, baby." Then his hands wrap around my neck, and his lips come crashing down on mine. I spread my legs and grip his suit jacket, pulling him closer. I relax when I feel the warmth from his body on my thighs. His tongue swipes along the seam of my lips and I part them. He tilts my head back to deepen our kiss, claiming me with every movement.

"Does this work?" he growls against my lips, pulling at the zipper that goes all the way down the front of my dress.

"Yes," I answer breathlessly. He doesn't hesitate to pull the zipper all the way down, shoving the dress off my arms, leaving me in nothing but my bra, underwear, and high heels. I hold his shoulders as he grips the waistband of my thong, lifting myself up for him while he pulls them down.

For a split second, I wonder, who the hell I become when I'm with him? If you would have told me a month ago I'd be sitting half naked in my office, about to get fucked on my printer by the guy I yelled at for stealing it once, I'd have said you were delusional. But I know who I become when I'm with him. I become his—to do with as he pleases—because there's nothing he's given me that I haven't been eager to take.

Which is why I move swiftly to unhook his belt, pulling his pants down just enough to free his cock, that's already hard and glistening with precum for me.

I wrap my hand around him, pumping at a painstakingly slow speed. "How bad do you need me, Fitz?" I tilt my chin up, seeing his eyes darken and the muscles in his jaw tighten.

"More than air, Trouble. I might stop breathing if I'm not sinking into your pussy in the next thirty seconds." He presses his hips forward, but I tighten my grip on him, causing a growl to rumble in his chest.

"Say please, Fitz."

"Please, Trouble. I'll fucking beg if I have to." I slowly tease my entrance with his tip, and his hands grip either side of my ass. "But I really don't want to have to beg."

"Why not?" I narrow my eyes on him and slide just his tip inside.

"Because I want you to need me just as badly." Before I can respond, he uses his grip on my ass to plunge into me and my mouth falls open with a silent scream. "Fuck, I love the way you fit around me." He looks down between us, watching as his cock slides almost all the way out of me before he sinks back in. I hold onto his shoulders as he picks up his pace, causing the printer to hit the wall with every thrust.

"Don't stop, don't stop," I plead with him, feeling my climax inching closer and closer. He pulls one of my breasts out of my bra, sucking it into his mouth without losing his rhythm. The sensation is almost too much to handle. I can feel him everywhere and I just want *more*.

"Yes. Harder."

"Someone is going to come barging into this office with as much noise as we're making," he tells me, keeping the same pace as before.

"I don't care. You better not stop." The devilish smile on his face at my words has me wrapping my hands around his neck to pull his lips back to mine with urgency. He pulls my other breast out, palming it as he thrusts so deep inside me, tears spring to my eyes. I've never felt anything like this with anyone before. The desperation to feel someone the way I feel him. His hands on my body, his lips on mine, his scent all over me, and his cock hitting places I never knew possible before him.

"V-V-Vince." I can't even catch my breath as my climax travels from the tips of my toes, all the way up my back until I'm gripping his shoulders for dear life, trying to keep from screaming his name.

"I've got you, baby. Soak my cock with your sweet cum, I'll swallow every one of your screams." Then his lips are back on mine, and he does just what he promised. Every moan that tries to escape me he swallows. Then he pulls away and wraps his hand around my mouth, tight, as he fucks me even harder. His eyes travel down my body, watching from where we connect, to where my tits bounce freely, back up to my face—where there's a longing in my eyes I'm sure he can see.

"Your eyes have always been one of my favorite things about you, but fuck. They're even prettier when they're begging for me." He smirks at me and my body is on fire again as another orgasm hits me out of left field. I moan into his hand and he thrusts twice more before I feel him empty himself inside me. He moves his hand from over my mouth and leans in to kiss me. It's soft and sweet in comparison to the way he just absolutely railed me. When he pulls out and takes a step back I hear something that causes my eyes to widen. Fitz helps me down, and his cum leaks down my leg as he picks my dress up from where I was sitting. I turn around and my hand flies to my mouth when I see the absolute trash pile that is my printer.

It's completely busted, the small screen on the front is glitching and the paper tray is holding on by a thread.

"You actually put a label that says *Property of Lauren Long* on your printer?" he snickers and I turn around to glare at him.

"You literally just fucked my printer to death and *that's* what you're worried about?" He gives me a playfully defensive look.

"Well don't make it sound like I had my dick in the cartridge holder, that's weird." I snatch my dress from his hands and start getting myself dressed.

"You owe me a new printer." I zip my dress up and fluff my hair, trying to *not* look like I just had office demolishing sex. Fitz is smirking at me as he rights himself as well, fixing his suit jacket and running his fingers through his dark locks. Then I pick up my phone and scroll through to catch up on everything, smiling at the picture Shane sent of Hendrix, Cece, and Poe in the kiddie pool at their house.

Fitz clears his throat. "Should I be jealous of whatever you're smiling at?" I look up at him, locking my phone before I toss it back down on my desk.

"What are you doing right now?"

He frowns. "That didn't answer my question. But nothing. I.T Steve can get fucked." My face falls and he shrugs. "What's up?"

I roll my eyes, sitting in my chair to finish up the email I abandoned earlier. "Well, the group wants to go out this weekend and I want to go shopping for something to wear. You wanna go with me?" I expect him to regret telling me he had nothing to do and say he's actually going to go finish helping IT, but I'm surprised when I look up to see him smiling.

"Hell yeah. I'll drive."

"We have an hour and a half before my showings start, think you can handle it?" I hit send, lock my computer, and grab my bag from beneath my desk.

"This may surprise you, but I *have* been shopping before."

I smirk at him. "Not with me you haven't." He gives me a confused look, but when I go to walk around my desk, my expression soon matches his.

"What's the matter?" he asks, stopping at the door.

"Where are my panties?" I whisper, catching a glimmer in his eye.

"Where they need to be." He pulls them out of his pocket and my eyes pop.

"Fitz. I need my underwear back. What if I have to try on clothes?"

He shrugs. "Then you can have them back then. For now, they're staying with me." He shoves them back in his pocket and opens the door, waving a hand for me to walk out first. I catch Luther standing in the hallway with his mouth hanging open.

"We're heading out." I wave a finger between me and Fitz and he raises his eyebrows suggestively.

"Happy hump day." Then he looks Fitz up and down, and I move in front of Fitz, tilting my head at Luther before pushing Fitz out the front door.

"You're cute when you're jealous, Trouble," he whispers in my ear before opening my door for me.

I roll my eyes at him. "I'm not jealous…" I kind of am, but I know it's stupid to be. I adjust to the feeling of his cum between my legs as I sit down and he leans in closer to me.

"I would *never* break Luther's printer." He winks at me and I have to fight the smile trying to creep onto my lips.

"Shut up and get in the car."

"Yes ma'am."

Girl Gang Group Chat

TAY

Lauren, Do you think Fitz would be down to line dance this weekend?

SHANE

Is it a miracle that we're hanging out twice in one week or am I dreaming?

RUBY

100% a miracle. Betty is so looking forward to having them all over again.

LEAH

This is all subject to whether Lauren and Fitz can make it or not. You know she's a travel girly now.

RUBY

I will personally come punch him in the nuts if he says no and ruins this for us.

TAY

Maybe you shouldn't, since your son just called him a bastard like four days ago. That might give him a complex.

RUBY

Secure men don't get a complex from a seven year old's comment.

LEAH

As a teacher I would like to debunk that myth right the fuck now. I have cried from things my kindergarteners have said to me.

SHANE

I would also cry if a child was mean to me.

RUBY

We are WOMEN. We are historically more sensitive than men. Tell him to grow a pair, grab a cowboy hat and fucking DANCE.

SHANE

attachment 1 photo

RUBY

Awww. my BABIES 🥹

ME

Y'all are absolutely insane. He doesn't have a complex 😌 I'm shopping for something to wear on my lunch, I'll be there and if Fitz wants the privilege to strip me out of whatever I find, he'll be there too.

TAY

Have I told you lately I'm obsessed with you?

ME

No, actually and now I'm pissed about it.

TAY

I'll make it up to you tomorrow night. 😉

SHANE

Yay for plans working out!!

"We're at a thrift store." I look over at Lauren after parking in the lot she told me to pull into.

"No. We're at my *favorite* thrift store." She unbuckles and goes to open her door, but I reach across her and shut the door again.

"Absolutely not." She frowns at me and I unbuckle my seatbelt. "I'll get your door." Her smile returns and I smirk.

"Okay. So, line dancing this weekend. You in?" We walk up to the door and I open it for her.

"If you're there, I'm there, Sweetheart." I can't read her expression when she looks up at me, then she turns around and continues talking.

"Perfect. We can look for something for you to wear too. Taylor requested a cowboy hat, but I don't trust thrifted hats." Her nose scrunches as she grabs a cart. "Okay. Let's go." She walks with purpose and I follow her to a section with color-organized tops. She thumbs through them quickly, picking out a few tops that have me dying to know what she would look like in them. When she picks up a blue and white checkered tank top with lace trim around the neckline, and turns it around to reveal a single tie in the back, leaving the rest open I grab it from her hands and throw it in the basket. She quirks a brow at me.

"It's the same color as your eyes." Her cheeks turn red and she takes a breath and looks around the store.

"Okay. If we're both going to have time to shop, we're going to need to split up." She peeks her head up over the aisle and points in the opposite direction. "Men's clothes are over there. Think, western throwdown, yee-haw, going to the rodeo outfit, and pick something accordingly."

I snort and nod. "I think I can manage to find something to wear line dancing."

"Go." She shoos me away and I laugh. I make it through the entire men's section and when I make it back over to her, my arms are full.

"Do you see this?" She looks up from examining a pair of jeans and smiles. "They have this shirt that still has the tags on it for *three dollars*. Then this." I put it in the basket, holding up the next item. "A whole freaking collection of designer dress shirts that look brand-fucking-new, all in my size." Her smile grows as she watches me. "I even found this pair of boots over there that look like they just need a little bit of polish and they'll be good as new." I hold up the pair of square-toed boots and her expression changes.

"Well, looks like we both had a successful trip. I am getting that top you picked, these jeans, *and* how cute is this?" She holds up a brown suede fringe jacket. "It'll match my boots perfectly." She lets out a happy sigh. "I love thrifting."

"No shit. It's like finding hidden treasures."

"You're not joking. I found my favorite pair of designer pumps here for *ten dollars*!" I stare at her blankly so she elaborates. "They're almost a thousand dollars retail."

"Jesus Christ." My eyes pop. "I want to see you in them tonight." I smirk at her and her expression turns sad.

"Unfortunately, that won't be happening. Ginny chewed them up the night I brought her home. I cried for two days about it." She checks the time and turns the basket around. "Oh, time to go!"

"Hey Lauren, find anything good today?" The woman at the counter asks with a smile on her face.

"I always do," Lauren answers with a wink.

"Well, I know you didn't find *him* on the rack, I would have kept him for myself." The woman sizes me up and I chuckle.

"Ms. Margaret, are you hitting on my man?" she teases, but I stay hyper-focused on how that sounds coming from her mouth.

"Well, out of all the things we have come through here, you two are by far the prettiest. Y'all sure would make some pretty babies." Lauren laughs and shakes her head. "Those blue eyes and that dark hair? Oh, what a little angel."

"You have quite the imagination, you know that?" Lauren hands the woman money for our things and I curse myself for not paying enough attention to beat her to it.

"It keeps life interesting for me." Lauren smiles at her and squeezes her hand.

"I'll see you Sunday."

"See you Sunday, dear." I grab the bags from the counter and we walk out into the summer heat as Lauren pulls her sunglasses from her purse, sliding them onto her face as she waits at the passenger door for me.

"Smart girl. I'm proud of you for learning so quickly not to touch your bags or door handles when I'm around." I kiss her temple and open her door as she slides into her seat with a smirk on her face.

"So, Margaret is fun." I sigh when I settle into the driver's seat. Lauren lets out a laugh and pulls her seatbelt on.

"Yeah. She lost her husband to cancer a few years back and opened the thrift store not long after. I saw it on my way home from work one day, stopped in, and we ended up talking until closing. I think she's lonely, you know? I just want to make her feel…less lonely." The sadness on her face as she looks back in the window of the store makes me love her even more. Her heart is so big.

"We *would* have some cute babies, you know?" She shakes her head and pulls out her phone.

"Drive the car, Fitz." I can't read her expression, but it seems this is a conversation we won't be having… For now, anyway.

I went to Lauren's showings with her today, simply because I haven't heard from my father since his birthday, for work or otherwise, so my workload is light, to say the least. We're back at her place now and she's just gotten out of the shower when I come back in from being on the phone. She's standing in her towel staring at the clothes hanging in her closet. I walk up behind her, inhaling every bit of her scent that I can.

"What's the matter, baby?" I rest my chin on her head.

"What do you mean?"

I turn her around to face me, appreciating her natural beauty. "You seem…nervous?" She exhales and I know I'm right. I just don't know *why* I'm right.

"Well, that's just a side effect of these dinners as a whole. It has… very little to do with you."

"Me?" I frown.

"Not *you*. Just my parents meeting you. I just… I hope they're nice, that's all." A forced smile appears on her face and I would do anything to turn it into a real one.

"I promise, everything is going to be fine. Okay? I have thick skin. They could call me garbage and I'll stay by your side until you're ready to go. Then we can go buy me a shirt that says *Hefty* on it." Her brows pull together in confusion when I run my forefinger and thumb across my chest. "Like, the trash bag brand?" I explain and she starts laughing.

"There's that smile." I grab her face and pull her lips to mine. She finishes getting dressed, and I match her style accordingly. She's wearing a blue dress, much like the ones she would wear to work, with a pair of tan booties, and her hair straight, so I chose a pair of cropped khaki slacks, my white sneakers, and a navy blue sports coat with a simple white T-shirt underneath.

She stands back and assesses me, arms crossed over her chest as her head tilts. "You might be the only guy I've ever liked in khakis."

"Thank you?" I squint in confusion.

"Ready?" she asks, grabbing her bag from the kitchen counter, petting Ginny's chin before heading for the door.

"Let's go, good lookin'." I slap her ass and she looks back, her hair whipping around her face as she rolls her eyes at me.

Lauren demanded she drive us tonight, and at first, I didn't know why, but when we pull into the mile-long driveway with a circle drive and a fountain in the center of it, I'm even more confused than I was before. Whoever lives here is absolutely fucking loaded. You won't find a place like this in Nashville for anything under a million dollars. I look at her in confusion, seeing her throat work as she swallows.

"Welcome to my childhood home."

Well… I didn't see that coming.

Chapter 53

Lauren

I'm going to throw up.

"This is where you grew up?" Fitz stares at the massive house we're parked in front of, then looks over at me in surprise.

"Yep." I pop the p, trying not to pass out due to my anxiety.

"I don't understand…"

I open my door, stepping out onto the gravel drive, as he does the same. "You will." We walk up to the front door and I ring the bell. I can feel his eyes on me, but force myself not to give in and look at him. My mother swings the door open, looking me up and down before a smile finally forms on her face.

"Lauren," she practically sings in delight.

"Mother." I smile and her gaze moves to Fitz.

"And you are?" *Ugh.*

"Mom, this is Fitz. Fitz, this is my mother." My mom holds her hand out and Fitz shakes it.

"Nice to meet you, Mrs. Long."

My mom smiles brightly at him. "You can call me Anna, Mrs. Long makes me sound ancient."

Fitz smiles and nods in agreement. "Of course."

"So, are we having dinner on the front porch, or can we come inside?" I ask as the smell of whatever dinner has been prepared finds its way outside.

"Of course we're not, don't be ridiculous." Mother turns around, leading the way to the dining room, expecting us to follow her. I close my eyes and take a deep breath, trying to brace myself for the night ahead. Fitz closes the door behind us and I hang my purse on one of the hooks in the entryway, taking his hand as we walk to the dining room.

"John, Lauren and her *boyfriend* are here." I roll my eyes at her tone, feeling Fitz squeeze my hand. My dad enters the room a moment later, walking straight over to us.

"John Long." He holds his hand out and Fitz shakes it firmly.

"Vincent Fitzgerald. Pleasure to meet you."

"Oh, Vincent. What a lovely name. Why did you introduce him as Fitz?" My mother looks at me questioningly and my teeth grind together.

"Because that's what he goes by." My father nods and turns his attention back to Fitz.

"*So,* what is it you do, Fitz?"

Here we go.

I hear that same tone from him as I heard from my mother earlier and I start to question why on earth I ever agreed to this.

"I own a skateboard shop." I almost choke at his response, looking up to see him wink at me.

"You do?" The absolute horror in my mother's voice brings me joy.

"Oh yeah. I've owned it for about five years now." My father looks at me, desperate for the punchline.

"It's a joke, guys. Calm down." I assure them, seeing them both physically relax.

Fitz clears his throat, shoving his hands into his front pockets casually. "Sorry about that, I couldn't resist. I'm actually in real estate, same as Lauren."

"Oh, well. That's fine." My father's tone drops and I scoff.

My father gives me a scolding glare and I feel myself emotionally shrink while wishing I had the ability to *physically* shrink. I look at Fitz apologetically and he turns back to my father.

"Actually, my father owns The Fitzgerald Firm in New York, maybe you've heard of it?"

"Oh, yes! It's one of, if not the most, prestigious firms in New York," my mother chirps.

"And growing by leaps and bounds if the articles I've seen are correct," my dad chimes in.

"That they are," Fitz confirms. My parents' faces light up so much we could practically screw them into the chandelier. "And I'm supposed to take over as CEO next month."

"Oh, how wonderful." My mother links her arm through Fitz's and walks him further into the dining room. "You know, we always encouraged Lauren to do more with herself."

"It's true. We could have gotten her to any Ivy League or top school of her choice. She would probably be running my law firm by now had she applied herself. Much like you'll be taking over for your father. Such an honorable career choice—taking over the family business." My father cuts his eyes to me before taking a sip of his drink.

"I mean, she had every resource imaginable at her fingertips. She could have done something truly amazing had she just taken what we tried to give her, don't you agree, Vincent?" She bumps Fitz with her elbow, and I am so close to coming unraveled. Every stitch in the armor I've made over the years to deal with my parents, slowly falling apart as they make digs about my life to the one person I've ever felt comfortable sharing it with.

"I'm sorry." Fitz laughs humorlessly. "Is this some kind of joke?" My mother's face twists and my father tilts his head in confusion. I look up at him, wondering where he's going with this.

"What do you mean?" Mother asks.

"You daughter is one of the most down-to-earth, capable, kind, and hardest working people I've ever met in my life. She could out-sell some of the best agents in New York, myself included, if she so wished because she pours her heart into her work. Hell, she could probably run the damn company if that's what she *wanted* to do. I'm proud of her for taking a chance on herself. Have you ever thought, for one moment, she's doing exactly what she wants to do, and doing it *well*? Have you taken even a single second to admire the fact that your daughter is completely self-sufficient? That she didn't *need* an Ivy League school, or your connections and resources, to build an admirable life for herself? Shame on you, shame on both of you, for ever making her feel like she isn't good enough, simply because she didn't choose to live her life the way *you* wanted her to." I'd kiss him right here and now if I could see to get to him.

"How dare you come in here and insult us this way? Who are you to tell us we shouldn't want more for our daughter? Maybe you'll understand when you have children one day. When you're a parent you do whatever it takes to make sure they are doing their best in life—"

"No. That's where you're wrong." Fitz cuts him off. "I would do whatever it takes to make sure *my* kids knew they were loved, that I was proud of them, and that no matter what they did—skateboard shop owner or CEO of a company—that I was fucking proud of them."

"Funny to hear you say that when you are who you are—wealthy, well connected, inheriting an entire company. Self-sufficiency and capability will only get her so far in life. A well-established career in something, knowing people who could help her if she ever got in a pinch, these are things that will take her farthest in life. Don't you dare come in here telling us we've done anything less than our best for *our* daughter, when you're being handed exactly the life we tried to give her."

"Enough!" I yell, pulling everyone's attention to me. "How dare you speak to Fitz that way?"

"Did you hear the way he spoke to us?" The disbelief on my father's face is priceless.

"Yes. I heard it. I also heard, for the *first* time in my life today, that someone was proud of me. I will not let you sit here and speak to him like you know who he is when you have no *idea* who he is—and you don't deserve the chance to get to know him the way I do. We're leaving." I grab Fitz's hand and pull him behind me, hoping I can make it to the car before I completely fall apart. I'm in such a hurry to get out of the house that I forget my bag.

"Shit, I forgot my purse." I turn around to get it, but Fitz's hands land on my arms and he stops me, holding up my bag in his right hand. I finally bring my eyes to his and I completely lose it. "I am so sorry, Fitz." He pulls me closer, his hand cradling the back of my head as I bury my face into his chest.

"Shh. Don't you dare apologize for them." His grip tightens on me and I let myself fall apart in his arms. I've never cried like this in front of anyone, not even my best friends have seen me in pain the way Fitz is right now. "Look at me." I pull away, blinking past the tears waiting to fall from my eyes, and he gently pushes some hair out of my face. "Why didn't you tell me?"

"I didn't know how." I sigh, running my hands over my cheeks. "I don't talk about this part of my life. I only see my parents every so often for Friday night dinners, though I'm starting to wonder why I've even been doing that. I know they don't approve of how I live, but I guess I always thought if they saw how successful, or happy I was that...I don't know. Maybe they'd realize their way wasn't the only way." I meet his gaze again.

"I just hate that you felt like you couldn't tell me. Of all people, you should have known I would understand."

"I know. I know, I'm sorry." I hide my face in my hands, but he pulls them away just as fast.

"Baby, stop apologizing." He ducks his head to catch my eye.

"I guess I just got scared. I didn't want you to think differently of me. I've separated myself so much from this life that it doesn't even feel like part of me anymore."

"I know exactly who you are, Lauren Long. Nothing your parents say or do could convince me that I don't." He leans down and kisses me, taking every bit of my anxiety and sadness away with the simple touch of his lips on mine.

Today was the last straw for me. I'm never coming back here. If they want their daughter back, they're going to have to prove themselves to *me*, not the other way around. Not anymore.

"Take me home, Fitz. Make me forget about today. Please."

Of all the reasons I imagined Lauren was so nervous about going to her parents' house, them being rich assholes who don't know what an amazing person their daughter is definitely didn't make the list. I've never seen her cry, not like that at least. It makes me want to march back in there and punch her dad in the nose, but instead, I focus on her. The way she stares out the window as I drive her car back to her house, how I hear her sniffle every now and then before trying to hide the fact that she's still wiping her tears away. I can't park the car fast enough and pull her door open, scooping her into my arms before she can even put her foot on the ground.

"What are you doing?" There's no giggle in her tone, or mischief in her eyes. Just a gray version of who she usually is as I approach her front porch.

"Do you trust me?" I ask, placing her feet on the ground and unlocking her door.

"Yes." I take her hand and guide her inside, closing and locking the door behind us. I toss her keys on the entryway table and she kicks off her shoes, so I do the same. Then I lead her into her bedroom, and stop her at the far corner of the bed, angling her to face her massive, full body mirror that's propped up against the wall. I walk behind her, watching as her eyes stay locked on me.

"Look at yourself." Her eyes glisten and she shakes her head no. "Yes." She takes a sharp breath and finally moves her gaze to her own reflection.

"Tell me what you see." Tears stream down her cheeks again, and I can see the plea in her eyes not to make her do this.

"Failure. Disappointment. Never good enough." Every word out of her mouth is like a knife in my heart. I run my hands along the length of her arms, pressing my nose into her hair, inhaling her scent to center myself.

"Let's fix that." I kiss her head and she sniffles.

"Tell me something you've done that made you feel successful."

"I don't know." She sobs, and it's taking everything in me to stay on task.

"Think."

"I bought my own house." She shrugs and I smile.

"Good, what else? Name as many as you can think of."

"I helped Tank and Ruby buy a house before they brought Poe home. I've done that for a lot of families, actually. I've been the top sales agent at Coleson for three months straight."

"Success. Not failure."

"Tell me something you've done that you're proud of."

"Planned Tank and Ruby's wedding in two days. Helped Amy figure out what season she is." I have no idea what the hell that means, but I'm not interrupting the process to ask. "Planning your birthday surprise." Her eyes find mine again, and I smile, nodding for her to look at herself again.

"Satisfaction. Not disappointment."

"Tell me something that makes you feel confident." Her lip quivers and she rolls her eyes in frustration. "Don't be embarrassed. Anything that makes you feel confident. Anything at all."

"Knowing I can take care of myself and Ginny. Putting together the perfect outfit or getting my hair or makeup just right on the first try." She turns around to look me in the eye. *"You."*

My heart bursts wide open as I look into her sad eyes, so full of truth and longing. "What?" I ask in disbelief.

"You make me feel most confident, Fitz. Anytime I'm with you, I feel invincible."

"I want you to feel that way every single day. You are successful, without the help of *anyone* else. You bring so much joy and satisfaction to so many people's lives, you have every right to feel proud of yourself. And you are the best person I've ever met in my life, the world doesn't deserve you, Sweetheart. You are more than enough, and I need you to start believing it." She reaches up and kisses me, and I completely melt into her touch. It's soft and desperate like she just wants to make this moment last.

Her hands move to slide my jacket off my arms, pulling at the hem of my T-shirt as soon as it's on the ground. I move away from her long enough to pull it over my head, then I pull her dress over her head before my lips are back on hers. She moves to unbutton my pants and when her hand slides into my underwear, wrapping her cool, slender fingers around my cock, it pulses in her grip. I reach behind her and unhook her bra, desperate to have her completely naked. When she steps back to drop her bra, she keeps my gaze as she slides her panties down her beautiful, tan legs. I follow suit, letting my pants and boxers fall to the ground, taking a step towards her. Those baby blue eyes are locked on mine, and as much as I love her looking at me, I want her to know she's the focus tonight. So I turn her back around to face the mirror.

"Do you even realize how fucking perfect you are?" I trail kisses from her neck all the way down her shoulder, moving in front of her to continue my path along her breasts and stomach. When I'm tongue level with her pussy, her fingers glide through my hair, and her legs part, inviting me in.

On my knees for her, I lift one of her legs over my shoulder, holding her steady by the grip I have on her thigh and ass. She moans when my tongue splits her entrance and the taste of her has me starved for more. I kiss and suck her clit into my mouth, plunging my tongue inside her tight cunt, until I can feel her dripping down my throat and chin. I'm so hard my cock is actually aching to be inside her. I fist it and pump a few times, trying to find just an ounce of relief. I hear her moan at about the same time and I look up only to find her watching me.

"Like what you see, Trouble?" She bites her lip and nods. I circle my tongue on her clit, increasing my speed until her legs are shaking and her fingers are gripping my hair so tight it stings my scalp.

"Yes, yes, yes. YES!" Her thighs squeeze around my head and I suck her clit again, making her scream. I stroke myself again as I slide her leg off my shoulder, standing to face her.

"Such a sweet pussy." Her cheeks are flushed and I love the way she smiles at me. I pull her up by her thighs, her legs wrapping around my waist, as I carry her a few steps to the bed. I lay her gently on her back, her legs never unhooking from around me, and I line myself up to her entrance, pressing into her slowly. Her eyes are on mine as she sucks in a breath and it's at this moment, I know with a hundred percent certainty, I never want to look into anyone else's.

I lean down and take her lips in mine, loving the way she opens up, allowing our kiss to deepen. With every concentrated thrust, every swipe of her tongue, I'm falling further and further into her orbit. I don't want to be anywhere but here, with her, surrounded by her, inside of her. My need for her grows stronger, and while I hoped I could keep things gentle for her, and show her just how precious she is to me, I can't hold back any longer. I bite her neck as I thrust harder, hitting deeper just the way she likes it, as her nails dig into my back.

"Fuck," I mumble into her hair, fucking her like I'm trying to meld our bodies into one.

"Vince." She whispers my name like a prayer and I'd absolutely bleed myself dry to ensure she never stops saying it. I lean up, grabbing her chin to turn her face towards the other side of the room.

"Look at us," I demand. "If you didn't see anything else in our reflection tonight, I want to make sure you see this."

Thrust.

"How desperate I am for you."

Thrust.

"How well you take me."

Thrust.

"How absolutely incredible you are. Tell me you see it." She nods her head, keeping her eyes on the mirror. "Tell me." She looks back up at me, her eyes falling to my lips before they meet mine again with a vulnerability I never thought I would see in them.

"I see it," she whispers.

I smirk at her and grip her hips. "I'm so proud of you." I let go of any and all control with her, bending down to kiss her again, palming her breast, pinching her nipple until her back arches into me. Then I move my hand between us, lifting up to watch her face be completely overtaken with pleasure as I circle her swollen clit with my thumb.

"Vince! Oh my god, don't stop. Please!" I see tears fall from the corners of her eyes as her hands grip the sheets. Her walls tighten around me and her body is writhing as I continue chasing my release, ensuring she enjoys every second of hers.

"That's it, cry for me, baby." Just as another orgasm causes her back to fly off the bed, I come so hard I can't fucking see straight. The only sound in the room is our labored breathing, and sweat is covering my entire body when I tuck her hair behind her ears, drying the remnants of her tears. "The only time I want to see tears filling those pretty blue eyes is from me making you feel so fucking good you can't help it. Not for anything or anyone else." A hint of a smile plays at her lips. "You are Lauren. Fucking. Long. Incomparable to all others. I want you to remember that the next time anyone tries to make you feel inferior."

Lauren

I really wish I had someone to talk to about the *fake* part of my fake relationship right about now. Fitz has been staying at my place more often than not, because who wants to sleep at a hotel every night? It's just been an unspoken understanding since the first time I told him to stay, but he still has things at the hotel. Which is where he currently is to get things he needs to go line dancing tonight, meaning I've been alone with my thoughts for a tad too long. Ginny makes the occasional noise when she scratches her kitty tower or starts chasing reflections around the room, but she isn't exactly the best at keeping me out of my head about what's going on with me and Fitz. I know Ruby would have great advice on the matter, but things just feel too messy with how everything started between us, and the fact that Tank practically hated him in the beginning. If they found out we've been lying this whole time, what would they think of him? What would they think of *me*?

Fitz comes stumbling back through the door with a huge suitcase, a duffle bag, and a rather large cardboard box in hand, causing me to turn on my barstool and stare at him.

"Um… Did you rob someone on your way in?"

"Ha. Ha. Very funny." He kicks the door closed, flinching when it slams. "Oops, sorry."

"Seriously, Fitz, what is all of this?" He drops the bags on the ground, carrying the box over to the counter to set it down before walking over to me.

"Well, I'm not going to be in town much longer, and I'm here most nights anyways so I was going to ask you if I could just stay here? Just until it's time for me to go back to New York." My stomach plummets when I think about the fact that he's supposed to be going back to New York soon. Our "agreement" isn't going to be up for a while, so technically we'll still be together, but we never actually discussed what would happen when he goes back. I would assume he'll be insanely busy running an entire freaking real estate *empire*, meanwhile, I'll be where? My same position at Coleson, just under the new company name? "If I misread the situation I am very sorry. I can take all of this stuff back before—"

"No! No. Sorry, I just...zoned out. Of course you can stay here." I smile at him and he steps up between my legs. I'm still in an oversized T-shirt and my underwear, since I always do my hair and makeup before getting dressed, but Fitz looks like a freaking stud in his dark wash blue jeans, cowboy boots, a belt buckle with a bull on it, and a T-shirt that says *Outlaw Rodeo*. "There is no way I bought that shirt for you. I would have remembered it in the pile of clothes."

"What? This old thing? I've had it for ages." He winks at me and I roll my eyes. "It was between this one and the *Save a Horse, Ride a Cowboy* shirt."

"Okay, *Cowboy*," I tease, hopping down to get myself dressed for the night. Once I have on my new top–courtesy of Fitz–jeans and boots, I call Fitz into the room and give him a little spin.

He leans on the door frame and whistles, taking me in. "Damn, Trouble. You sure you don't want to just stay home and dance?"

"You're going to learn that if I spend any amount of time making my face look this good, I'm not staying home." I circle my face with my finger and he pulls his arm, which was previously hidden behind the wall, into the room with a cowboy hat in his hand. He puts it on his head and I think I actually die.

"Fine by me, you can do your due diligence and save a horse when we get back." He walks into the room and dips me, kissing me as I try not to giggle against his lips.

Oh, I'm definitely riding this wannabe cowboy later.

"Take a picture with me?" I ask, pulling my phone from my back pocket.

"Have I ever told you *no* before?" A wide smile spreads across my face before I reach up and kiss him on the cheek. We take a few pictures in the mirror, obviously needing proof of his get-up. Vincent Fitzgerald, the man who never leaves home without his suit or cropped slacks, looks like a Wild West wet dream. I send one of the photos in the group text to the girls and tell Ginny goodbye, but before we make it out to the Uber Fitz ordered us, I check my phone one last time and smile to myself.

TAY

Oh, he's going to fit in juuuussst fine.

"Why are your hands so sweaty?" I look up at Fitz, holding his hand as we walk into Knockin Boots together.

"Why are you pointing it out?" he growls into my ear and I smile.

Aww. Is he nervous?

"There they are!" Taylor smiles at us when we finally reach them at the bar. "Loving everything about this." She waves her hand up and down, gesturing to our outfits.

"Right?! I didn't even have to dress him." I shoot him a playful look and he shakes his head at me.

"So, how was dinner last night?" Shane asks, sipping on her soda.

"We can pour it out right here if we need to, then dance the night away to forget about it," Ruby suggests and I smile, looking over at Fitz briefly before turning back to them.

"It was horrible. They literally talked about me as if I wasn't even there, and basically tried to coerce Fitz to agree with them about how I should have done more with my life."

"What, from the bottom of my heart, the fuck?" Taylor snaps.

"But *then*...Fitz kind of went off on them. He told them everything I wish I'd had the guts to tell them over the years. He stood up for me and I finally made the decision that I'm done with them. If they want me back in their lives, they can work for it. I'm done."

"I'll drink to that." Ruby wraps her arm around my shoulder and we all take a shot before hitting the dance floor.

Chapter 56

Fitz

I've never seen Lauren laugh as much as I have tonight, and to be honest, I can't remember the last time I enjoyed myself like this either. Her friends are hilarious, everyone gets along and can be themselves around each other, which seems like an anomaly with this many people. They're probably the most genuine group of friends I've ever been around. The girls hit the dance floor, but I hang back with the guys while we finish our drinks before joining them.

"Hey." Tank grabs my attention.

"Yeah?"

"I heard what Lauren was telling the girls about what you did at her parent's house last night. Good for you."

"Yeah, well, no one's talking about my girl like that if I have something to say about it. Not even her parents. I was inclined to go back in there and break her dad's nose once she started crying in the driveway."

"I fucking would have," he mumbles before taking a drink of his water.

"I believe that with every fiber of my being." He laughs and then his face turns into a scowl.

"Well, looks like you might get your chance to break someone's nose after all." He nods to where a guy is checking out Lauren, getting way too fucking close to her while they dance.

"Lucky me." I set my beer on the counter and head toward the guy, surprised to find Tank right behind me. When the guy tries to take Lauren's hand to start partner dancing, she pulls away and I can tell by the shake of her head she's telling him no. He grabs for her again and Tank and I share a look before we make it to them.

"Oh, come on, we're just dancing, what's the problem?" The guy laughs, trying to cover his sleazy intentions with fabricated innocence.

"The problem is she said no and you're still here."

He scoffs and shakes his head. "You know how girls can be, sometimes they just need to be persuaded."

"Look, buddy, unless you want that beak of yours broken, I suggest you leave my friend and his girl alone." I almost choke at Tank's remark. The guy gives us a nasty look, then goes to walk away.

"Whatever, there's hotter pieces of ass here anyways." He bumps into Lauren on his way past, and I hear the girls gasping, and cursing, pulling her towards them. Within a second I have my hand on his shoulder, turning him around before my fist goes flying into his face. Another guy comes out of nowhere, trying to pull me back, but Tank grabs him and throws an elbow in his face, sending him stumbling backward. Tucker and Max show up next, pushing the other guys off the dance floor while we deal with the guy who started this mess.

"Get the fuck out of here, before you no longer have the ability to do it without assistance." Tank points him towards the door and the guy stumbles out. I turn around and find Lauren staring at me, and walk over to her.

"You okay, baby?"

"Yeah, I'm fine." She smiles at me. "Think you can still manage to dance with me with that busted hand?" I look down to see the skin torn on my knuckle.

"I think I can manage." I grab her hand and she pulls me onto the dance floor, but the look on her face when I take the lead is absolutely priceless. We dance until we're both sweating, and the amount of times I've made her laugh tonight is probably record-breaking at this point.

"Ok, I need a drink!" she yells over the music.

"Just one more," I tell her, earning a glare from her, but she doesn't argue. I turn to wait for the bartender and hear Ruby come up from behind me.

"Um, okay. So this night has been wild. Not only did I just see Zander and Tana making out in the hallway, but Jackson is here with one of the new teachers—according to Leah—and guess who else I just saw?" Ruby says, her eyes widening when I turn around to face the conversation she was starting with Lauren.

"Who?" Lauren asks impatiently.

"Uh…" I raise a brow at Ruby but she makes no effort to answer.

"What a small world." This Australian motherfucker and his accent.

"Hugh? Oh my god, what are you doing here?"

"I'm in town on business and I heard so many locals talking about this place, I had to come check it out for myself. It's very loud."

"That it is," she agrees.

"I was surprised I never heard from you. My reason for being in and out of town is because…" A group of people behind me get frustratingly loud and I can't hear him anymore. Lauren must not be able to either because she turns her ear towards him and he steps closer to her— much closer than I'd like for him to be. I'm trying to remain civil, but I did already punch a guy for getting too close to her tonight, who's to say I wouldn't do it again. Her mouth pops open and she gasps and the look on his face after sets me off. I reach out and grab her arm and, very calmly, pull her into my chest. She's tucked safely under my arm as I throw back the scotch I ordered when Ruby came up, and she wraps her hands around my forearm instantly.

"Well, I wish I could help you, but me and this guy have been pretty busy traveling lately. Plus, I don't do a lot of commercial sites, but I have plenty of great recommendations I could give you if you'd like."

"That would be lovely. You can text or email them to me. You still have my number, yes?" I look down at Lauren but she just nods.

"I do, I'll send them to you."

"Well, I am going to find somewhere less crowded and with fewer peanuts on the ground. It was great seeing you all again." Hugh waves and heads towards the door.

"This guy?" I tease, and she turns around, looking up at me. I adjust my hat and her eyes watch the movement before finding mine again.

"What? It's like a term of endearment!"

"*This guy* is a term of endearment?"

She rolls her eyes, crossing her arms over her chest. "Well, I could have called you Lucifer."

I grab her cheeks with one hand, pulling her lips to mine, sliding my tongue into her mouth as I kiss her right in the middle of this bar. "One of these days you're gonna learn your lesson about rolling those damn eyes at me, baby."

She catches her breath and looks at me, eyes wild with desire. "What if I don't want to learn it?" She pulls her bottom lip in with her teeth and I clench my jaw.

"Brat."

The most devilish smile appears on her face. "Asshole." Then a more serious look washes over her features. "You heard me tell him I wouldn't work with him, right?" She's actually worried about me being upset, and I don't mind how much I enjoy that.

"Yeah, I heard." I smile, wrapping my hands around her waist. "I trust you, Trouble. I just...don't like looking at his face." She laughs and her hands come up to my cheeks.

"If it makes you feel any better, I like your face a lot more." I narrow my eyes at her.

"Just my face?" I tease.

"And your hands." Her hands caress the backs of mine.

"And your lips." She leans up and kisses me.

"The way you talk to me." She smiles, standing on her toes to reach my ear.

"The way you fuck me," she whispers, and goosebumps race down my arms.

"I like you more, Fitz. Every single thing about you, I like." I bend down and pick her up, squeezing her body to mine as I breathe in the faint smell of coconut on her skin.

"Wanna get out of here?" She nods in agreement and we say our goodbyes and head home.

Chapter 57

Lauren

"Pack your bags, Trouble. We're going to New York." I wake up to Fitz kissing my nose and telling me to pack a bag, but when I open my eyes I see that the sun isn't even up yet. If it weren't for the fact that I'm traveling with the guy about to own the company I work for, and the way Jack and Barbara don't care if I take off as long as I get my work done—which miraculously, I've been doing—I'd be worried about being jobless.

"Oh my god, this company has a lot of events. No wonder it's as big as it is." I groan, pulling my pillow over my head.

"Flight leaves in three hours, better get moving." He squeezes my ass and the way my heart starts racing wakes me up almost immediately. I pull the pillow off my head and give him a suggestive look and he smirks.

"Fuck it, we can be a little late." He pulls his shirt over his head and pounces back on the bed, making me scream out in laughter. "Better here than the airport bathroom, right?" He growls into my neck and I push him over, to straddle him.

"Right."

I look at Fitz and frown when I realize we aren't at the airport we usually fly into.

"Fitz, what on earth kind of event is out here?" He smirks and his face twists into playful confusion.

"Who said we were attending an event?" My mouth pops open but no words come out because...he's right. I did just assume we were coming for an event because that's the only reason we ever do. Maybe there's another acquisition happening and he's bringing me along for the job? After driving country roads with little to nothing on them, I start to second-guess my theory. "Here we are." We pull onto a dirt road and I look over at Fitz in complete confusion and shock. If he brought a tent for us to sleep in and didn't warn me, so help me...

"Welcome to Shadow Hill Ranch."

"What is this place?" I ask, just as we come into view of the most beautiful farmhouse I've ever seen. It's not like the modern farmhouses you see these days, though. It's original, with blue siding and red bricks, worn wood on the porch, and a swing blowing in the summer breeze.

"*This*...is *my* childhood home." He shifts the car into park and my mouth falls open.

"What?" I almost laugh the question out. I'm completely stunned.

"Time to get to know the last little bit of me, Trouble." He hops out and rounds the front of the car.

"I have no words," I mumble to myself just as he pulls the door open. He drapes his arm around my shoulders and when I look up I see the brightest smile on his face.

"You're going to love Gran and Pops." My stomach twists as we make our way up the stairs to the porch, and without even knocking, he opens the screen door and walks right inside. I'm about to meet the people who raised him, completely unprepared. Doesn't he know me well enough by now to understand he can't do this to me.

"Anybody home?"

"Vincent? Is that you?" I hear a woman's voice exclaim. He stalks through the house so quickly I barely have time to take it all in. An older woman with gray hair pulled back in a clip and an apron comes around the corner and screams with a smile on her face. "Ahhh! My boy! It's about time you came back home to see us." She reaches up and kisses his cheek and he wraps his arms around her, squeezing her tight before letting her go again.

"Gran, this is Lauren. Trouble, this is my Gran. Otherwise known as the greatest woman in the world."

"Seriously, Fitz, with the Trouble?" I mumble to him as I walk over to Gran.

"Oh, stop it." Gran swats his arm, opening her arms for me.

I lean in and she wraps her arms around me. "Hi! It's so nice to meet you." She smells like homemade bread and flowers and hugs me like she's got love to spare.

"I am so happy you could come. I've been dying to meet you ever since Vincent told me about you." I love hearing her call him by his real name. I raise a brow at him over my shoulder.

"You told her about me?" He simply winks at me without a word before someone comes stomping through the back of the house.

"Joann? Are you in here?" The gravely tone of voice makes me assume this would be…

"Hey, Pops." Fitz smiles as the old man's eyes grow wide.

"You rascal! What are you doing here, boy?" He comes over and bear-hugs Fitz, slapping his back with a thunderous sound that makes my breath stall.

"Well, I missed you guys. Plus, I wanted you guys to meet Lauren and to show her the ranch." Pops looks over at me and I smile, walking over to give him a hug.

"It's so nice to meet you."

He pats my back and laughs. "Well aren't you just sweet as pie."

"That she is." I feel my cheeks heat and while I'm sure Gran and Pops have no idea why, I can tell by the look on Fitz's face that he definitely does, and I'm blushing for a good reason.

"Oh, I'm just so happy you both are here. I still can't believe it." Gran puts her hands up to her face and smiles. "Come on in here and have a seat, I'm just getting something whipped up for lunch. Are you hungry?"

"Always," Fitz answers before I can, but I'm grateful he does. My stomach has been growling since we pulled in the drive. "I'm going to grab our bags, I'll be right back." He kisses my nose and runs outside.

I watch after him, seeing the screen door slam as he trots out to the car. My eyes scan the room quickly, taking in the country plaid couch with matching curtains, the fact that there are fresh flowers in old metal watering cans and mason jars on every solid surface, and the worn boots next to the bench by the door. Everything here would be considered antique to people my age, and I love every single thing in this house. The creaky wooden floors, the China cabinet full of matching dishes, the old record player in the corner, and the rug that looks like it's been around forever.

"So, Lauren. Tell me, how did you two meet?" I pause for a moment, turning back to face Gran while trying to remember the story we agreed to tell everyone else, but it feels like…I don't know, a sin or something, to lie to Gran. So I don't.

"Well, we actually met at one of the summer conferences The Fitzgerald Firm hosted last year." I lean against the kitchen counter, admiring the fresh food spread she has out while she works on lunch.

"Those are always a very big hit. Were you speaking there?" I laugh out loud, then cough to try and cover it up, catching a playful glance from her.

"No, nothing like that. I was one of two people chosen from my firm in Nashville to attend. I just happened to meet Fitz at a mixer that night." She smiles and continues working on lunch so I, of course, keep talking to fill the silence. "I was actually getting hit on by some other guy who didn't understand the word *no*, and Fitz kind of swooped in and saved the night." Her smile reappears.

"He's a good boy that way." Gran winks at me.

"Glad the manners we taught him seem to have stuck," Pops adds.

Warmth spreads in my chest at their appropriately placed admiration for their grandson.

"The best." Gran slides a bowl of fruit my way, handing me a fork along with it.

"What are my two favorite ladies talking about?" Fitz walks back into the room, standing behind me to rest his chin on my head.

"You," I answer simply, looking up at him.

"Uh oh." Gran and Pops laugh at his reaction.

Pops walks over and grabs Fitz by the neck, giving it a firm shake. "Why don't you come help me and Lochlan with the rest of the cattle?"

"I thought we were having lunch?" Fitz asks, and Pops picks up a small loaf of uncut bread and holds it to his chest.

"Lunch isn't ready yet and we'll be done before it is. The city is making you soft on me." Fitz shakes his head with a small grin. I can tell by the look he gives me next that he wants to make sure I'm comfortable staying with Gran—which I am.

"You boys have fun." I smile and he kisses my head, takes a *massive* bite out of the bread, and grabs an old cowboy hat from right by the back door before putting it on his head with a wink and disappearing outside. I watch after him, still not quite believing that this was his life up until college. I really have no idea who he is, do I?

"We keep his hat right there waiting for him until he finds time to come back home." A soft smile plays on her lips.

"Can I help you with anything, Gran?" I offer, looking around at the spread she has on the counter.

"You know what, as a matter of fact, you can. Would you mind squeezing these lemons for the lemonade?" She slides a bowl of lemons and a juicer my way. I hop up to wash my hands before returning to my seat to squeeze them. "So, tell me, do you enjoy working in real estate?"

"I do. I actually got kind of bored with it for a while before Fitz came along."

"Bored? How so?" She continues mixing what I believe is chicken salad.

"I guess I just didn't feel challenged enough? Coleson is such a small firm, and while we're highly sought after, it just got…"

"Boring?" Gran smiles at me and I laugh.

"Yeah. I don't know. I just… I have my strategies down to a science on when to reach out to past clients, and when it's time to find new ones. I make myself present on social media a lot more than the other agents so I get contacted more, meaning I know how to handle a busy schedule and get everyone into the houses they want to view, and I'm quick to get houses listed when it's time. I don't know. It sounds silly now that I say it out loud."

"It sounds to me like you're excellent at what you do, but that you've outgrown the position. How did Vincent change that, though?" I think back to all the things he had me doing when he first came to Coleson—making me go through training with him, only to put me in charge of leading training the next week. How he pushed me to do more and was constantly giving me scenarios to come up with a solution for, even though it would never be necessary, and how he would do anything to keep me from sitting on my ass for any length of time.

"He gave me more responsibility. He pushed me, and while at first I thought he was doing it just to piss me off, I realized how bored I was when he wasn't there."

"He's good at that, knowing when people can handle more, and entrusting the right ones to do so."

"Yeah, I guess he is," I think out loud.

"It sounds like he met his match with you. Sounds like you probably gave him hell during all of that *pushing*." She winks at me and I laugh, feeling my cheeks warm.

"I suppose he doesn't call me Trouble for nothing." She laughs out loud and it makes me smile. I wish I had parents, or grandparents, to talk to like this. "So, what was he like? Growing up, I mean."

"Wild. Funny. Sweet." She smiles, looking out the window to the backyard. "He would about give me a heart attack trying to climb any tree with a low enough limb to hoist himself up on. Always messing with Dexter and causing trouble with the cows."

"Who's Dexter?"

"Dex was his dog. They were thick as thieves, always running through this house like two bats out of hell. Then they'd fall asleep on the couch, or in a blanket fort he'd make with Pops and I'd catch a glimpse of the sweet, peaceful version of him." I smile thinking of a young Fitz running around here like that. "He would pull pranks on me all the time too, and while it made me absolutely crazy, this house was filled with laughter all hours of the day. He would go from taping the sink hose down to spray me when I'd start washing dishes, to bringing me a bouquet of wildflowers from the field. He would grab my face in his little dirt-covered hands, make me look him right in the eyes, and tell me *you're my favorite gran in the whole world.* The little stinker would make me cry every time." I see her eyes shimmer with unshed tears, and mine begin to sting as well.

"I don't think I've seen that sweet, boyish smile on his face since he started his senior year of high school. Not until today, at least." She wipes her hands on her apron, puts the food she's been prepping in the fridge, as well as the lemonade I finally finished, and turns back to face me. "I need some apples from the orchard. Care to join me?"

"You have an apple orchard here?" My eyes widen in surprise.

"The best one in upstate New York." She grabs two baskets from the corner of the kitchen, handing me one as she grabs her sunhat. Then she grabs another one and places it on my head with a smile. When she links her arm with mine, I selfishly wish I didn't have to prepare myself to lose her sometime in the near future.

Chapter 58

Fitz

Pops and I come in from working and I see Lauren and Gran laughing together in the kitchen, peeling apples. She's wearing one of Gran's aprons and from the looks of it, Gran is making her famous apple pie for an after dinner dessert. I've never loved the sight of something as much as I love seeing Lauren fit in here so well.

"There you boys are! Lunch is officially ready," Gran says. She slides two plates with chicken salad sandwiches and veggies over to us, and Lauren pours us both a glass of lemonade.

"If it doesn't taste good don't be too hard on me, I've never made homemade lemonade before." She raises her hands and I take a sip.

"You put your finger in this, Trouble?" Her eyes grow wide.

"Is it sour? I put the right amount of sugar in it." She frowns and I can't help but laugh.

"No, it's perfect, Sweetheart." I laugh, winking at her as I take another drink. She gives me a playful eye roll and I make a note to deal with her later over it. Pops and I are quiet while we stuff our faces and I watch as Gran gives Lauren step-by-step instructions on how to make the pie filling.

"You'll never be the same after having Gran's apple pie. Trust me," I tell her and Lauren smiles.

"I can't wait." I watch her, in the pair of linen shorts she changed into, a pair of flip flops, and a white boxy tee, with Gran's watermelon apron on, and can't imagine anyone else I'd ever want to share this part of myself with.

"Lauren told me about how you two met," Gran says, lifting her eyes to mine. "I'm proud of you for swooping in and keeping her away from men with ill intentions." I can't help but laugh, remembering the night I made the bold move of calling Lauren my wife, having no idea whether she would play along or slap the shit out of me for overstepping. Then I realize she told Gran the real way we met.

"Okay. I think I need to dance some of that off." Pops pats his stomach and stands from his seat, kissing Gran on the nose before walking into the living room.

I see Lauren's head swing in my direction and I dip my head, avoiding her gaze. I hear the music from their record player flowing into the kitchen a moment later and Gran wipes her hands off on her apron before Pops comes in, taking her by the hand and pulling her in close. I stand from my seat and do the same with Lauren, and before I know it the four of us are all dancing in the living room to Elvis's "Burning Love" while Gran and Lauren's laughter fills the room. I take Gran and hand Lauren off to Pops, spinning Gran around the living room while Pops dances with my girl, and I don't think I've ever been happier than I am right now.

"Whew! I think I'm ready for my nap now. Good food and good dancing will really take it out of ya." Pops kisses Gran and looks at Lauren. "It was a pleasure dancing with you young lady."

"The pleasure was all mine. You may give Vince a run for his money as my top choice for a dance partner." She smirks at me and I shake my head.

"Okay. I'll see y'all around supper time." Pops heads in the direction of their bedroom and I get an idea.

"I'll be right back." I kiss Lauren's temple and head to the loft, better known as my old bedroom, where I dropped mine and Lauren's stuff off earlier. I dig through my old dresser looking for the pocket knife Pops gave me for my sixteenth birthday and slide it into the pocket of my jeans. When I come back down the stairs I hear Gran's voice coming from the kitchen and just before I walk in, I hear her say something that stops me in my tracks.

"I never thought I'd see that boy fall in love, but it's clear as day that he has."

Well, damn, Gran. Way to tell her before I could.

"Oh, well…" I walk in, cutting Lauren off.

"There you are." I smile at her, but I can see the unease written all over her face.

"Well, this pie looks ready for the oven. You're a natural in the kitchen, dear," Gran praises Lauren and I smile. "Alright, I think I'm going to go tend the garden."

"Do you need any help?" Lauren asks, but I step in and stop her.

"Actually, if Gran doesn't mind, I'd like to show you the rest of the ranch." I take her hand in mine and she nods with a soft smile on her lips.

"Of course, you two go have fun. I'll see you at dinner." I nod to the back door and Lauren pulls her apron off, sliding on a pair of boots before following me out through the yard.

"You ever ride?" I ask, catching the flirty look in her eye.

"You know better than anyone that I have." I bark out a laugh and she smiles.

"I meant horses."

"Yeah, yeah. I know." Her eyes roll again. "No, I've never ridden a horse."

"Well, you won't be able to say that after today." We walk into the barn and I pull my old horse out of her stall. "This is Tina." Lauren snickers and I raise a brow at her.

"Sorry, that name makes me think of Napoleon Dynamite. Did you ever see it? When he's like *Tina, you fat lard, come get some dinner.*"

I love her.

"Would you believe me if I said that's who she's named after?" She falls into a fit of laughter and I pull Tina with us out of the barn. Once they're used to each other, I hop up on the saddle, pulling Lauren up behind me. "Hold on tight, Trouble." Lauren's hands snake around my waist and I sigh at the way her touch always calms me down. I click my tongue and Tina starts to walk.

I point to the garden where Gran is working, telling the story of how I helped build the greenhouse during my junior year of high school. Then we pass one of the fields where we keep the cattle. Next, I show her the chicken coops and the old barn that's been turned into a bunkhouse, before I let Tina pick up her speed as we start up the hill, stopping when we get to the one place I've been dying to bring her.

"Why does this look so familiar?" I smile when she immediately recognizes it.

"Because you've seen it before." I give her a minute to think, not surprised in the least bit when she figures it out.

She gasps, looking at me with amazement in her eyes. "It's the tree from the painting in your living room."

"That painting was the first thing I ever willingly spent a large amount of money on," I admit.

"Well, I understand why." Her arms readjust around me into less of a grip and more of a hug, her hand caressing my abdomen as we sit here.

"This tree is actually how the ranch got its name. Because no matter what time of day it is, or where the sun is in the sky, the branches are so big the whole hill stays shadowed."

"Shadow Hill Ranch. I love that." We hop down and I tie Tina up to one of the low branches and I walk around the tree until I find it—Gran and Pops' initials carved into the tree with a heart around it. "Aww. That is so sweet. How long have they been together?" She runs her fingers along the carved bark.

"Shit, I don't even know. Forever and a day." She laughs, nodding her understanding.

"They seem like they have the kind of love that lasts."

"What makes you say that?" I look at her curiously, wondering what her answer may be.

She shrugs, running her fingertips over the soft bark that's been carved out. "The way they look at each other, how they stop to dance with each other in the middle of lunch, the nose kisses." Her eyes meet mine, and my breath catches. "You'd have to be blind not to see it. He watches her when she's not looking and she acts like she doesn't notice, but you can see the smile on her face and you know that she knows. But, I don't know…maybe I'm just romanticizing things." She shrugs again and I take her face in my hands, tucking her hair behind her ears, even though I know she hates it. It gives me an unobstructed view of her beautiful face, and for that very reason, I will never stop doing it.

"No, you're absolutely right. They've looked at each other like that for as long as I can remember. And there's nothing wrong with romanticizing life, Sweetheart. It helps you to know exactly what you want out of it."

"Fitz?"

"Yes, Trouble?"

"What are we doing here?"

I frown in confusion, letting my hands drop to her arms. "I wanted to show you the tree."

"No, not *here*, at the tree. I mean. You and me. What are *we* doing?" I swallow hard, waiting for the bomb to drop. "I mean, you come to my house, asking me to be your girlfriend for a year, with no other details, just a blind agreement. What happens when you move back to New York next month? What happens when the year is up? Does all of this just…end? If so, why not just end it now? Because I don't know if I can just be a parental distraction anymore." I feel my heart constricting in my chest.

"Is that what you want? You want all of this to end now?" Her eyes fill with tears almost immediately and I see her head begin to shake.

"Why did you bring me here?" The pain on her face almost breaks me and I know I can't wait for her to tell me what she wants. She's guarding her heart, but I need her to know she doesn't have to. Not from me.

"Because—" I take a deep breath, gathering my courage. "Because I want to carve my initials into that tree. I want them to be right below yours and circled with a heart. I want them to be here in fifty-five years when we're old and gray, just like Gran and Pops, and I want to be dancing in the kitchen with you as sickeningly in love with you as I am right now."

"What?" she chokes out, as the first tear falls from her pretty blue eyes.

"I love you, Lauren Long. I'm so in love with you it fucking hurts sometimes. I can't sleep if it's not next to you. I think of nothing but you when we aren't together. I crave your touch and to see your eyes roll, whether it's *at* me or *for* me. I love your attitude and the way you love your friends. I love that you made me feel special on my birthday, and have made me feel just as important every day since then. I love every single thing about you."

"So it…it wasn't all fake?" The crack in her voice makes me want to hold her until she can feel just how real my love for her is.

"Sweetheart, I could never fake the way I feel about you. This may have started as a favor or an agreement, or whatever the hell you want to call it. But it's real. You can't tell me you don't feel the same way. Please tell me you feel the same way."

She takes in a shaky breath, her bottom lip quivering. "I do. I feel the same way." More tears fall from her eyes and she smiles through them, my heart freaking soaring when she reaches up and caresses my cheek. "I love you, Vince. I love you so much." I wrap my arms around her, picking her up off the ground as she grabs my face and pulls my lips to hers.

I've kissed her in every single way imaginable—soft and slow, firm and needy, but this time when I kiss her, I kiss her like she's mine.

Really mine.

I savor every moment, putting her feet back on the ground so my hands can caress her face, arms, and hips. I'm scared that if I let go, she'll disappear. That I'll suddenly wake up and it'll all have been a dream.

I press my forehead to hers, still trying to catch my breath. "I've wanted to tell you this so many times, Trouble. You have no idea how it's been killing me to keep it in."

"Well what the hell were you waiting for?" she laughs through her tears, and I take her face in my hands, feeling my heart open even more for her while I get ready to bare my soul.

"I've been waiting for acceptance for so long, from so many people in my life, that I guess I wanted to know that you'd accept me for who I really am. Every single part of me. Not just the rich, real estate empire heir, but the guy who herds cattle and dances with his Grandma in the kitchen with dirt on his boots. I've come so close to telling you so many times, baby. But I needed you to know this part of me first. That's why I brought you here, to make sure you could love every part of me."

"Vincent Fitzgerald. What on earth ever made you think I wouldn't love and accept this part of you?" She hits me in the chest and I laugh. "I love you even more, seeing how happy you are out here. I know the real you, Vince. No ranch or real estate office is going to change my mind about that."

"You're perfect, you know that?"

She smiles up at me. "Carve our initials in the tree, Vince."

I'm convinced that this will forever be my new favorite moment. I've had a lot of memorable ones in life, but none of my favorite ones have ever involved something directly happening to *me*. Most of the best moments in my life were me being happy about things happening to my friends—my self-proclaimed sisters. But this moment? This one's for me and Fitz. We lay under the giant oak tree, staring at the initials Fitz carved into it, LL + VF with a heart surrounding them, while he holds me close to his chest. I can hear his heart beating wildly and it makes me giggle.

"I would have thought your heart rate would have slowed down by now, but it sounds like a rabbit thumping his foot against my ear." I look up and see him smile down at me, my own heart picking up speed at the sight.

"Well, I'm a little anxious I'll wake up and this will all have been a dream. I'm just holding on for as long as I can." I sit up on my elbow to face him, running my fingers gently along his cheekbone.

"You can hold me as tight as you need to, but even if you let go, I'll still be right here." He wraps his hand around the back of my neck, pulling me down to kiss me. The leaves rustle from the summer breeze, blowing through, making this moment even more perfect than it already was. We stay out here a while, silently enjoying the moment—*our* moment. Shadow Hill Ranch might just go down as my favorite place in the world—especially if I'm here in the arms of the man who gave me the one thing I was always so scared to want. The nauseating kind of love.

"So…is this why your only tattoo is a bull?" I ask, making his chest shake with laughter.

"Yeah. This would be why." I nod my understanding, then he sits up, pulling me with him, and turns me to face him.

"You finally going to tell me about why you memorized every state bird and flower?"

My mouth pops open to argue but I see the look in his eye and I know I won't win this one, no matter how hard I try. I let out a defeated sigh. "Someone in my class called me dumb. I foolishly believed them and wanted to learn something no one in our grade had learned yet. So, I memorized the state birds and flowers. At the time it felt like very powerful information."

I expect him to laugh, but the frown on his face is serious. "Who called you dumb? I'll kick their ass."

I have to think of the name for a minute before I can recall it. "Leslie Winkleman."

"Oh. Well…never mind. You're absolutely brilliant, Trouble. I'm sure you always have been." He kisses my nose and I smile. "List all the state birds, right now." I laugh at his demand and shake my head.

"No!" I giggle, pushing him back down to lay my head on his chest again.

I pull my phone out and take a photo of the tree from my point of view, full green branches with the tiniest bits of sunlight shining through the leaves, posting it to my story, tagging Fitz and our location before sliding it back into my pocket.

"You ready to head back to the house?" Fitz continues playing with my hair, and I'm sure if we stayed here five more minutes, I would fall asleep in the grass with him.

"Would you judge me if I said no?" I feel his chest jump with a laugh.

"Not at all, Trouble. If I'm being honest, I don't want to go, either." He kisses the top of my head. "However, I do want Gran and Pops to get to know you and spend as much time with you as possible before we head back into the city tomorrow." I look up at him and frown.

"I didn't know we were going back to the city." He sighs and readjusts his head on the arm he's been lying on.

"I have been hoping to find a way out of it, but seeing as how my work is directly related to my father, I don't see me using work as an excuse."

"Get out of what?"

"My mother's birthday party."

"Wow. You guys have birthdays *really* close together." His expression is blank as he stares across the fields. "You know, I've only picked up on bits and pieces of what your relationship with your parents is like. Since I understand complicated parental relationships I never wanted to pry, but I can tell there's tension there. What happened? I mean, I know a little bit about what happened with your dad, with him not letting you choose what to do in life and all, but what about your mom?"

"My mother just goes along with whatever my father says, always has. When he suggested I live here with Gran and Pops until I was ready to start learning the family business, I could tell she was upset to see me go, but she also seemed…excited? Which just fucking hurt, you know? What mother doesn't want to raise her own child? I never really got to have a relationship with either of them, and I think I've resented them both for it ever since. When I came to New York last Christmas, she suggested we go shopping together, which was weird, but…I guess the little boy in me wanted so badly for the facade she was putting on to be real, that I allowed myself to lower one of my walls. Only to find out it was a plan made up by my father to convince me to settle down."

"Wow."

"I never understood why she wouldn't fight for me to stay with them. Why she didn't want me around, why she didn't visit me more.

Then one day, I eventually stopped caring. I realized I had the best people in the world raising me. They loved me and taught me all of the lessons in life worth learning. They taught me how to be a hard worker, how to be kind, and how to take care of not only myself, but others as well. I wouldn't change the way I was raised, I just sometimes wish…" He trails off and I sit up to face him.

"Sometimes you just wish your parents were different."

He scoffs, a small smile playing on his lips. "Look at us, two peas in a pod."

I snort. "A trauma pod."

He laughs out loud, making me smile. "Oh, my god. That's a horrible way to put it."

"It's also very accurate. And when have I ever been one to sugarcoat things?"

"Literally never," he answers a bit too quickly. I glare at him and he sits up, our noses brushing against each other when he leans forward. "And I love that about you the most. What do you say, Trouble, be my girlfriend? For real this time." I roll my eyes and he gives me a warning look.

"Yeah, I guess."

"You *guess*?" He grabs me around my waist and rolls us over to pin me to the ground. "Do I need to help you find a more convincing answer?"

"And how exactly would you do that?" I challenge him and he grins.

"I can think of a few ways I've made you scream the word *yes* before." I bite my lip, trying to hide my smile. "Shall I try them again?" he practically growls above me, and I simply can't help myself. I shrug, my expression full of indifference.

"Yeah, I guess."

"You little brat." His smile is devilish when he buries his face into my neck, proving me right when his methods work. I enthusiastically agree to be his girlfriend beneath the giant oak tree, before he takes us back to his grandparent's house for a shower before dinner.

"Gran, no one makes homemade ice cream like you." Fitz practically licked his bowl clean, after having his apple pie and homemade ice cream, and I honestly can't blame him. Everything she made today was to die for. I wish I could stay here for a week or a month, or however long it would take for her to teach me everything she knows in the kitchen.

"He's right, everything was delicious," I agree. Gran waves a hand dismissively.

"Oh, please. You're the one who made the pie, dear." She smiles at me and Fitz grabs my hand, kissing the back of it.

"That's right! The apple pie was perfect, Trouble. You did good." I don't understand why, but every time Fitz tells me I've done something well, my stomach and my vagina take turns fluttering.

"Sorry to interrupt—" Someone comes walking through the back door, stopping when we all turn at the table to face him.

"Lochlan, we didn't know you were still here. You should have come in for supper," Gran scolds him in the most loving way.

"I uh—" His dark eyes stay on me, and I suddenly wonder if I have food on my face.

"Stop looking at her like that, Lochlan. She's mine." Lochlan shakes his head and laughs nervously.

"Sorry. No, I just… You've never brought a girl home, so I was just surprised."

"As were we all," Gran agrees with a smile on her face.

"Was something wrong, Boy?" Pops asks, shifting the conversation back to why he came inside to begin with.

"Oh, right. Mabel is about to have the calf. You said to let you know before she did but if Vincent is here…" I look at Fitz in surprise when he tosses his napkin on the table.

"Are you…are you going to help a cow have a baby?" My eyes pop and he laughs.

"Don't wait up." He winks at me, then he and Pops rush out the backdoor with Lochlan. My mouth is hanging open when I turn back to face Gran.

"You want to go too, don't you?" Gran observes as I look back out the door.

"Yeah, I kind of do," I admit shyly.

"Well, if I know Mabel, she'll still be a bit before that calf is coming. Why don't you and I get things cleaned up in here together and put on a pot of coffee. I hear we don't get you for much longer." We begin moving around the kitchen table, clearing plates, and washing dishes as she puts the small amount of leftovers in the fridge.

"That's what I hear, too. He just told me today we have to get into the city for his mother's birthday tomorrow."

"Mmm. Have you met them yet?" Gran asks, still moving effortlessly around the small space.

"Briefly. I've only spoken to his father a couple of times, not enough to really get to know them." I finish drying our dinner plates and hand them to her. "Do you mind my asking, which one of them is yours?" A sadness fills her eyes as she pauses her movements briefly.

"Lena."

"Oh." Is all I can manage to say.

Then she shakes it off and continues her task. "As much as I hate to say it, I know they're hard people to get along with. Lena wanted nothing more than to get away from the ranch from the moment she was sixteen years old. Always said she wanted *more* out of life. When what she really wanted, but wouldn't say, was to marry rich and not have to lift a finger like we made her do around here. It broke my heart the day she left, but she got what she wanted." She lets out a sigh, then turns to face me, placing her hand on mine. "Do me a favor, if you don't mind."

"Anything."

"Don't judge Vincent any differently when you *really* get to know them."

I smile at her reassuringly. "You don't have to worry about that,

Gran. If we judged each other based on the way our parents behaved, he would have left on two wheels after meeting mine."

Her face turns solemn and she pats my hands. "I'm sorry to hear that, sweetheart."

"It's okay. I realized that night that there are people in my life who will accept me exactly as I am, and it was refreshing to know I have the choice to no longer surround myself with the people who won't. Even if those people are the ones who raised me."

"Well, I know we're a bit more than a drive from Nashville, but you will always be welcome *and* accepted here at the ranch." She gives me a wink with the sweetest smile on her face.

"Thanks, Gran." My eyes begin to water, and she pulls me in for a hug.

"After all, any girl Vincent finds important enough to bring home is one I expect to see again." She gives me a shake and I laugh, feeling more loved than I probably ever have before. Gran offers to get our coffee poured while I run to the restroom, and when I pull my phone out to set it on the counter, I see my message notifications and decide to open them before I end up forgetting.

RUBY

Tell us about the ranch!

TAY

I've only seen tree branches and I already want to
visit.

SHANE

Not to be the odd one out, but WHY are y'all at a
ranch?

LEAH

Valid question. I was kind of wondering the same.

ME

He brought me to meet his grandparents.

RUBY

Tell. Us. Everything.

ME

They practically raised him here. They're cattle ranchers, they have chickens and goats and a greenhouse and everything. He has a horse named Tina, who I rode. He took me to the tree where the ranch gets its name "Shadow Hill Ranch" and he told me that he loves me. 🫠

TAY

AND?!?!?!?!

RUBY

Wtf do you mean AND?! Was that not enough information to have you screaming?!?!

TAY

AND...do you love him too??? 🙂

SHANE

👀

LEAH

👀 👀

ME

Yeah. I really do.

TAY

AHHHHHHHHHHHHHHHHHHHHHHHHH!

RUBY

There it is.

RUBY

I may or may not be able to see out of my eyeballs.
I'm so happy for you.

SHANE

"May or may not" is for rookies. I am full on sobbing rn.

LEAH

LAUREN IS IN LOVE!?! OH MY GOD, THE STARS
HAVE ALIGNED.

I almost sent them the photo I took of mine and Vince's initials carved into the tree, but at the last second, decided I'll keep that to myself, just for a little longer at least. I hear the screen door open then slam shut and hurry to finish up so Gran doesn't think I've fallen down the drain. Or worse, that I'm taking a shit.

Chapter 60

Fitz

I didn't think it was possible to fall more in love with my girl. Then she came outside last night in a pair of Gran's old work boots, her hair clipped back, and helped us deliver a calf. We took one last trip out to the tree before we packed our bags to head back into the city. Taking her to the ranch was the last piece of the puzzle for me. Seeing the way she fit in there, helping Gran in the kitchen, riding Tina with me, the way she just jumped in with Mabel's delivery. I've never been more sure of anything in my life, than I am that Lauren has been, and will be, the only one to have my heart. Her fingers have been intertwined with mine the whole drive back into the city, and just as we turn onto my street, I hear her stomach growl.

"Why didn't you tell me you were hungry?" She shrugs and leans over, resting her head on my shoulder.

"I was just ready to be home."

I glance down at her, watching her eyes flutter closed. "You know, you've called my place here in New York *home* twice now."

"Mmm. Have I?" I laugh when I notice she never opens her eyes when she asks.

"You have."

She finally lifts her head, looking into my eyes. "Weird." There's a sweet playfulness in her eyes but she just smirks at me. When I kiss the top of her head, her stomach growls again.

"Why don't I grab us some food from Milano's while you head up and take a shower?"

"Are you sure? I can go with you."

"Baby, your eyes are barely open right now. Go up and shower and I'll be back in twenty minutes." The car comes to a stop outside of our building and I give her the key, making a note to give her one of her own. If she's going to keep calling this place home, I want it to feel that way to her in every sense of the word.

"Twenty minutes. I'm counting." She points at me and I smile.

"I won't make you wait a minute more." I wink at her and she smiles, running up to the entrance. I'm almost to Milano's when my phone starts ringing, and the smile on my face from the anticipation that it may be Lauren disappears when I see that it's my mother.

"Hello?"

"Fitz, honey! So glad I caught you. Are you busy?"

"Only always. What's up?" I hop out of the car with a sigh.

"I just wanted to make sure you were coming tomorrow."

"Yes, we'll be there." There's a pause on her end of the line and I look down to see the seconds on our call still ticking by.

"Okay."

"Okay?"

"I don't want to keep you, we'll see you then." My brows practically meld into my hairline in shock.

"See you then."

The line goes dead and I waste another minute of time, wondering what the hell that was about. If I know anything about how my parents react to things, I'm sure I'll figure it out tomorrow night. I rush into Milano's, order our food and drinks, and barely make it to pick up a bottle of Lauren's favorite wine before getting back to the apartment with a minute to spare. Keeping my promise to someone has never felt so important and rewarding.

When I walk through the door she's fresh out of the shower, wearing one of my T-shirts, a pair of her underwear, and socks, bundled up on the couch with a spot open for me. I don't even bother fighting the way I love her. Eating pizza and watching her favorite shows, rubbing her feet until she's falling asleep, and getting to make love to her without the fear that it'll end all too soon any more, makes me happier than I can even comprehend. I can't wait to surprise her with what I have planned tomorrow—*before* the dreaded party we're here to attend, that is.

If it wasn't for the fact that my body and mind are both completely relaxed when Lauren is wrapped in my arms, I wouldn't have been able to sleep a wink last night. I was up an hour ago, pulling clothes from her bag and laying them out for her, before brewing our coffee and starting breakfast.

"Oh my gosh, something smells amazing." She shuffles into the kitchen in her silk nighty and her hair clipped back, causing me to pause and take every bit of her beauty in. Her bare face, rosy cheeks, and hard nipples teasing me through blue silk.

"Get over here, beautiful." She gives me a playful look and skips over to me with her bottom lip pulled in with her teeth. I lift her onto the counter and her legs part, allowing me to move closer. When I squeeze her ass as her arms drape over my shoulders, and the look in her eyes has me completely mesmerized. I kiss from her neck, down to her shoulder and when my lips begin trailing down her chest she giggles, pulling my chin up and my eyes meet hers.

"You're going to burn our breakfast."

"I'll make more if you let me taste you, first." She bites her lip and nods eagerly.

"Just—" she stops my quick descent down her body. "Turn the burners off first at least."

"How about I make you a bet?" Her eyebrow lifts, curiously.

"I'm listening."

"If you finish before the bacon burns, you can't ask any questions about what I have planned for us today."

"Okay," she agrees almost immediately.

"And you can't tell me no about any of it."

"I'm slightly more hesitant about that one," she teases.

"Come on, Trouble. Don't you trust me?" She rolls her eyes and I grab her thighs, pulling her to the edge of the counter before she can even answer. She catches herself by slamming her palms against the countertop. "You know the rule, baby. You roll your eyes, I give you a reason to." I lift her silk dress, and my cock throbs when I see she's already wet for me.

I waste no time diving in to devour her. Her back arches, and her head falls back as sweet moans, that might as well be music to my ears, fall from her lips. The more I taste her, the more I crave her climax to satisfy us both. I grip her hips, biting, kissing, and licking her from entrance to clit until she grips my hair and begins grinding her hips against my face. I flatten my tongue, teasing her until she's writhing on the counter, screaming my name. I'm startled when she grabs my face with both hands, pulling me up to her.

"More," she pants, kissing me in a way that sends my head spinning.

"Tell me what you need, baby." I nip at her bottom lip and she moans.

"You. Inside me. Now." She pulls my sweatpants down, grabbing my cock with a grip that's both gentle, yet completely demanding. She's going to take what she needs and fuck if it isn't the sexiest thing I've ever experienced.

"Take what you need, Trouble." Her eyes slowly find mine and she releases me, sliding off the counter until her chest brushes mine and I'm towering over her again. Then she takes my arms, turning us until my back is against the counter. She lifts a brow, tipping her chin to urge me up onto the counter. I slide myself up and she crawls up next, straddling me. She guides my cock into her slick entrance, her grip around me still as tight as ever. The tiny straps on her nighty fall down, as do pieces of her hair from the clip she's wearing, as she rides me. She goes between biting her lip and her mouth popping open, then she readjusts her position, bouncing on her feet now instead of her knees.

"That's right. Use me, baby." Her nipples harden against the blue silk fabric that's a second away from falling down. "Keep going, just like that." I feel my balls begin to tighten, seconds away from emptying myself inside her, when the smoke alarm starts going off.

"Shit. The food!" Lauren's movements begin to slow and I grip her hips. Thrusting into her.

"Let it fucking burn, but don't you dare stop." One of her breasts falls free just as her tight cunt squeezes around me. "Shit, baby. You fuck me so good."

"Vince, I can't. I'm coming!" I take over when her legs give out, gripping her hips as I thrust so deep, she completely soaks me. She grinds her hips against me as my cock continues to pulse inside of her and when we've finally reached the peak of our climax, I slide us off the counter and switch the burners off.

I'm still seated inside of her when she looks at me and smiles. "You lost."

"The bet was off the moment those eyes rolled, Trouble." Her mouth pops open in disbelief.

"What! That's not fair." I squeeze her ass and press my cock deeper inside of her, causing her to moan and rock her hips against me.

"I think you got exactly what you wanted. Didn't you, baby?" I softly kiss her lips, then her neck, lifting her just enough to reach the breast that fell out of her dress while she was riding me, sucking her nipple into my mouth until I feel her walls tighten around me again.

"Let's get cleaned up, then we can go grab breakfast. I have a busy day planned for us and we're actually out of bacon." I grimace and she laughs.

"Um, did you lay my clothes out for me?" She hikes a thumb towards our room.

"Yes. I did." The smile on her face is enough to tell me that she'll wear it. I only hope she's as excited about where we're going as she is about me picking out her clothes for her.

Chapter 61

Lauren

Fitz could hardly stop smiling during breakfast this morning. Whatever he has planned for today he must be *really* excited about. Which is making me equal parts anxious and excited. We went to the cutest little café just a couple of blocks away from his place, and the breakfast sandwich he ordered for me was heavenly. He was practically dragging me out the door before my coffee was even half gone. The outfit he picked for me to wear is simple, comfortable, and honestly, I've never felt this cute. I'm wearing a navy blue, short-sleeved, T-shirt-style mini dress with a plaid button-up flannel wrapped around my waist, a pair of white sneakers, and my hair clipped back. I assumed he wanted my hair clipped like this when I saw the matching blue claw clip right above the dress on the bed—sitting right next to a key to his apartment that I'm trying to stay calm about. It's safely attached to my keyring, but I want to get him one to my place too before I say anything about it.

"Now, remember, you're not allowed to tell me no today," he reminds me as we pull up to the shops on 5th Avenue.

"I don't love that you said that when we just pulled up *here*. Fitz, you know I don't spend a lot of money on clothes. I can't imagine paying 5th

Avenue prices on something I'll likely end up dropping a taco on." He laughs and wraps his arm around my shoulder, kissing my head.

"I know, but for one, *you're* not spending a penny while we're here, I'll buy you whatever you want, or whatever I want you to have if you won't pick something. Two, the one thing I know I already know I'm getting you, won't be anywhere near a taco…trust me." I glare up at him and roll my eyes, protected by the sunglasses I've slid on my face since getting out of the car.

I sigh in defeat. "*Okay.* You're in charge."

"Mmm. I like the sound of that," he growls in my ear, making me smile. We walk through the doors of Bergdorf Goodman, and I have to consciously ensure my mouth doesn't fall open as I take in the massive store. "Come on, Trouble. The fifth floor awaits." I look up at him and my brows pinch together.

"What's on the fifth floor?"

He smirks and leans down to whisper, "Shoes." I can't even deny how excited that one word makes me. I expected us to browse through the shoes until I found something that caught my eye, but instead, Fitz walks with purpose to a certain display. I immediately fixate on a pair of black pumps that look just like the ones Ginny chewed up and I finally allow my mouth to pop open.

"See something you like?"

"These." I point to the pair I'm looking at. "They're the exact ones I had that Ginny chewed up."

"You're joking." He laughs. "When I came here last Christmas, I saw these exact shoes, and the first and only thought I had was, *I need to see Lauren in these shoes.*" I look at the shoes again and process the timeline. Realizing he'd only just come to Coleson, and we were still in… unfriendly territory.

"Are you serious? We didn't even really know each other back then," I say quietly, still fixated on the shoes. I can feel his eyes on me and look up.

"Maybe so, but from the moment you snapped at me about being on my phone during a meeting, I knew that I wanted to." He winks at me as an associate approaches us.

"Hi there. See anything you'd like to try on?"

"These, in a size seven. Thank you," Fitz answers, making me blush over the way he speaks with such confidence. Remembering my shoe size, insisting on buying me a replacement pair of my favorite shoes—whether he knew that before two minutes ago or not, still means a lot to me. "Do you see anything else that you like?"

"What? No! These shoes are a thousand dollars, we're leaving after this." I argue, catching a warning look from him.

"Sweetheart, I'm just getting started spoiling you. Why do you think I picked your most comfortable shoes for you to wear today?"

"Vince, you don't need to do this," I whisper, and he takes my face in his hands.

"I know I don't need to. Which is exactly why I *want* to. Please just let me spoil my girl. Just for today. Then we can go back to Nashville and thrift everything else we ever buy if that's what you want." I've never had someone spoil me. Or call me their girl. Or offer to thrift for themselves just to make me happy. Who the hell am I to tell him no?

"Fine. You can spoil me. But I reserve the right to remind you whose fault it is if you ruin me and I remain spoiled afterward."

"I can live with that. Let's get to shopping. This is only stop number one." He wags his brows and I'm suddenly much more worried about what is coming after this.

"Fitz, there is no way this is all going to fit in the trunk of the car." I look at the associates who have their hands full of shoe boxes and bags of clothes—well half of it is actually lingerie, but the other half is a mix of work and weekend clothes.

"You underestimate my ability to make things fit." My mind goes somewhere else at the statement and he moves past me to start loading the car. No matter how much money Fitz just spent on me, I smile knowing he's still the same guy I fell in love with, working with the Uber driver to get everything placed in the trunk of the car, high-fiving him when they get it all in and the trunk closed. "Told you." He lets out an exhausted sigh and I laugh.

"A modern-day hero." He walks over to me, wrapping his arms around my waist, kissing me before looking at his watch.

"We even have enough time to get all of this stuff dropped off before we have to be at our next stop."

My stomach is completely empty after shopping for the last three hours, and it's on the verge of growling louder than the traffic behind us. "Please tell me that our next stop involves us getting lunch?"

"You think I don't know when I need to feed you, Trouble? Of course it does."

We pull up to the front entrance of our next stop and if I had a million guesses of where we were going, I would have gotten it wrong every single time.

"We're going to a baseball game?" I look over at him in surprise.

"Not just any baseball game. The Dodgers are playing the Yankees today." I smile when I see how excited he is as he slides his Dodgers cap backward. "Now I know baseball isn't everyone's thing, but just give it a chance? For me?"

I shrug when I answer. "I can't tell you no today, right?"

We walk through the gates and immediately the smell of ballpark hot dogs and popcorn fills my senses. The announcer on the loudspeaker is informing everyone about things happening around the park, kids are screaming while they play, and people are laughing in every direction you turn. I breathe it all in, loving every single second.

"Burger, hot dog, or nachos?" Fitz asks, pulling his wallet from his pocket as we stop at a concession stand.

"Hot dog, french fries, and a beer, please." I smile up at him and he kisses my nose, reminding me of the way Pops did the same thing with Gran.

I'm so glad he grew up around them.

"Yes ma'am." We make it to our seats, which are so close to the dugout you can practically smell the sweat and sunflower seeds, just as the teams are starting to warm up. I scan the field carefully, watching as each player exits the dugout when Fitz's voice brings my attention back to him.

"Are you disappointed?" My head snaps in his direction, seeing the guarded look in his eyes.

"What?! No. Why would you ask that?"

He shrugs. "I don't know. This isn't—" Something catches my attention on the field and I gasp embarrassingly loud when I look over and see who just ran out of the dugout.

"Fitz, shut up. Look! It's Shohei Ohtani!" I slap his arm and watch as he begins warming up with the rest of the team. After a minute, I remember that Fitz was in the middle of saying something to me and I look back over at him. "I'm so sorry. I interrupted you. What were you saying?"

"Um. What the fuck, Trouble? You…I. I don't even know what to say." My head falls back with laughter, wishing I had a picture of his face right now.

"You're not the only one full of surprises, babe." I bump his shoulder with mine, lowering my glasses to wink at him.

He laughs, sitting back in his seat like he's actually needing a minute to process. "So…you like baseball then?"

"Yep. I dated a guy in high school who was on the baseball team, and that's when I first got into it. After we broke up I stopped going to the games, obviously, and wound up missing it more than I thought I would. So I started watching college and pro games instead." He shifts in his seat like he's too excited to sit still.

"Do you have a favorite team?" I scrunch my nose while I think.

"Not really. I'm more of a fan of the players than I am of a specific team. I feel like that limits your support. Like, for instance, Yadier

Molina was one of the greatest catchers of our time, and you won't change my mind about that. He was damn near impossible to run on. Then you have Barry Bonds, one of the best hitters ever, even naturally he's one of the hardest batters to pitch against. Then, of course, my guy Shohei. He's a great pitcher but as a DH? Forget about it. Love him." I pop a French fry in my mouth and look over to see Fitz with an unreadable look on his face.

"I think I just fell in love with you again." I laugh, rolling my eyes at him and he wraps his arm around my shoulder, pulling my ear closer to his lips.

"I saw that, Trouble."

Lucky me.

GRUMPY BUNCH GROUP CHAT

UNKNOWN NUMBER

Okay, maybe you can settle this argument for us.
Which is worse. Sitting on one of your balls, or zipping
your dick in your jeans?

UNKNOWN NUMBER

Who the fuck is wearing jeans without underwear?

UNKNOWN NUMBER

Sometimes there's just not time.

UNKNOWN NUMBER

WHEN?! WHEN IS THERE NO TIME TO PUT ON
FUCKING UNDERWEAR?

ME

Who is this?

UNKNOWN NUMBER

First number is Tucker

Second number is Max

Third is Tank

Fourth is Sawyer.

ME

Why am I not surprised it's the brothers that have an
issue with their dicks getting zipped?

SAWYER

😅 I didn't even notice that.

MAX

Seriously? Did your father not teach you how to put on
underwear before your pants or is this a conscious
decision you've both made?

TUCKER

I'm going to play the dead dad card and say no, he
didn't.

TANK

That's a little messed up, bro. And that's coming
from me.

ME

Is leaving this group chat an option?

SAWYER

Afraid not. You're one of us now. So…what's your
vote? Sitting on a nut or zipping your dick.

ME

As a tried and true underwear-er, I'm gonna have to go
with sitting on a nut.

MAX

HA!

SAWYER

Thank god this is over.

TUCKER

Whatever. Come back when you forget one day and
zip that motherfucker up in a heavy duty denim zipper.

TANK

💀 industrial zipper wearing ass.

ME

leaves group chat in spirit

SAWYER

follows *holds the door for Max*

MAX

tips hat in appreciation

Chapter 62

Fitz

This weekend has been absolutely life-changing. I never pictured myself as the guy who would fall in love and settle down, mostly because when my parents began shoving that narrative down my throat all I wanted was the exact *opposite* of that. I didn't want to live my life the way they did. I didn't want someone in my life who would have to suffer through me becoming exactly like my father, but I also never met someone who made me *want* to settle down. Someone who reminds me I'm nothing like the man I feared I'd become. Someone who makes me want to be better. Running the family business as a bachelor always seemed like the perfect fit for me. Until I met Lauren.

Now I don't see my future without her in it. No matter what I do, in any scenario I can think of, she's always by my side. Running a real estate empire in New York? She's there. Helping deliver baby cows on the ranch? She's there. Thrift shopping in Nashville every weekend? We're there together. Whether we travel the world or stay in one place, it never changes. After the baseball game, we came home and showered then fell asleep until my alarm went off telling us it was time to get ready for my mother's birthday party, and I had no desire to get up. I have been absolutely dreading this event, but knowing I'll have Lauren on my arm and in my ear, is the only thing helping me make it out the door tonight.

"Well well well. Don't you clean up nice." I turn around, immediately wanting to fall on my knees and worship the ground this woman walks on. She's wearing a blue long-sleeved party dress with bell sleeves, and the shoes I bought for her today—the same ones I've dreamed of seeing her in since the day I first saw them. Only, I've been picturing her in nothing *but* them. Her dress stops on her mid-thigh, allowing her tan legs to be on full display like the true work of art that she is.

"How the hell did I get so lucky?" She rolls her eyes at me and I'm tempted to bend her over the kitchen counter before we go, but when I check my watch I see that we don't have the time. "You look breathtaking, Sweetheart. Undoubtedly the most beautiful woman I've ever seen." I hold my hand out and she places her fingers in it, allowing me the chance to bring her hand up and kiss the back of it.

"I guess your charm isn't so fake after all." She winks at me and grabs her clutch from the counter. "I wonder if you'll still be as much of a gentleman when you see what I'm wearing under this dress later." She pulls me behind her, sending my mind spinning with excitement, as we walk out the door.

My parents have never been the type to do small events, so it's no surprise that my mother's 60th birthday party is probably the biggest event I've been to this year. We make our way around the room, and I'm pleasantly surprised by the fact that Lauren manages to keep some kind of contact between the two of us the entire time. As if she knows the effect she has on me even though I'm almost positive I've never told her.

"You have been absolutely amazing tonight, you know that?" I whisper in her ear as we make our way over to one of the open bars in this massive venue.

"What do you mean?" she asks, her hand still wrapped comfortably around my bicep.

"You have no idea the difference your presence at these events has on me. I no longer feel the burning desire to bolt for the door five minutes after being here. Nor does your touch make my skin crawl the way…*others* used to." I worry for half a second that she'll be upset about me mentioning being with other women before her. Until she laughs so beautifully, the rest of the room fades away.

"Well, with the amount of time I spend touching you, I sure hope you don't feel that way." I pull her into me, letting my hands rest comfortably on her ass as I lean in and kiss her. I hear someone clear their throat behind me and look up to see Frank, turning a hilarious shade of red.

"So sorry to interrupt you both, but Fitz, may I have a word with you?" My brows furrow and I look at Lauren.

"You okay on your own for a bit?"

She nods and smiles at Frank, her cheeks also blushing. "Sure. I'll be around."

"I won't be long." I wink at her and follow Frank to the opposite side of the room, stopping when we reach a sitting area that is mostly vacant. "What's going on, Frank?"

"Remember that old saying *don't shoot the messenger?*"

What the hell?

LAUREN

I have to say, this event is fancy as hell. There's a live band on one end of the room, set up right in front of a dance floor, that you can tell was put in solely for this event. There are two locations for open bars, several places for people to stand at pub tables, as well as couches in small areas around the back of the room, most of which are empty right now.

"Lauren!" I hear a woman's voice that I don't recognize, call from behind me. I spin to face her, wine glass and clutch in my hands, soon realizing it's Fitz's mother.

"Mrs. Fitzgerald. Happy birthday." I smile, hoping I'm not as transparent to her as I am to her son.

"Oh, thank you. This is all just…too much, but West insisted." I have no idea whether or not to believe her. Knowing what I do about how desperate she was to get away from the ranch and how desperately she wanted this life, I wouldn't be surprised if she's just trying to seem humble when in reality she's the one who's planned this whole thing. Then again, maybe she does feel that way now and this is just her husband's way of keeping up appearances. Either way, it's not my business and I don't really care to find out.

"Well, I'm sure he means well," I offer, politely looking for an exit strategy as I take a sip of my wine.

"So are you having a good time?"

"I am, yes." I nod, and she smiles.

"That's good." She leans in closer to me, like we're two friends sharing secrets and it makes the hair on the back of my neck stand up. "I am honestly surprised to see you here tonight. Especially after the announcement coming out today." My stomach twists uncomfortably at her words as she sips her champagne and I stupidly take the bait.

"What announcement?"

She laughs sympathetically. "Oh, dear. Well, it's no wonder you're still here." I stand frozen, still unsure what she's talking about, but *very* sure that I don't want to see whatever it is. Apparently, she can't read my mind though, because she pulls out her phone, clicks two little buttons, and turns the screen in my direction.

There's an article illuminating much too brightly in my face:

New York power couple, Vanderbilt Hotel heiress, Jessica Vanderbilt, and soon-to-be real estate CEO at The Fitzgerald Firm, Vincent Fitzgerald to announce engagement soon, sources say.

There are multiple photos attached to the article, including a family photo of them with their parents, as well as one of just the two of them that I quickly realize is from the night of Fitz's birthday. My face burns with embarrassment, remembering that was the night I showed up to surprise him. Was he there with *her*?

I read a little further.

The two have been photographed several times over the last several months, looking mighty cozy during Fitzgerald's trips back home from managing acquisitions in other states. Company-wide takeovers seem to call for a little extra love when coming back home, and Vanderbilt clearly has plenty to spare for her hard-working fiancé.

I'm going to throw up.

"This is just gossip." I try to argue, but then she scrolls down a bit, showing photos of them together in a coffee shop, more from Fitz's Dad's party, and another of them kissing on a boat. I can feel the warmth of the tears in my eyes as I see them together. Mr. Fitzgerald joins us, and while I think she might change the subject, she doesn't. Making this feel like a complete ambush and less like a conversation of happenstance

"When are you going to realize that you don't belong here, Ms. Long? My son needs someone who is more compatible with him. Someone who knows his world, and will be able to help guide him as he runs this empire. What can a sales agent from some small firm in Tennessee bring to the table for someone like Fitz? Jessica and Fitz are made for each other. He's been with her before, and he'll realize soon enough she's exactly what he needs. Especially when he reads the contract stating the company will go to Frank unless he agrees to the terms of the merger for Vanderbilt Hotels and The Fitzgerald Firm. A merger that will, in fact, include their nuptials."

He'll lose his right to the company if he stays with me?

"If you truly care about him, surely you wouldn't allow him to lose everything he's worked his whole life for. Would you?" I regain my composure and straighten my spine as I look at them both in their smug faces.

"Wow. You both are unbelievably disgusting human beings. You can play mind games with me all you want, but I know Vince better than you think. He is by far the best person I know. He's hard-working, loyal, kind, and he would never lie to me the way you're suggesting he would. Our relationship aside, what kind of parents would manipulate their son this way and watch him give up everything he loves? Just to become just like the people who shipped him off to be raised by someone else until he was old enough to be groomed into what *you* wanted him to be. He is *more* than capable of running this company with or without a wife, he'll probably do it better than you, if we're being honest, yet you still make every effort to tell him what he's doing wrong, instead of giving him the slightest bit of encouragement for everything he's done *well*. Shame on both of you." I take a deep breath, seeing his mother turn a deep shade of red, meanwhile, his father just smirks, looking over my shoulder. I glare at him, then do the thing I shouldn't do—I turn around. Just in time to see Jessica Vanderbilt and Fitz making out.

"Excuse me." I don't turn back around to face his parents before I slam my glass down on a table, marching towards the table they're standing at.

Chapter 63

I'm filing a fucking restraining order on this woman as soon as I leave this building. After what Frank shared with me about the article that came out this morning, and her cornering me at my mother's birthday party, while I'm here with Lauren, no less, is the last straw. If I lose Lauren over this, I'll burn the entire company to the ground, along with everyone who played a part in my losing her, inside of it.

"Come on, Fitz. You know you two won't last once you're back in New York for good. Just accept that this is going to happen. Everyone already expects us to be together, we make sense together, why can't you just see that?"

"Jessica, I—" Before I can tell her to fuck off, or anything else for that matter, she digs her claws into the back of my neck, and slams her lips to mine. It's forced, uncomfortable, and unwanted in every single way possible. I wrap my hands around her arms and pull her off me. My heart stopping when I look to the side to see Lauren standing next to us with tears in her eyes. I hear a noise come from Jessica, likely accompanied by a smirk, but I refuse to take my eyes off Lauren.

"Excuse us, Jessica. I need to speak with Fitz. *Alone.*" Her tone is calm and shakes me to my core.

"I'm not so sure I want to leave my fiancé with some random girl." I open my mouth, ready to tear into her about how delusional she is when Lauren beats me to it.

"It'll only take a minute."

The fuck?

Jessica drags her hand slowly down my arm, Lauren's eyes watching every movement before I shrug her hand off. Then she disappears into the party leaving Lauren and I standing in the hallway together.

"Fitz, what am I doing here?" Her eyes are filled to the brim with unshed tears, breaking my heart and infuriating me all at once.

"You're here because you're my girl. That wasn't what it looked like, okay? Jessica came out of nowhere and ambushed me and… I swear I'm filing a restraining order against her when we leave here tonight." The first tear falls down her face and she blinks more away.

"I don't belong here, Vince. We can pretend all we want that I do, but you and I both know that I don't."

I grab her arms, ducking to catch her eye when she tries to avoid my gaze. "Yes, you do. You do belong here."

"No, I don't! Look around us. Everyone here is at the top of a corporate or social ladder. People who will help you succeed in life, in your career, and then there's me. A sales agent with anxiety and a favorite thrift store. I'm not a socialite. I don't fit this image, I don't even live in New York! I have nothing to offer you, Fitz. You shouldn't be with me, you should…you should be with someone like Jessica."

"No! Everything you just said is exactly why I love you. If you don't belong here, then I don't either." She shakes her head and I can feel her slipping away and I'm pissed the fuck off that I can't seem to catch my grip on her.

"Yes, you do, and I can't do this. I can't be selfish and ruin everything you've worked so hard for. I'm going to go back to Nashville, and you're going to stay here, and you're going to do so many amazing things at this company." I shake my head, refusing to hear any of this. "And I will always be so proud of you for it."

"What are you talking about? I don't understand." I grip her hands tight, willing her to snap out of whatever she's thinking. "Don't leave me. Please. I thought…I thought you loved me?" More tears fall freely down her face and I can feel my heart screaming for her to say she's only joking. That she isn't going anywhere.

"I love you more than I have ever loved anyone, Vincent Fitzgerald. That's why I have to leave. Please forgive me." She reaches up and kisses my cheek, but I move and pull her lips to mine, begging her to stay with every movement. Then she pulls away and runs out the door.

My entire fucking world just walked out the front door, and I have no idea why.

But I'm sure as hell going to find out.

She said she couldn't let me lose everything I've worked so hard for, and outside of working on getting her to fall in love with me, that can only mean one thing. Losing the firm. My mind is foggy as I walk through the party looking for my parents, knowing they're the only ones who could have provoked this sort of reaction out of Lauren. When I finally see them at the bar together I take my opportunity to interrogate them about what happened—or that's my plan at least—until I hear clear as day the absolute fuckery they're discussing.

"I'm telling you, it worked. I just saw her running out of here and right after we told her what would happen if he didn't end up with Jessica. Her seeing them kissing was just icing on the cake. There's no way she'll come back after that. Everything is going to work out just as planned when Fitz realizes it's in his contract that he will lose the company if he doesn't agree to marry Ms. Vanderbilt, everything will be fine, dear. Now, enjoy the party. We have a lot to celebrate tonight."

These motherfuckers.

They have no idea what they've done.

Lauren thinks I was at risk of losing everything, but she clearly doesn't realize I lost it the moment she walked out the door. I manage to turn around without a word to my parents, for now, to head home and get my girl. On my way out I catch a worried expression from Frank, but I don't have time to deal with explaining things to him right now. The only person on my mind. Is *her*. But when I get back to the place she's so easily called home, it's empty.

"Fuck!" I yell, folding my hands behind my head. I walk to the bar cart and go to pour myself a scotch when my phone begins to ring.

"What, Frank?" I snap.

"What happened?" I've always loved the way Frank just knows when something's wrong and actually cares enough to check in.

"Too fucking much to explain, but I need you to be straight with me about something." I abandon my unmade drink, standing to look out the window at the city below.

"Always am, son. You know that."

"Do you know what all is in the contract for me to take over the firm?" He sighs and I know my answer already.

"I didn't until tonight. I asked your parents about the article I told you about when I saw you at the party with Lauren and they told me. I was on my way to find you when I saw you leaving."

"Fucking assholes," I grit out through my teeth.

"I had no idea before tonight though, I swear. I've always seen you like a son, Fitz. I would have never kept this from you had I known before." A warm feeling spreads across my chest at his words.

"We need to meet."

"Tell me when and where and I'm there." I give him a time and a place, hanging up the phone before heading straight out the door. I can't stay here without Lauren. It feels too fucking empty and I hate it.

Lauren isn't answering my calls. She isn't responding to my texts and she turned her location off, again. It's like she turned into a ghost last night. The contract for me to take over the company is supposed to be signed by the end of the week, which is the *only* reason I am not already back in Nashville, busting down her door. Instead, I'm stuck in New York, trying to find a loophole in this god-forsaken contract.

"Are you serious?" I sit across from Frank, looking over the paperwork, seeing the undeniable condition that the merger between Vanderbilt Hotels and The Fitzgerald Firm includes Jessica and I getting married.

Over my cold, dead, body.

"I'm afraid so. It states that within 30 days of you becoming CEO that you two set a date, and that if within a year you two aren't married, then..." he trails off, likely too worried to finish saying that the company will go to him.

"Only my parents would even consider something as insane as an arranged marriage just to further the success of their career. It's not even going to be *their* career anymore so why the *fuck* do they care?" I throw the contract across the office, making Frank sigh. I snatch my glasses off my face, pinching the bridge of my nose in frustration.

"You trust that this wasn't my idea, right Fitz? I would never want to take this away from you. This is going to be *your* legacy, I only ever wanted to be here to support you." I do. I trust Frank more than I trust most people who have been in my life for as long as he has.

I look over, my eyes narrowing on him. "You really mean that Frank?"

"Scouts honor." He holds up his fingers and I chuckle.

"Then we have to fix this. Now."

Chapter 64

Lauren

I barely made it into a taxi before completely breaking down after leaving Fitz standing in the hallway at his mom's birthday party. I know him far too well and he would have thrown everything he's been working so hard for away if he'd known what his parents were up to. I know he'll find out eventually, and when he does I want his decision, whether it be to take on his new company with Jessica, or to leave it all behind, to be made with a clear mind. I don't want him to lose what he's meant to inherit because he feels like he has to choose me or his career. I've never been that girl, and I won't start now just because I've fallen in love. Becoming CEO has been his plan all along, I wouldn't be able to live with myself if I knew I was what stood in his way. Gran even said it herself, he's great at what he does. He deserves this.

I grab my phone out of my clutch and call the only person I can think of right now.

"Chattahoochies, what's your poison?" A sob breaks out of me at the sound of her voice and she immediately knows it's me. "Max. I'm taking this in the office." I hear her tell him, then a few minutes later she's back.

"What's the matter? What happened?" I can't even speak. I just cry my eyes out on the phone with her for at least five minutes, and she just listens. Reminding me to breathe when I get close to hyperventilating.

"I don't even know where to start," I admit.

"Okay, well…if he hurt you, just know he won't live to see the end of the year."

"He didn't hurt me. I—I broke up with him." The words burn my throat when I say them.

"What?!" I take a deep breath, almost losing it all over again when we pull up to his apartment building and I look down at the key he got made for me this weekend.

"I have to pack and get on a plane. I just…needed to cry."

"Come straight to my house when you land. I'll have everything we need. I love you, Lu, and I am so sorry you're hurting right now when I can't squeeze you. Please text me updates as you can." I nod my head even though she can't see me.

"I will. I love you too."

I haven't stopped crying since I got into the taxi in New York. I cried the entire time I packed my bags, leaving behind everything that wasn't a necessity, including the key I used for the first time when I got there to leave. Then I cried through the entire wait at the airport while I changed my wallpaper and hid all the photos of Fitz and me in my phone, only stopping when I fell asleep on the plane. I've been a zombie ever since I landed, barely remembering ordering my Uber from the airport to Ruby's house. I text her that I'm here since it's currently three in the morning and I didn't want Maverick to wake anyone. Two minutes later the door swings open and the tears start falling again.

"I miss him already." My voice is hoarse from crying so much and she holds onto me so tight it's like she's trying to keep me from physically falling apart, the way my heart already has.

"I know, sweetie. I know." She runs her hand through my hair, and we stand in the doorway while I cry a little more. "Come on. I have wine and snacks. You can tell me what happened at your own pace."

We curl up on the couch, bundled in blankets, while *New Girl* plays in the background. Our wine glasses are full, there's a new box of Kleenex on the coffee table, and her attention is solely on me.

"So I guess I should start by telling you the truth." She frowns at me and I feel the nerves spark to life in my stomach. "When Fitz and I started dating, it was all…fake."

"Fake?!" Her eyes pop in surprise.

"Yeah. You remember when he was my date to Taylor's wedding? He did that as a favor because I didn't want to go alone."

"Lauren." She tilts her head sympathetically.

"I know. It's so embarrassing thinking about it now, but he offered, and I said yes. When he said I would owe him, I thought he meant something work-related but he came back the next day and asked me to be his girlfriend for a year to get his parents off his back."

"Off his back about what? Being single?"

"I wondered the same thing, but apparently they wanted him to end up with some hotel heiress so the companies could collaborate or merge or something. I don't know, but I met the girl and I could see why he didn't want to be with her. So we played the part and we played it well," I say sadly.

"So then what happened?"

I shrug, feeling the emotion creep back up my throat. "It stopped feeling fake." She stays silent as I try to regain my composure. "I fell for him, Ruby. I fell *so* hard. I thought he was just some rich dick that would keep my parents from trying to set me up with random guys whose *texts* gave me the ick, but he wasn't. He was everything I've ever wanted and never had. He made me feel…" Hot tears stream down my face. "He accepted me for who I was. He *loved* me, exactly as I was. The bratty attitude, thrift shopping, horrible parents, workaholic that has a cat and friends who are a dealbreaker, and he never made me feel anything but wanted."

"Shit," she whispers, making me laugh ironically. "So then… Why did you leave?" I meet her eyes and anger and sadness overwhelm me.

"His parents won't sign the company over to him unless he's with someone from *their world*. Basically, someone who can offer him more."

"Something more than love? Love so deep that you'd leave him and break your own heart in the process just so he doesn't lose everything he's worked his whole life for?" I'm filled with gratitude for the way she recognizes how fucking hard this has been.

"They don't care about love, Ruby. They care about status, climbing the corporate ladder, and making sure he stays at the top. From what I gathered at least." She sits with the information for a minute, then looks at me.

"Do you actually think he'll do it?"

"What?"

"Marry someone else just to take over the company?" My heart cracks straight down the middle at the very mention of it.

"I don't know." I take another long sip of my wine.

She tilts her head, looking at me expectantly. "Lauren."

"What?"

"Think back over the last few months, and tell me if the man you fell in love with would really marry someone else just for his career."

"I don't want to think about it, Ruby. I just want to go to sleep and wake up from this nightmare." She gives me a sympathetic look and nods.

"I'm sorry. Get some sleep. I can't guarantee the nightmare will be gone when you wake up, but I'll be here when you do." We snuggle up on her couch, turning the volume up on the TV and I silently cry myself to sleep. Because while I know I made the right choice in leaving, the choice to not be selfish and give Fitz the space he needs to make a clear-minded decision about what he wants for his future, my heart is still scattered in a million pieces all over New York. And the only person who could pick them up, is still there as well.

And is now calling me for the fifteenth time since I left him at that party.

"I'm not going to wake her up." The sound of Ruby whispering wakes me, but I can't manage to open my eyes.

"Well, it's not fair that you got to nurse her broken heart by yourself last night. You should have called us." Taylor's unmistakable voice catches my attention next. "I work the night shift, I'm used to dealing with unstable patients on very little sleep."

"Okay, well I'm sorry you guys, but she cried herself to sleep last night so she's probably exhausted. I'm not waking her."

"You already did, you troll. You can't whisper for shit. And I'm not unstable." I groan, pulling myself to sit up on the couch, seeing Taylor, Shane, and Leah standing in the kitchen with Ruby, coffee, and breakfast bags in hand.

"Hiiii," Taylor coos. "Of course you're not." I roll my eyes at her as she hands me a coffee, then my face turns down and my lip starts quivering.

"Maybe I'm a little unstable." I shove the coffee back at Taylor and I can see the confusion on her face.

"What the hell did you do?" Shane whispers, not so quietly.

"I handed her her favorite coffee," she answers cautiously.

I take a deep breath, grabbing one of the tissues from the almost empty box.

"He paid attention to what I liked, you know? Like, for so long I thought he was up my ass at work to piss me off, but then—" I take a few shaky, sniffly breaths. "Then he took me to get tacos one night and then started bringing me my favorite coffee. It's a hard order to remember, you know?" They all shake their heads, even though I probably sound insane right now, rubbing my arms in a comforting way while I lose it over a fucking cup of coffee.

"What happened, sweetie?" Shane asks, and I motion for Ruby to tell them because I physically do not have it in me to go through everything again. It hurts too much.

"So she left him, to make sure he didn't lose everything," Ruby concludes.

Well, shit. It hurts just as much hearing it as it does saying it.

"Well, lucky for you, we're all free as a flock of birds today and we're going to do whatever you want. Manicure? Pedicure? Day drinking? You name it," Leah says, brushing my hair out of my face. I roll my head and look at her.

"Re-start last night's episode. I am part of this couch now." They all give me a sad, yet understanding look. "And give me my coffee." Taylor hands me the coffee then picks up the box of tissues, handing it over as well.

"Just in case," she whispers with a wink, pulling my legs into her lap and snuggling up next to me as the curls from her messy bun flop around. The rest of the girls pile onto the couch, and we stay there for the rest of the day. Tank brings us food and informs me that he's fed Ginny for me. Hendrix snuggles me and brings me his favorite stuffy to make me feel better, and my girls don't leave until they absolutely have to.

They're the truest form of family I've ever had.

Chapter 65

After sitting with Frank until I couldn't see straight, one simple phone call from the ranch gave me clarity on what the final stipulation would be for the contract we rewrote. The plan Frank and I have set in place has given me an insurmountable peace, which was all I needed before storming into my parent's house to let them know exactly what I think about the shit they've been trying to pull.

"Oh, Mr. Fitz, we weren't expecting you today." My parents' housekeeper greets me with a smile, turning a bit worrisome when she sees my hardened features.

"Nice to see you, Mags. Tell the kids I say hi, won't you?" I give her a quick smile, seeing her instantly relax, then walk into the sunroom. My parents are sitting on opposite chairs, Mom is flipping through a magazine while Dad looks at something on his phone. From the way he's swiping, I can only assume he's playing some sort of game.

"Fitz, honey! We didn't know you were coming by today." My mother abandons her magazine, walking over to me, while my father simply looks at me over his glasses. Before my mother can come in for a hug I hold my hand up to her, glaring at her in a way I can only hope she feels pricking her skin.

"Well, that's why they call it the element of surprise, Mother." She rears back, glancing at my father quickly before turning back to me.

"Is everything alright? You seem…tense."

"Tense? No. Livid. Yes." My father pockets his phone, finally standing from his chair to show interest in my presence.

"What is this about?" he asks, seeming bored by my answer already.

"Lauren left me. Any idea why she may have done that?" I ask, rhetorically.

"Well, honey, maybe she finally realized she doesn't belong in this world." I glare at my mother. "I mean, we all saw you with Jessica at the party Saturday night. She probably came to her senses and ended things before she got too attached." The audacity for her to lie straight to my face has my blood boiling.

"What about me? Huh? What if I was attached? Do you really not care about what I want? In any area of my life?"

My father scoffs, causing a raging fire to shoot down my spine. "Don't go getting sensitive about a piece of ass, son. You'll do just fine without her."

I take a calculated step towards my father, meeting him eye to eye. "Don't you *ever* speak that way about the woman I love, *ever* again. I don't care who you are, I will knock all of your teeth out, so help me god."

He chuckles darkly, putting his hands on his hips. "I'd read your contract a little more carefully boy, before making threats that bold."

"Oh I read the contract. I have no interest in merging The Fitzgerald Firm with Vanderbilt Hotels, or marrying Jessica to do so. Frank can have the company, we sent the new contract to your lawyer this morning. As soon as it's approved which—" I look down to check my watch. "Should be happening any time now. I'm no longer obligated to be your little puppet."

"Have you lost your mind? After the years of work we've put into this company, you're willing to just give it away? For what? For *her*?" Disapproval drips from his tone.

"No. You're right. I wouldn't just give it away." I see relief wash over him, but only for a moment. "I would burn the whole fucking company to the ground, for her. She is the single best thing to ever happen to me, and the fact that you'd willingly destroy that just to make yourself look good; makes me embarrassed to be your son." My mother stands frozen next to us, looking a mix of ashamed and scared. Meanwhile, my father just looks completely unphased. Fucking sociopath.

"Then consider the papers signed. Frank can have the company. I know he'll do right by it." He pulls his phone out of his pocket, clicking away as he takes his seat, ignoring me completely.

I look at my mother who is nervously twisting the pearl bracelet around her wrist, and a piece of my heart seems to chip. Like a fragile teacup that's been hit on the edge of a counter. "Gran and Pops would be so disappointed in you." Her lip quivers, but she composes herself again quickly, taking her seat and flipping through her magazine. I think of a million things I want to say to both of them before I go. How I want to scream at them and ask why they never cared? Why they still don't. How they could let the love of my life walk out the door and be *proud* of what they've done to us. Instead, I turn on my heel and walk out the front door, for what will likely be the very last time. I call Lauren again, but of course, she doesn't answer. I've lost count of how many calls have gone unanswered, or how many texts have been left unread.

When I finally get back home, after spending the last two nights on the couch in my office, reality sets in even further. I see the key I gave her on the island and the Taylor Swift record we'd been listening to while getting ready Saturday on the record player. The blanket I got her when she was sick is tossed across the back of the couch as well as one of her claw clips on the coffee table.

Fuck, I wish she'd just have come home.

I walk over to my bar cart, grabbing a bottle of scotch before falling onto the couch. Her blanket still smells like her shampoo and body lotion and I feel myself on the verge of tears as I lay my head back on it. Breathing her in, even though she isn't here, feels like the cruelest form of punishment when I can't reach over and pull her into my lap. I turn the bottle up, unlocking my phone to call her—again—hoping one of these times, she'll answer and I can tell her everything will be okay.

Lauren

It's embarrassing how long it took me to get myself to work this morning. I cried from the time I got in the shower, until I pulled into the parking lot, my tears returning with force when I realized the acquisition was complete and the rebranding had already begun. His name is going to be everywhere today, and I'm supposed to keep my composure somehow. My hair is a mess since I let it dry naturally, it looks somewhere between a lion's mane and a pom pom, and my face is completely free of makeup. I didn't quite see a point in wearing any since I knew I would end up with tear streaks anyway.

"Honey, you *know* you're my icon, but you look *rough*." Luther closes the door behind him as he walks into my office, taking a seat in one of the armchairs across from my desk.

"Thanks, Luther. At least I know I look how I feel." I give him a tired smile and his brows pull together.

"Tell me everything." He beckons his fingers, encouraging me to talk.

I let out a tired sigh. "I'm afraid I don't have it in me to explain, *again*, how I got my heartbroken, but I'll be okay."

He jumps up from his seat, rounding my desk. "Heartbreak? Why are you even here today? You should be a pint of ice cream and at least two showings of *The Notebook* into grieving."

He pulls me into an embrace and I feel myself letting my protective walls down, just barely. "I ate all the ice cream yesterday, and no to *The Notebook*, they wind up happy at the end."

"What can I do to be here for you today?" he offers, shaking himself into fix-it mode. My lip turns down, while I fight like hell not to let myself cry again.

"Can you just…hang with me? I don't have showings today but everything around here makes me think of him."

"Like the sex printer?" He points to the corner where my broken printer sits next to the brand-new one that I never had time to take out of the box.

My voice cracks as I look at it. "That was such a good day."

"Bitch, I bet it was. Look at this paper tray." Luther flicks it and it falls completely off, hitting the ground with a *clink*. I can't help but laugh when it does, and as weird as it feels to do so, it also reminds me that I still *can*. "Okay. Sex printer is out of here. Then I'm going to make sure nothing with the F word on it comes through that door, then we're going to play some music and…" He looks around the room trying to get an idea. "Plan your birthday party?"

"I don't think I'm supposed to plan my own party, am I?" His head whips in my direction and he purses his lips.

"As if that's ever stopped you before."

Luther and I spent the day listening to every playlist he had with the least amount of sad songs on it, to keep me from crying, while we planned the outfits we'll wear for my birthday party, instead of the party itself. Then got lunch at Spurs Diner. It was exactly what I needed to distract me from my own thoughts today, but that's all it was…a distraction. Not a cure for the heartbreak that awaits me when I'm alone. I walk into my house, tossing my stuff on the floor by the door, not bothering to hang anything where it goes, before calling Ginny over to lie on the couch with me. I barely make it onto the couch before my front door flies open. I jolt upright and gasp, my heart rate only slowing when I see Leah walking my way with a bottle of wine and takeout from Casa Taco. She moves around the kitchen, dropping everything on the counter before kicking off her shoes and making her way over to me all while she talks.

"Before you ask, yes I was stalking you to know exactly when you got home. I didn't want you to be alone for too long, because being alone with a broken heart—" she flops down on the couch next to me with a huff, "is for people without best friends. And you, my dear, have too many of those to go through this alone." She tucks a piece of hair behind my ear and I fight to stop the memory of Fitz doing that same thing so many times before.

"I don't know what I ever did to deserve a friend like you."

She hums playfully, tapping her lips. "I think you said *I like your hair, do you want one of my chicken tenders?*"

I laugh in disbelief. "How on earth do you remember that? It was like three lifetimes ago."

She smiles and shrugs, grabbing one of my hands. "I'd never forget how I met my bestie."

"Meanwhile, I'm over here unable to think of a time there wasn't a me without you." She wraps her arms around me, and I do the same, relaxing a little more.

"Okay! You go get your comfy clothes on. I'll plate our food and pour the wine, and then we can watch—" She raises a brow at me, waiting for my show request.

"*Ginny & Georgia.*"

She nods in agreement. "You got it." She pulls me up from the couch and slaps my ass, making me laugh as I head towards my room to change.

We make it through a whole bottle of wine and two episodes of *Ginny & Georgia* before I realize I can't find my phone. I wanted to take a photo of Ginny watching the show with us, but when I went to reach for it, it wasn't there. We flip all of my couch cushions and dig through my purse twice before I find it still outside in my car. My stomach twists and my heart aches when I see new notifications from Fitz, only this time the missed calls are accompanied by one new voicemail. He hasn't left one of those yet and I've had my texts from him muted to keep myself from giving into the temptation while he figured things out.

"Oh good! You found it." Leah sighs as I walk back through the door. I look up at her, my face emotionless. "What's the matter?" She walks over to where I'm still lingering in the doorway, looking down at the phone. I hover over the play button for his voicemail and she looks up at me.

"Are you going to listen to it?"

I swallow past the lump in my throat. "I don't know. Maybe it's important?" She takes my phone from me, swipes out of my voicemails, and clicks into my call log and texts.

She shoves the phone back into my hands. "Um. I'd listen to it." My eyes lock with hers and she smiles at me encouragingly. I take a deep breath and click the play button just as Leah grabs my hand for support. She looks on with anticipation and tears fill my eyes as soon as I hear his voice. A few words in, I can tell he's drunk. He doesn't sound like himself at all.

"Trouble. Please answer your phone baby." He lets out a heavy sigh. *"I really need to see you. This blanket still smells like you, you know. You left your scent and everything, all over the damn place. You left your key on the counter and that hurt so fucking much. You're not coming back to me, are you? How am I supposed to be okay when you're not here? I need to see you. I have to— There's just so much you need to know, but I… I just need to see you, Sweetheart. I love you. I'll always love you, you know. Fucking bottle is empty."*

Something crashes right before the line goes dead and I immediately wish I knew if he was okay.

"What did he say?" I sniffle, blinking away the few unshed tears that have pooled in my eyes.

"Um. He said that he missed me. He kept saying he needed to see me, and that uh… That he still loves me." My voice shakes as I speak.

"What are you going to do?" I run my hand through my hair anxiously.

"I don't know, Le. What can I do? I left so he could figure out what he wanted without me being in the way and making him feel like he had a tough choice to make."

"Babe, by the amount of texts and phone calls he's left you, I think his choice is pretty clear." I look at her blankly. "It sounds like he's choosing *you.*"

"What if he isn't, though? What if he just got drunk and was rambling nonsense?" She grabs my arms and looks at me with that calming smile of hers.

"What does your gut tell you?"

Shit.

"That I want to go see if he's okay."

Her smile broadens. "You book a flight for the morning, I'll help you pack. Then I'll stay til you fall asleep so you can get some rest before you leave."

"I love you, Le."

"I love you too."

Chapter 67

Fitz

I wake up to the sound of my alarm echoing in my head so loudly; I know I had to have finish the bottle of scotch I opened last night. I told myself I would do this right, that I would finally leave her alone, get things squared away here, then go back to Nashville to talk to her in person, but when I got home last night and I saw her key sitting on the counter, I lost the last sliver of composure I'd barely been hanging onto. I know that I called her last night, but I can't remember if she answered or not. I'm just glad I don't have any texts this morning telling me to leave her alone.

I look at the clock and see that I have about thirty minutes before I need to be at the office when I hear a knock at my door.

Please tell me I ordered coffee in my sleep and didn't remember.

I swing the door open and my knees almost give out on me when I see my girl, standing right in front of me with a suitcase in hand and a nervous look on her face.

"Lauren, what are you doing here?" I see the pain so clearly in her features and I wish more than anything I could just take it away.

"Um… I just… I got your message last night and it kind of worried me. You didn't sound like yourself and you just kept saying you needed to see me. I wasn't sure if—um, I can just go. This was a mistake. I'm so sorry." She turns to walk away but I grab her arm, making her stop.

"You came?" My voice cracks and a small, sad smile pulls at the corner of her lips as she shrugs.

"You called."

My hands grip either side of her face and my lips come crashing down on hers with a need I've never felt before in my life. When her arms wrap around my waist I feel like, even if just for a moment, everything is okay.

"I shouldn't be here," she whispers against my lips, but I shake my head in disagreement.

"You're exactly where you need to be." I pick her up by her thighs, kicking the door shut behind us, leaving her suitcase outside as I carry her to my bedroom and lay her down on my bed.

"Vince, I really didn't come here for this." I stop and look at her in confusion.

"Then why did you come?" My heart feels like it's going to beat out of my chest as I see her pulling back. The walls she used to put up with me, slowly getting higher.

"I just…wanted to check on you."

"And that's it?" Her tear filled eyes meet mine when I snap the words out.

"I don't know," she whispers, confusion washing over her face. I take a chance and start to undress her, knowing she'll tell me to stop if this really isn't what she wants. But fuck it, I miss her and I need to show her just how much.

I slide her shorts down her legs, pulling her panties off with them, then reach for the hem of her sweatshirt, and when her arms raise, the hope deep within my chest skyrockets. I pull the sweatshirt off and just the sight of her naked body in my bed has me hard. I grab her chin and tilt her head back, bending down to kiss her. The tiniest moan escapes from her throat and I caress her breast, feeling her tight nipple between my fingers.

Releasing her chin, I drop my sweatpants and fist my cock, watching her tongue wet her lips as if on instinct. I lay her down, sliding my fingers between her legs to see if she's wet enough for me, pleased to find that she is. I climb over her on the bed, taking my time to appreciate seeing her hair fanned out over my sheets again. I slide between her legs, looking straight into those baby blue eyes I'm so obsessed with, when she spreads her legs further to let me in. I pump into her slowly, my body entering a euphoric state as I sink into her over and over again. Her eyes water and her hands slowly caress my biceps as her legs wrap around me.

"I missed you so fucking much, baby." I lean down and kiss her, seeing one single tear fall from the corner of her eye when I look back down at her.

"I missed you too," she whispers. Her words light a fire inside me.

"Don't leave me again."

"Vince." I know she's about to argue with me, but I'm not taking no for an answer. I lean down and take her lips in mine, claiming her with my tongue while my cock sinks so deep inside of her she moans into my mouth.

"Do. Not. Leave. Me. Again," I say with every punishing thrust. "Do I need to remind you where you belong, Trouble?"

"Maybe you do." I pull out of her, hearing her whimper from the rapid loss. I walk over to where my suit is hanging for today, yanking the tie from around the hanger before I make my way back over to the bed. That fire I missed so much is back in her eyes.

"Hands out in front of you." She holds her wrists out, and I work the tie around them, tightening it before wrapping it around one of the rails on the footboard of my bed, putting her in the doggy style position.

"What's your safe word?"

"Dancing." I smile, remembering the night we first established it. I move behind her on the bed, loving the view of her ass and soaking wet pussy. I slide back inside of her with ease, pulling her back until there's resistance on her restraints. Her knees part, allowing me to hit deeper and I groan at the sensation. I slap her ass, feeling her walls tighten around me as she gasps.

"Why did you leave me, Trouble?" I grab both of her hips, unrelenting as I fuck her from behind.

"Vince, please."

I slap her ass again. "Why?"

"Because!" she screams out when I hit that sweet spot—so I hit it again.

I lean forward and grab her neck, pulling her head back towards me. "Because why?" I growl in her ear, thrusting into her once more time.

"Because… I love you!" I release her neck, leaning back to slap her ass one more time before I pull out and flip her on her back, the tie tightening with her new position. I spread her legs, sliding back inside of her before pulling her thigh up on my hip, wanting to be as close to her as possible.

"Then promise you won't leave me again. If you love me as much as I love you, then don't make me live without you, baby."

"D…D—"

Don't say it.

I thrust into her harder, making her scream out in pleasure when her orgasm hits her. Pleasure creeps up my spine as her walls tighten around me, her cum covering my cock and I find my release at the same moment my entire world crumbles.

"Dancing." I look down to see tears falling freely out of her eyes.

"No," I whisper, and she turns her head away from me, squeezing her eyes shut. I untie her hands and cup her cheek, turning her face towards mine.

"You want this to end, Trouble?" She pulls her bottom lip in with her teeth, silencing her cries as she shakes her head no.

"I want you to get everything you deserve in life, Vince. I can't be the thing to stand in the way of that." She leans into my touch and I know in my heart I haven't lost her.

"Then I need you to do something for me."

She nods. "Anything."

"Marry me."

Chapter 68

Lauren

Marry Me.

Leave it to Fitz to not ask, but demand that I marry him.

"What?" The question comes out as a half laugh, half sob. He slides out of me—because he *would* tell me to marry him while still inside me—and reaches over to his nightstand, pulling out a little velvet box. My hand flies to my mouth, eyes wide with disbelief. When he opens it the most beautiful ring I've ever seen in my life sits inside.

"Marry me." I'm not usually one to be left speechless, but that's exactly what I am right now. How can I marry him? Knowing everything I know. Even though everything inside me is screaming *yes*.

"Vince, I ca—" Tears flow down my face as I shake my head and he takes the ring out, sliding it onto my finger. "You're not supposed to do that until I say yes."

"Then for the love of God, say it. Say yes." I meet his eyes, swallowing past the answer on the tip of my tongue. "Every other circumstance aside, the company, my shitty parents, the reason you felt you had to leave me. If none of those things were in the way, what would you say?"

I'm getting kind of sick of crying so much.

But, even still, warm tears stream down my face.

"I would say yes. Without hesitation. I would say yes."

"Then that's all I need to know."

"What do you mean? It isn't that simple. You'll lose everything, Fitz. I can't be the reason you lose everything."

"The only way that will happen is if you leave me again. Woman, when are you going to realize that *you* are everything to me. I don't need this company, the penthouse or the stupid luxurious lifestyle if I can't have *you*. All I want, all I *need*, is you, Trouble. What else do I have to do to prove that to you?" I look down at the ring on my finger, that somehow fits perfectly, and my heart bursts wide open. Knowing this is how he feels, that this is what *he* wants, my answer is immediate. I look at him, biting my lip before I answer with a playful tone.

"Say please, Vince." With misty eyes, he smiles, grabbing either side of my face.

"*Please*. Please. Marry me, woman."

"Yes! Yes, I'll marry you!" I giggle and his lips land on mine, this time when my tears fall, they're from pure joy. "I love you, Vince," I whisper against his lips.

"Say it again. Say you'll be my wife." His forehead rests against mine, and I smile.

"I can't *wait* to be your wife." His arms wrap around me, squeezing me in a way that feels like I've finally made it back home.

"I hate myself for saying this, but we have to get dressed. We're late." He jumps off the bed, leaving me there gaping at him.

"*We?* You didn't even know I was coming. Late for what?"

"Come find out, future wife." He winks at me and grabs his tie from the end of the bed, making my eyes fall back to my left hand.

I'm getting married.

Fitz helped me pick out what to wear, which I'm kind of beginning to love, dressing me in a black and white pencil dress, with the same heels

I wore to his mom's party. It's nothing to get too excited about, but I think the heavy diamond on my left hand is what's making me feel invincible today. We make it to The Fitzgerald Firm, and I'm not the least bit surprised to see the amazing corner office Fitz has, with a full city view in every direction you turn. It's exactly the kind of office the CEO of a company should have, and my stomach twists knowing he may be giving it all up for me.

"No frowning, Sweetheart. Today is a good day." He winks at me, grabbing something from his desk, and then he grabs my hand, pulling me right beside him as we walk down the hall to the conference room. Upon entering the room I'm shocked to see so many familiar faces— faces of people I've spoken to, or marketed with during the events Fitz and I have attended together over the last couple of months.

"Good morning everyone, sorry we're late." There are murmurs across the room, everyone seeming pleasantly unbothered. "We had some business to attend to this morning on the way in." My cheeks warm as I fidget with my engagement ring.

"Meeting doesn't start 'til you're here, boss," one guy says, earning a sly smirk from Fitz.

"Ah, yes. What a perfect segway into why we're here in the first place." Fitz takes his place at the head of the table with Frank directly to his right. There's a seat open to his left and Fitz motions for me to sit there, so I do. Silently smiling at everyone else around the table. "As most of you may know, effective as of yesterday, Frank has been announced CEO of The Fitzgerald Firm. My father has given him sole ownership of the company."

"What?" I gasp, my eyes wide as I glance between the two of them. The smirks on both of their faces confuse me even further, but Fitz just winks at me and continues.

"You all know me very well, you have seen me work day in and day out to prepare to take on the role of CEO, but when it came down to it, Frank was just a better fit for the job… For now, anyway. Frank." Fitz gives Frank the floor to speak, giving him an encouraging clap on the shoulder as the two of them stand next to each other.

"Thank you, Fitz." Frank clears his throat and addresses the room. "I was honored by Fitz's decision to sign over the rights to The Fitzgerald Firm to me. I've been here since damn near the beginning, and I've always considered this young man right here like family. Watching this place turn into the empire it is has been…well, downright mind-boggling. I have no doubts that Fitz knows what he's doing, and that is why I have agreed to act as CEO for one year, starting today, and then I will retire, leaving the company to my acting COO."

Holy shit. The whole company is going to someone at this table.

Fitz takes the lead again, with a smile on his face. "The Fitzgerald Firm will keep its name, and our family legacy will continue, so long as the COO, and future Mrs. Fitzgerald, agrees to her promotion."

Who?

Oh my god.

Does he mean…

"Me?" Laughter floats around the room at my surprise.

"Lauren, you are very extremely overqualified to be a sales agent. You have impressed every single person at this table, without even knowing it, with your knowledge and capability. The simple conversations you had with the people in this room, which you may recognize upon closer inspection, were enough to prove you are a perfect candidate for the open COO position. I have no doubt that within a year's time, you'll be ready to call this company your own. If you want it." Frank's words sink deep within my soul as I sit with my mouth hanging open, likely still in shock from being told I'm being handed over a million, possibly billion, dollar company.

"What do you say, Sweetheart? You down for the challenge?" He knows just which buttons to press to get me to say yes, doesn't he?

"Are you sure?" I ask the general presence in the room. Everyone, *everyone*, nods their heads in agreement.

"The board, the people in this room, have already discussed the matter, and we all agree that you're the top choice for this position, but just to prove it to you, we'll take it to a vote. All those in favor of bringing Lauren Long on as acting COO for one year, with all intents and purposes to name her CEO after that time, raise your hand."

It's unanimous.

"It's yours if you want it. And not because of that ring on your finger. Because you've fucking *earned it*. You remember that, above all else." My eyes fill with tears again and I'm thankful I chose to wear waterproof mascara today.

"I am so honored that every single one of you has the faith in me to do this job. May I have the night to think it over? It's just been…a very crazy morning." I laugh, raising my left hand to my forehead, unintentionally showing my engagement ring, causing others to giggle along.

"Of course, take the night. Take the rest of the week if you need to. The position is yours if you want it." Frank holds out his hand and I stand to shake it. "I always knew you were a good fit for him." He nods towards Fitz with a wink and I laugh.

"Wait…" I look over at Fitz, my brow furrowing. "What position will you have?" He smirks and looks back at everyone else.

"You all are dismissed. Thank you so much." I narrow my gaze at him, wiping my face of any curiosity when people quietly congratulate me, smiling on their way out. When the room is empty, and the door latches behind Frank, I turn back to face Fitz.

"Well?" I ask impatiently, making him laugh.

"How would you feel about me running the ranch?" The surprise and joy on my face are immediate, followed quickly by concern.

"Are Gran and Pops okay?"

"They're fine, I promise. Pops called me Sunday night, telling me that he's and I quote, *getting too old for this shit,* and wanted to know what my thoughts were on handing things over to Lochlan. That's when my wheels started turning and…"

"You told him you'd do it." The admiration on my face is clear as I smile at my future husband.

"Lochlan isn't quite ready to take it all on by himself, but I know he could get there eventually. I know it's a bit of a commute between the ranch and the office, but I know some really great people in real estate, and we could find a house somewhere between them—" I put my finger to his lips, stopping him from rambling.

"We can worry about the details later. You're going to run the ranch!" He smiles so wide I think his cheeks might crack.

"Yeah?" he asks, wrapping his hands around my waist.

"Yeah!" He picks me up, spinning me around in an embrace before planting my feet carefully back on the ground.

"Have I told you lately that you're my favorite person in the world?"

I scrunch my face. "I don't think you've ever said that, actually, and I need you to start saying it more often," I tease him.

"I love you, Trouble."

"I love you, too, *Cowboy*." He rolls his eyes and I grab his cheeks with one hand. "Do I need to give you a reason to make those icy blue eyes roll, Vince?"

"Please, god, yes," he groans, burying his face in my neck and making me laugh.

"What a day. I got engaged, got the biggest promotion of my life, and found out I'm marrying a cowboy, not a millionaire."

"Billionaire."

"*What?!*"

"Thoughts?" He raises a brow at me.

I let out an exasperated breath. "I need a taco."

"Not in those shoes, you don't."

Chapter 69

Fitz

Today went better than I could have ever imagined. It's been a whirlwind of emotions ever since I opened the door to see her standing in front of me. From her saying she shouldn't be there, to saying she would be my wife, and I wouldn't have it any other way. We wouldn't be us if there wasn't a little push and pull before finally giving in to what we wanted, and knowing she wants to be my wife makes everything that got us here worth it.

We walk down the sidewalk, her right arm wrapped around my left, while she holds her hand out and stares at her ring. "It looks sort of like an antique mirror," she says, looking up at me and I smirk.

"Do you like it?" I stop, turning to face her and she does the same.

"I love it. It's beautiful." Her eyes are practically sparkling as she smiles at me.

I lean down and kiss her nose, making her giggle. "So are you going to FaceTime them, send a photo, or should we be packing for a flight to surprise them?" I raise a brow and she bites her lip.

"Ok, I have a plan." She pulls me to the side of the sidewalk getting us out of the way of the passersby and pulls out her phone. "Stand right here and don't move." I'm off to the side and I watch in amusement as she fluffs her hair, adjusts her ring, and then clicks into the group chat to FaceTime them all at the same time.

"Finally! I haven't heard from you since you landed. Are we kicking ass or what?" I peek around to see Leah on screen first. Shane, Ruby, and Taylor join soon after and all greet her with concern.

"Is everything okay? Did you guys work it out?" I see Lauren's throat work as she swallows.

"I'm officially not his girlfriend anymore." I watch as she puts on the performance of a lifetime, and the girls all gasp, saying how sorry they are and asking if she's okay, then the most beautiful smile spreads across her face and she turns around, allowing me in the frame with her, as she holds her ring finger up to the camera. "Because I'm his FIANCÉE!" she yells, as screams break out from every end of the call.

"You bitch! You had me ready to sick Tank on him," Ruby yells.

I lean closer to the phone. "Please don't. I haven't recovered from the first time he beat my ass. But don't tell him that."

"Too late, Lucy. I'm right here." Tank's face enters the screen with a big ass grin.

"Of course you are."

"Congratulations you two," he says, before disappearing again.

"Thank you!" Lauren calls back.

"Oh my god, let me see it again," Shane says, holding her fingers against her lips. Lauren holds her finger up to show them.

"So, when are you coming home? We need to celebrate!" Taylor claps her hands together and Lauren smiles.

"I'm not sure. Fitz has some work stuff to handle here so I may just stay with him for a while. I'll be back in time for my birthday, we can make it a double celebration!"

"Ok, fine! Well, I better see pics of this on your feed ASAP so I can stare at it a little more." Lauren laughs and agrees before everyone shouts their congratulations one more time and hangs up. Lauren lets out a happy sigh, sliding her phone back into her purse.

"You didn't tell them about the job offer," I say, raising a brow at her. She bites the corner of her lips and a look of conflict washes over her.

"I'm not ready yet. Because telling them about the job means telling them I'm moving almost a thousand miles away." I wrap my arms around her and kiss the top of her head to comfort her, trying to fight a smile.

"So, you're taking the job?"

She pulls away, looking up at me as her head nods. "I'm taking the job."

"I'm so fucking proud of you, baby. You're going to make an amazing COO."

She bites her lip, her eyes soft on mine. "I'm proud of you too, Vince."

She has no idea what those words do to me.

"Let's get some food, future wife." I wink at her and we turn to continue the way we were headed earlier, only to run straight into Jessica with a couple of her friends. Her mouth is hanging open like she's trying to catch flies.

"Future *what?*"

Guess the news that she won't hold that title hasn't reached her yet.

"*W-I-F-E,*" Lauren says slowly, drawing out each letter, and a chuckle slips from my lips before I can stop it. She rubs my arm with her left hand and Jessica's eyes fall to her ring. I take Lauren's hand in mine and kiss it, winking at her before turning back to Jessica.

"Have a lovely day, ladies." Lauren smirks at her and we walk around them. I'll let my parents deal with the fallout with the Vanderbilts, seeing as how they're the ones who started that shit to begin with. I regret ever having anything to do with Jessica, but how was I supposed to know what one summer hookup would turn into my parents thinking we were end game?

No, the woman on my arm who lights up my entire life, she's it for me. I begin and end with the love we share, and if I were to ever lose that, I am convinced I would lose myself. She taught me that I am capable of loving and being loved for exactly who I am. The good, the dark, and the terrible. Because the right person will always look beneath it all, and light you up from the inside out. She'll always be the sun to me.

Chapter 70

Lauren

September 5th—Lauren's 30th birthday

"I can't believe you have waited this long to tell them." Fitz shakes his head, watching as I anxiously try to fix my hair for the fifth time today. I'm one more attempt away from throwing this brush at the mirror, but God love him, Fitz is giving me the space I need to freak out about this.

"It's only been two weeks," I argue weakly. He leans against the doorframe, crossing his arms over his chest.

"And how long has it *felt*?" I point my brush at him in a very hostile way.

"Like two eternities. I haven't wanted to touch my phone or respond to the group chat because I feel like I'm going to vomit every time I say something to them that isn't *oh my god I got promoted to COO of the company I'll one day OWN, and OH YEAH, we're moving to New York!*" My heart starts to beat erratically in my chest.

"Sweetheart, you need to breathe or you're not going to make it to your party." Tears well in my eyes and I sigh as my shoulders drop.

"What if this is my last birthday with them?" My voice betrays me, cracking as Fitz walks over to wrap his arms around me.

"Baby—"

"What if everyone is too busy raising the babies I'll never get to see, or running bars, and veteran centers, and we only see each other once a year at Christmas? Or worse! What if our Christmas traditions end because I move a thousand miles away?" He strokes my back, trying to calm me down, but how can I calm down? When I'm on the verge of a panic attack over leaving the people who have been the only true family I've ever known. "I won't get to take Hendrix on Auntie Lauren dates anymore, or do tea parties with Cece, wearing crowns *much* too small for my head. I won't get to hear Poe say his first words or get to watch Shane and Max's new baby grow up. What if I can't do this without them?" The reason I've waited so long to even tell them about the move is because I'm scared I'll chicken out when the truth is finally out there and not want to go.

"You and I both know you won't have to do this without them. You guys will talk all the time, you'll FaceTime and send so many pictures and voice notes that it'll be like they're right there with you. You will absolutely be keeping your Christmas traditions because I need to be a part of at *least* one of them. You'll have a jet you can take any time you miss them, and you can fly them out to us whenever their schedules allow. I know how hard this is going to be for you, but I'm going to be right by your side—tonight and for the rest of our lives. I know you'll miss your life in Tennessee, but I swear to you, Trouble, I will do everything I can to give you a life you'll love in New York." I feel myself relax at his words. That's how I know he's right for me. Because it won't be my friends that I call first when something happens, good or bad, Fitz will be. I'll *always* need my best friends in my life, but Fitz is the missing piece I was always trying to fill with someone or something else. I look up at Fitz, as he runs his fingers through my hair, and I smile. "I love you. Thank you for letting me freak out."

"I love you too. I'll always let you feel whatever you need to, and be right here to calm you down when it's needed." He kisses my forehead and I let out a sigh of relief, then push off him to face the mirror.

"I don't know why you let me cry after I did my full face of makeup though." He chuckles at me and I smile back, salvaging what I can of my makeup. Someone knocks at the door and we both look at each other in confusion.

"Are you expecting someone?" he asks, but I shake my head. "I'll see who it is." Ginny jumps up on the counter next to me and I take a deep breath, petting between her ears before grabbing a Q-tip to get the mascara from under my eyes.

"Sweetheart?" I spin to face a troubled-looking Fitz.

"Yeah?"

"Your mom is here." My heart drops into my stomach and I freeze.

"What? Why?" I whisper, unsure if he let her in or not.

He shrugs. "She just said she needed to see you." My mouth pops open a few times as I think, then when I can't think of a reasonable explanation for not seeing her, I nod and we walk together into the living room. When I see her standing in the doorway I'm not sure how to feel. I'm not as nervous or anxious as I used to be when she would visit, waiting for the impending jabs at my life or my home, instead, I'm just…curious.

"Lauren." She smiles and it surprises me. "Thank you for seeing me, sweetie."

"Is everything okay?"

"Yes, everything is fine…" she stops herself, shaking her head. "Well, I suppose that's a lie, isn't it? Everything isn't fine." She walks further into the house, no longer waiting for an invitation to do so. She sets her purse on the counter and takes a deep breath, squaring her shoulders as I've done so many times when I need a boost of confidence. "I came here to apologize to you, Lauren. For the way things ended the last time we saw each other, and for every single thing that your father and I did or said that led up to that point."

I think I'm hallucinating.

I look at Fitz, trying to figure out if this is really happening, and he wraps an arm around my waist, silently supporting me like he always does.

"I don't… What?" I'm completely lost for words, waiting for the *ha-*

ha moment where she takes it all back and tells me why she's really here.

Her eyes glisten, but her voice remains strong. "You, my darling girl, are perfect, just the way you are. You have always been the smartest, most talented, kind, and beautiful girl I've ever known. I regret ever making you feel like you were anything less than that." Tears fill my eyes and my throat is tight as she speaks.

"Then…why? Why did you? Why did you and Daddy push me so hard and never tell me that what I was doing was good?" The regret in her eyes seems genuine and I see her nostrils flare as a tear falls from her eye too.

I don't think I've ever seen my mother cry.

"I couldn't begin to tell you. But your father and I know now that we shouldn't have projected what we may have wanted in life onto you. We should have listened and supported you. You built your own life here, Lauren, and even if it was out of spite, which I would understand, you did it all on your own. I have never been as proud of someone as I am of you. Your father is too."

I scoff. "Then where is he? Why couldn't he come here to tell me himself?"

"He wanted to come, I promise he did, but I told him it may be better if I came alone so you wouldn't feel overwhelmed."

"You're proud of me?" My voice shakes with every word and Fitz's grip tightens on me.

She nods, blinking away her tears as she sniffles. "I am so sorry, Lauren. I hope one day you can forgive us for the way we've treated you and the way we made you feel. You are more than enough and you should never feel like you have to prove yourself to us. To anyone, for that matter." I look over at Fitz and he smiles softly at me.

"We have somewhere to be tonight, but maybe we can talk about this another time? With Daddy here too?" She nods eagerly, a smile finding her lips.

"Yes! You just tell us when and we'll make it happen." I nod, watching as she grabs her purse and turns to leave. My heart sinks a little that she forgot—

She turns around to face me. "Happy birthday, baby girl. I hope you have the best night with your friends."

"Thanks, Mom." When she leaves, I fall into Fitz's arms and cry, hardly able to believe that that just happened.

"I'll let everyone know we'll be a little late. Let it out, baby." He strokes my hair, letting me feel it all. Just like he promised he would.

We made it to Topgolf twenty minutes late but spent the entire night drinking, golfing, and laughing until my cheeks hurt. I was so glad Luther and Reggie made it to celebrate with us, even though they had to leave right after our game and couldn't come back to Chattahoochies with us.

"Last drink for you tonight, Trouble," Fitz whispers in my ear, sending a chill down my spine. I like that he keeps me from overdoing it. I spent so long drinking to cure the ache of disappointing my parents, or feeling alone, and now he reminds me that I no longer have to drink to feel better—I have him for that. Plus, I think not remembering the first time we slept together really adds to his reasoning.

"To the birthday girl and future Mrs. Fitzgerald! Thirty is going to be your year, babe!" I smile at Ruby, lifting my glass to clink it with the other nine.

"Man, what a year. Taylor and Tucker *and* Leah and Sawyer got married, Shane got pregnant again, and Lauren got engaged. Damn... We didn't do anything interesting this year." Ruby frowns at Tank and he laughs.

"Woman, I already gave you a baby, what else do you want from me?"

"Well, that's actually not all." All eyes turn to me.

"Oh my god! You're pregnant too?!" Shane exclaims, holding her palms together by her mouth.

"Oh, god no," I say immediately catching a frown from Fitz. "I mean, I'm not opposed to kids…someday. But—" Now is not the time to be having a secret conversation with my future husband about whether or not I want to have kids. Shaking my head in frustration, I continue, "That's not the point right now. No. I'm not pregnant. I got offered a new job." I rush the words out and all the girls gasp, while the guys give me encouraging congratulations.

I swallow hard, forcing out the next words. "As COO of The Fitzgerald Firm." The girls all gasp and squeal in excitement.

"Holy shit." Ruby's tone drops to one more serious and the energy begins to shift.

"But that means…" Shane starts.

"You're… Are you—" Leah tries to get out, but her voice is already thick with emotion.

"You're moving to New York?" Taylor's voice cracks in disbelief and my heart starts to do the same.

I nod, confirming for her. "We're moving to New York."

"That's not… I mean, you can't move to New York. Your favorite taco truck is here." Taylor is trying her best to lighten the mood with jokes, all while wiping her tears away angrily.

"The tacos in New York are okay too. Maybe you can come try them sometime?" I shrug, tears falling from my eyes as I look at Ruby. She's the only one who's managed to crack a smile, and my brows pinch in confusion.

"What a fucking badass. You're the COO of The Fitzgerald Firm in New York!" I laugh gratefully, as she pulls me in for a hug. All the girls join in, holding me tighter than ever—like they're scared to let me go this time.

"We'll definitely come try your New York tacos," Shane says.

"And that pizza place Fitz is obsessed with," Taylor adds, and I catch Fitz throwing his hands up from the corner of my eye, making me laugh.

"I'll bet you have some swanky new office you could show us too," Leah says.

"We'll be regular tourists for you." The girls giggle, but when I catch Ruby's eye, and see this warrior of a woman with tears streaming down her face, I freeze.

"You better not forget about us," she warns.

"Are you kidding? I could never." Her lip quivers and I look around the bar, smiling as I remember the night we first came here. The guys move to stand next to their wives, and Fitz pulls me into his lap on his barstool.

"When do you move?" Shane asks, sniffling as she wipes her face.

"I start in two weeks, so…before that." Everyone silently nods.

"Hell yeah. Packing party this weekend." I look at Max gratefully.

Tucker claps, pointing finger guns in the air. "Be happy the number of us has multiplied since Taylor moved in with me." We all laugh, finishing our drinks as we reminisce on the last few years. Starting from when Shane moved back to Nashville and needed to drink away a crappy weekend, we came to Chattahoochies to do just that, and four tequila shots and a key lime martini later, we wound up here—one big family that we found along the way and pieced together little by little. I'm going to miss them more than they'll ever know, but I know that moving to New York is what I'm supposed to do next. Because while my heart aches thinking about all I'll miss when I'm gone, I have so much peace over what I'll experience in New York with Fitz. I may not be down the street anymore, but we'll always have our Nashville nights.

Chapter 71

Fitz

The packing party

Lauren and I got all the boxes assembled last night so they would be ready for us to pack up and load onto the moving truck. Then ran out and grabbed coffee and breakfast sandwiches for everyone this morning, giving Lauren the chance to cry over how much she's going to miss her favorite coffee shop. I know we'll go through the grief of everything she's leaving behind, but I'm fully prepared to listen and comfort her until she starts to love the places around our new home. The door swings open and Taylor walks in with packing tape and bubble wrap in her arms.

"Packing party is here!" she yells. Lauren runs over and they wrap their arms around each other, and Tucker and I bump fists. Ginny jumps up onto the counter next to us and Tucker jumps.

"When the fuck did you get a cat?!" Lauren and Taylor burst out laughing. "Hey, kitty kitty," Tucker coos, picking her up and petting under her chin, making her purr. They rub their heads together and the three of us just stand back watching them. "What's her name?" He looks at Lauren.

"Ginny."

"Let me keep her." The girls fall over in laughter again and I shake my head, laughing with them.

"I told you!" Taylor yells.

"Told her what? Stop talking shit. She loves me. She doesn't wanna move to New York. Do you Ginny?" Tucker lifts her up and she meows. "See."

"Ginny loves New York, actually. You can't have my cat, Tucker." Lauren tries to take her from him but he turns in the other direction, blocking her from being able to.

"I just met her, let me hold her a little longer. Stingy ass."

"You're unbelievable." Lauren rolls her eyes at Tucker, walking back over and stopping by Taylor. "Please take him to the animal shelter when you leave here."

"Nah. I think I'll keep him." They laugh as the rest of the crew comes flooding through the door. Ten adults, three kids, and Ginny makes for a crowded ass house, but the laughter that fills every inch of this place is something I wouldn't dream of taking away from my future wife.

"Did I ever tell you guys about the time that Tucker almost killed Zander in front of my house?" Taylor asks, taping up a box full of Lauren's clothes.

"Really, Darlin'? That's the topic of conversation you're choosing during a lull?" Tucker sighs, and Taylor shushes him.

"That doesn't surprise me, but details please." Leah leans over the counter in the kitchen, where she's boxing up kitchen supplies Lauren is donating to the thrift store.

"It was the night he finally took me on a proper date, and we ran into *both* of my exes. Michael was the waiter, but y'all knew that already. Then when we got home, Zander's drunk ass was on my porch talking shit, so Tucker choked him out and was going to leave him in the bushes while we ordered takeout. We had to send him home in an Uber so the takeout guy wouldn't think we murdered someone." The girls burst out laughing and the guys in the room all shrug in solidarity. Meanwhile, I'm realizing just how crazy my new friends are.

"Y'all remember that time Max punched Pete when he showed up at Black Hearts? I think I fell in love with him that night."

"I thought you were already in love with me. I didn't know the violence is what did it for you." He slaps Shane's ass and she pretends to be mad, swatting his hand away with a grin on her face.

"Has anyone here *not* assaulted someone for their wife?" I ask and everyone laughs.

"Yeah, pretty much," Sawyer says, making Leah roll her eyes at him as she wraps her arms around his waist.

Ruby appears from the bathroom with a box in her hands. "Tank kind of takes the cake when it comes to wife-related violence—"

"Please reword that." Tank cuts her off, and she corrects herself.

"When it comes to violence *on behalf of* his wife."

"Thank you."

Ruby waves the Sharpie she's been marking boxes with around and continues, "I thought for sure we were covering up a murder the night he hunted down my ex at the trashy motel one town over." My eyebrows bounce to my hairline.

"He was an abusive piece of shit that was low-key stalking me for like a year. Then he showed up at work and put his hands on me." How the fuck does she say that so casually?

"Jesus. I'd hate to be that guy," I mumble, stacking a few more boxes by the door.

"But look at us now, all happily married, or engaged, to men who would quite literally burn down the world for us, with friends who are more like family, and an army of babies in the making." Shane smiles and rubs her stomach at Leah's words. "Speaking of which…" Leah pulls a piece of paper from her back pocket and the whole room gasps. "We're adding another one to the baby gang."

"SHUT UP RIGHT NOW!"

"OH MY GOSH THAT'S AMAZING."

"Thanks! We just found out for sure yesterday." Sawyer kisses Leah's forehead and she smiles up at him.

"Can we *please* get a dog? I feel left out, dammit." Tucker's response has the whole room laughing.

"Congratulations you guys!" Lauren runs over and hugs them both, and I follow to do the same. "You better call me as soon as you feel the slightest contraction so I don't miss this baby's birth. You know how I feel about birthdays." Lauren holds Leah's stomach, even though she isn't showing yet. It takes a while to get back to packing, but once Lauren turns the volume up on her music, the whole house gets moving, and within two hours, everything is ready to go to New York or the thrift store. The girls all took turns taking things from the donation boxes, filling bags for themselves of Lauren's stuff. It's literally like she has four sisters.

When the house is completely packed we all stand in the kitchen, looking at the empty space while the girls sniffle and fight back their tears.

"One last trip to Spur's?" Lauren asks.

"Fuck, yes. I'm starving." Max agrees, immediately. Grabbing Cece from where she's playing with her blocks on the floor. "I'll be in the car." Shane shakes her head, laughing as she grabs the diaper bag from the counter.

"We'll get a table, apparently. See you guys there." Everyone gathers their stuff, leaving Lauren and I standing alone in the quiet house. Today was such a fun day, and I do hate that we won't get to have days or nights like this regularly with them. But I know as soon as we're all together again, it'll be like no time has passed. These aren't the kind of friends you lose that type of connection with.

"Still sure you want to do this?" I ask, praying she hasn't changed her mind.

She rests her head on my shoulder. "I'll always be sure about my life with you, Vince. I'll miss my friends, but I'll be fine as long as I have you." She looks up at me and I take her face in my hands, kissing her softly.

"For as long as you'll have me, I'm yours, Trouble."

Epilogue

Lauren

one year later

I've been awake, running my fingers through Fitz's dark hair, for almost an hour. Staring at my engagement ring as I take in the fact that we're getting married tomorrow. I know everyone is going to be getting here soon to get ready for bachelorette night, but I'm trying to savor this quiet moment with my future husband while I can. We've spent the last year adjusting to our new life in New York, and while I spent the first two months being emotionally unstable at times over being so far away from my friends, Fitz never stopped being the supportive man I fell in love with. I've absolutely loved seeing him run the ranch and learning my new role at The Fitzgerald Firm has been just the career change I needed. I quickly noticed that Frank is more like a dad to Fitz than his real father ever has been, and it's been an honor to work so closely with him this past year. I'll miss him when he leaves, but luckily he's assured us he'll never be too far.

"Please don't ever stop. This feels so good." I smile as Fitz wraps his arms tighter around my waist.

"Well, you've always spoiled me with foot rubs and played with my hair to put me to sleep, I thought you should know how good it feels." I kiss the top of his head and he finally sits up, cupping my face and taking my lips in his.

"When is everyone supposed to be here?" he growls against my lips.

"Umm..." I hear a knock on the door and he groans.

"No! I need more time." I laugh, pulling him out of bed with me.

"And the rest of our lives isn't enough?" I tease, stopping right in front of the door. "No amount of time with you will ever be enough, Trouble."

"We can hear you! Open the door!" Taylor yells and I laugh, kissing Fitz once more before swinging the door open.

"AHHHHHHH!" All four girls and Luther pile into the house screaming, wrapping me in a hug that pushes Fitz off to the side.

"No no, I'm fine over here, thanks." Luther pulls away from the group and hums.

"Oh, *please* get your fine ass in on this hug." His eyes take in Fitz in his sweatpants and shirtless body, and I suddenly regret letting him come to the door looking like that.

"*Actually–*" I stand in front of Fitz, covering his chest and blocking Luther's view. "He has to go grab his stuff and head out."

"Party pooper." I turn around and kiss Fitz, sending him off to our room, biting my lip as I watch him go.

God that man is sexy.

"That jet was insane. I am ruined for commercial flights now," Ruby says, bringing my attention back to them.

"Oh, one hundred percent. I'll never be the same," Taylor agrees, putting a brown paper bag down on the counter.

"Did Loretta make it too?" I ask, looking in the hall before shutting the door that was left open.

"You know she wouldn't miss it for the world. We dropped her and the babies off with Marilyn and Tony at the ranch before we came here." Fitz and I have been building our own house on the ranch, wanting Gran and Pops to keep their place there. It didn't feel right to take the place they've always called home, so we've been staying at our place in the city while it's being built. The contractor said it should be done by the time we make it back from our honeymoon, but Gran and Pops had a couple of empty rooms and offered them to Leah and Taylor's parents for this weekend.

"I'm so glad they all made it and I'm extremely grateful they were willing to watch the babies tonight so we could do this." I pull out my phone to text them both as much, just as I hear something rattling across the kitchen.

"It's the last bachelorette party so you know what that means," Taylor sings as she shakes a box.

"PEEN PASTA!" they all yell together. I bury my face in my hands, before walking over and taking it from her.

"I cannot believe you remembered."

"Um, duh. It's a tradition at this point." She snatches it back and starts directing us all, in true Taylor fashion. "Okay, Shane has our matching pj's. Ruby has the drink mix. I'll get started on the pasta, and Leah, you get the music going. Luther, grab the skin-care items. This might be our last girls' night for a while, let's make it count." She winks at me and I pull her in for a hug, the rest of them quickly run over to join us. "Oh my gosh! I forgot to show you." Taylor gasps, pulling her phone from her pocket. "We have puppies!" She turns her phone around to show me a photo of the cutest bunch of puppies I've ever seen. Tucker and Taylor ended up getting a dog the same week I moved to New York, and then got another one a week later. Now they have puppies, apparently.

"Your husband's wedding gift will be ready in six to eight weeks." I smile at her gratefully.

"Ginny is going to hate this." I laugh, pulling the phone closer to look at the little fur balls.

"Ok. Enough staring at puppies. We have shit to do. Our girl is getting *married!*" Shane squeals.

This is it. I'm really getting married.

FITZ

I never had a lot of friends growing up. I spent most of my time on the ranch, and when I went to school I was a little anti-social, if you will, and didn't really care to make connections with anyone. As I made my way into adulthood, nothing really changed. I was fine not having anyone to grab a beer with, and I spent every waking hour at work anyway, so I never realized what I was missing. Until this bunch of lunatics came around as a packaged deal to the woman I'm marrying, and now I can't imagine not having them around.

"What did you guys do for your bachelor parties?" I ask from my end of the pool table. It's not exactly Chattahoochies, but the pool hall we ended up at is proving to be a good time so far.

"We did a cigar lounge and night vision paintball for Max's. Tank didn't have one because he got married so damn quick, and I'm pretty sure we did exactly what we're doing now for mine only we were at Chattahoochies," Tucker concludes, pointing a finger at Sawyer. "Then this bastard surprised us all with his fucking wedding ceremony the night of. We thought it was a celebratory dinner for winning the Stanley Cup, but *nooo*, so we didn't do shit for him either."

"Sounds like you've really been robbed, man," I tease, slapping him on the shoulder, causing the other guys to snicker.

"Whatever. Not like I wanted to do anything super cool for you assholes anyway. I'm getting too old for this shit."

"Well, I don't like extravagant shit, and I'm definitely not one of those guys trying to go to a strip club for my bachelor party. I don't believe in that *last night as a free man* bullshit."

"My man. Me either." Max holds his fist up and I bump it.

"Yeah, whoever came up with that idea probably shouldn't have gotten married in the first place," Sawyer adds, setting his beer down to take his shot.

"Hell yeah. Welcome to the whipped men's club." I almost choke on my drink as Tucker grins, pumping his fist in the air.

I tilt my head, laughing. "Happy to be here."

"How's everything going at the house?" Tank asks.

"Finished, actually. Lauren still thinks it won't be done until we get back from our honeymoon, but I'm surprising her tomorrow after the ceremony."

Max asks, leaning against the pool table, leveling me with a stare. "You ready?"

"I've never looked forward to anything the way I'm looking forward to this day."

"Let's get this man home. Don't want him too tired to remember his vows tomorrow." We rack our pool cues and I laugh.

"That's why I wrote them down."

Even though there's no way I would forget everything I want to vow to her tomorrow.

MAX

Dude, where are you?

TUCKER

I know rain is good luck on your wedding day, seeing the bride is bad luck, but I'm not exactly sure what to qualify not being able to find the groom??

SAWYER

If Lauren finds out? A category five disaster.

TANK

We'll be there soon, shit. Calm down.

TUCKER

You're WITH him? I thought you were taking the world's longest shit.

TANK

Why? Why would you think that?

TUCKER

SAWYER

He better not be delivering or butchering an animal.

TANK

His phone is literally off, you're all just talking to
yourselves.

MAX

Technically, we could be talking to him if you'd just
relay the fucking message.

TANK

I'm the best man, not the mailman.

TUCKER

I'm still not sure how that happened. Didn't you used
to hate him?

TANK

Dude, you realize he WILL see these messages
eventually right?

TUCKER

Watching Lauren adjust to our new normal over the last twelve months has been nothing short of astounding. Her first day as COO I had people calling and texting me non-stop that I better not do anything to lose her because I couldn't possibly do better—all things I already knew. She took on her new position, has been involved in every step of the building process of our house at the ranch, and planning our wedding without so much as batting an eye. Today, I get to make this amazing woman my wife. Tank and I rushed to make it to the hill after I put her wedding gift in our honeymoon bag. It's the desk plaque with her name and *Chief Executive Officer* on it and a new pair of red-bottomed shoes for her first day in her new position as owner.

She planned the wedding on Shadow Hill, requesting it be a small ceremony with only our closest friends and family, and I wouldn't have it any other way. I walk Gran to her seat next to Pops on the front row, then take my place. My heart feels like it could run laps around this entire ranch with the anticipation of seeing Lauren in her wedding dress. Tank stands next to me, along with Max, Tucker, Sawyer, and even Hendrix. Little stinker weaseled his way into my heart over the last twelve months and there's no way I wasn't having him up here with us as I marry his Aunt Lauren.

All the baby boys, Poe, Theodore, and Alex, are in the crowd with Taylor and Leah's parents, whom I've come to realize are like the group's parents. Cece walks over the hill first, holding Ruby's hand while she throws yellow and blue flower petals on the ground, her sweet little smile lighting up the hill. They take their place at the front next to Frank, who is officiating for us today, then Shane, Taylor, Leah, and Luther walk up, falling in line behind Ruby. The pianist, whom I still have no idea how Lauren convinced to haul a piano all the way up this hill, begins playing a familiar song for her to walk down the aisle to. All I can hear as it plays is Lauren singing along the day I played it at our place in the city. When she tops the hill with her arm linked through her dad's, I feel the emotion creep all the way up my chest, and into my cheeks as I fight to see through my tears. She's a vision in white silk, her dress hugging her curves until it flares at the bottom, the sleeves falling elegantly off her shoulders with a veil tucked into the loose bun she wears in her hair.

Fuck it. I'm not fighting it.

A full sob racks my body and I squeeze my eyes to let the tears fall, not wanting to miss a moment of my bride walking down the aisle to me. When I meet her gaze, her baby blue eyes are sparkling with tears as well, and her bright smile, which heals every bit of my torn and tattered heart, fills me with more joy than I ever knew I was capable of feeling.

"Wow. She looks like a princess," Hendrix says from down the line, and I laugh.

"Yeah, she sure does," I agree. When she makes it to the end of the aisle, I step down to take her hand, and her father gives me a nod. I'm thankful they were able to mend their relationship, even if I wasn't able to mend things with my parents. I get to start a new family today, and

I'll be everything for Lauren and any kids we might have in the future, that I wish my dad had been.

"You may be seated," Frank announces. I can hardly focus on anything but her the entire time Frank speaks. I've always had a problem focusing when she's around, but today? Impossible. I take in every detail of her dress and veil, the pearl necklace she wears around her neck, matching the small ones on her ears. The way her cheeks shimmer with blush, makes me excited to see the natural blush she'll wear for me later tonight. The way her thumb caresses my hand as we stand at the altar, and how the whole world fades away with her—until Frank gets to the vows.

"Lauren, whenever you're ready." She smiles at him and pulls her vows from the pocket of her wedding dress. She wags her eyebrows at me and I know that was the selling point of this dress for her.

Vince,

You may not know this, but when you came into my life, I was
at my very lowest.
Me not remembering our first meeting may have been a good
giveaway of how I was handling things,
but I was bitter and angry, and to be honest, I didn't like
myself very much. When you showed up, you pushed me at work,
started pressing every button I had, and drove me absolutely
crazy. Then when you weren't around, I realized I missed your
annoying presence. The things I thought I disliked about you,
were the very things that would brighten my day.
Then after an emotional morning and mindless rambling, you
offered to take me to one of my best friend's weddings so I
wouldn't be alone and you haven't let me feel alone ever since
that night. You took every snarky comment, every hangry
attitude, every eye roll and quirk that I had, and showed me that
they weren't flaws, but things that simply made me the woman
that you loved. Meanwhile, I fell in love with you too. With the
way you command a room, with the way you encouraged me and
paid attention to the things I liked and disliked. I fell in love
with the way you were always yourself when you were with me.
The day you told me you loved me, was the best day of my life.
Because I secretly wanted every single thing you claimed to want
that day as well. To grow old together and dance in the kitchen
to old records playing, and to be nauseatingly in love with each
other. Your initials were carved into my heart long before we put
them into that tree, and I've never once wanted to remove them.
Today, I vow to love you for exactly who you are, for the rest
of our lives, to always roll my eyes at you, and to dance in the
kitchen, whether there's music or not. I vow to never stop
encouraging you to chase your dreams, and to always remind you
how proud I am of you for going after them. I vow to love you
unconditionally, for better or worse, and when the day comes
that we're turning into wildflowers underneath this tree, even still,
I will love you.

LAUREN,

YOU'VE BEEN A TROUBLEMAKER EVER SINCE THE FIRST NIGHT I MET YOU, AND I'VE NEVER WANTED TO CAUSE TROUBLE WITH ANYONE AS MUCH AS I WANT TO WITH YOU. I KNEW FROM THE MOMENT I FIRST SAW YOU, THAT YOU WOULD BE A FORCE TO BE RECKONED WITH, AND DAMMIT WAS I RIGHT. GETTING YOU TO REMEMBER ME WAS THE SINGLE BEST ASSIGNMENT I EVER HAD, AND THE PAYOFF WAS GREATER THAN ANY THAT CAME BEFORE IT. YOU ARE SMART AND KIND. LOYAL AND FIERCE. FUNNY AND EMPATHETIC. YOU FILL MY LIFE WITH SO MUCH JOY THAT I NEVER THOUGHT WAS POSSIBLE FOR ME. YOUR SMILE HEALS ME, AND YOUR TOUCH STEADIES ME. YOUR VERY EXISTENCE IS A GIFT TO THIS WORLD, AND I FEEL LIKE THE RICHEST MAN ALIVE THAT I GET TO BE THE ONE TO CALL YOU MY WIFE. I HAVE WATCHED YOU FALL APART AND PUT YOURSELF BACK TOGETHER. I'VE SEEN YOU SHOW UP FOR YOUR FRIENDS WHEN YOUR OWN HEART WAS BROKEN AND I'VE WATCHED YOU SACRIFICE YOUR OWN HAPPINESS FOR THE WELL-BEING OF THE PEOPLE YOU LOVE MOST. TODAY, I VOW TO NEVER LET YOU GO THROUGH LIFE FEELING LIKE YOU HAVE TO HANDLE IT ALL ON YOUR OWN. THE PAIN, THE JOY, THE SACRIFICE, AND THE REWARDS, I WILL SHARE THEM ALL WITH YOU. I VOW TO NEVER STOP PAYING ATTENTION TO YOU AND TO TAKE CARE OF YOU EVERY SINGLE DAY, THE WAY YOU'VE ALWAYS TAKEN CARE OF EVERYONE ELSE. I VOW TO NEVER STOP REMINDING YOU HOW PROUD I AM OF YOU AND TO NEVER STOP LOOKING AT YOU THE WAY I HAVE SINCE THE VERY BEGINNING. LIKE YOU'RE THE SUN THAT HAS LIT UP MY WORLD SINCE THE MOMENT YOU STEPPED INTO IT. I TOO, WILL LOVE YOU, EVEN WHEN WE'RE TURNING INTO WILDFLOWERS BENEATH OUR TREE.
I LOVE YOU, LAUREN. WITH ALL THAT I AM, AND ALL I'LL EVER BE. MY HEART HAS ONLY EVER BELONGED TO YOU.

The exchange of rings happens, and when Frank tells me I can kiss my bride, I kiss the *hell* out of my bride. I dip her as my tongue slides into her mouth, and our friends and family cheer. When we finally stand again, we get announced for the first time as—

"Mr. and Mrs. Vincent Fitzgerald."

A phrase that I never in a million years thought I would happily hear.

Lauren Fitzgerald, in all her troublemaking chaos, came into my life and turned me into the version of myself I always hoped to be, giving me the family I always dreamed of having. I've gained so much more than a wife today, I've gained the life I was never brave enough to go after for myself.

Until her.

Trouble.

My wife.

My life.

I can't wait to take it all on with her.

The End.

Ivan's Chicken Pot Pie

1/3 C margarine
1/3 C all purpose flour
2 tbl chopped dried onion
1/2 tsp salt
1/4 tsp pepper

1 3/4 C chicken broth
2/3 C milk
2 C cut-up cooked chicken
1 can drained "veg-all"
2 deep dish pie crusts

1. Heat margarine over low heat until melted. Blend in flour, onion, salt and pepper. Cook over low heat, stirring constantly until smooth.

2. Remove from heat. Slowly stir in broth, making sure to keep mixture free of lumps. Add milk.

3. Heat to boiling, stirring constantly. Boil and stir one minute.

4. Stir in chicken and vegetables. Pour, filling one deep dish pie crust (unbaked). Use other pie crust to cover pie. Seal edges of crust by pressing with a fork.

5. Cut pie in center to allow steam to escape.

6. Bake uncovered on 425° until brown. 30-35 minutes.

ACKNOWLEDGMENTS

I can't believe this is the end for our beloved found family from the Nashville Nights series. When I first started writing Waiting for Sunshine December of 2022 I never imagined what this series would bring. The friendships, the inspiration, the community of readers who have loved and supported me along the way. You guys have completely blown me away and I am forever grateful for you all. I am going to miss this gang so much, but I am excited for what's to come next in the Sarah Pirtle universe.

Pirtle, I've acknowledged you in every single book, and my love and adoration for you and your support of my dreams only grows with every one. Your insight, the way you help me plot and process when I'm stuck, the hype you give me for every book I write, your unfailing determination to never let me give up on this dream of writing, I truly couldn't do it all without you. I know it hasn't always been easy to find balance, with three kids and some major crunch time deadlines, but you've never let me down, making sure I love them and spend as much time as necessary to make sure the story feels right before publishing. I love you, my best friend and real life book boyfriend (husband.)

To my parents, Keith and Karen, who have supported me, told me they were proud of me, and celebrated every victory I've encountered. Your love, wisdom and humor inspired so many aspects from our favorite Nashville Night parents (The Clarks and The Gates.) I am grateful I got to grow up experiencing that love, and that I'm blessed enough to still experience it today. I love you both so very much.

To my babies, who gave me inspiration at every turn for Hendrix and Cece, I love you more than life itself. Your excitement when I finish a book always brings a smile to my face, and I hope watching me chase my dreams of becoming an author, helps all of you remember to never give up on your own. I will always support you, no matter what those dreams may be. Reach for the stars, then catch a planet.

Courtnee and Tabitha, my found family. My book besties. My girls. I am so unbelievably grateful for you both and your friendship. Who would have thought writing about some best friends would allow me to find ones of my very own, but it has and I'll never take that for granted. For all of our girls nights, group chats, and family traditions, I hope you know how much I love you.

Kate, you have been with me from the very beginning, and I couldn't imagine doing this without you. You were one of the first people to read Waiting for Sunshine, then you brought it to life through your designs. I could not be more grateful that Erica gave me your name when I was looking for a designer, because the FRIEND I got out of what started as a working relationship is something I cherish dearly. Thank you for sticking with me through it all, for never failing to make my books so beautiful and for alpha reading and giving me the constructive criticism I need to make my work it's best. I love you so much!

Keri, my girl. The best PA I could ask for, I simply could not get through life without you. Not only because you do all the things I hate (spreadsheets. ick) but because your alpha reading gives me life, our group chats and text messages brighten my day and our four + hour midnight FaceTimes heal my soul. You get me in ways most people don't and I love you more than words. I am so glad you're my smut soul sister.

Erica, where do I begin? I simply love you so much. Connecting with you changed my life, and I will be forever grateful to have you on Team

Sarah Pirtle, and being one of the founding members of it. Working with you has been a dream and your support means the world to me. I hope you know I will always support you just the same and I cannot wait til I get to squeeze you again!

To the many author friends I have made along the way, Mollie Goins, Brianna Remus, Kat Singleton, SJ Sylvis, and Laura Pavlov—who have helped guide me in the right direction, answered my endless lists of questions, and cheered me on, thank you, I love you.

To my ARC and Content Teams who have created beautiful content and reviews, hyped up every book I've released, helped spread the word for new releases and loved my books and characters the same way I have, thank you so much. I wouldn't be able to keep publishing if it weren't for your love and support.

To the readers who pick up my book by happenstance and stuck around to this acknowledgement, I hope the words I've written have brought you some kind of comfort, whether in the love of Mama Marilyn, the giggles from the group chats, from the healing of heartbreak from past loves, or traumas, to the undeniable love between the characters. I hope you had plenty of 'kicking your feet' moments, as well as fanning yourself from the spice. That you had plenty of tissues on standby for the hard moments, and that you found a smile on your face during the happily ever afters. I have poured my heart into every single story from this series, and I hope you all enjoyed it.

I can't wait to bring you something new in 2025. Who knows, maybe we've even seen a peek into what world we'll be entering next. I've been told I drop easter eggs like the queen Ms. Swift herself... hmm. I guess only time will tell.

All my love, Sarah Pirtle

More From Sarah

Waiting for Sunshine (Nashville Nights 1)
Grumpy x sunshine
Workplace Romance
Military MMC
Grief Bonding

Waiting for Healing (Nashville Nights 2)
Friends to Lovers
Road Trip Romance
Only one bed
Navy Seal + ER Nurse

Waiting for Redemption (Nashville Nights 3)
Marriage of Convenience
Former Marine + Bartender
Second Chance
Single Mom

Waiting for Fate (Nashville Nights 4)
Childhood friends to lovers
Hockey Romance
Virgin Heroine
Second Chance